Bitterwood Commons

Marieke Mitchell

Cover designed by Marika Mitchell

This book is a work of fiction. Names, characters, places, and incidents either are products of the author's imagination or are used fictitiously. Any resemblance to actual persons, living or dead, events, or locales is entirely coincidental.

Marika Mitchell
Visit my website at Bitterwoodcommons.com

Printed in the United States of America

First Printing: January 2019

CONTENTS

This book is dedicated to my Thomas who is my rock in this journey through life.

Finally, brothers and sisters, whatever is true, whatever is noble, whatever is right, whatever is pure, whatever is lovely, whatever is admirable—if anything is excellent or praiseworthy—think about such things.

— PHILIPPIANS 4:8

Chapter 1

Voices in the Wind

*J*ust as it had occurred a little over a week ago, the sound materialized, once again, out of what seemed to be the abyss of my imagination. A distinct voice resounding through the wind which penetrated through to my very soul, "Come to me . . . Please . . . You must come to me." It was tremendously coercing, as I shook my head, refusing its urging. What was going on with me? I stopped dead in my tracks. I was a middle-aged woman with two adult children . . . A seemingly strong person with the mentality that could take on anything that life had to dish out; or so I liked to believe. Was I going insane with the emergence of these voices? The breeze continued blowing as I resumed my run, eventually reaching the lengthy driveway that led to my rural Michigan home. I paused a moment, shrugged off the bizarre incident involving the voice, and proceeded home.

My Victorian manor, my dream home, usually stood empty these days. My kids, now 20 and 21, had taken on their own independence. I feared that they had moved out as soon as possible due to my callous attitude, but I got solace in calling their absence independence. It was a rarity if I heard from either of them these days. I kicked off my shoes and gazed at the table in front of me that was once faithfully set for five. It was now a mere gathering place for books and other collectibles that had seemed to find their way into my life.

My ex-husband, Daniel, and I had started a business some time ago buying estates. We'd never know what we'd find buried away behind this or that. Sometimes the contents of an entire estate could be purchased for a mere $5,000.00 just out of sheer convenience from the inheritors of not having to deal with it. Now, our business employed 15 people full time, and Daniel was going as far as the East Coast to obtain properties. He insisted that it was his responsibility to be there sorting and categorizing each new lot, enabling each individual piece of the estate to get to its prospective buyer.

Daniel had proprietors waiting all over the world to get their hands on antique furniture, glassware, and just about anything you could think of. All the truly unique things, however, such as jewelry, figurines, coins, stamps, letters, etc., were sent to me. Too many times, I had been known to keep something that would have brought a good price, like the antique necklace I had come across a few weeks ago. After all, I figured I was entitled to some perks along the way and, frankly, business was flourishing and I knew I'd get far more pleasure out of keeping the necklace than the money we'd receive in selling it.

After showering and putting on some comfortable lounge wear, I placed Rachmaninoff in the CD player, turned down all the other annoyances, lit up a cigarette, popped my nightly meds, and sat down by the computer to get the day's auction results. A storm seemed to be brewing outside. I lived in a very rural area and I was unsure if I'd stay connected to the Internet with the wind picking up as it was. As I looked at the computer screen, which was the only source of light visible in my office, a brilliant glare ricocheted from the large, orangey-pink stone which hung from around my neck and then bounded back to the screen. It reminded me that I needed to get an appraisal done on the necklace within the next week. It was funny how the value of things didn't seem relevant to me anymore. I got to see so many expensive pieces, some dating back to the 16th century, that their worth consisted more of their sentimentality to me than their value. It was the reason why I was so fascinated with this piece of jewelry.

I had discovered it in a box of letters Daniel had found in a barn in one of our purchased estates in northern Indiana. The letters dated back to the early 1900s. The day I received the shipment of this particular lot, I stayed up the entire night reading of a stranger's longings. This poor lonely soul, named Arie, had apparently met the woman of his dreams during this long-ago age. She was definitely his soul mate, his one and only. For him, it had been love at first sight, even though I wondered from the tone of the letters if he had ever become physically close to the woman he had given his heart to. He grew more and more obsessed with her and wrote her constantly, creating beautiful poems and sonnets from his heart. From the way it sounded, she was never able to be with him, or truly understand how he felt. The letters were never that clear, and I wasn't certain that they had ever been sent. I even got the impression that it could have been an almost forbidden love. Whatever it had been, the 673 letters had abruptly stopped around the summer of 1918. At least, through reading the letters, I now knew that a sapphire necklace had been obtained for Arie's soul mate in the event that their lives publicly meshed in reality. In one of the last letters Arie wrote, he referred to the exact sapphire necklace in detail.

Someday, it is my prayer that you can claim, as your own, this man who gave you the necklace that holds the unusual stone of sapphire's brilliance, my precious flower. To my knowledge, there is no necklace on earth like it, and I believe it was meant only for you. Please, wear it proudly signifying my purest love in your heart. When it is finally around your neck, I'll be able to heal your mind, and it is my oath that I will find you; no matter what the circumstance, through all time, through all space, through all eternity.

It was just such a heartbreaking scenario. These letters had become priceless to me, and I'd pay any amount of earthly currency to uncover the outcome of Arie's life. I could only hope to find the necklace described in these letters. It would be much more than a mere piece of jewelry if I found it. It would be a token of dedication and love from a bygone era. Never, however, was the necklace that I had, and now wore, mentioned in the letters. The stone in my necklace appeared to be rare, orangey-pink in color, but definitely not sapphire; I wasn't sure of the gem. It was, however, one of the most beautiful stones I had ever envisioned. I just felt in my heart that it also had something to do with Arie.

These letters were definitely a maze cutting through time and emotion, mentioning places and people with faces unbeknownst to me in this life. Perhaps these letters were the release I needed. Perhaps a place within my subconscious where I could go, even if a century faded the path to get there. If I could sooth my own sorrows and feel the love and passion that had been so missing from my life for so many years, then these letters were worth obsessing over. I just had to find the missing sapphire necklace mentioned in the letters, and I had to uncover the origin of the necklace I now wore as well. No, I could never part with this necklace, or these letters, ever!

The wind continued howling through the few open windows in the house, rattling the shutters against the panes as I heard something crash to the floor. I rose to go into the kitchen to investigate when, to my revulsion, that familiar voice within my brain began chanting to me once more, "Come to me . . . Come to me." I closed my eyes trying to ignore its captivating pleas. I ran to the kitchen and discovered that a vase of wildflowers, which I had just picked the previous day, had fallen from the windowsill from a gust of wind. I began cleaning up the spill when the voice overtook me, engulfing everything around me. Nothing else seemed important. "Come to me," it hauntingly commanded, sending shivers up my spine.

Suddenly, through the wind's clamor and all the confusion, the computer in my office began giving me a notification signal that I had mail. It was repetitious as never before, and freaked me out since I was sure I had turned the speakers off on the computer when I put my music on. At least it had interrupted another one of my bouts of insanity, or as I liked to put it, my lack of enough antidepressants. I let the spill go; thinking what could happen next, and returned to my office to relieve the ongoing, high-pitched, chiming announcement of mail.

I checked the speakers. Just as I thought, they had been turned off. I thumped the computer loudly, thinking there must be a loose circuit, hoping it would fix the sound, but it continued its shrill annoyance. I stood there for a moment in a frenzy, holding my head, thankful that at least the unearthly voice from within my brain had withdrawn from my presence! I could deal with the computer. The speakers had evidently malfunctioned.

I looked up my new mail, and in a moment I found the usual postings: end of auction results and confirms from clients who had received their merchandise, but as I scrolled down something caught my eye, Lonely on the Prairie," it stated. "What could this be?" I asked myself aloud. "Could it possibly be from Daniel?" I proceeded to open it without hesitation, swiftly reading the passage with utmost interest:

My Dearest:

The prairie grasses once again are turning
amber from the early summer's heat.

Another day passes and I yearn to
spend eternity with you.

How I long to touch your hair of
blackest night, and hear your voice crack-
ling with innocent laughter.

*I only want to hold you each night
as the moonlight illuminates my window, and tell you that I'd give you anything just upon your asking.*

*For, if you were mine, I'd give
you the world; now I can only attempt to give you my soul.*

*Please take from me this pain of want-
ing... Take me from this pit of despair. Bring
me into your precious arms where I'll be safe
and content forever and forever in your love.*

*Follow the prisms my love, follow the light,
and never stop smelling the eternal flowers of
my soul. I don't want to roam and search for
you anymore. Oh, dear God, please help us!*

Arie

Oh dear Lord! Daniel had found the sequels to the letters that I had cherished so much! Apparently, he had copied one of them and sent it to me through email. I stood there glued to the screen, reading the words again. Were there more letters where this one had come from? What was this light he referred to? Quickly, I hit, reply, and began typing a response ... Daniel, I see you found more letters. Please send them all to me as soon as you can. You know how preoccupied I am with them. Thanks much, Em.

I clicked, send, confident that it would get to Daniel, but an error message appeared on my screen. Your mail could not be sent. Please type in an address. I quickly scanned the Lonely on the Prairie email, noticing that there was no web address where it had been sent from. I couldn't respond because there was nobody to respond to. Now, how did Daniel do that? Presently, I typed in Daniel's email address and then forwarded him the very same message. He'd surely have an explanation for me before night's end.

I printed out the letter before I signed off the Internet, shut the windows, and took the letter upstairs where the others were stored in their original box. The tone of the letters was unmistakably the same, and now I was certain that Daniel had found at least one more of the missing letters. I yawned and began reading some of them again for what seemed to be the hundredth time. And, as always, they took me back to a place a century ago, and I totally lost track of time. Whatever happened to this gentle stranger, I repeatedly asked myself, cradling the antique necklace in my hand. Did he and the love of his life ever marry? Did they ever share intimacy, a longed-for kiss, or even get the chance to embrace?

I closed my eyes, romanticizing of this precious love that Arie so desperately wanted to give. I wondered if I was becoming too consumed with this life from so long ago, and with this love that was so pure and abundant and wanting to be shared. I could only dream of having that in my life! Perhaps these ongoing episodes with the voices, etc., were all part of my so-called insanity as of late . . . My crazy imagination drudging up wishes from my subconscious. Now that I thought about it, it was right after I had begun wearing the necklace that the voice began to emerge in my head. Now, it was all beginning to make sense, and I became relieved knowing that I was still capable of solving all of life's complexities; something I prided myself in. With the source of the problem found, I was certain that the voice would now go away, or at least that I'd be able to subdue it. I gently nestled under the bedcovers, continuing to read and mentally consume the precious sonnets from yesteryear. Dreams once again intertwined with my existence. I fell to sleep in the peace of that moment.

Chapter 2

Unanswered Questions

$\mathcal{M}$orning took me by surprise as I awakened to the sun shining directly upon me. One of the louvers in the mini-blind had caught on the lace curtain, creating a hole where a ray of sunlight found its way to my pillow and directly to my face. The old letters surrounded me on the massive poster bed. The one I had printed from the computer was still haphazardly in my hand. I reflected on my night's visions . . . Dreams that brought fantasy, yet, a yearning for explanation . . . The ivory gazebo, the town, the unnamed faces. These were the same apparitions I'd been experiencing nightly for the last week. It was like I was being transported back in time in my dreams through the letters! I was either literally going crazy or, for the first time in fourteen years, had found something that finally preoccupied my mind. I wondered if Daniel had responded to my letter from last night. I pushed the letters aside, stretched, and made my way downstairs to my office. Anxiously, I typed my password into the computer and waited to be connected to the Internet. Quickly, I scanned through my mail . . . faster and faster, until I found one from Daniel. I impatiently clicked on to it, yawning and rubbing my eyes as I read:

I'm sorry about the letters, Em. Not to my knowledge have any more been found. I have no idea who sent that letter to you, and I guess I don't know exactly what you are even talking about. Actually, I'm not in Indiana anymore. I have two estates to look over in Illinois. Peter's still in Indiana, however, but, I think he's pretty much through taking care of that lot. If Peter, or I, do find more letters, or the sapphire necklace you're looking for, I'll surely let you know. I'm worried about you, Em. What's going on with your fascination with these letters anyway? I've just never seen you have such an interest in this stuff before. Maybe it's a good thing? Okay, hope all is well with you. I'll try to call within the next few days. Daniel.

I closed Daniel's email as a shaking sensation began to rise up my body. "Arie!" I screamed, "Who are you?" I stood up and walked over to the window. A sort of fog intermingled through the rays of sun, drying the humidity from the previous day's heat. I stood there staring blankly, then vigorously rubbed my face. Wait a minute, Em, I said to myself...Get yourself together. Going into the bathroom, I moistened a washcloth, gently wiping the sleep from my eyes and smearing yesterday's mascara. What could I possibly be thinking? Peter, our longtime friend and associate, was in Indiana, not Daniel. He had to have been the one who found the letters. He was the one who emailed me! The computer was definitely not working properly, that was evident from the night before. I wondered how I could get myself so worked up when there was always a logical explanation for everything if you looked for it. Still, I was excited that someone had found another letter and had sent it to me. Now, I was even more obsessed to know where it had come from, and the finality of this love affair.

I walked into the kitchen, finding the fallen vase of flowers that I had partially cleaned up from the prior evening. As I bent down, I noticed that the flowers I had picked earlier had dried, but fresh ones seemed to have taken their place. I picked one up and studied it. They were flowers I had never seen before! What in the world was going on? I thought my brain had fried! Throwing the flower to the floor, I quickly went, took my morning medications, and decided that a journey had to be made this day. I was being drawn into another dimension, another time element in this world. Could I blame it on my imagination, my unstable emotional state, or was it a cruel caper that someone was playing on me from long ago? Who knew? I only knew that my heart was pounding with excitement for the first time in years, and I had to find out what happened to this Arie, this stranger who had somehow occupied my very being!

I showered and gathered a few things together. In an hour I was on the interstate heading south. I knew where Daniel had found the letters. It was in a small town called LaPier, in northern Indiana. Peter, Daniel's longtime associate, and my forever friend, was apparently still there taking care of business.

My mind was in a dither as I went by the signs, stating one city and then the next. Before long, the Welcome to Indiana sign appeared. In four hours I turned off the highway near my destination. LaPier appeared to be a rural farming town, yet I knew it was only a few communities away from the bustle of the Chicago suburbs. The houses stood far and few between here. I searched the surroundings, trying to find any sort of familiarity as to what Arie had penned in the letters. Where was the ivory gazebo that he mentioned in so many of them? I glimpsed the faces of people in their cars, studied the few pedestrians on the streets, and wondered if they were relatives of this man I was searching for. What puzzle was hiding here? What love was never found, or what love was still waiting to be found? My heart thumped wildly, unlike it had done in ages, and I felt somehow akin to this place. After all, Arie had spoken explicitly of things in this very town, and towns couldn't change that much, could they?

I took out my little box and popped another pill. Perhaps it was out of anxiety, but I didn't seem to function anymore without my little security blanket hidden within the confines of a doctor's prescription. I knew I was addicted, but I had reason for this addiction, and that was excuse enough.

I followed a curvy, hilly road until it came to an abrupt halt. In front of me stood a park encased in an old, decorative, wrought-iron fence. I could tell from its huge oaks and maples that the park had been here for some time. Two stately stone towers, draped with climbing vines, welcomed me into the park. There were play areas in the front of the park with swing sets and tennis courts, and even places to sling horseshoes, but I couldn't see to the back. I parked my car; got out, and began walking on the hardened-gravel walkway. A young woman and two small children were coming my way.

"Excuse me," I interrupted as they neared. One of the little girls gave me a gleeful smile. "I'm from out of town," I began, "but I'm trying to find something that I'm not sure exists anymore."

The woman gave me a rather peculiar look.

"I know this may sound absurd," I continued, "but I own a box of letters dating back to the turn of the century. The letters were found in this town, written by a gentleman who I'm trying to find out about." She smiled and looked mildly interested. "Anyway," I resumed, "in the letters, the gentleman spoke of a place in the middle of town which had a gazebo. Are you familiar with any such place? I would really love to find out if it still exists."

"Mommy, Mommy, Jenny's kicking me again," the littlest girl blurted out.

"Natalie, please be quiet for one minute if you can, please!" The woman grabbed the curly-haired girl's hand, wiped some ice cream from her face with a tissue, and then looked directly at me. "There is a gazebo here in Bitterwood Commons. Did you know that? It's quite a large one, and has quite a history!"

I looked at her, overwhelmed. "Where is it?" I spouted out.

"Well," she continued slowly, as I wanted to pull the words from her mouth, "If you keep following this path over that hill, continue going by the historic churchyard and it will eventually take you to the other side of the park. You'll see a place where the one-room schoolhouse used to stand. There's not much left of it, just the granite stones from the foundation, but across from that you'll find the gazebo. It's closer to the other gate. The gate that comes in from State Street."

"State Street, you're kidding, right?" I said, startled.

The little girl pulled her hand from her mother's grip. Soon, the two children began running circles around the woman continuing their silly songs and attempting to trip each other. She shook her head. "No, I'm not kidding, it's State Street all right. The county road that comes in from the interstate turns into State Street from beyond the park."

I shivered, for I now stood in the very neighborhood that Arie spoke of. It may have been the place where he had walked. How could I forget the address neatly printed on each and every envelope? 89 State Street was the destination of the 673 letters. Ironically, it had also been but one number away from my departed great grandmother's address in Rolling Falls, Michigan. My mother possessed many letters sent to 88 State Street in my own home town. They were treasured heirlooms sent directly from war-torn Europe during WWI, penned by my great grandfather. I guess I would never forget either of these addresses! Perhaps it was an omen of some kind.

"Well, I've gotta run," the woman said, firmly taking both girls by the hand. "I hope you find whatever it is that you're looking for. It truly sounds... might I say, fun?" She smiled again and began to walk away.

"Thank you so much," I replied. "But, it goes much, much further than fun. I believe it's an obsession!" I gave a laugh as though joking, but I knew in my heart otherwise. I could hear the songs the little girls sang grow distant as I approached the hill along the gravel pathway growing impatient with each step. Soon, my walk turned into a fast paced run. I was umbrellaed by huge shade trees, decorated with beautiful climbing vines, as I passed by all the things she described until the gazebo came into view. I ran, panting from the summer's heat, until I reached steps leading up to what looked like a newly painted structure. There was a plaque at the base of the gazebo. The plaque sat upon an unusual type of crystal stone. It read: May this gazebo erect new hope and new beginnings.

There I stood, wondering and taking inventory of the place. I walked up the steps and encircled the area, touching each part as I went. "This couldn't possibly be a century old," I whispered to myself. I made my way to the other side and sat down on one of the built-in seats. Well, here I was in Indiana, sitting inside an ivory gazebo and yet still unsure of everything as I had been before. The sun made distinct streaks through the oaks, creating shadow- pictures on the gazebo. I couldn't help but notice how the bright rays ricocheted from the stones on the base of the dedication marker in front of the gazebo, creating rainbow effects wherever it touched. It was unusual and pretty, and it kept my interest. The hills and massive trees surrounding the gazebo, in this Bitterwood Commons, as it was apparently called, deadened the noise from the nearby street. I closed my eyes and felt a sense of familiarity here, a sense of belonging, and I was very glad I had made this journey.

I sat in the gazebo until late afternoon, smelling the smells, watching the sun's effects on the gazebo, and listening to distant sounds. I guess I was waiting for someone to just pop out at me and lead me on the path to recovering Arie's past life. Slowly, and with a heavy heart, I left the gazebo and the park. My car was hot from the afternoon's sun as I drove through the arched rock gate, continuing on the road that turned into State Street. This area south of the park grew more rural, and I squinted my eyes, trying to make out addresses on houses which now stood even farther apart. I had to be nearing the address so embedded in my thoughts, so I began looking for Peter's truck. When I found it, I would also find the discovery place of Arie's precious letters.

Sure enough, around a small curve in the road I spotted the bright red pickup with Estate Consolidators printed on its side. I turned in the drive of the modest old farm home as I saw

Peter walking from the barn in the back.

"Hey, you," I yelled, waving my arm out the window. I pulled into the driveway.

"Em! . . . Are you kidding, is that you?" Peter asked, as he approached.

I quickly put out my cigarette, throwing it out the window, and got out of my car, "Yeah, it's me," I replied with a smile.

"What in the world are you doing here?" He shook his head as he drew closer to me.

I put out my arms, and we embraced as usual. "You're probably going to wonder why I'm asking you this," I said, "but, you didn't happen to send me an email with another one of those letters that Daniel found in this lot of stuff, did you?"

"First and most importantly, you need to answer my question." Peter replied. "What are you doing here? And, what in the world is this I see?" He kicked the smoldering cigarette that I had thrown out the window.

I shrugged my shoulders, acting like it wasn't a big deal. Peter grabbed my arm. "Ya know, perhaps this isn't any of my business, but you promised me that you'd quit the drugs, the drinking and the smokes after our little episode last month."

I took a few steps away, reminiscing about how Peter had found me a little over a month ago at an estate job in Michigan. I had totally blacked out from apparently taking too many pills; at least that's what they told me. I had done a terrific job of blocking out the incident, even from myself. Why did Peter have to remind me? I hadn't seen him since then, and I guess I had avoided talking to him on the phone as well.

Peter kicked the ground, dispersing my thoughts as he looked up. "I worry about you, Em...you know that." He paused for a moment. "Now, if I haven't scared you away with my GREAT welcome, what were you asking me? . . . Something about an email?"

"Yeah," I responded, ignoring his prior words. "I just wondered if you had copied to my email another one of the letters you may have found from this estate."

"I sure didn't, Em. Why, what's going on?"

I lit up another cigarette. I could tell Peter was less than impressed with me, and yet in his own tender way he always seemed genuinely glad to be with me no matter what I did.

"Em." Peter interrupted my addicted pleasure with a gentle nudge.

"Oh, . . . I'm sorry, Peter," I said, flicking the ashes from my cigarette. "Nothing's going on. I just felt an overwhelming urge that someone has called me here to LaPier."

"Called you to LaPier?"

"Well, I received a very strange email that sort of pertained to this lot of stuff," I continued, "and I guess my curiosity got the best of me. I just had to come down here! It's almost like someone put a map from yesteryear in front of me that I feel I must follow. I guess it's hard to explain. You know how these old sentimental things seem to get the best of me! Well, actually you probably don't; this is the first time I am genuinely obsessed!" I laughed and rolled my eyes, continuing to flick my cig.

Peter displayed a counterfeit smile. "Listen, Em, you're welcome to go into the barn or the house and look through anything that's in there. There's not much left. I think today or tomorrow will be it for me here. But, Em, you may be searching for something that doesn't exist."

He kicked the ground again, sending a small pebble flying. "Everything will be shipped out within the next few days," he continued. "I've surely been keeping my eyes open for ya, though. Daniel told me to be on the lookout for anything that might be of interest to you: more jewelry; letters, books, anything regarding this estate."

Peter started making his way over to the truck. "Well, listen, if you don't mind, I'm supposed to meet some guy in town for dinner tonight to discuss another estate sale. Just a small one, so Daniel wanted me to take care of it. I guess I'd better run and go and get cleaned up before the meeting."

"That's fine, Peter. Don't mind me," I replied. "I may just snoop around a while."

"Are you okay, Em?" he questioned. "I mean really okay? I'm not talking about you being here searching for things; I mean your health. I haven't stopped thinking about you since what happened last month."

I laughed in a cocky manner, leaning against the truck's door, "Sure," I said, smiling, "I'm always okay. You should know that!"

"I don't know that, Em, that's what frightens me." Peter started up the truck as I stepped back. "I'm staying in the old brick hotel right on the corner of town if you need anything, Em. Oh, and here, I'll give you the key to this place. Lock her up when you're through with your search or whatever you're doing here." Peter reached into his pocket and pulled out a chain full of keys. He sorted through them then fed one around the thin metal circle releasing it from the others. He handed it to me awkwardly, laying his hand in mine. We looked at each other, and he waited for a few seconds before drawing back. His hand was warm and for a moment it gave me chills feeling his skin next to mine. "Don't hesitate to call me, okay?" Peter said, as he began to back up.

"Thanks, Peter," I replied, following closely beside the truck, "Ya know," I said, "you'll probably never believe I'm say- ing this to you, but you've meant a lot to me all these years."

Peter shrugged, "Nope, I can't believe you're saying that to me. What happened to you anyway? What happened to little Em who never gets close to anyone or lets anyone know what she's thinking?"

I was hoping that our talk would continue, but Peter, pulled out of the driveway, leaving me alone with all of my demons.

I looked around and noticed the dilapidated address plaque hanging cockeyed on the house. Surprisingly, this was not the address written on all the letters. 89 State Street apparently was the house next door, and this house was in obvious disrepair. There was virtually no paint left on the clapboard siding, and the shutters hung collapsed over each other. I walked to the rear of the house and saw vast fields so flat that they seemed to go on forever. The crops had begun turning amber from the early summer heat, just as Arie had written in the letters. This place truly resembled everything that I had ever heard or read about the prairie.

The house next door stood much closer than the distant ones on the other side, and I couldn't help but notice an elderly woman in a wheelchair in the back yard. It would be a miracle, but perhaps she had known the recipient of the letters, or even perhaps, Arie. I began walking in her direction when a yard full of unintended flowers captured my attention. They were very unusual! I gasped, taking special notice. They were the very flowers that had appeared in my fallen vase back home. I was sure! I shivered. Bending down to admire the graceful blooms that must had been planted in the neglected plot years ago, I was suddenly startled by the old woman's voice.

"Are you the one who I've been waiting for?" she yelled out in a shrieking tone, staring straight at me.

"Excuse me," I said, as I walked over to the elderly woman. "Were you speaking to me?"

She sat there with a blanket wrapped tightly around her legs with a haunting, blank expression on her face.

"Ma'am, excuse me," I said once again, as I bent down, touching her arm, trying to awaken her from her spell-like stare. My necklace dangled from my neck, emitting prisms of orange colors from its stone. When the old woman saw it, she gasped. Then she reached for it, clasping it in her hands as if it were her long-lost friend. I was scared that her roughness would break the chain. Her eyes slowly peered from my necklace to my face. Then she turned and seemed to be glaring at the fields.

"He is waiting for you," she babbled quietly, still holding the necklace in her hands. "Please, bring him the necklace ... It is you he waits for, and you can still save her life."

"Arie?" I questioned in a loud whisper. "Are you talking about Arie who waits? PLEASE, oh please, tell me about him!"

A screen door squeaked open and a woman about my age, very plain but strikingly pretty in her own way, came out of the house.

"Hello," I said, carefully trying to untangle the necklace from the old woman's grip. She finally let it loose as I turned to face the other woman. I offered my hand, and the woman shook it softly. "My name is Emma Barker." I continued, "I hope I'm not bothering you. My ex-husband was the one who bought the estate next door."

"Oh, okay, my name is Jill . . . Jill Vandenberg. We wondered what all the commotion was about a couple of months ago. I think I finally talked to your ex-husband or someone and he told me that the place had been sold. I try to distance myself from things around here. I'm originally from Ohio. My grandmother fell ill some years ago with dementia. My two sisters and I have been taking turns caring for her."

"I see," I said bewildered. "Life has its way of making us take on things we never dreamed, doesn't it?"

"Yes, but I have to believe that it's all in a bigger plan . . . God's plan, you know?"

I chuckled, closing my eyes and rubbing my face with my hand. "I don't believe in that plan anymore. If there is a God, why does He let these things happen?"

"Oh, I can't answer that," the woman replied, "but I do know that there is a purpose for everything that happens in life, even if it's unexplained. I know it doesn't always seem fair. Frankly, this town frightens me to death, and I sometimes have to wonder where God is. I certainly don't like coming here so often to care for Grandmother, but I really have no choice. Grandmother won't leave this place. We've tried to take her to our homes, but she throws tantrums at the least attempt to leave; almost died once . . . refused to eat. It's really strange because she doesn't seem to know anything or recognize anyone, but she will not leave this farm."

She bent down and kissed her grandmother on her fore-head. My curiosity regarding the old woman's remarks was killing me as I interjected, "When your grandmother saw me a minute ago, she asked me if I was the one she's been waiting for. She also seems to recognize my necklace, and spoke of a man. I was wondering if that man may have been named Arie? I believe he knew the woman who lived in your house many, many years ago. Do you know any reason why your grand-mother would have mentioned those things?"

She rubbed her grandmother's arm and replied, "She sits out here almost every day. She'd even come out in the rain or snow if we'd permit her. It's almost like she's expecting someone." She bent down and looked at her grandmother and then turned back to me. "My grandmother's name is Joy. I hope she didn't frighten you. Lately, whenever Grandmother comes in contact with any woman she always asks them if they're the one she's waiting for. I don't know what she means, and I doubt anyone ever will. As for your necklace, she always seems to look for necklaces on anyone who comes here. It's al-most as though she's looking for something that she's lost and is waiting for its return. Since the dementia hit her, she speaks of a necklace much, and seems obsessed with finding it. She sometimes acts as though it's a life-and-death situation. But, I truly don't think she's capable of understanding much of any-thing anymore."

"But she spoke of a man," I said, bending down to let the old woman hear his name. "Do you remember Arie?" I re-peated, gazing at her.

There was a long pause with no response from the woman.

"I personally never knew of an Arie," Jill replied as she looked up at me. "I'm sorry. If this Arie did know someone who lived in our house, perhaps Grandmother knew him, but I'm afraid she could never tell you that. The estate your hus-band purchased..."

"My ex-husband," I quickly interrupted.

"Oh pardon me, your ex-husband, I meant that...Anyway, it has been in the Peterson name for years. It was kind of like Grand's farm here. This house was kept in our family also, yet abandoned for much of its existence, similar to the one your ex-husband purchased. In the past, Grand did, however, mention many times the man who lived next door to her when she was growing up. He was the town parson. I know his name wasn't Arie...it was Justin. Grand absolutely loved him; he was very gracious to her. Are you looking for something specific about this Arie, or his ancestors?" She looked at me as though genuinely interested but continued before I could answer. "I only met one of the Petersons for a brief moment, but perhaps there was someone, or is someone, who knew this Arie in the past. I wish I could tell you."

"Well, I'm trying to find out anything and everything about him," I replied. I proceeded to tell her how I had obtained the box of letters in the estate we had purchased, addressed to 89 State Street, which ironically was their address. And, how Daniel had come across my alluring orange-gemmed necklace, also within the purchased estate. I think she could tell how consumed I had become with all of this. "Anyway," I continued, "today I was drawn here by a force that I can't explain, for a reason that I can't explain."

Just from telling the story, I could feel my tears welling up. "As you can tell," I said, "I'm very passionate about this venture."

Presently, the old woman looked up at me and spoke with what seemed to be authority, "He wasn't the one who always left flowers for her, you know? Now, go to him. . . He waits for you at the gazebo."

Goose bumps prickled my arms as I looked at her adamant face.

"Grandmother, what are you talking about?" Jill questioned. "What gazebo? The one in the park?" Jill sighed. "Please, like I said, don't mind her. Sometimes she scares me! She must remember so much that everything gets scrambled inside. It's funny that this subject even came up . . . Almost ironic! I was just thinking about this stuff yesterday, for within a short time it will mark the anniversary of my great-grandmother's death. Come over here with me a minute." Jill took my arm and led me away from her grandmother.

"I guess I have a story that you may be very interested in hearing. It takes a lot for me to tell it, but if anyone should hear it, I know it must be you. You see my grandmother was originally from LaPier but moved to Ohio when she was 11 years old. Your story about the letters, the necklace . . . It makes me shudder. There are too many coincidences from things I've heard, but I'm scared to know the details. I always have been, especially after my parents' tragedy. You see, I fear for the truth. I feel an eerie evil amongst all of this, but I assume you'll want to hear it anyway."

"Please, if you don't mind, I would love to hear your story. I NEED to know your story," I acknowledged.

"Well, I remember Grand taking me to a large celebration here, in LaPier, with my mother when I was a young girl. They dedicated the rebuilding of the gazebo in the town park at that time and said it had been replicated from the original one that stood in town until not long after the turn of the century. They even took a piece of the beautiful stone footing from the original gazebo and had it mounted on the base of the memorial plaque in Bitterwood Commons. I remember the event well because my grandmother told me all sorts of stories about my great-grandmother, Natalia, and how she would sit in the original gazebo. I'll never forget it, for she always referred to it as being, their meeting place. Of course, I really didn't know what she meant by that, and I guess I never totally will.

"My great-grandmother, Natalia, always told Grand many strange stories. They were stories that were never understood, like two people who are the same, but are very different; life existing of no time or no space . . . Time travel, the ability to change events in history, you name it! They were stories straight out of a radical imagination or a demented mind. From what we've come to understand through the years, my great- grandmother suffered from extreme mental illness, probably schizophrenia, and back then . . . Well, you know, that sort of thing just wasn't revealed or understood, or for that matter, talked about.

"Anyway, believe it or not, I'm just getting started with the history of our little gazebo. There was also a man. Sometime in the early 1900s, it was documented that he was tragically stabbed to death in the original gazebo. If you ask around even to this day, I'm sure the majority of people could tell you stories of the spirit, or soul, of Bitterwood Commons, who left flowers at the gazebo for precisely two years after the stabbing. It was also right after this man's death that the crying sounds began to be heard bellowing through town late at night. The little town even became notorious for it! Nice thing to become famous for, huh?"

I raised my eyebrows.

"Well," Jill continued, "Quite ironically, the unexplained flowers and the phantom's cries completely stopped the very day my great-grandmother passed away in a tragic fire. She perished in that horrendous blaze! And, take a guess where all this happened?"

I shrugged my shoulders.

"In the infamous gazebo!" she declared. "From what we've heard, there was ample time for her to escape, but she just stayed there and let the flames engulf her. By the time help arrived, the gazebo was about to cave in. I guess that was when her husband, who was my great grandfather, Gerrit Kappan, and his child began witnessing the hellish event. It has been told that the whole time she was being engulfed in flames she kept searching for something and screaming at the top of her lungs. Then, for some strange reason, it was said that she just stopped, and she seemed contented.

"Some of the witnesses even claim to have seen the shadow of an angel in the smoke floating right next to her;

even holding on to her! Of course, some claim it was a demonic force, due to Natalia's mental health, but I choose to believe it was angelic. Natalia was seen through the glow of the fire and embers with a peaceful expression on her face right before the gazebo collapsed on top of her. I guess the reason I'm telling you all of this is because the words that Natalia screamed were said to be Arie, Arie. Pardon me a moment."

Jill walked over to check on her grandmother, leaving me with so many thoughts that I didn't know where to turn. The old woman sat gazing at the amber fields as Jill kissed her forehead and then walked back to me.

"Grand, of course, if you haven't already figured it out, was that child who witnessed all of this. She was only 9 years old when she watched the terrible death of her mother. Not only did she have to endure all of that, but her own father died just two years after the fire. Most people claim that he died a broken man of a shattered soul. It was this evil, Emma, this evil that I've heard over and over about, that did my family in. My grandmother went through so much agony with all of this. She finally was sent away to live with an aunt in Ohio. She grew up there, married, and raised her only daughter, my mother, in the Akron area. Grand would, however, return to LaPier whenever she could. She adamantly refused to sell this farm. You see, back in those days people had very little money. They were immigrants, like most, and after the tragic death of my great grandmother, Natalia, she was laid to rest on this very property. My great grandfather's body is also here. You've probably noticed the flowers blooming in the yard that have spread through the years from Natalia's grave?"

"They are beautiful," I responded.

"Yes, they are beautiful, and yet as mysterious as everything else," Jill replied. "Anyway," she continued, "after my grandfather passed away, my grandmother, Joy, insisted on returning here to live. I now try to protect her from these memories as much as I can, much as she used to do for me when I was young. You see, my grandmother raised my two sisters and me after our parents were killed in an automobile accident. There's a curse; I'm telling you, a curse on our family. My mother also tried to figure all of this out, Emma. She probably knew more than any of us regarding these things. If she was aware that there was a way to make things right through time travel, or whatever these mystical powers were, then I'm sure she would have. Apparently she was unable to, for she's dead along with my father! Anyway, I never married, so I care for Grand the most. I owe her so, so much! She was a wonderful substitute for a mother.

"All of these events regarding my great-grandmother, Natalia, have recently surfaced once again since the dementia hit Grand. She never spoke much of this during our growing-up years; just little bits and pieces would surface. I'm thankful for that. I think she also believed there was some sort of curse or evil embodied in all of this and tried to keep it from us. But, now that she's at the end of her years, it's like she's obsessed, even though she may be obsessed through a limited mental state. She'll blurt things out, just as she did with you, and it makes you wonder.

"But I'm too scared to take anything to heart. She just keeps saying over and over that it's almost too late to save her, and that she must find the prisms to go to her! Whatever in the world that could mean; I don't know! I believe that she's talking about saving her mother, Natalia. I blame it on the dementia, but sometimes I know that those scrambled-up pieces of information must have meaning. Perhaps, in her mind everything is clear and she's trying to get me to understand before it's too late. Anyway, I still can't tell you who Arie is. I certainly wish I could, but now you know some gruesome nostalgia regarding LaPier and my family."

I listened intently as I yearned for more and more information. "Oh Jill, I so appreciate you sharing these things with me," I replied. "I had no idea what you or your grandmother had gone through. I'm just in awe at your story. However, don't you wonder about this necklace and my letters? Perhaps they all belong to you. Don't you want to try to sort it out? After all, they were addressed to your home!"

"There is nothing in my eyes to sort out, Emma. After experiencing all the deaths in my family, and feeling this evil that seems to encompass this town, I want nothing to do with any of it. I'd be careful if I were you. Strange events seem to walk on this pathway. Your ex-husband purchased those letters and that necklace; they're yours now. I just wish I had a more pleasant tale to tell you, but that's the way it is. Well, if you'll excuse us, it's getting late. It won't be long and the fireflies will be flying and the dew will be settling . . . Another thing Grandmother used to say to me." Jill grabbed ahold of the wheelchair and turned it toward the porch door.

I gave the old woman a hug and looked at Jill. "It was good meeting you," I concluded.

Jill looked at me as if to say something else, when her grandmother became very nervous as though she needed to get my attention. Her movements began making the wheelchair tip from side to side.

"Grandmother, what are you doing?" Jill hollered. "You can't stand up! . . . Your hip . . . Remember, your hip!"

Jill tried to get the old woman nestled back in the chair, but again she fidgeted, using all her powers to try to stand and turn to me. Jill quickly turned the chair back in my direction and that seemed to settle her down. Her eyes became glazed as they peered almost corruptly into mine.

"I returned the letters to the house when I was a child; to the secret place," she whispered once again. "Go to the hill and follow the stone's prisms. You now possess the power to help her. It's wrapped around your neck! I've begged and pleaded to make the journey again, but without the stone it's too late! She left a note behind her countenance in the pearly frame. . . . The way to get to her!" Her whispers turned into screeching. "You'll find him. I know you will, and he'll discover a way to save her soul. I let him use the necklace, and it has somehow made its way to you! Use the prisms. Listen to me, Go! It's in your hands now!"

Jill shook her head, "What's the matter with you tonight, Grand? I'm scared enough after telling Emma about LaPier, and now you're scaring me more." Jill shook her head again. "I'm sorry Emma, I don't know what she's talking about. It could be partially true, could be fiction. She really needs to get some sleep. She's just all worked up."

"Well, if your grandmother does settle down, could you ask her about the parson, and try to find out anything else about him? I know she probably won't be able to tell you, but it would mean a great deal to me."

"Well, you know his name was Justin Peterson, but I don't know what else Grand could tell me now."

The ninety-plus year-old Joy continued wiggling in the wheelchair like she needed desperately to answer, but she couldn't. Her mind was trying to help me unmask something, but her lips were unable to utter the words.

"It's late," Jill said as she took her grandmother into the house. "Be careful if you stay alone in the old place tonight. I don't think it's in the best repair. I'm sorry if I frightened you with the stories. Sometimes I guess it's good for me to get it out. I just wish my heritage was different. It's not much to be proud of. Well, if you need anything, we're here. Nice talking with you, Emma. Good night."

And with that, the door was shut, with my only source of information from that bygone era locked deep inside.

After hearing all the stories, I wasn't at ease staying in the rickety old house. The electricity was shut off, and my only means of illumination was from a left-behind oil lamp and a flashlight that I had brought from home. I was exhausted from all the events of the day! I changed into sweats and rolled out my sleeping bag onto the floor of the old parlor. After popping a couple of my pills, I crawled into my temporary bed. I looked through the shadows that the lamp seemed to produce and tried to envision what this place had looked like in better days. Perhaps Arie had stood in this home and gazed into the eyes of his only love. How I wished that I could have lived 100 years ago and met this humble, passionate man. It was crazy, but in a weird and very strange way, I had fallen into some sort of freaky love with this stranger from the past.

I tossed and turned, facing one direction and then the next. I had no idea what time it was, but I was certain that morning must be near. Finally, I closed my eyes and searched within for answers. Why couldn't life be easy? Why was I so desperately searching for this perfect love that Arie so wanted to give? Perhaps I wanted to find it in hopes that it would loosen the weights that had encased me for fourteen years. I rolled over as today's events continued rumbling through my mind like a massive runaway freight train. Thankfully, and slowly, slumber rescued me and took me into its vast chasm of tranquility.

Chapter 3

Lillian Post

*E*mma, Emma." I could hear a muffled sound of someone calling me through my sleep, but I would not
give in to the voice's influence. Suddenly, someone
banged on the door, making my heart throb and sending me
bolting from the floor to see what was going on. I looked
through the window, shaken from the sudden awakening, and
unlatched the make-shift bolt which allowed the door to
slowly swing open.

"Did I wake you?" Jill was standing there as I looked up at
the sky. The sun stood high already, and I realized that I had
slept way into the late morning.

"No, it's fine. Thanks for checking on me, Jill," I said, with a
yawn. I stretched and rubbed my aching neck. "Wow, I'm not
used to sleeping on a hard floor!"

"Yeah, I can imagine." Jill smiled. "Well, the main reason
I wanted to catch you before you left was because I was looking through some of Grand's old things last night after we had
talked, and I came across some greeting cards that Grand had
saved. I was looking through them and found one from an old
friend of hers. This friend is just short of 100. Anyway, she and
Grand grew up together here in LaPier and have stayed friends
throughout their lives. She resides in a nursing home called
Pinebrook Manor; just west of here. I wrote down the directions for you. Lillian's mind is still clear, although her health

has much deteriorated as of late. She is bedridden, I believe, but still enormously enjoys company. I was thinking that she would be the one for you to talk to regarding many of your questions."

"Oh Jill, that would be great!"

"I thought you'd be happy to hear the news. Her name is Lillian Post. You may want to call the nursing home first just to see if she can still accept visitors. I haven't seen Ms. Lillian for a few months. My sister and I took Grand to visit her toward the end of winter. She was grateful to see Grand again, although it saddened her to realize that Grand didn't recognize her anymore."

The news from Jill overwhelmed me. Could this be a link to Arie? "Ya know what, Jill, I'm going to call Pinebrook Manor ASAP and see if I can go and visit her today."

Jill handed me a folded piece of paper. "I thought you could use the directions and the number to the nursing home."

"Thanks, ... You know Jill, I've never felt this way before," I admitted. "Am I screwed up, totally obsessed, or what?"

"You're not screwed up, Emma." She chuckled. "Well, I guess I don't know you well enough to say that for sure, but you may be totally obsessed! You're definitely on a mission from your heart from what I understand of the whole thing. I know you think it's romantic, but you may find it isn't as lovely as you perceive. Believe me, I've known others who've tried to investigate this whole thing, and in some cases it didn't turn out too well for them. Look at my parents. Just be careful, please!"

"I know what you're saying, Jill, but the more I think about the whole thing the more compelling it seems to try and find out even more about Arie, the letters, LaPier, the screaming sounds, the flowers, and, most of all, the necklaces! The whole thing is rather frightening, but I guess the urge and romance to solve the mystery outweighs my fear from it all."

"I guess I understand," Jill said, backing away from the door and taking a step down. "Well, listen, let me know what you find out if you talk to Mrs. Post. I've gotta run. I can't leave Grand alone for too long."

"Okay, Jill, thanks so much for the information. Hey, you didn't happen to run by your Grandmother anything regarding the parson last night, did you?"

"I was talking to her when I was going through her things, and I did ask her if she remembered him. Emma, she doesn't respond, it's always a one-way conversation, but like I told you, I know she thought a lot of him. I wish I could get into her brain and pull out all the information. I just think of all the missed opportunities I had to find everything out from her through the years and didn't. There are so many things that I'd like to know and have answered about my family's past also, but I guess I've always been terrified to ask, and now it's too late. Maybe it's for the best. It's just so frustrating."

"Well, thanks again, Jill, for everything you've done. I'm not sure when I'll see you again; I really don't feel comfortable staying in this house. I'm going to do some investigating of my own, probably get a hotel here in town for a few days, but you can be sure that I will let you know anything I find out."

"That would be great," Jill concluded. "Then we'll chat later, okay?"

"Sounds great," I said, shutting the door, "See ya!"

There was no hesitation as I grabbed my phone from my purse and quickly dialed the number connecting me to Pinebrook Manor. Soon, I was talking to the nurse and inquiring about the health of Lillian Post. I was informed that she was a very energetic and loved company. That's all I needed to hear. I needed a shower, but I wasn't about to impose on Jill for that. I took out my stuff from my overnight case and prettied myself up as much as I could. It felt as though it was going to be a humid day, so I put on a fresh tank top and the skirt I was previously wearing. I was such a driven woman that I had forgotten to take my meds; something I hadn't neglected in a decade! I pulled them out and swallowed them, gagging and dry-coughing a bit until they went down. I was getting good at that.

The sun was hot as I got into my car. I noticed a little note tucked under the windshield wiper and got out and pulled it off; tearing the corner.

Think we could get together while you're in town? Remember, I'm staying at the only hotel in LaPier. Hope to see you, Peter.

What was this all about now? I laid the note down on the car seat as my heart began to pound. I felt a little like a schoolgirl again. What was going on with me? I had hidden my emotions for years! I chuckled and pondered the situation a little further then I went on my way.

Pinebrook Manor Nursing Home was located precisely as Jill had indicated, just west of town. I could see the sign as I approached the entrance. My heart was pounding fast in expectation of what Lillian Post might tell me. The aromas of cleaning solutions and room freshener greeted me as I hurried in.

"Can I help you find someone?" a rather robust woman inquired from the front desk.

"Yes, that would be kind," I responded. "I am hoping to meet with Ms. Lillian Post. I spoke with someone earlier today and they told me that she was able to receive guests."

"Yeah, Lillian would love to have you visit. She's in room 124, just down the hall and to the right."

I was already heading in that direction as I looked back and thanked her.

The door was ajar in room 124. A woman sat in a wheelchair at the base of the bed. She didn't appear as bedridden as I had been told. She was attempting to comb out her long, sparse locks of kinky, silvery hair. It appeared that it had been braided; probably wound up on top her head. I could tell she was having a hard time getting her shoulder to cooperate with her combing motions.

"Hi," I said, as I entered the room.

"Well, greetings to you," she said, in a rather firm, deep

voice. It sounded differently than how I would have perceived it to be. She gently put down her comb. "And, who do I have the privilege of meeting?"

I put out my hand. "Name's Emma Barker; I'm pleased to meet you." Her hand was warm and didn't seem to want to let mine go.

"Likewise, my dear. Do I know you?"

I observed that Lillian Post looked tired and fragile, just the way I would think a 100 year-old would look, but her mind seemed as sharp as a woman's half her age! "You don't know me," I continued. "I am a friend of Jill Vandenberg."

"Oh gracious," she said, as her face lit up. "How is her grandmother? I miss her so."

I smiled. "She seems to be doing rather well, although Jill tells me it is frustrating. The dementia, you know?"

"Poor dear; she's been such a precious friend through the years. Perhaps the dementia has finally taken her out of her sorrows. I miss our talks. I'm sorry; I forgot to mention my name. It's Lillian, but then you must already know that."

I nodded, "Yes. You're probably wondering why I'm here?"

"Any friend of my Joy's, or her children, is welcome here," she stated with a smile. "Now, what can I do for you?"

I sat down on the bed, picked up her comb and gently began combing out the knotted hair at the back of her head where she couldn't reach.

"I'm here mostly because of these." Putting down the comb, I picked up my straw bag and proceeded to show her some of my treasured letters. "I have 673 letters addressed to Joy's home from a gentleman named Arie. The letters are all from the early 1900s. They are beautiful, heart-absorbing love letters and sonnets. Ms. Post, I am totally absorbed with these letters. They don't make direct sense to me, but they are written in such a fashion that I can't put them down. I want to read them over and over. I believe there may be more letters also, for someone tried to contact me regarding them; at least I think they did. I just can't explain to you how I want to find out about them. This poor man in the letters…This Arie … He was so in love, and I know that the woman he loved had to love him as well. In the letters there is reference to a sapphire necklace."

I pulled the chain out from under my tank top. "I found this necklace in the box of letters. It's obviously not the sapphire one, but I've never seen such a beautiful stone in my life."

"Emma, let me see that!" The old woman jolted forward in her chair toward the necklace as she adjusted her glasses and peered. "This necklace … This necklace, I've seen it before! I've held it, and even wore it when I was a child! Joy showed it to me but made me promise to never let anyone know she had it! It belonged to her mother. I remember Joy telling me that her mother loved it dearly and would wear it almost always. She seldom took it off, yet she kept the history of it such a secret. Joy told me many times that this necklace had special powers, and she knew how to use them!

"One day, to Joy's surprise, she found the necklace lying on her mother's dresser. It was the day of our Summer Picnic and Joy took it over to show me. We tried the necklace on and pretended we were royalty. Joy ended up wearing it to the picnic but on the way home she lost it somewhere in the woods. She was frantic! We searched and searched for it, but never found it. It was that night that her mother came up missing and was later found in the Bitterwood School. I remember that day well. All of the people in town were searching for her. Your necklace has such an unusual stone with the exquisite gold scrolling that it makes me know that it's got to be one and the same! It's the one, I'm telling you!"

Lillian finally stopped peering at the necklace and looked up at me. "We never found the necklace, but to Joy's relief, and total surprise, the next day her mother was wearing it again. Neither Joy nor I could ever figure it out. If only that necklace of yours could speak!"

"I knew that this necklace had significance in all of this!" I said excitedly. "I felt it in my heart and soul. Now if only I could find the sapphire piece of jewelry that the letters are referring to. Oh Lillian, I know that I'm asking a lot from you, but Jill thought maybe you could answer some questions for me. Would you be so kind?"

Lillian sat gazing at me, then reached into my straw bag and pulled out a letter. She adjusted her glasses again and stared at the letter. I waited, watching in anticipation, wondering if she could truly see it.

"My Dear, Ms. Emma Barker," Lillian began, looking up over her glasses, "This is incredible. I was visited many times in years past by Jill Vandenberg's mother. This, of course, was many, many years ago. She would have been so very interested in seeing these letters and your necklace. Was there ever a name stated for whom these letters were addressed to? I see on this letter it is simply addressed to "My Love.""

"There has never been a name mentioned on any of the letters," I explained. "At least not a name for whom they were meant. But Arie was the name used to sign each of them."

Lillian turned the page, scrolling down to verify what I had told her. "Arie, again, huh? Who might that be, I wonder." She wrinkled her forehead in thought, and now I could confirm that her reading abilities were intact!

"Are you familiar with a woman named Natalia Kappan?" Lillian asked. "She was Joy's mother; Jill's great-grandmother; the owner of your necklace."

"I am," I answered.

"Natalia Kappan was a troubled soul. I knew her and heard many, many tales of her throughout the years. My mother and I knew bits and pieces of her whole life because Joy and I were around the same age, and very close. It's a small town, you know; rumors thrive. Joy and I went to Bitterwood School together and were inseparable; closer than sisters. I was devastated when she was taken away to Ohio. Natalia was a beautiful woman. She had olive skin and night-black, satin hair. She almost looked to be of partial Asian heritage, but the inside was a different story. Some even say she was possessed by demons. You say that these letters were addressed to the State Street address of Joy's home?"

"Yes," I said, "In fact, almost all of them are in envelopes ready to send. However, there is no stamp, and none of the envelopes have been sealed."

"I would almost be certain then, Ms. Emma Barker, that these letters, from the date, the address, etc., would have most definitely been meant for Natalia Kappan."

"That was my conclusion also," I interjected. "The only logical conclusion there might be. But Natalia had a husband and his name definitely was not Arie. Is that correct?"

"Joy's father was named Gerrit. He was of Dutch ancestry. He was a soft-spoken gentleman if you knew him. However, rumor had it that he was a very violent man and he had an awful temper. But then, we don't know what Natalia put the poor man through, either. We just don't know the details. Joy used to tell me horror stories about her parents' fights. Many times they were physically abusive. The poor dear...what she didn't endure. If it would have been this day and age, I'm sure she would have been removed from that family because of violence, but it was another era."

"I find this fascinating," I responded as I finished combing out her hair.

"Well, my dear, it may be fascinating, but I've only begun. Are you sure you want me to open up this can of worms? It may spoil all the romance of your letters."

"Lillian, I've driven quite a distance here to LaPier, because I need to know the truth. God knows that I am very aware that life isn't always pretty. I'm divorced. I'm a mess inside. I drink and take drugs to get me through each day, and I have a deceased child. This obsession I have with these letters, believe it or not, may be a good thing. At least I think it is. So you see, I will sit here with you for two weeks straight if need be. I want to know everything, everything, even if it's bad, about these letters."

Lillian gave me a subdued smile and stroked my face,

"Such a pretty young woman, to have all these troubles. Oh, my dear, if you want to listen, I will tell you what I know."

"It's a deal," I said as I made myself more comfortable on the bed, preparing to be there for a while.

"Now you must realize that I am an old woman," Lillian began. "I do pretty well mentally; wish I could say the same physically. I may be a little slow at recounting everything. So, bear with me, my dear." She sighed as if pondering many things, and then began again. "Okay, I'm going to start from when Joy and I were in the old school together. Like I said, from the time my family moved to LaPier, which was when I was right around 7, I believe, Joy and I were soul mates. Are you familiar with the park named Bitterwood Commons here in town?"

"Yes," I answered. "Actually, I spent quite a bit of time there yesterday. I was lucky enough to find out about the gazebo there. I should tell you that a gazebo is mentioned many times in these letters."

"Yes, our renowned gazebo! That's not the original gazebo that would have been mentioned in those letters, if they are as old as you say. You're aware of that, aren't you? It burned many, many years ago."

"I was told about that by Jill Vandenberg." I replied.

"She told you about the gazebo?" Lillian looked very surprised.

"She only told me vague things, no details or anything; no names. But, she did tell me that her great grandmother burned to death in a horrendous gazebo accident."

"Jill has had many problems throughout her life." Lillian said, shaking her head slowly. "All three of the Vandenberg girls have had their problems...mostly depression issues. They truly believe that their family has been cursed, and I guess they have reason to believe that. They lost their parents at quite a young age, you know? Joy took right over as their mother figure, tried her best to cover up all the things regarding LaPier and her family's history. She and the doctors at the hospital where the girls were treated just didn't think those girls were up to hearing about it or, for that matter, needed to. I'm sure they've heard their share, but I know Jill tries to leave it in the past. She does remarkably well now; all three of them are doing well from what I understand. They all take turns caring for Joy. They have been such a blessing to her."

"Jill does seem to leave everything in the past." I agreed. "Although I do believe she wishes she knew everything now. I guess it makes me understand why she doesn't know so many things. But, how do you live not knowing? I'm consumed by it already, and I'm a stranger! These letters, Lillian; they are amazing. You really should read them. I can leave them for you if you'd like?"

"I will say that the letters do intrigue my interest immensely. Yes, that would be fine if you could leave them. I could study them a bit more that way. Now, where was I?" Lillian questioned.

"You just started telling me about you and Joy as children."

"Awe, yes, Joy and I! Well, our family's home stood just outside where Bitterwood Commons is today. It wasn't a park at that time, more like a little burg within LaPier. All of the park's land was owned by our town's parson, Justin Peterson, and upon his death, by his request, the trust converted the land to a historic park. It was said that our dear parson inherited quite a sum of money sometime in his life, but you would have never known it by the way he lived or acted. I guess I'm not quite sure when the inheritance took place. Anyway, getting back to the subject...it was only a short jaunt over to the Kappans' home from where I lived. The granite stone blocks still can be seen inside the park where the old one-room schoolhouse sat. Bitterwood Schoolhouse is what they called it. Funny name, huh?"

"Indeed it is."

"It got its name quite by accident you know. Legend has it that one of the first settlers here in LaPier planted a vine. It produced a flower and fragrance that were inconspicuous yet yielded beautiful ornate berries. It was divided and shared with neighbors throughout the town. It was thought to have been called Bitterwood, but in essence we now know better. It was Bittersweet. Anyway, the Bittersweet vines trail up many of the trees in the park. Most interestingly, the vines were known as Bitterwood by so many people in these parts, for so long, that the name just stuck. The school was wrongfully named after it, and later the park. It's kind of ironic that the word bitter is amongst our town's heritage with all the bitter, weird things that have abounded. I didn't mean to get off the subject, but I guess I did...Just sharing some of our history."

"No, I find it most fascinating," I interjected, "tell me everything!"

"Okay, when I was a child, Joy and I did almost everything together. State Street, as I'm sure you know, runs right down the center of LaPier...Huge, huge town." She chuckled, rolling her eyes.

"We had lots of fun in those days. They were days of innocence when you're a child, you know? LaPier was a nice place to live before all the happenings occurred. Down the road from Bitterwood Commons on State Street right before you'd come to town is where the original gazebo used to stand. It was a regal structure. All of the town gatherings occurred there...The ice cream socials, many of the town's weddings, political events...You name it; it was hosted there. Our parson, Justin Peterson, even did some of his Sunday worship services from that gazebo during the hot summers. He was a wonderful preacher! He converted many."

"Lillian," I interrupted, "The parson...is he the one who lived next door to Joy?"

"He did end up living next to the Kappans, however; originally he lived in a small dwelling closer to the Bitterwood Schoolhouse. Bitterwood School was also Bitterwood Church on Sundays. But, yes, later on, he did build a home next to Joy. And, I might tell you that she absolutely loved that man. I believe that it was his kindness to her that brought her through all the tragedies and made her the woman she was. Our parson was indeed her father figure, although I remember something happening between

him and Gerrit Kappan that prevented Joy from seeing him for a time. Anyway, that man was the salt of the earth. I don't think he could do any wrong! The parson never married; his church was indeed his love and his family. He made such an impact on our little town, cultivating so many close friend-ships. Especially to a certain young man who had become converted at one of his rallies. I believe he befriended him quite soon after Natalia's death. He became like a brother to him."

"It's all so interesting," I interjected. "What do you know about the murder, Lillian?"

"Ah, yes, I'll elaborate on the murder in a minute! I'm try-ing to recall Justin's friend's name. I believe they called him Maddy. He was always somewhat of a mystery to our town but did a lot of good here. He just wasn't the type of man who would let anyone get close to him, or know his heritage; no one except for our parson, that is. He later moved away. It was said, he went to do God's work."

"So the parson's name was Justin? Jill had told me of him also."

"Yes, Parson Justin Peterson. Oh, my dear, I just can't re-member where I've left off and where I've begun."

"Is this tiring you out, Lillian?" I asked. After all, I had to remember that I was talking to a remarkable woman who was almost a century old!

"It's fine, my dear, if you can put up with me. My mind just isn't what it used to be."

"Lillian, I only hope my mind is a third of what yours is when I am your age!"

She gave a little chuckle, shaking her head. "Shhhhh, now let me think a minute. Okay,...Joy and I, and many of the town's children, used to play a lot at the gazebo. There was a funny little chant that all the kids would say there. Funny, I haven't thought about this in so many years. Let me see if I can remember how it went."

Lillian rested her head on her hand, propping it up with her arm, and closed her eyes in thought. I didn't say anything, even though after quite a while I wondered if she had fallen asleep. Finally, she opened her eyes and squinted, "It went like this, I believe: The stones upon foundation stand for sun to prism onto land. And if you're in the perfect place, you'll be transported to another place.

I had a pen and paper on my lap and quickly tried to jot the saying down; along with other points I wanted to remember.

"Silly, huh?" Lillian questioned. "We'd all hold hands and chant that adage as we skipped around the gazebo. I don't know for sure where that saying came from. Some of the children said they first heard Natalia Kappan saying it, and they mimicked her, but I always kept that rumor from Joy. Anyway, when we were but youngsters we'd truly believe that when the sun was in the perfect spot and hit the crystal stones used on the foundation, we'd stand in that glow of the prisms and pretend we'd be taken somewhere in our imagination. You could never envision the places we'd go! And, they seemed so real; perhaps they were!" She gave a subdued laugh. "Oh, to be a child again!"

"It's amazing that you remember that, Lillian."

"Amazing? No, I think not. It's more because I grew so fearful of that place. Some things just become imbedded in our memory; never to leave." She sighed loudly. "Now, getting back to the Kappans. I truly believe that Natalia Kappan loved Joy, even in her depressed mental state. Joy told me that her mother loved her. How could a mother not? But, honestly, I don't think that Mr. Kappan ever had much to do with that poor, dear child of theirs. Natalia had a history of mental illness. She had been an orphan. She was put on one of those orphan trains out of New York when she was young. That's how she came to live with a family here in LaPier. Gerrit Kappan married her when she was very young. My mother told me that Natalia was but a child herself when the poor dear gave birth to Joy when she was only 15! There were peculiar things that happened that were never exposed. Some have questioned if Gerrit was even the true father.

"Joy told me, in confidence, a few times of a strange man she'd see lurking around their house. That's why the letters don't surprise me. I gave her my oath that I would never tell, and why I'm telling you this now, I can't explain." Lillian sighed and rolled her eyes. "Natalia didn't love Gerrit Kappan, which was very evident. My mother said it over and over again. I, along with all the other children of LaPier was terrified of her. Natalia just did the strangest things, and yet I can remember a time or two that she seemed perfectly fine, even rather pleasant and kind. It was almost like she took on different personalities from time to time.

"Many times, Joy would come over to our house crying. Mr. Kappan would come to fetch her home, or my father would escort her back. Joy never wanted to leave, and it broke my heart when she had to. There isn't much more to tell about our childhood. We played and were best friends. She told me many secrets, some I'm sure I've forgotten. But, I know without a doubt that Natalia Kappan loved to sit at that gazebo. Almost every evening when all the children would leave to go home, we would see her walking to the gazebo. My mother said she'd stay there sometimes until long after dark. All of us children always wondered if perhaps she went there to let her imagination take her away.

"In later years, Gerrit put a stop to her leaving the house, and it caused uproar in that family, but so much for that. Now, I'm going to tell you when the real drama started." Lillian paused and took a deep breath.

"When I was just about nine or ten years old it was a stormy, summer evening; late at night. We had been having storms all that week if I'm remembering correctly. We were still awake because there had been a terrible lightning storm earlier, and father was out sawing a limb that had come down onto our house. We saw Doc go by in his carriage, heading into town at a fast pace, trying to avoid the downed limbs. The next day we found out that someone had been stabbed to death in a bloody fight. The body was found lying in the gazebo. We right away thought of Natalia, but it ended up being a man. Apparently, his face was so disfigured, so mangled, so ripped into shreds that he was never identified. No one in town ever came up missing, and the case still stands unanswered to this day, as far as I understand.

"The only evidence left was a bloody letter opener. It had been bent from the sheer force of the stabbing. They wanted to question Natalia Kappan, but Gerrit assured the sheriff that she had not left their home that evening, and Joy verified it as well. I even asked Joy and she told me too that her mother had never left. Besides, the authorities were quite sure that the murderer had to have been a man with great strength. It was the only way the dull letter opener could have done that much bodily harm to a human being. Parson Peterson had a somber, Christian burial for the corpse. A few of the town's people showed up out of due respect. I remember how everyone said that it impacted our parson more than anyone could believe. He was never the same after that stabbing. The body is buried in the town's churchyard, ironically in Bitterwood Commons. Only a tarnished silver cross gives witness that the body is even there."

"And when did this happen, Lillian? Do you know what year that would have been?"

"Well, if I remember right, it would have been right around 1918."

"Bingo," I said, "My letters stopped in 1918! I wonder if it has any connection?" A shiver went up my spine!

"As you can imagine," Lillian continued, "My parents, and the parents of the other children in town, didn't want us to play anymore at the gazebo, but it intrigued us even more now. We'd walk by it and sometimes linger a bit. There was even a ceremony one summer night at the gazebo. It was supposed to have been a healing ceremony to free the town from the bad memories that had happened there. I guess it helped a bit because events began happening again. The rest of the children and I were absolutely fascinated with the place. Funny how when you're a child and something scares you how it also brings such interest to you as well."

I nodded in agreement. "Even when you're an adult it appears to happen! I'm proof of that right now!" I smiled.

"I guess you are," Lillian said, stroking my arm. "Another interesting event began occurring within months after the stabbing. Flowers began appearing on the benches of the gazebo randomly. I found them a few times, and once brought them home, to my mother's horror. They were somehow seen by the townspeople as something horrible...like a cultish sign or something. Other children would find them, and we'd even see Natalia, in her dazed frame of mind, walking home with them. I remember my father telling me that they were flowers unlike any he had ever seen. My father was a gardener and had every book on horticulture imaginable in those days but, I can remember him saying that he could not trace them to any specie.

"It was after the stabbing that Natalia would go to the gazebo even more. In fact, she seemed to become infatuated with sitting there! People began saying she was obsessed with death. It was said that Mr. Kappan had a ritual of going there late at night to bring her home. And, do you remember the little chant I told you about earlier that we as children would say at the gazebo? We began finding Natalia there when we'd get out of school. She'd be circling the gazebo with tears streaming from her eyes reciting that very chant, sometimes screaming it from the top of her lungs! Joy would run to her mother and clasp onto her legs. She'd hold on to her, but it was as though Natalia didn't even realize she was there. Joy didn't let go and was forced to encircle with her, faster and faster. I can still hear Joy pleading, please, come home; please come home,

Mama.

"The bizarre screams also began happening after the stabbing. I heard them many times. They were the most intense screams you've ever heard! They've always been blamed on Natalia, even though many times Natalia had been in someone's company during the screams, proving them not to be hers. I think in later years, after Natalia was gone, it was just convenient to blame them on her. Truthfully, the screams sounded more like a man's screams of agony than any screams that Natalia was capable of making."

"Gees, Lillian, this is truly freaky!" I admitted. "Sounds like it's right out of a movie!"

"Indeed," she said, shaking her head.

"So, what about Natalia? What exactly happened to her?"

"Oh, Emma, it was the most horrendous event I've ever experienced!"

"You were there?"

"I was there along with my parents and many other people from the town. The screams were especially loud this particular evening, but that of a different tone; of a woman's tone. My father oftentimes would go outside when they were so loud, to try to hear where they were coming from. This night, the screams came from the gazebo. Father also noticed a bright, luminous light glowing down the road and told mother and the rest of us kids to get ready and get on the wagon, so we could see what it was. We hurried down to the road, following the screams, and finding the bottom of the gazebo ablaze! The screams this night were definitely from Natalia. I can see her as if it were yesterday standing in the middle of that gazebo. It was the most haunting sight.

"Flames ripped around her, but hadn't reached her level of the gazebo yet. Townspeople tried their best to get to her, but the flames began to encircle her. My father called to her, but it was as though she couldn't, or wouldn't, respond. I watched as she appeared to be searching for something on the floor of the gazebo. As she did, she screamed. Some say she was screaming out a name, and the name they believe she was saying was Arie!

"It was then that Mr. Kappan and Joy appeared. Gerrit Kappan was burned badly trying to save her; even lost his right eye in the attempt. There was just no getting to her. I guess what stands out in my mind the most is right before the fire engulfed her, she stopped screaming and stood tall amongst the flames. She was beautiful, embellished in a long, white dress. It had caught on fire. She even had flowers in her hair. There she stood with the most peaceful expression on her face. Her long, black hair glowed from the fire's frenzy. That's when the apparition within the flames appeared. My mother told me it was my imagination, but I know I saw a fleeting figure within the flames with Natalia! Then, almost as suddenly as it had begun, that was it, Emma. The whole thing collapsed on top of her, and she was gone. Our poor Joy had watched it all."

"Wow, that is some story!" I said, sighing. "So what was the explanation for it? Why did they say it happened?"

"No one knows. No one will ever know. But, right after that, Gerrit Kappan went into a crazed state of mind. His physical pain was excruciating, and I don't think he ever recovered. He didn't talk anymore, he didn't go out anymore, and, worst of all, he didn't want anything to do with Joy anymore. Not that he ever did that much, but it was far more evident now. They say the burns he encountered never healed, and he refused to let anyone see him. His face was so scarred and raw that he would wear scarves around his head when deliveries were made to his house.

"For the next years Parson Peterson and my folks looked after Joy most of the time. Somehow, after Natalia's death, or perhaps it was right before it; I just can't recall anymore, the parson and Gerrit seemed to reconcile their differences. It was even said that Justin was the only one who Gerrit allowed in his house after the accident. Natalia's death was blamed on her insanity. No one knows how the fire started. Broken glass from an oil lamp was found in the remains, and speculation was that she had dropped it, setting off the fire. But, most still claim that it was suicide. The flowers stopped appearing after the fire, and the screams also quit the very night of Natalia's death. No one could ever explain it. But, did Jill happen to tell you about Natalia's grave?"

"No," please tell me, Lillian," I said with much anticipation.

"Flowers began appearing at her grave right after her death. Many flowers; the same lovely ones that used to appear at the gazebo. They were the peculiar ones that no one could ever identify. I've heard that they were a cross between the Bittersweet vine and some type of exotic flower...a Lotus Flower, perhaps. This happened each spring and summer for years. The seeds from the flowers took root and now, if you'll notice, the entire acreage where Joy lives is covered in blooms around this time of year. Another funny thing that I've heard is that various townspeople tried to harvest the seeds from these flowers to grow at their own homes. They are truly beautiful flowers. But, not to this day have I known anyone to succeed in growing them. They've never been known to grow anywhere except for on the land by Natalia's grave!"

"Amazing that you're telling me this! I have encountered the flowers twice now myself." I shivered and wondered what it meant.

"As you may or may not know, Gerrit Kappan ended up passing away approximately two years after Natalia's death. So many rumors abound as to the cause. Some say it was the pain from his burns, and though they were terrible, my mother always said he died of a broken heart. I know this is crazy, but I truly think he was overcome with Natalia's beauty and loved her despite everything else. My father often said that Gerrit Kappan told him that he believed one day he would make Natalia love him. But, I'm convinced that it never happened.

"It was after Gerrit's death that Joy was sent to live with family members in Ohio. Oh, my dear Emma Barker, I hate to tell you this, but this old woman has grown weary and tired. I didn't realize how this story still affects me. You have churned up memories I haven't thought of in decades. If you don't mind, I believe I'll take a rest. If you could call for a nurse, I'd like to slip into bed."

After we got Lillian comfortable, I put the letters on her lap.

"I'll stop by tomorrow to see how you're doing. Feel free to read the letters, Lillian."

"I hope I've helped you in some way, Ms. Emma Barker," Lillian remarked. "You can be sure that I will read the letters, or at least some of them. After meeting you, I knew in my heart that I couldn't go to my deathbed without telling my story once again. You see, I did reveal all of this to Jill's mother, Jean, at one time. But, I think it was buried along with her memories upon her death in that accident. It isn't fair to those in the family for me to keep silent. I may be the only one who knows. Please see to it that the truth is known. I have the feeling you are the right person to be entrusting this information. I will try to think of some more things to tell you tomorrow. Now, I am very tired."

I kissed my new friend on the cheek and proceeded down the hall and out to my car. This was an amazing story, and I was overwhelmed by it. I popped some of my meds and sat there reminiscing in the heat of the summer afternoon.

Chapter 4

Padparadscha

*J*t was growing late in the afternoon, and I needed to get a room. I drove into town looking for a hotel. Gazing down on the seat next to mine, I grabbed Peter's note...Think we could get together while you're in town? Remember, I'm staying at the only hotel in LaPier. Hope to see you, Peter.

Reading it over made me want to be with him, yet I blamed this unfamiliar longing on the romance and intrigue of this place. The ringing of my cell phone interrupted my thoughts. "Hello, this is Em."

"Hi, Em, it's Daniel. Where are you? I've been trying to reach you via email and on your home phone for two days."

"You won't believe me if I tell you. I'm in LaPier ...at your estate."

"What? ... What are you doing there?"

"Oh, Daniel, I'm investigating...that's what I'm doing." I tried to act as though it was nothing.

"Have you seen Peter?"

"Yes," I answered a bit apprehensively.

"Well, tell me what you've come up with...What did you find? Did you find out where that letter came from?"

"No, I still haven't uncovered that. I thought Peter may have sent it to me, but he didn't, either. Daniel, there are some really strange happenings going on here with this estate, my necklace and these letters. I mean really strange things, like deaths, prisms taking you places, chants, angelic or demonic powers...you name it! I'm going to stay here until I find out some more. Why did you want to get ahold of me? Are the kids okay?"

"I'm assuming the kids are fine. I haven't heard from them. ...Deaths, prisms, chants, Em? That sounds like pretty far-fetched, frightening stuff! I've been worried about you; guess it was rightfully so. So, besides everything else, what's going on with Peter? Is he leaving soon?"

"I'm not sure," I answered, "Maybe I'll see him before he leaves. I'll probably stop by the estate again either tonight or tomorrow."

"Well, tell him I said hi, and that he did another excellent job, will ya? And Em, take care of yourself...I mean it, dear."

"Everyone pretends to be worried about Em," I said with a chuckle. "But, then I wonder if anyone really does care."

"You know I do, Em." Daniel said with all sincerity, acting a little aggravated at my accusation.

"Yeah, yeah, you're a good guy, Daniel. I gotta run. I think I just passed the only hotel within 80 miles!"

"Okay, well, be careful."

"Always," I said, laughing, "Byeeee."

I made a quick U-turn in the next driveway, skidding my tires and proceeded back to the hotel. I looked around but didn't see any sign of Peter's truck. The hotel looked like it had just came out of the 1900s itself. It sat on a corner and was connected to the other buildings that continued down Main Street. It was a two-story brick building with what looked to be a neat little suite on the very top, creating its third story. As I walked through the double oak doors, time seemed to be on hold once again.

"How are you today?" I was greeted by a middle-aged gentleman behind the counter.

"I'm fine, thanks. I need a room for the night. Would you

have that available, and what's the cost?"

"It will be $65 for a room with a double bed."

"Sold," I said, popping out my credit card.

As the man processed the paperwork, I questioned him. "Are you the owner?" I asked.

"Indeed, I am. "The Hotel Saint Denis' has been in the family for years and years." He returned my credit card. "Please sign the guest book if you would."

"Thank you," I replied. I couldn't help but notice that Peter's name was just three up from mine. It definitely was not a busy hotel. "You have a quaint place here. LaPier is a very unusual town. I've heard lots of stories."

"...Bet you're talking about the legends here, right? The Gazebo...The screams . . . Are you a writer?"

"I wish I were, but no, not really." I answered. "I'm not here to write anyway, if that's what you mean. Our business bought the old Peterson Estate just out of town a ways."

"I see," replied the man. "The reason I asked is because we had a gal here...Oh, it was many years ago now. She said she was gathering information and was going to compose a book about our little town."

"Really?" I said with much interest.

"Yeah, she stayed with us about a week...Real nice gal."

"Well, I hope she found what she was in search of," I said as he handed me my room key.

"You're in 2-3. It's on the second floor, third room to the left."

"Thank you," I said as I began climbing the open stairway.

"Oh, and by the way, you did say the old Peterson Farm, didn't you?

"Yes," I said as I turned around.

"We have another guest staying here that's been working on that."

"Yeah, that would be my friend, Peter. What room is he in?"

"Let's see...think I put him in room 12." He looked over

at the keyboard, "Yup, 12. He's leaving tomorrow, though. He said he's almost all finished up here."

"I'll check up on him," I replied. "Thanks very much."

It felt so good to take a shower. No matter how dated the room was, I was genuinely anxious to sleep in a real bed tonight. I don't think the room had been remodeled in a good 50 years, but at least it was clean and comfortable. The décor fit perfectly with the events of this trip. I was totally worn out from constant thoughts of solving the mysteries looming here. I brought in my laptop, plugged it in and began going through my mail. "You've got to be kidding." I said in a panic as I quickly opened up another Lonely on the Prairie email.

You now wear the necklace, my love; I told you that I would find you through all eternity. We are so close to being together; please come to me. Follow the prisms to my heart. Come!

"This is freaking crazy," I said as I quickly closed the mail. "Who are you? What do you want with me? Follow the prisms? How do I freaking follow the prisms?" I banged my hand on the table. Who in the world knows I'm here. Who's doing this to me? I sat there perspiring, thinking of all the things I had learned in the past couple of days. Suddenly, the chant came to my mind. I ran over to my purse and pulled out the crumpled piece of paper that I had written the words on. The stones upon foundation stand for sun to prism onto land. And, if you're in the perfect place, you'll be transported to another place. The foundation wasn't at the gazebo anymore. It had been pulled out after the fire. But Jill did say something about them using the stones in the memorial plaque. Come to think about it, I remembered seeing rays of light protruding from it yesterday. Immediately I grabbed my keys and headed to Bitterwood Commons once again.

The sun was still bright at 6:30 in the evening in early July in Indiana. I rushed down the walkway toward the gazebo. There it stood. It was a stately structure, but I was paying closer attention to the marker this time. The gazebo stood alone, but what I noticed was how the sun was creating prisms through the crystal-looking stones on the marker. I stood in one direction and then the other, feeling the heat from the sun ricochet off the stones, and then onto me. It was amazing. I pulled out my scrap of paper and began reading the words aloud...The words that Lillian had told me that they had chanted. Thank God I was alone, or someone would surely have me committed. Slowly I began encircling the gazebo, chanting out loud as I went. Shivers penetrated my soul. I was truly mimicking what Natalia Kappan used to do. Was she so desperately trying to find her Arie, just as I now did? I continued circling.

"Are you okay?" Someone said, laughing. I was quickly brought back to reality by a couple of teens.

"Oh, I'm fine, thanks," I answered, feeling totally embarrassed. "I was just reciting something that I was told had been recited here a long time ago. I probably looked foolish; I didn't mean to frighten you."

"Just checking," the young man answered. "We know a lot of the stories as well. If you really want to see that thing glow," and he pointed at the marker, "you should come back here around 1 in the afternoon. It prisms the light right over to that hill over there! It's really cool. Anyway, have fun with your little game." He continued laughing, and the girl who was with him rolled her eyes. "Oh, and be careful that the Boogeyman doesn't get you!" They walked away holding hands.

The Boogeyman, huh? Maybe I need the Boogeyman to rescue me; I'm ridiculous! When they were gone, I once again began encircling the gazebo. Each time I made it to the front, the prisms from the marker landed on my face. I stood there taking it all in. I gazed in front of me at the hill that the young man had just told me about. One o'clock, aye? I'll be here! I made a conscious date in my head for tomorrow.

I was starved by the time I got back to the hotel. I thought it would be fun to see if Peter wanted to grab something to eat. He was on the first floor, but I couldn't remember what room; not that there were that many to choose from.

"Excuse me," I said, approaching the front desk." What room did you say that Peter Lanar is in?" The man looked up, focusing his attention behind me, and then smiled. At that moment, I was nudged from behind.

"Peter…I was just coming to look for you!"

"Well, look no more, here I am."

"Are you hungry?" I asked. "I was hoping that we could do the town tonight, even though the town looks pretty small and pretty shut-up." I laughed.

"Sounds like a plan to me. Frankly, I could eat about anything right now. Where would you like to go?"

"Where would I like to go?" I said, raising my eyebrows in question. "Since I have no idea what is here, you better tell me."

"Not much," he admitted, "but, I'll show you what there is. Are you ready to go? …You need to change or anything?"

"I'm ready," I said.

"Well, let's just walk down the street and see what we'll find then." Peter and I started for the door.

"Have a good evening," the man at the desk said.

A dry breeze swept down the sidewalk. "Oh, wow," I said, holding my skirt down. We laughed.

"You trying to put on a show, are you?"

"Not intentionally," I answered.

Peter laid his arm on my shoulder as we walked. "So, I take it you got my note?"

"I did."

"Well, I'm so glad we are able to be together."

I quickly lit up a cigarette. I was feeling anxious.

"Em, there have always been feelings between us. You had to feel them, too, especially yesterday."

I closed my eyes and shook my head and grabbed Peter by the arm. "I can't talk about it now," I said, ignoring his question and pointing across the street. "Come on, I see somewhere that I want to go."

Most of the town was closed for the evening, except for an antique shop that we had passed. But, as I pulled Peter across the road, I noticed there was still activity in the jewelry store.

"We gonna buy an engagement ring?" Peter asked with a snicker. "I had no idea I had impacted you that much!"

"Shut up, Peter," I said, giving him a little push. "Now, come on."

I was relieved that Peter was willing to joke. It took off some of the pressure of perhaps being more than friends. It was now close to 8:30, and I was surprised the store was still open. I flicked out my cigarette and we entered. A couple, arms draped around each other, was looking at the diamond ring on the girl's finger as they walked out. They smiled at us and I could feel their joy. We would now be the only customers in the store.

"Can I help you?" An older woman approached us.

"I'm certainly hoping so," I exclaimed. "I recently, sort of, inherited this necklace." I pulled it out from under my blouse. "Peter, could you unclasp it for me?" I lifted up my hair.

It took him a minute to untangle the chain from some short locks underneath my long ones. He carefully unloosed the clasp and laid the necklace in my hand. I placed it gently on the glass counter and the woman picked it up.

"Exquisite piece," she said, studying it. "May I get my eyepiece?"

"Oh, please do." I agreed, "I'd love to have you tell me anything about this necklace that you can. I will be glad to pay you for your efforts."

"You're not closing soon, are you?" Peter inquired.

"No, not until nine," she answered, returning with the eyepiece. As the chain dangled down, she held the gem incased in its delicate setting and inspected it closely. "This is very old...

appears to have been through a fire at one time."

"A fire?" I questioned, getting the craziest sensation throughout my body.

"Ah ha; someone did a wonderful job of cleaning it up, but there is evidence of a fire. This is a grand piece of jewelry. I'm guessing its origin was about the 19th century... perhaps even older...24 karat gold." She continued studying it.

"What I was wondering," I interrupted, "was what kind of a stone is it?"

"You don't know?" she said, looking up at me. "It's the most incredible Padparadscha Sapphire that I've ever seen!"

"A SAPPHIRE!" I shrieked, looking at Peter.

"Settle down, Em," Peter said with a chuckle.

"But, I thought sapphires were blue?"

"Oh, sapphires come in a variety of colors. Blue, of course, is how we think of them." The jeweler kept turning the stone in various directions. "Yours is very rare. It must have been cut from a very large stone! It has been stone-cut in a half-dome shape. Did you notice that when you move the stone, there is a light phenomenon, which seems to dance magically across the stone's surface?"

"I've noticed many things about it, most of all that it's the most beautiful necklace I've ever seen," I replied.

"Well, it is lovely," the jeweler agreed. "Sapphires like these are called gemstones of the skies, because they rest, hidden away in only a few places on earth ... places such as Madagascar and Tanzania. Their hardness is only second to the diamond. Did you know what the sapphire symbolizes?"

I looked at Peter, shaking my head, and then looked back to the woman, giving her the same cue.

"It symbolizes loyalty and faithfulness, but also expresses love and yearning. It's a very romantic gem."

"You can say that again," I said, sighing. "So, this Paradea thing that you called it..."

"Padparadscha," she corrected.

"What exactly does that mean?"

"It means that it is an orange variety of sapphire with a pinkish undertone. And the poetic name of Padparadscha simply means 'Lotus Flower.' But, I better warn you," she said, looking at me with a gentle smile, "There are rumors of gemstone lovers who have everlastingly and sincerely lost their hearts to the rarity of these sapphires."

"That would be me," I said giggling, yet feeling tears welling up in my eyes.

"Well, if there's anything else I can do for you ...show you a watch, perhaps, or a sapphire ring? I wouldn't have anything to match this incredible piece, but I do have some beautiful selections."

"Oh, you've done more than I could ever express!" I began, attempting to reattach my precious necklace. Peter took over the job for me. I opened my purse. "Please let me give you something for your appraisal."

"Oh goodness me, there is no charge. There was no appraisal done. You'd have to leave the necklace with us for a written appraisal if you need one. It would take about a week, and then we would charge you. Written appraisals are mainly done for insurance purposes. And, I would highly recommend you having one done on this piece. Like I said, it is quite exquisite!" She laid her eyepiece down on the counter. "I thoroughly enjoyed looking over your necklace for you. I don't come across things like this too often."

"In all honesty," I said, "I don't care much about its monetary value. There are emotional ties to this necklace that are invaluable!"

"I kind of got that impression," the woman said softly, approaching the door and turning the sign around from OPEN to CLOSED. "You two have a good evening, and if I can help you with anything, please come and see me."

I put my hand out and shaking hers, said, "Thank you so much."

Chapter 5

Prisms

*P*eter and I ended up having a very enjoyable evening. We resorted to a late, fast-food dinner, not by choice, but because nothing else was open. After eating, Peter showed me the remnants of an old pumping station. I guess it all tied in with my journey into the past, except for the fast food, of course! All evening, for some strange reason, I kept noticing that I was having reflective moments regarding Daniel.

The feelings were especially prevalent when Peter and I had entered that little jewelry store in the middle of LaPier that evening. When I first saw the shop, it reminded me of the crazy time when Daniel and I had gone to the Upper Peninsula in Michigan and stumbled across an Ojibwe, Native American, souvenir shop. We had been dating just 4 months when he dragged me into the doorway of that shop, passionately kissed me, in front of, he didn't care who, and then, seemingly jokingly, proposed marriage. It was just one of the most wonderful, spontaneous times in my life. I told him yes, in the same joking manner, and he bought me a ring, right then and there, but insisted on picking it out himself. I was sent back to the car to wait for my surprise. He picked out a little turquoise ring; the only type they sold there, and I can still see him coming out of that shop with the biggest smile on his face with that ring on his pinky. We didn't marry for almost two years, but I still think of that little ring as my true engagement ring, even to this day. Well, until we were divorced, that is.

Peter and I made it an early evening. We sat in the lobby of the hotel for a while talking, but I needed sleep. Tomorrow I had many things to accomplish, and many mysteries to hopefully solve!

Today was a new day and I was very curious how Lillian Post had reacted to the letters I had left with her. I was also overwhelmed and amazed after learning about my necklace from the jeweler last night. I was so amazed that I couldn't wait to get my letters back from Lillian. I had awakened throughout the night thinking of all the pieces I had to put together. I had decided that Natalia Kappan had to have been wearing my necklace when she was burned in the gazebo. There was now proof of that on the necklace, but then how did it get back in with my letters? And, where was Arie, and, who was Arie, when all of this transpired? I was also curious as to what the hotel owner had told me about the woman who had come to LaPier wanting to write a book. Who was this person that would know to come here, unless she knew the things that I did?

There were many questions I needed to get answered today. I would start by driving out to Pinebrook Manor. Then I was to meet Peter at the gate of Bitterwood Commons at noon to say goodbye. It should give me just enough time to get to the gazebo by 1 o'clock to see what the prism business was all about. It was another sunny day, so at least the prism effect would be working...I hoped! I hurried down the steps to the first floor of the Hotel Saint Denis' and approached the front desk.

"I hope you're rested?" the same gentleman from yesterday asked.

"Oh, indeed, I feel much better," I replied. "I will be needing to keep my room for at least one or two more nights, if that will work out for you?"

"That's fine, we don't usually fill up this time of year too often . . . Only when the county fair is here, and sometimes when the LaPier Summer Fest arrives. They're both next month, so not to worry. I'll just put it on your tab and you can stay as long as you'd like. Just make sure you see me before you check out."

"Thank you very much," I said, and started to leave. "Oh, I almost forgot. I was hoping you could help me with something you said yesterday. You mentioned a woman that came here to write a book. Would there be any way you could give me her name and where she was from?"

"It really isn't our policy to divulge that information." He pushed his glasses down away from his eyes. "I'm trying to sound formal," he said, laughing. "Truthfully, I'm not sure I even have that information any more. I don't keep the receipts after three years, and that must have been decades ago. I was working for my father here at that time. I do remember her distinctly, though. She was from California. Her name was something like Rebecca or Amanda or something."

"But you have the guest books, don't you?" I reminded him.

"I guess you're right, I do keep all the books. I actually have all the guest books going back to the early 1900s."

"That is just wonderful. Nice memories for your hotel!"

"I'll tell you what, if I think of it, I'll mosey downstairs this afternoon and see if I can find anything for you."

"That'd be great, Sir, I'd appreciate it." I replied as I left the hotel.

I was starting to know my way around LaPier pretty well, as I turned into Pinebrook Manor Nursing Home. I couldn't stay too long today; I had gotten a late start, and couldn't forget to meet Peter. Down the hall to the right, room 124, I said to myself. I was hoping that it wasn't too early to make a call on Lillian. It definitely wasn't early, but maybe the residents in a nursing home would think it was. I found Lillian still in bed with her nightclothes on. I quietly approached the bed.

She looked to be asleep. Just as I was about to leave, I heard her voice.

"Ms. Emma Barker, is that you, dear?"

I turned around, "Lillian, I hope I didn't wake you," I said in dismay, returning to her bedside.

"You should be glad that you did wake an old woman like myself! At almost 100 years old, I'm amazed each day when I awaken to a new day." She chuckled in a low toned pitch. "Come closer, my dear, I have things to tell you."

"And I have things to tell you, too, Lillian," I said. "I found out last night that my necklace, the necklace that you said Joy showed you as a child, had been through a fire. And, you know the orange stone? I pulled the necklace away from my shirt to let her see it again. "It's a sapphire, believe it or not! The jeweler in town told me. Here I came to LaPier in hopes of finding the sapphire necklace, and it was around my neck all along."

Lillian raised her eyebrows and gave me a surprised look. She struggled to sit up, so I helped her get comfortable by bunching some pillows behind her back. "Your letters are wonderful, my dear. I thoroughly enjoyed them. I just can't for the life of me imagine who this Arie was. I have thought and thought of who he might have been to no avail."

"I have no idea, Lillian, but now you can see how I want to find out."

"I definitely understand," she agreed. "I never married, but if I had, I would have wished my husband could have wooed me with poetic verses like that." She sighed. "How I would have loved a romantic man, but it was never to have been. I just never found the right one." She gave a faint smile. "Well, I do have a couple of things that I wanted to make sure to tell you today. First of all, and I don't know how I forgot to tell you this yesterday, but right before Natalia died in the fire, she came to our door one day. She was carrying a box, a soiled, broken, old hatbox, and asked my mother if she would be sure to give it to Joy in case she vanished or something else happened to her. My mother told her that was ridiculous, that people don't just vanish, but of course Natalia wasn't right, wasn't normal. Natalia insisted . . . She so insisted that my mother finally accepted it, and promised that she would give it to Joy if that circumstance occurred. Natalia politely said thank you and left. I do believe that was the last time we ever saw her alive."

"So, Lillian, what happened to the box and the contents?" I quickly asked.

"Maybe it wasn't right, but, I remember my mother coming in the house and untying the ribbons which held the box closed. I believe that she thought it was her duty, because my mother was worried that something was going to happen to Natalia. She opened it immediately. The only things inside the box were a framed picture of Natalia and some very strange clothing...Clothing that seemed to be from another age."

"Another age?" I said, surprised. "And Lillian, did Joy ever get the box?"

"Oh yes, my mother gave it to Joy right before she went to Ohio. I guess she treasured that picture. I remember seeing it at her home many times. It would always be setting atop her marble, claw-foot table."

"Do you think she still has it?" I inquired, "I'd love to see it."

"I would be very surprised if she doesn't. I imagine the girls have it now. Perhaps you could ask them. There was something else I was going to tell you, too, but wouldn't you know, it has completely slipped my mind."

Two aides entered the room. "Lillian, it's time for your bath." One of them approached her, and the other one waited with towels in her arms.

"An old lady has to go and get clean now." Lillian smiled. "Please, my dear, don't forget your letters." She pointed to the floor next to the wheelchair.

"Lillian, I'm going to leave you with my cell phone number. You can call me anytime. I'd love to hear anything that you remember." I bent down and scribbled it on a menu planner that was laying on her table.

"I will do that, dear," she said, as the women got her into the wheelchair. "So sorry to make you leave so suddenly."

I kissed her cheek. "We'll keep in touch, okay?"

"Okay, and thanks again for sharing the letters," she said, as I walked out the door.

I once again drove into Bitterwood Commons past the big stone towers on each side of the entrance, and parked my car. I looked at my watch. 11:45; I can't believe I'm early, I thought to myself. I started to recline my seat to relax when I heard a truck pull in next to my car. It was Peter.

"We're both early, huh?" Peter said, getting out of his truck at the same time I got out of my car. "So what has little Em been up to today?"

I looked at Peter and smiled. "Well, I picked up my letters from the woman in the nursing home that I told you about. She gave me a bit more information...Just what I needed! And, that's about all...Now, I'm here.

"I wanted to meet you this morning before you left because I wanted to show you the gazebo. Can we walk down there together? ... Do you have time?"

"Well, ... I'm awfully busy," Peter said, in a flirtatious manner as he began pushing me down the path. "But I guess I can make time for you!"

I had never really told anyone: Peter; Daniel; anyone, all the details of why I was in LaPier. For some reason, I felt compelled to share the entire mind-boggling story with Peter today. The sun was shining brilliantly and it was another warm July day as we stood by the gazebo. I began blabbering on and on and on and, after some time, I finished the whole, compelling story. I stood, looking at Peter, awaiting his conclusion.

"Well, you know what I have to say about all of this, don't you, Em?" Peter said as he grabbed both of my hands in his. "I think you're way over your head. I don't think you should believe half of it. And, furthermore, I think you need to go home, even though I know you won't take my advice. I will, however, say one thing positive about this little trip of yours... Well, two, since we were able to be together for a while. I will say, I haven't seen anything spark your interest like this in so long. You remind me of the Em I used to know in college, and that's a very good thing."

I smiled at Peter, wondering how he came up with some of the conclusions that he did, and walked over to the gazebo marker. The sun was beginning to hit the stones underneath on an angle, prisming the light in different directions. I looked over to the hill and noticed that the light was almost reaching it. I looked at Peter as he watched me. He stood there with a big smile on his face, shaking his head.

"Are you planning on leaving this earth today...Time travel perhaps?" He chuckled and I was sure he was recounting the story I had just told him. Then he walked over closer to me.

"Peter, seriously, before you leave, I need to say something. I'm just not ready for any kind of relationship yet. I still haven't forgiven so many things. I'm still so angry, and I don't know how to make all this crap go away. You're right about my obsession with these letters. It is the first time since I lost Anthony that I've had something to think about that helps me to release the pain. It's crazy that I'm admitting this to you. I can't remember the last time I uttered Anthony's name aloud. I don't know what I'm going to find here, but something or someone is telling me to look. I will always love you, Peter, as my friend ... Please understand."

Peter stared at me for some time. He walked over and sat on a nearby stump. Neither of us said another word for what seemed like five minutes. Finally he got up and came over to me. "I'm going to take off then, Em, okay?" I could sense a sort of resentment in the way Peter looked and sounded.

"Peter, please..." I tried to continue, but he interrupted.

"Find what you're looking for here. Get rid of your anger, your pain, and your bitterness...all of it. And you have to forgive before you will ever get on with your life. You will never be able to love again, Em; not really, not totally, until you forgive. When that happens, maybe you'll think differently of me, or even Daniel for that matter. I told you that Daniel loves you. Even with all you have been through together, he still loves you. And you have children together; please remember those kids."

I closed my eyes, shook my head, and then looked at Peter. "You know, you don't have to remind me. I know I have kids far too freaking well." I quickly lit up a cigarette.

"Em, I care for you enough that I want what's best for you. If that includes me in your life, as more than a friend then, that would be great. But if it doesn't, I'll live with that, too. I just want you happy."

Peter headed down the gravel walkway. "I'll be thinking of you."

I didn't say a word. I just stood there holding on to the marker in one hand, as it were the only thing holding me up in this world, and holding my cigarette in the other. I felt angry. I watched Peter continue down the path until he turned the corner and was gone behind the tree line.

I read the words on the marker once again: May this gazebo erect new hope and new beginnings. "Yeah, right," I said, throwing down my cigarette and beating it repetitiously with my foot into the ground.

After a while, I went and sat in the gazebo. I hadn't uttered Anthony's name aloud in years, and after I said it to Peter, it made me miss my boy again with even more excruciating pain. He was such a beautiful child. I could still see that little 8-year-old boy as if it were yesterday as he looked up at me with his vibrant green eyes. They were unusually beautiful eyes; the type that even passing strangers would comment on. Why had Daniel allowed Anthony to fall from that fishing vessel on Lake Michigan while the undertow was at its peak?

His little body had been swept far under the cold water and hadn't been recovered for over two months. When we got the call that he had been found on that beach, the only recognizable item still clinging to his faded, torn shirt was a little firefighter badge that he always wore. The toy gold plating had rubbed off from the coerce of the deep waters, but on an area of the badge engraved within the plastic was the name "Anthony" that I had painted on so painstakingly only days before the drowning. I was furious that I had painted his name on that badge, for maybe then I wouldn't have had to claim that lifeless little body. I guess there was so much anger that I harbored deep within that I was unable to love anymore.

Tears blurred my eyes and I could barely make out what was in front of me. I closed my eyes, rubbed them, then looked up and tried to focus. I looked at my watch. I had spent more time with Peter than I had thought. It was going on 2 o'clock, an hour later than I had wanted to be here. The hill was in front of me, and it was just as the young man had promised yesterday. The sight was spectacular! The prisms from the sun reflecting on the stones under the marker were shooting directly upon the hill. I quickly got up, walked over a short distance, and climbed the small knoll. I had to close my eyes at times; the rays were so intense.

I pulled the wadded-up piece of paper out from my purse and began reading the words aloud. "The stones upon foundation stand, for sun to prism onto land. And, if you're in the perfect place, you'll be transported to another place." I stood there, still rubbing my teary eyes, and gave a sarcastic laugh. Then I said the chant again. This time I said it from memory. "The stones upon foundation stand, for sun to prism onto land. And, if you're in the perfect place, you'll be transported to another place." Instantly one of the prisms ricocheted from the marker, hitting the middle of my sapphire necklace. When it hit, it felt as though a bullet had shot through my chest and made me gasp for air. The ray of light instantaneously ricocheted back to the stone on the marker, and I fell to the ground as if dead. I lay there, and it was as though a kaleidoscope of events, from my early childhood until now, encircled my memory. I couldn't move, no matter how I tried, and I was so fatigued. Finally, after what seemed to be an hour, I was able to partially move my limbs. Slightly at first, and then I was able to get up.

Oh my Gosh, where was I? Everything had changed. What had happened to me? I brushed the dirt from my clothes and stumbled down the hill trying to stay on the path. It wasn't a gravel walkway anymore. It was a small dirt trail. If I was still in Bitterwood Commons, where did the gazebo go? What happened to the towering trees? I felt around my neck, searching for the chain of my necklace. Frantically, I searched...My necklace was gone! I quickly ran back up the hill to where I had fallen and searched the ground, but it was nowhere to be found. Suddenly I was taken aback by the sound of children coming up the trail. I stood silently as they approached. They saw me and hesitated, staring for a few moments. Their clothes! ... The girls...This couldn't be happening to me!

"Lillian, look what that lady is wearing!" One of them commented.

"We can't worry about that, Joy! We must continue looking for the necklace! I will be in so much trouble! It must be over here...Come on!"

I couldn't believe what I was hearing as the girls hurried down the trail. Had they somehow known that I had lost my necklace? Then, I suddenly realized who the two little girls named Joy and Lillian were! They were about 90 years younger from when I had seen them the last time! I WAS HERE! I was definitely here! I had traveled to the past! The prisms, the chant, it wasn't a hoax, it worked! This was absolutely ludicrous! What was I to do now? I wanted to scream. I looked down the hill and spotted what looked like, a one-room schoolhouse.

I wandered slowly toward the white, wooden building, dragging my feet and watching the trail as I went. I felt weak and clumsy, blaming it on my fall. Suddenly I spotted something. I quickly bent down and swept through the greenery with my hand. I was looking for a glaring object. There it was ... My necklace! I wondered how it had gotten over here. I hadn't walked in this area since I had arrived in the past, but then perhaps I had been too mixed up to even notice. Quickly, I put it on, struggling a bit to get the clasp shut, and then I continued over to the schoolhouse.

I peeked in the first of three windows, on the side of the building. It looked as though there had been a summer party and the children had just left. A very proper-looking young woman was cleaning up. The things I saw were not from the period of time that I was from! This was amazing! Could it be that I was the only one to have ever time-traveled? I continued watching as the woman packed up some papers, placed them in a linen-look bag, and began to head to the door. I hid around the corner of the building. Soon, I heard the door shut, and I saw her continue down the trail. The trail must lead to town.

Quickly and quietly, I opened the door, went inside, and closed it behind me. The wooden desks sat neatly in three rows with allowance for two children to sit at each desk. The blackboards went almost across the entire front of the room, and an American flag hung proudly above the boards. The teacher's desk sat in the middle front of the schoolroom.

There was a calendar hanging from the wall and a date was circled. On that date someone had written Bitterwood School Summer Party. The date was July 7, 1920. I was now living in the very time period that I had wished to be in! I closed my eyes, trying to shake myself out of this place, but I went nowhere. I was exhausted! I just wanted to sleep. In the corner some blankets and quilts were stacked on a shelf. I pulled a couple of them out and placed one on the floor, covering myself with the other. It smelled of 1920, sort of musty, sort of disturbing. I began to cry. How would I ever get back to Daniel and my family? All of a sudden, I missed them terribly. I closed my eyes, pretending it was a dream.

Chapter 6

Transformations

atalia...Natalia, please wake up..."
I could faintly hear some words as I opened my eyes a notch.

"Natalia!"

I awakened to find a man looking to be in his early 30s nudging my shoulders, pleading with me to awaken. I took a deep breath. "Who are you?" I asked.

"Natalia, you know who I am. I'm Justin Peterson, the parson. Wake up; please...the whole town has been searching for you."

I looked at the stranger and I looked at my surroundings. I suddenly realized that this was far more than a nightmare. I quickly felt for my necklace. It was still around my neck. I shook my head and flinched my body hard, trying to find reality. Why was this man calling me Natalia?

"Where am I?" I asked, confused.

"You're in Bitterwood School," he answered. "You must have fallen asleep here last night. Your husband and daughter are so worried about you. Like I said, the whole town has been searching for you."

"I'm ... I'm sorry," I said hesitantly. "But please answer me. Why are you calling me Natalia? That is not my name." I couldn't figure out why he seemed to evade my questions. I got up from the makeshift bed, glancing to see that I was still clothed in my short skirt and tank top from a century yet to come. I assumed it would be quite inappropriate clothing for this day and age. Keeping the quilt tightly around me, I watched as the young man seemed to struggle with words to say to me.

"Natalia, we've got to get you home," he said, staring at me earnestly.

I was trying to keep calm and find understanding as to why he was calling me Natalia, and yet, crazily enough, it was as though it all made complete sense. It was like I belonged here, and I almost felt at home in these new surroundings.

"Would it be okay if I took the quilt along with me?" I asked, trembling from fear. "I'm very, very cold," I lied, trying to justify the shivers. "I will return it to you without delay."

"Yes, ... Yes, take it with you. I hope you're not becoming ill, Natalia. Would you like me to walk you home? I really don't think you should be wandering the countryside today in your condition."

"I would be indebted to you if you would," I answered as I began to walk toward the door with my new acquaintance helping me.

"Do you remember why you stayed here last night, Natalia?" he asked as we left the schoolhouse.

"I can't remember last night," I answered. "Everything is a blank until you awakened me this morning." I yawned. "Oh ...Wait. I do recall something. Yesterday, I recall stumbling upon two little girls just before I got here. They had to have been the girls named Joy and Lillian. They saw me, but they didn't recognize me. They were looking for something in the woods."

"Well, you've had quite an ordeal staying in the school-house all night. I'm sure you'll be glad to get back home." Parson Peterson spoke with sweetness and consideration in his voice.

We walked and walked, and it was so hot that I could

feel the sweat dripping from me even though the trembling continued. I, however, kept the quilt wrapped tightly around me so as not to divulge my attire. Eventually we approached a wider gravel road which I assumed led into town. I could see a few houses in the distance. We were on State Street, I was certain, the very location in my letters and the place within my dreams for quite some time now. I hardly spoke and the parson hardly spoke, although there were myriads of questions I wanted to ask him! As we started up a small hill, a man and little girl approached.

"Natalia!" the man hollered. "Where have you been?" As the little girl hurried toward me, I realized it was the girl I assumed to be Joy, who had passed by me in the woods the previous day. When she reached me she hugged my legs tightly.

"Mama, Mama, we were so worried. Why do you have that quilt around you when it's so warm outside? Papa," Joy hollered, turning back to her father. "She's sweating!" Tears streamed down her face.

"Your mama's cold," answered the parson. "She may be ill."

Why was this little girl calling me Mama, I thought to myself, especially when she hadn't recognized me yesterday?

I bent down and looked at her. She should have been a mere stranger to me, but I could somehow sense, that in this life, she seemed to love me very much.

"Your necklace!" Joy said, as she saw it dangling from around my neck. "Where did you find it, Mama?" Her face flushed with surprised.

"What about my necklace?" I asked.

"Nothing, Mama, nothing....I'm just glad you didn't lose it...that's all."

By that time the man had caught up. He stood there gazing at me. He was a gruff-looking, older man. Not given to pleasant appearance, about six feet tall with longer, thinning, graying hair and a stubbly beard.

"You have got to stop running away like this, Natalia," he said softly, catching his breath. He took my hair in his hands and began stroking the long strands with what seemed to be affection. It made me very uneasy, and as his hand continued caressing my hair, it made me take notice of something strange. My hair was no longer blonde and curly, it was straight and jet black! Was I no longer who I used to be? I began to freak out and felt faint. This was so confusing, so unbelievable! I needed to look at my appearance; I needed so many things! I began crying.

"I'm going to leave you with your family now, Natalia," the parson said as he patted the man on the back and smiled at the little girl.

I couldn't help but notice how the parson kept his right hand clasped shut, even when he reached out to pat the other man on the back. I also, for the life of me, couldn't help but wonder why these people didn't think it strange that I, being an adult woman, was crying and sobbing. Why didn't anyone console me? Could this just be the normal way that Natalia acted? Did they just ignore her? It was unbelievable!

"But, wait...please wait," I interjected, looking at the parson. "How am I going to get home?" I continued crying.

"Mama, we'll take you home, you know that," the little girl said sincerely. She took my hand and started leading me away.

"I'll let everyone know she's been found during the service today," the parson whispered to the man. "She was sleeping at the schoolhouse. She claims that two little girls passed her in the woods yesterday...claims they were Joy and Lillian. Joy never said anything about seeing her, did she?"

"No, of course not," Gerrit quickly interjected. "If she had, I would have come for her. She did say something about seeing some peculiar stranger, come to think about it, but never Natalia."

"Strange, don't you think?" the parson questioned.

Gerrit nodded his head in agreement.

"Well, take her home and she'll probably feel better," the parson continued. "I'll check back on your family on my way home after services."

I watched the two talk as the parson nodded at me. "Take care, Natalia." And, with that, he headed back in the same direction we had just come from.

I was still crying when we finally reached 89 State Street. Reality was beginning to baffle me. I knew what had happened to me, even though it was freakily unbelievable. But what was even more puzzling was that the longer I stayed in this new era, the more my memory from my past life seemed to be fading. We reached the door of the house where I eerily, but barely, remembered talking to Jill VanderBerg and her mother just days ago. Now, however, it was a new structure!

"Please show me to my room, little girl, if you would be so kind." I directed my words to the girl who I thought must be Joy. She had been holding my hand the entire way home. She looked at me queerly and her lips began to quiver.

Without warning, Gerrit's fist slammed on the table in front of us. He winched and cradled his fist in his other hand. I could tell the man was in pain from his action. "Natalia Kappan, this is your daughter...Your daughter, Joy," he hollered. "She's not a stranger! Why do you call her little girl?" His soft-spoken tone had greatly changed. "Why must you torment us the way you do?" He kicked the table leg, sending the table thumping against the kitchen floor. "I do nothing but kindness for you and your daughter and yet you leave, and we don't know where you are! An entire night you were gone! Do you ever think that we worry about you? Your daughter cried the entire night. She never slept, because she didn't know if her mother was ever going to be coming home again." The man came toward me.

"Please, please, know that I am so sorry." I whispered through terrified tears, "I... I didn't know...Please, can I go to my room?"

"Go...Get out of here! You sicken me so!" he answered, turning away.

The little girl ran to me, grabbing my hand, and I followed

her up the stairs. The quilt was still wrapped around me, as I stumbled a bit getting up. It was a very narrow, steep stairway as we got to the top.

"Joy, you must listen to me. I am not feeling well. I didn't mean to hurt your feelings, darling, by calling you little girl." I knelt down, gently brushing the tears from her cheeks.

"I know, Mama," she answered. "But why do you do the things you do? You know my name is Joy, and yet you call me little girl as though you don't even know me. I just want you to be like a regular Mama."

"Oh darling, what can I say?" I closed my eyes, grasping my face in my hands, trying to get my composure for the dear little person in front of me. She most definitely had to have been through more than most children her age. I remembered all the things I was told that Natalia was known for.

"Come, Mama, I put new water in the wash basin, so you can freshen up. You can use the new soap that Aunt Agatha made." Joy tried to pull the quilt from around me, but I held it tight.

"It's hot today. You don't need that blanket around you. You're not ill, are you?" Joy stroked my back and put her little hand into mine again. I got up and followed her into a room that was in front of us.

The room was modest but clean and sunlight streamed through the windows. In one window hung a large fern, and below that was a little sitting bench built within the dormer area. There was a bed in one corner, draped with what looked like a hand-sewn quilt. I noticed the bed at once.

"Joy, if you could tell me, dear. Does your father share this room with me?" I knew there wasn't any evidence of it, but I was so fearful. I needed to ask.

"No," she answered. "Papa's room is down there." She pointed to the room down the hall. "He told you that it was your room too, whenever you wanted it to be, remember?"

"Of course, honey, how could I have forgotten? And do I share it with him frequently?"

"Mama, you never go in there. Papa gets so mad."

I gave a sigh of relief. As I scanned the room I noticed two dressers; one with an ornate mirror. When I saw my reflection, I screamed and grabbed my face. Joy was horrified and screamed as well. I could hear Gerrit quickly come to the steps. "Is she okay, Joy?" he hollered.

"Yes, Papa," Joy answered, looking at me and then in the direction of her papa's voice. "I think so." Joy's face was so pale.

She turned back to me. "What now, Mama? What's wrong?" Joy looked so sad.

"Joy," I said, "What do you see when you look at me? Have I always looked this way?" I couldn't get my eyes off the mirror. I kept moving to test if the mirror was telling me the truth. I was young again. I was gaunt but beautiful, and now I was apparently Natalia Kappan!

"Mama, it's you," Joy said softly, rubbing my arm with her hand. She went over to the dresser and picked up a couple of pictures, one in a pretty pearl frame. She brought them over and handed them to me.

"These are pictures of Natalia?" I questioned.

"Yes, Mama, these are pictures of Natalia and Natalia is you. Please Mama, please be okay."

I looked at the photos and then I looked in the mirror, over and over again. Joy sat quietly watching me from the bed. "Joy, did you see me in the woods yesterday? I saw you and another little girl leaving the school."

"No, Mama," she answered. "Papa already asked me that question. Lillian and I lost something very important after the party, and we were looking for it. We passed a stranger, but we had never seen her before. She had funny clothing on. Almost like undergarments; like a colorful corset and slip, but nothing over them. Why, where were you, Mama?"

"Oh, you must have been in a hurry and didn't see me," I answered. "I was walking to the school. You didn't recognize the stranger, Joy? Did you look at her face?"

"No, Mama. I had never seen her before. She had fair-colored hair and was older than you."

I tried to figure out my transformation. When had it taken place? All I could figure out was that I must have turned into Natalia Kappan the moment I put the necklace back on after finding it along the path. Could this tremendous love that I felt for this Arie have taken precedence from Natalia Kappan's love for him? Could this love have somehow summoned me to join him here in this time, confusing me for his true love? Could it be that the real Natalia was absent from this time period at the very split second that I had come? Perhaps she, too, was seeking something in another time, just as I had, and because of this void in this sequence of seconds, I now had become her! And, what was the explanation for the necklace not being around my neck when I got here, and then me finding it along the path? Nothing made sense!

"Please Joy, could you leave me alone for a while? I asked. "I really need to be alone."

"Yes, Mama," she said, as she promptly got up. I followed her to the door. I began to close it, when she reminded me sternly, "Papa doesn't let you have the door shut...remember?"

"And what will he do if it's shut?" I inquired.

"Mama, you know he'll get mad."

"Please don't tell him, Joy. I desperately need the door shut for a little while. Please understand, dear. Maybe I'll feel better then."

"I won't tell, Mama," she whispered. "But he will see."

"We'll deal with that then, dear." I shut the door quietly, leaving the little girl reluctantly on the other side. I stood at the door for a few minutes but didn't hear her leave. Finally, the sound of footsteps faded away down the stairs. I threw the quilt off and quickly began rummaging through the dressers searching for something to wear. I pulled out what looked to be a matching two-piece dress outfit. I undressed and quickly got rid of my other clothing, hiding it behind some garments in the back of the dresser. I hurriedly dressed in the new clothing. All the buttons took forever to fasten.

There was an armoire in the corner next to the bed, and I opened it, finding more apparel. On the dresser sat a wash basin and pitcher of water. I guess Joy had already reminded me of that. I needed to freshen up so badly. I poured some water into the bowl. Cupping my hands, I wet my face. The lukewarm water burned my eyes. I had done so much crying that it stung. I dried with a little fringed, embroidered towel that hung next to the basin and continued to look at myself in the mirror. I brushed out my long, black hair with a silver brush that sat next to a matching comb.

I couldn't fathom why all of this was happening, but I couldn't help believe that I was the one responsible. I had said the chant. I had said it over and over. Of course, I secretly wanted to come, but who would have thought it would have happened? Now, the only thing I could do was to deal with it. I guess the strangest thing besides everything else was that I was starting to get a sensation of truly being Natalia Kappan. I even had feelings for that little girl downstairs beyond what I should. I opened up a sterling silver rectangular container and gently patted my face with the powder inside. It was almost routine... how did I know what was in there!

Peculiarly, all of the things on the dresser seemed familiar, even the perfume bottle. I opened it and smelled the scent. It was fresh and pure and made me think of love...made me think of Arie! "Arie, you're here; you're in this world, aren't you?" I watched my mouth say those words as I looked at myself in the mirror, and it frightened me. Yet it made me long for him like never before. He had made a promise in so many letters that he'd find his true love through all space, through all time, if she only wore the necklace. Here I was! I embraced the precious stone in my hand and held it tight to my chest, looking at it in the mirror.

All of a sudden, something occurred to me. I was now living in the past from where I had come. The future I had known had not yet happened. Before I was taken back, or whatever was going to happen to me, I had to make an attempt at something before it was too late. I frantically looked around for some paper and an envelope. I found something resembling parchment paper, neatly tucked away in the top drawer of the dresser. I quickly jotted down some words, dipping the pen in ink as I went, and sealed the message inside the envelope. I addressed it appropriately, then hid it under the doily on the dresser.

Suddenly, the door to my room burst open. I could see through the reflection in the mirror that Gerrit was standing in the doorway. I had hid the envelope just in time.

"Natalia," he said, in the same soft tone as when I first met him. "You are not to leave your door shut. I've made that perfectly clear to you. What are you doing in here?"

Just then, Joy came into sight, standing beside him. "Mama, why are you wearing your Sunday clothes?"

"Take those clothes off and put something appropriate on," Gerrit insisted.

I began to cry once again. I didn't know what kind of clothes to put on! "This is too much for me...Where are my pills? Why am I going through this?" I wept.

Gerrit quickly spoke up. "Joy, go down and get your mother her laudanum."

"Papa, please, leave Mama alone right now." Joy whimpered. "I will go get her medicine in a minute, but just let me sit with her right now. Let me help her to change her clothing."

"Always the same!" Gerrit shrugged. He turned around and left once again, leaving Joy and me alone in the room.

Chapter 7

Fading Memories

oy helped me to change into a less fancy dress. Of course, I had no clue as to what was in style in this age. Besides, it seemed to me that none of the clothes Natalia Kappan owned were on the fancy side, making them all seem appropriate. I did, however, spot one dress in the armoire that was an exception. It was all white, simple, but extremely elegant. At once, for some strange reason, I felt a longing to wear this dress. I felt that it was a part of my near, yet unknown, future.

"Do you feel better now, Mama?" Joy asked.

"Yes, Joy, I do," I answered, giving the little girl a subdued smile. Something strange was continuing to happen to me. The more I tried to remember things from my other life, the harder it was to comprehend them. I still had love for my kids, for Libby, Collin, and even my precious deceased Anthony, but I was also beginning to love this little soul that sat so patiently with me. I was beginning to have a bond with Joy that I couldn't explain.

"Joy," I said, turning to her. "I have forgotten so many things. Could you please tell me about my life? I know that may sound strange to you, but I need for you to tell me all that you know."

"Mama, I try to tell you things and explain things to you all the time, but you forget so much!"

I was trying to grasp what Joy meant. Was Natalia Kappan's mind incomprehensible? Was she so mentally ill that she was unable to reason? My mind still belonged mostly to Emma Barker, and yet I feared that I was slowly dissolving, both mind and body, and perhaps even soul, into the depths of Natalia Kappan. While I believed that my thoughts were still somewhat coherent, remembering both past and present to some degree, at this moment; I knew I was slipping away. I needed to make as much sense out of things as possible in a very short time.

"Joy, do you know someone named Arie?" I continued. "He must live around here."

"No, Mama, NO; there is no Arie!" she said adamantly. "Please quit saying his name, it makes Papa so angry!"

"Do I say his name much?" I continued to inquire.

"Papa has to wake you up all the time from your sleep. You always are yelling out Arie in the dark of night. Papa always has to bring you your laudanum to get back to sleep. We don't want to know who he is, Mama. Papa says you made him up because you don't love us enough."

"No...no, that is not true." I shook my head. "I love you, and don't ever forget that."

"Mama, please, stay how you are right now. You have never talked to me like this before. I like you how you are right now." Joy gave the porcelain-faced doll that she was holding a hug.

"What do you mean, Joy? How is it that I act?"

"Mama, you are always wanting me to fetch the letters. You wake up in the morning and ask me if the parson is gone so that I can get them for you. You run away all the time and papa has to bring you home. You start screaming and won't quit no matter what papa does for you. You stay at the gazebo day and night. The children are scared of you.

They see you, you know? They see you chanting. I try to make you stop and you don't listen. They say things about you to me. They ask me why you don't come to Sunday worship service, and tell me that you have the devil in your soul. They call you a murderer, Mama! They even say that you're the one who screams through our town."

I was at a loss for words and paused, contemplating what I had just heard. "Joy, I'm so sorry, Dear. You just have to listen to me now, just in case, again, I become as you say I was. I can talk rationally to you right now. You can believe what I am saying, and I do love you, Sweetie. Do you understand?"

The little girl nodded her head yes.

"Now, please tell me of the letters that you talk of; where are they?"

"Mama, you know that they are in the barn. Parson Peterson keeps them hidden in the barn. I found you getting them out before. You know where they are."

"And how did we originally find them?"

"It was I, Mama. I found a couple of them on the ground one day when I was leaving Parson Peterson's house. Don't you remember? I took them to you, and you read them and cried and cried and even screamed. You made me promise to never tell Papa that I had found them. You made me take the letters back to Parson Peterson one night, and tell him that I discovered them. He asked me if anyone else had seen them. I did what you said, Mama, I lied and told him, no. It was that night that papa and I found you, without a lantern, watching the parson through the window in the barn. The next day, when the parson went into town and Papa was gone, you made me climb up in the loft in the parson's barn. You told me the letters were hidden under a door up there, and sure enough, they were, just as you had said. Mama, you read the letters whenever you can."

Joy whispered as she spoke, and kept turning to the door as though to be watching for her father to appear. "I know that the letters are signed by Arie, but Mama, who is he? Do you love him? Is that why you don't love Papa?"

"I don't know who he is," I said, crying. "And, Joy, I am sorry for everything." I took the little girl in my arms and hugged her tenderly. I sobbed, thinking of what kind of life she had endured.

We sat on the bed together for some time, and I fell asleep with her cradled in my arms.

"So, you're getting along all right then?" I awakened, hearing talking downstairs. Quietly, I picked up Joy. She was still lying against me, asleep. I lay her on the bed and went to the doorway to listen.

"Natalia's been acting differently since she came home. She hasn't lapsed into her screaming bouts and hasn't demanded her medicine that much. She's been asleep upstairs for the better part of the afternoon without taking her laudanum. I've been keeping my eye on her. She even let Joy sleep with her this afternoon, cuddled in her arms. Natalia seldom gives Joy much attention; you know that."

"I noticed it too, Gerrit," I heard the parson reply. "She talked to me coherently while I was with her today. However, she kept asking me why I called her Natalia. She even gave me permission to walk her home, something Natalia would normally never want. She always insists on being alone as though she's waiting for someone to appear and take care of her. Maybe a miracle has happened, Gerrit. We'll just have to wait and see."

"I guess we will. So, the service went good today?" Gerrit asked.

"It was fine. The choir sang nicely, but we missed you and Joy, as always," the parson answered. "Hopefully, Natalia will continue to get better and you all can join us! That continues to be my prayer."

I needed to ask this man downstairs so many questions. For some reason, I trusted him. I imagined it was because of what had been said about his faithful character from the people from my previous lifetime. I grabbed the letter that I had hidden under the doily on my dresser, tucked it in my dress, and quickly ran down the stairs.

"Well, hello, Natalia, are you feeling a bit better?" the parson questioned. "I was scared you were getting ill."

"Yes," I answered briskly. "I was wondering if you had a moment? I would like to speak with you in private."

"Natalia, whatever you have to say can be said in front of all of us," Gerrit said softly.

"No, I need to talk to the parson." I grabbed his arm, noticing once again that he kept his hand tightly closed.

"Natalia, let him go," Gerrit continued in his soft tone.

I continued grabbing Justin Peterson's arm anxiously, and quickly exited the house, practically pushing him out the door with me. I walked over to where the picket fence stopped by the road and stood there. We were far enough away from the open windows. I didn't think anything could be overheard inside from what I was about to say. Looking in the window of the house, I could see Gerrit sternly watching, marching back and forth.

"Please, you must help me." I pleaded, looking at the parson, then back at Gerrit in the window. "I don't know how I've acted in the past, but Joy tells me that I am much different right now. I can't explain this to you, but I can feel myself turning back to becoming the other way. I desperately need to know some things. I need to know about my life. Could you please help me?" I scratched my head in dismay. "I feel as though I can trust you." I looked at him with what I'm sure were insistent eyes.

"Natalia, of course you can trust me. I want you to know that! What's brought about this change in you?"

"Things that you would never understand, or, I'd ever be able to explain to you," I stated. "I am at a loss for words to explain it myself."

He looked at me somberly, "Well, where do you want me to start? Are you sure you can't take this up with your husband?"

"NO," I said loudly. "I want to hear it from you. Start with everything you know about me," I pleaded, as I nervously kept looking back and forth at Gerrit in the window.

There was a pause as if he was considering telling me or not. "All right, but this could take some time. I can tell you what I know for sure, but I'm certain that there are a lot of things I don't know about you." He sighed.

"Just start telling me, please," I begged. "I don't know how long we'll have alone before Gerrit will come out."

"Well, you came to LaPier, as I understand, when you were young. You were orphaned as a child. I understand that you had a foreign-born mother. Gerrit was told that she was of Russian and Asian descent, and was unable to care for you. And, please know that this was not unusual for children to go through in those days. Natalia, I'm sure your mother had the best of intentions. So many different ethnicities, religions; just precious souls, immigrated here to the East Coast, and then were unable to find jobs, or care for their young. I'm sure that's what happened to your mother. She only wanted a better life for you. You used to live in New York City. In those days, they rounded up the children that were living on the streets that needed homes and placed them with people throughout the States. You were put on a train and placed with a family here in LaPier, named the Sloans. Do you remember any of this?"

"No," I said blinking my eyes. "Indeed I don't," and yet, fragments of pictures and voices invaded my thoughts. Some were violent; some were beautiful! "Please go on," I insisted.

"My family also is gone, Natalia," Justin continued. "Do you remember me telling you the story about that?"

"No."

"They died of the cholera on route, ironically, to New York City also. My father was going to establish a tannery there. I, like you, was the only one in my family who I thought survived. My family was originally from Colorado. My uncle owned a mining company there. I was the oldest of four children and my parents left me with him to learn the mining trade. I've always asked God why He let me live and took everyone else."

"That is amazing, Justin, so much suffering in this time period, but, you said you thought survived. Did someone end up surviving?"

"No, no...No one else." He shook his head and seemed to quiver as he spoke.

"So how did I ever end up with Gerrit Kappan?" I looked at him intently, awaiting his answer.

"Gerrit Kappan cares for you greatly, Natalia. He married you when you were very young. You must remember that he cares for you, although I know it's hard for him to show his true feelings."

"I'm sorry to say, I haven't felt that." I paused and looked down. "And what about my daughter? I must have given birth to her when I was very, very young."

"Indeed you did, but those things are better left in the past. You have a dear, dear daughter, Natalia. Are you sure you don't remember anything more?"

"No," I demanded, yet again, pictures that were very violent entered my subconscious. I looked again to the house. Gerrit still stood in the window watching.

"Please start coming to worship service, Natalia," the parson said. "The thing that freed me from all my grief was going into the ministry. I started doing tent revivals along with my uncle's parson right after my uncle's death. We traveled all around, and then I began doing them on my own. It's amazing to watch people's lives transformed. This little city right here is where God has called me. I've had to deal with so many tragedies, as you well know. But, then again, perhaps you've forgotten all of it. I have learned, right here, how to forgive and love through the toughest measures."

"I'm glad it helped you; religion just never seemed to help me," I replied.

"You have to give it a chance," he insisted.

"I used to be religious, shall we say, in another life, but

that's another story. It's a huge unbelievable story. I must ask you one more important question," I said in haste. "Do you have any idea who Arie is?"

The parson bent his head, closed his eyes, and suddenly seemed very troubled.

"Natalia, why do you ask me that? Don't you remember?"

"No, you must tell me," I begged.

"If you don't remember, it's better if it's left as it is."

I grabbed his shirt. "I need to know." I looked at him pleading, and bit my lip.

His face turned solemn. "Natalia, do you remember anything that happened at the gazebo in times past?"

I squinted my eyes, trying to remember. "No," I replied.

"If you don't remember, then keep it that way. Perhaps you're feeling better because you have forgotten. We all need to forgive, or life is not worth living. Please trust me. I need to go now."

"But you can't just leave me here with all my questions. Especially, with a man that I don't know and don't trust." I grabbed onto his shirt. "You can't just leave me here," I shrieked. I looked at the window and noticed that Gerrit was gone.

"Could I count on you to do something very important for me?" I asked nervously, letting go of his shirt and pulling the letter out from within my clothing. I looked to the door and could see Gerrit on his way out.

"Take this letter and please attach appropriate postage. I beg of you to mail it for me. Don't ask any questions or say anything, just mail it, please." I slipped the sealed envelope in his hand, hoping he'd adhere to my wishes. At that moment, Gerrit and Joy began toward us.

"Everything okay?" Gerrit asked. I knew he had heard my elevated voice, and I wondered if he had seen from the window how upset I had gotten.

"Everything is fine, right, Natalia?" the parson assured him.

I nodded my head. "I will be needing to talk more with you." I said.

"Natalia, Justin is a busy man," Gerrit replied.

"I'm next door if you need anything, Natalia. Good day, everyone." And Justin Peterson departed for his home.

"Let's go in and get something for dinner," Gerrit recommended. "You must be very hungry." He took me by the arm and showed me back into the house.

While I had been asleep upstairs, this man, who was my husband in this life, had prepared a meal for us. The table was set, and I could tell that Joy was very excited.

"We're going to eat together tonight, huh, Mama? We never eat together!"

"It looks like we are." I answered.

There was chicken, potatoes and carrots, and I was surprised at how hungry I had been. Throughout the entire meal, however, there was an uneasiness that loomed over me. Gerrit was civil, and though Joy talked the entire time, only a few words came from Gerrit's mouth.

"Papa, after we clean up, could we all go into town tonight? Those singers are going to be giving a program at the gazebo. Lillian's mom says that they're hoping that it will bring healing to the town. It will be the first gathering since...."

"Shhhh, Joy," Gerrit said, as he put his hand over her mouth.

"But Papa, remember, I told you that Lillian's mother told me all about it?"

"Yes, Joy, I do remember, but we don't need to be reminding your mother right now. You'd better ask her how she'd feel about going into town. She hasn't been to an event in town with us in years, although she likes to go and visit that gazebo alone...that's for sure." His sarcasm was apparent.

"I will go," I answered directly.

They both looked up, shocked. Soon, Joy lunged from her seat, giving me a hug.

"Mama, tonight you can wear the dress you had on today. Everyone won't believe that you are with us! You will look so pretty!"

As the day unfolded, I had to concentrate to remember anything from my past. It was like a slow death was consuming my recollection. I didn't want my memories to fade, but they were doing so without me being aware. Every time I looked at Gerrit Kappan I wished I had my Daniel again. I still remembered Daniel, to some degree, and the things that felt so terrible at one time in my previous life seemed to look better and better now. I didn't know how I was ever going to get back to him, or if I'd just eventually forget that I even lived another life. It felt as though I could cry constantly, and yet the new person I was becoming was starting to take over. I could feel the hardness in her heart from all she'd been through and that hardness helped to scorch some of the tears.

"Are you ready to go?" Joy asked, as she came up to my room and inspected how I looked.

"Almost," I answered.

"You look so pretty, Mama! You even have the flowered comb in your hair that Papa gave you! He will be so surprised. I can't wait until Lillian sees you!"

We descended the stairs and were met by Gerrit in the parlor. He had shaved and looked much better than before, although I couldn't figure out why Natalia would have married a man such as he was. He looked to be in his early 50s, and I presumed that I was still very young.

"Mama, don't forget your wrap," Joy said, as she quickly grabbed her sweater laying on the chair by the table. This little girl definitely acted older than her young age. It was apparent that she was used to, or I should say forced into, taking care of things in this house.

Gerrit gazed at me and then approached. He raised his hand and touched the comb in my hair, and then continued down my back with his hand.

"You look lovely tonight," Natalia. I looked at him, feeling troubled, and turned away.

"Are we walking tonight, Papa? Can we please?" Joy said, jumping up and down.

"Natalia, do you feel up to walking?" Gerrit said rigidly; looking at me.

"That's fine with me," I agreed, as Joy continued jumping right out the door.

It was a balmy evening and I couldn't imagine needing a wrap. But then, I remembered all the references to the cool prairie breezes in the letters from Arie. I closed my eyes and felt the air hit my face as we walked down the very road I knew Arie traveled. I checked my necklace to see that it was still in place. A picture came into my mind of a man, and I stopped for a moment's time to reflect. It was a vivid picture; he was young and handsome. My love for him seemed to be replacing the love I had for Daniel, and I suddenly got a strange but wonderful feeling inside.

Joy skipped and sang a little song all the way down the road until we reached the hill. Soon I could see all the way to town. Between here and town stood the elaborate gazebo in all its grandeur. It was the gazebo mentioned in so many of the letters. The sun was beginning to go down a bit, and there were very pretty colors within the sky of pinks and light yellows. We continued walking as I noticed all the activity. There were wooden chairs arranged all around the gazebo. It was still decorated with bright flags and patriotic colors from the Independence Day Celebration. Families were arriving in buggies and more townspeople were beginning to drive automobiles that were also arriving. Blankets were being placed on the ground and people were passing homemade goodies out that they had prepared for the event.

"Mama, there's Lillian!" Joy yelled out. "Can I go and see her, Mama?"

"Ask your father, Joy," I replied.

"Go, child, go and play," he said, looking down as he spoke.

As we approached, I could sense many people looking at

us. Not only were they looking, but also they were talking amongst themselves, and then looking directly at me. It was obvious that I was creating a stir. What kind of impact did Natalia

Kappan have on this little town? As we got closer, people began to comment and say things to me.

"Nice to have you with us, Natalia," a lady in a peach-colored hat said.

"Thank you, Mrs. Griffin," I replied. I knew this lady's name! How could it be? I had traveled almost a century, and I knew this lady! I now realized that I was taking on Natalia's very soul.

"Gerrit ... Natalia....over here! I've saved you seats," a stout, vivacious lady hollered from the other side of the gazebo. I knew her, too. It was Mrs. Sloan, the lady who had taken me in some years ago. She was, in essence, my adoptive mother, although I never thought of her in those terms. She never gave me love, only used my work abilities to help her out. Although the Sloans had children older than I was, I was the one that cared for the younger Sloan children, while Mrs. Sloan slept or cooked, organized social events, or did whatever she liked to do.

I squinted my eyes and remembered something else: Mrs. Sloan was also Gerrit's sister. That was a fact I had just recalled. I was beginning to remember so many things, and yet so many specifics were still blurred. We got to the seats, and I reluctantly sat down next to my husband, and my husband sat next to his sister. I marveled at how she kept a constant conversation with anyone and everyone around her. I marveled even more, however, at how I kept hearing other things, some unpleasant, being said within the crowd about me. Didn't people know I could hear?

Before long, a group of people took their position on the gazebo, "Welcome, everyone!" they said, as the people scurried to take their seats either in the chairs or on blankets scattered on the ground. The chattering calmed.

Joy quickly appeared with Lillian. The two girls were holding hands. "Doesn't she look pretty, Lillian?" Joy said loudly, as she stroked my skirt. I was embarrassed. I noticed many people gaze our way. I couldn't help but stare at the young Lillian, who had a small birthmark on her fair-skinned cheek. It was the same one I had noticed on the wrinkled-up skin of the old Lillian in the nursing home.

"How are you, Lillian?" I asked, as I noticed Gerrit quickly turning his head around to look at me. "Always remember what a special young lady you are won't you? I promise, you will have a good, long life."

"Thank you, Mrs. Kappan," she replied, in the same low-tone voice that undeniably belonged to her.

The program began with some short talks by various people including the mayor as to how this would be an evening of healing for the town and the gazebo. Patriotic songs and country gospel music followed the speeches. Joy and Lillian sat at my feet, every once in a while giving me a glance and a smile. I now lived in the year 1920, with hardly a glimpse left from the future. God help me!

Chapter 8

$\mathcal{D}efilement$

$\mathcal{I}$ couldn't believe all of the people who insisted on talking with me during the intermission of the program and afterward. It seemed it was the entire town. Gerrit just stood there looking at me in amazement. I wondered how differently I was acting than Natalia usually did. It was almost as though people were talking with me to test me to see how I would respond, instead of making genuine conversation. I did hear Gerrit comment to various people that; Yes, she was indeed doing well. I caught on quickly that the she he was referring to, had to be me.

We had an invitation to the Sloans' house afterward, along with several other people in attendance at the program, for cake and lemonade. Mrs. Sloan strived to be the socialite that everyone looked up to. She was the one who always knew all the news anywhere around LaPier, be it true or made up. Gerrit told his sister that it probably wouldn't be appropriate to come, but she later asked me, and I welcomed the invitation. I've never seen a child more excited about anything in my life as Joy was when she heard we were going for company. She asked if Lillian could come along, and Gerrit told her, yes.

The Sloans had driven their buckboard to the event, so all of the people who had been invited over were instructed to hop on and they would take us to their house. There would be plenty of room on the large wagon for everyone to fit. The only bad part was that we'd have to walk home. Joy assured me that it wasn't a bad thing at all, and that it would be a beautiful walk on a night like this.

The Sloans lived on Engle Road, just west of State Street. It was the place where I lived for a good six years. Joy was so excited to go to their house because Gerrit had been telling her that they were one of the first rural homes in the Bitterwood Commons area to install electricity. Even though there was electric throughout most of the city now, it had not yet come to many houses in the country; including ours. On the way, there was much talk going on amongst the people on the wagon, but I couldn't tell you one word they said. I sat quietly, reminiscing, looking at the countryside as the horses found their way home. No one bothered me, or interrupted my thoughts or visions. It was almost as though everyone knew to keep their distance. As we turned into the driveway of the farm, all sorts of emotions bombarded me.

I definitely did not consider this my home. Although, Mrs. Sloan never gave me love or affection, Mr. Sloan was a different story. He'd hug me whenever he had the chance, sometimes holding me for several minutes. It was very awkward for me, but I had decided that it was his way of trying to make up for Mrs. Sloan's aloofness. Even still, that was the extent of the affection I felt from him as well. Mental and heartfelt love, from either of them, was never given to me. They did, however, keep me warm and fed and provided for. I had to give them credit for that but; still, I always felt more like their servant than their daughter. In the six years I lived with the Sloan Family, I was never told to call them Mom or Dad. I was directed to call them Mr. and Mrs. Sloan, which I still did to this day. I guess the life I had here was better than I could have expected on the streets of New York. At least I had to convince myself of that.

I began remembering more and more. I could now envision being very young when my mother dropped me off at a large, multi-story home in the middle of what must have been New York City. She talked for a long time to an old woman at a desk who tried to interpret my mother's broken English. My mother told me that she'd come back for me and assured me that this lady would care for me until that happened. I must have been so young, yet these memories were all of a sudden so vivid. Everything was rushing through my brain, and I was trying to grasp every minute piece of information while I could.

"Natalia," Gerrit said, interrupting my thoughts. "You going to do some more day-dreaming, or are you coming with us for refreshments?" I looked up, and Gerrit was standing there ready to help me get out of the wagon. I hadn't even noticed that everyone else had already left, or for that matter, that the wagon had come to a halt.

I looked at him and answered, "I need to stay here for a few minutes if you don't mind, Sir."

"Do as you wish, then. I'll be down by the barn," Gerrit said, pointing in that direction. "Are you sure you're okay here, Natalia? I can have the girls keep an eye on you."

"I would appreciate it. And yes; I'm fine," I concluded. I wondered why Gerrit seemed so concerned about me being here.

"My memories...where was I?" I whispered to myself, as I watched Gerrit walk down a path on the side of the house that led to the barn. This was an amazing journey I had taken. It was as though I had entered the pages of a book with everything already written down as to what had happened. I just had to let my brain read through it. I leaned my head back on the wooden board and watched as twilight captured this era. Suddenly, I felt weak. I didn't know if there was something within the breeze from being at this familiar place, or just the sheer strain on my body from everything that had occurred, but that same voice that had commanded me to come to LaPier once again invaded my head.

You are so close, now, Natalia......Please come to me, it

said with authority.

I shivered.

"Where are you?" I yelled out.

I must have drawn the attention of a couple of the Sloans' grandchildren who were playing nearby in a mud puddle. They looked at me in fear and ran back toward the barn. I got up and slowly started on the path. I felt very, very funny. This was a place that I held close to my heart. I could feel it. I had my first kiss here! I sighed.

"Thomas!" It was the first time in this life that I had remembered who I was in love with! His name was Tom Abendroth. It wasn't Arie at all! I continued walking and saw a fence. On the other side of the fence was a large hill that dropped off into a wooded area, and I could scarcely see the outline of a pond below. I went to where the fence was broken down and began searching. I looked and looked some more. "I know it's here!" I panted. Then, I found what I was looking for! It was a pathway overgrown with weeds that wandered off into the woods. I kicked some of the growth aside and began following it, as best I could, slowly down the trail. This was our pathway. I could hardly see as night had fallen, yet, the moon lit the way almost eerily. I stood there as the voice overtook me once more.

Come to me, Natalia, it instructed.

There wasn't only a feeling of love here; there was a definite presence of evil here, too. I could sense it. It abounded all around. All of a sudden, I remembered being 14 years old. Someone claiming to be Thomas threw a stone at my bedroom window and awakened me. Thomas had often gotten my attention in this manner. Now, it was all coming to me. I used to meet Thomas on this path. He was my everything. We grew up together in New York; he took care of me there when I had no one. He came back here to find me! I would sneak out of the Sloans' house and walk this path with Tom. I remembered so vividly now. Even at my young age, he was my only refuge; my only hope was to be with Tom. I could see him now in the reflection of my mind. He was tall and lean, with dark, wavy hair. He had a cute little smile that made his nose turn up when he laughed. Tom was kind and good, and I loved him! Where was he? I still couldn't remember. I went a little farther down the path when I heard something that startled me.

"Joy, is that you?" I said. "Joy...Lillian?" I wondered if she and Lillian had followed me down here.

I continued hearing swishing of leaves and crackling of sticks. Perhaps it was Tom. How I wished!

"Thomas," I called out. "Are you there? Please, answer me, whoever you are."

I turned and unexpectedly came face to face with a figure. He peered at me and softly uttered the words, "Please forgive me." I stood silent. I could make out his silhouette, yet it was too dark to make out any details about him. For a moment I was numb, then I screamed. He ran.

"Thomas, is that you? I'm sorry I screamed." I continued to cry out, but there was no answer; just crackling of the woodland in the distance. I stood there alone in the moonlight listening as the crackling got farther and then distant. Soon, the sound quit. What had just happened to me? I was so frightened, yet I had hoped it was Tom who I had just come across. But, why would he have appeared to me, and then fled as he did, if it were him? Perhaps my scream frightened him away. What did his words, forgive me, mean?

I started making my way back up the path, feeling very lonely inside. I had so many emotions that I didn't know where to turn. I had finally remembered the love that I had longed to find, although I wondered why his name hadn't been Arie. I still craved to find out about this man who had written my letters, and that I had come so far to find. Ironically, however, this terrible evil still loomed inside of me. It made me shiver as I continued up the darkened path.

I could see the fence just up the hill. A dim light illuminated the sky ahead. It must have been coming from the barn and the newly installed electricity. At least, I had almost made my way back up to the house without too much bad coming of what I had experienced. I wanted to tell Gerrit, or Mrs. Sloan, or anyone, what I had encountered with the person in the woods, but I was sure that no one would believe the disreputable Natalia Kappan.

I sat down on the murky path and propped my chin in my hands, balancing my elbows on my lap. "Please, I need to understand this," I said quietly, directing my prayer to whatever higher power would listen. The moon glared above, and frogs in the pond below croaked, when suddenly I heard the most excruciating sound imaginable. In the far distance I heard the screams of a man. They brought me immediately to my feet and made me want to run for safety. I stood there frozen, and listened. The screams came from the direction in which the man had run. They were like the sounds of someone being tortured! I ran up the hill and stumbled on a rock that was partially embedded in the ground and fell, hitting my knee rather hard. The screams continued as something very sinister began to happen.

Rapidly, a dark figure, that seemed so real but lived within my mind, pounced on me. "Please," I screamed. "Get away, get off of me!" The figure tore off my blouse as the screaming in the distance and the screaming from my very soul continued.

"Just pretend I'm your young man." he whispered. He hastily tied something around my mouth, so that I couldn't scream. I struggled with all my might, but there was no getting him off of me. I gashed him with my nails and kicked and kicked. I frantically searched all around me with my free hand for the rock I had just stumbled on. I pried it out of the dirt and quickly raised it to hit him in the head. He grabbed me, twisting my arm and making me release the stone. The stone thumped me hard on the head. There was a ringing sound and I heard him say, "I've wanted you for so many years, Natalia." Then, all was totally quiet. I had blacked out.

I awakened stiff and battered and bleeding. I was terribly hurt. I tried to untie the linen material from my face, but it seemed to no longer be there. I began screaming uncontrollably. "I need help! Please, please, help me!"

Almost immediately, I could hear a tiny voice. "Mama, Mama!" I looked up and Joy was there with her friend. "What's the matter?" She stood there looking at me. Soon Gerrit and the Sloans and many others at the house came into view. They stood there looking down at me lying on the ground, some holding illuminated kerosene lamps.

"Please," I begged. "Don't gawk at me. I need something to cover with." I tried to hide myself by rolling up in a little ball. "My clothes are torn off, and I'm bleeding." I continued screaming. "Please help me!"

"Natalia!" Gerrit said, as he bent down. "You are okay! Your clothes are fine, look at them…you have them on…you are not bleeding!"

I continued screaming, hearing muffled talk in the background. I was trembling and hysterical and tears dripped down my face. I felt flush.

"Natalia!" Gerrit yelled as he shook me.

I looked down at the clothes I was wearing. They were all intact. Gerrit lifted me up and brushed some dirt from my clothing. The people in the background continued talking.

"She's the same old Natalia," one of the Sloan children whispered.

"I thought the poor dear was doing better," I could hear another person saying.

I kept trembling as Mr. Sloan approached Gerrit. "We'd better get her home. Why on earth would she make something like this up?"

Gerrit shook his head, "Yes, we'd better get her home."

Then, just as though the bellowing person could feel my pain, I began hearing frantic screams in the distance again. I rose suddenly as Joy darted to Gerrit, clasping his legs. Lillian clutched Joy. I was now even more terrified and could tell that I wasn't the only one feeling that way by the expression on the children's faces.

"It's all right, child," Gerrit said softly. He looked at Lillian: "It's okay" he assured her.

"What is that?" I shrieked, as Joy reached out and took my hand while continuing to hold onto Gerrit.

"It's at it again," Mr. Sloan commented.

"Where's it coming from this time?" another questioned.

"Mama, it's the ghost!" Joy said, looking at me.

"Quiet, child," Gerrit yelled.

"I may have just seen him," I cried out. "It was in the woods, down by the pond. He looked at me...I saw him!"

"Just as your clothes were torn off, and you were bloodied?" Mrs. Sloan said with a taunting smile, as she focused on the people around her. "I'm sorry, I shouldn't have said that." She shook her head and looked to the right at her friend in a peach-colored hat. Her friend gave Mrs. Sloan a caring pat on the arm.

"No one has ever seen this person who screams, Natalia," Mrs. Sloan's friend, Mrs. Griffin, said. "You must be a very privileged person to have him directly appear to you. Please tell us what he looked like, will you?"

"I cannot tell you what he looked like," I replied. "It was too dark."

The ladies stood looking at me, with unbelieving expressions on their faces, and it angered me to not be believed.

The men kept trying to figure out what direction the sound came from. Soon it dissolved into emptiness, as quickly as it had begun.

"We could go down there, but you know what happens... We'll never find him, or it," Mr. Sloan acknowledged.

"You're staying right here," Mrs. Sloan demanded. "Besides, you need to take

Natalia home."

There was far less talking on the wagon ride home. All the families except for one had decided to walk home, which had been the original plan. And, the couple who had decided to ride lived only a few minutes from the Sloans. They had already been dropped off. I wondered if it was because of me and my actions that so few wanted to ride in the wagon. I couldn't imagine walking anywhere in the dead of night with the screams we had just encountered. I guess the screams had gotten to be quite a routine thing around here. I could tell that Gerrit was upset, yet he seemed to always be a troubled man. He sat up on the seat with Mr. Sloan, and I could hear them whispering. Joy sat holding hands with Lillian across from me. All of their chatter had stopped.

I sat there feeling dirty and battered. There were no two ways about it; I had been defiled on the Sloans' property at some time in my life. Apparently, tonight's episode was my memory recalling the brutal attack, but I knew, without a doubt, it did happen! It had all come back to me in such vividness. I looked over at my daughter sitting so innocently on the other side of the wagon. She saw me look at her and raised her hand, giving me a little wave. I waved back. Now I knew what I was trying so hard to not remember. I was assaulted when I was 14 years old. Joy must have been the result of that crime. How could a child so beautiful be the outcome of something so evil?

We got to our home where all was dark. Mr. Sloan told Gerrit that he would take Lillian home. "She can ride right up here on the seat with me," he said, lifting the little girl up. "That Natalia and her imagination," he continued, shaking his head and looking at Gerrit. "There is just no reason for her to make things up like that. She was always so well taken care of at our home. She was so loved!"

Gerrit helped us off the wagon. I had heard the snide comment, but I pretended I hadn't. What good would it do for me to say anything?

Lillian waved and said her goodbyes to Joy, and she and Mr. Sloan took off down the road with the horses leading the way.

Gerrit lit the house as we entered, and I quickly ran upstairs. Joy followed closely behind me, lighting the lamp in my room. I shut the door.

"Mama, remember the door." Joy said reminding me of Gerrit's wishes for me to keep it ajar.

"It will be fine, Joy," I answered. "I desperately need to wash up.

"Tomorrow night Papa will bring in the tub," Joy answered. "I can't wait for a bath. Do you want me to go and get you some water from the kitchen?"

"If you would be so kind, Joy, I would appreciate it." Quickly, the little girl grabbed the pitcher from my stand and skipped over to open the door, anxious to help me. I began to take off my clothes while looking at myself in the mirror. My precious necklace sparkled in the reflection. I grabbed the silver brush on my dresser and began brushing out my long black hair. I was hot and felt so dirty and abused.

I continued to unbuttoned the blouse part of my dress and underclothes, letting them fall to my waist. I went to the window and opened it a bit higher. I raised my arms, tucking my hands behind my head and stretched, letting the late-night breeze caress my breasts and bare skin. It felt so soothing. I gazed back at the mirror and noticed that Joy had left the door wide open when she left. Gerrit's face stared at me in the looking-glass. I was horrified. He must have been standing a slight distance down the hall, watching me the whole time in the reflection of the mirror. I was thoroughly disgusted! I quickly pulled my clothes back up around myself and ran to the door, giving it a shove. Just as the door was shutting, I spotted Joy at the base of the stairway with a pitcher of water. I held the door open a crack and noticed that she could barely make it up the steps. Struggling to hold my garments around me, I ran down and helped her by taking the pitcher from her hands. She followed me back upstairs and into my room. I went to shut the door when Gerrit held it open.

I looked at him with one hand still holding up my blouse to cover my breasts. My back was bare. In my other hand

I held the heavy pitcher. "I need my privacy," I said quietly. "Please honor that."

"We all need something, don't we, Natalia? It's sad that we don't always get what we want or what we deserve. Your door is NOT to be shut!" He turned away and headed down the hallway. I shoved the door hard and it rebounded with a crack. Joy was beside me and pushed it shut to where there was about an eight-inch opening.

"Papa will be okay with that," she tried to assure me.

"Do you want me to get your nightgown out for you, Mama?" the sweet little girl asked.

"Please, if you would," I directed.

I dimmed the lamp making it hard to see, and got out of my clothing. If Gerrit was somehow still watching, there would be little he could make out. I dumped the water from the pitcher into the basin and used a linen towel to dab it up and wash with. The water was cold, and now with the breeze from the window blowing, it made me shiver. I dried myself, and Joy brought me a nightgown she had gotten from my dresser drawer. "Why don't you wear this one tonight, Mama?" she advised. "You never wear this one."

I put on the sheer, white, one-piece gown as I watched Joy turn down the sheets on my bed. When I was all dressed, I raised the wick in the lamp. Once again, the room lit up. I looked down at the nightgown and was amazed at how pretty it was with its silver embroidery and lace cut-outs.

"You should wear your pretty one every night, Mama." Joy sat on the bed, her face beaming.

"Thank you for all your help today," I said to her. "Will your father tuck you in?"

"No, Papa always tells me to help you into bed, then he tells me to help myself. It's okay; I'm used to it. Parson Peterson says to say my prayers every night, and I don't ever forget, Mama. That's how I tuck myself in. Did you know that I never forget to pray for you?"

"Thank you so much, Joy," I said, as I closed my eyes and

gave out a sigh. "I could tuck you in tonight if you wish?" I felt so sorry for the tenderhearted little girl.

"Papa probably wouldn't like that," she answered. "Sometimes he comes to tuck you in, though. Please, don't scream for Arie if he does tonight, will you, Mama? It scares me so much when you scream."

"I... I won't," I said, puzzled. "Do I scream for Arie often?" I got into bed and pulled the sheet over me.

"Yes, Mama, you scream for him almost every night." She sighed. "Good night, ... It won't be long and the fireflies will be flying and the dew will be settling." She lowered the wick in the lamp until it almost went out.

I sat up in amazement. That saying...I had heard it before. "Joy, where did you learn that little saying?"

"Well, Parson Peterson always says it to me. Why, Mama? Why do you ask?"

"It just reminded me of something, that's all," I said. I pondered for quite a while digging inside my thoughts. It was as though I had two different lives, although I knew that was foolish. Why did I keep thinking there was something more important? How could there be something more important than the here and now and my very own daughter, Joy? There was such a blur in my mind, like I was forgetting the very depths of my being. What Joy had just said brought back a glimpse of something which seemed important, yet so cloudy. I guess if there had been something imperative that I was to remember, it had now been forgotten for good in my mind. I had a hard enough time just remembering my life here in LaPier.

"Good night, Mama," Joy said again.

"Be careful in the dark hallway," I directed her, as I heard my door swish as she left.

I had been so very tired that I couldn't wait for bedtime to approach. The iron bed was very small, yet, comfortable enough, especially being as tired as I was. For some time, I could hear the sounds of Joy getting ready for sleep, then all was quiet except for the sound of the breeze blowing in my window. I lay there for what must have been an hour. I couldn't get warm even after I pulled the large quilt over me. I must have caught a chill from the cold water I had used to bathe with. I rose to shut my window. It creaked and I hoped I hadn't awakened anyone. As I went back to bed I heard footsteps coming down the hall and then into my bedroom.

"You can't sleep?" I heard Gerrit question softly as he entered my room.

"No...I mean, I just got up to close my window."

He approached me, and I was frightened. "I can't sleep either, Natalia." He took my hand in his. Everything was in shadows, as the wick in my lamp was very low. Most of the light came from the moon through my window.

"I keep thinking of the comb you wore in your hair tonight...The one I gave you," Gerrit murmured. "I thought that maybe you were trying to tell me that you care for me. I wait for you every night to come to my room, you know. How long must a man...a husband wait? For years I wait for you. Why must I always come to you and have you reject me? Do you know what that does to a man like me?"

I shivered as he drew me to him. "Please... please, this is NOT what I wish for ... I'm not ready for this." I quivered. "Please let me go." He held my hand so firmly that it hurt.

"But you're my wife and you've been acting differently today," he replied, forcing me to look at him by holding some strands of my hair. "I saw your nakedness tonight, and I must have you." Then, he forcefully kissed me, throwing me onto the bed.

"Please, I don't want to scream, it will awaken Joy. Please, sir, I don't care to be with you."

He continued holding me while he kissed me wherever he could get his lips.

I screamed.

"Come on," he said loudly. "When are you going to start screaming for your precious, Arie?" He continued holding me down by grasping my hair, and tried to pull off my nightgown.

I reached out my hand and began feeling on my nightstand for anything that might subdue him. I grabbed something long and sharp.

"If you don't quit, sir, I will stab you." I shrieked, getting his attention. I stuck the point of what I was holding to his neck and held it tightly there. I was frightened it would penetrate his skin and yet, I was willing to do anything to detour him. Gerrit stopped and looked at me.

"Is this something that is a pattern for you now, Natalia? Stabbing people with letter openers when they get in your way?"

I kept the point to his neck. He was panting uncontrollably, but finally got up. "Trying to mimic the murder night, I see," he said, trying to catch his breath. Then he got up. "One day, Natalia, like it or not, you will be with me. I will promise you that."

I lay there with my legs tucked beneath me, still holding the blade in front of me. I was in disbelief as to what I might have been capable of doing had he not left me alone. Quickly, I bound the quilt tightly around me as he began to exit my room. He turned once more before leaving as though to be coming back to me, but, then just stood there. Through the shadows I could see his disgusting silhouette. For the second time this day I had been defiled. It was no wonder that I felt evil looming in this place!

Chapter 9

A World Unconnected

I was out on the porch early the next morning waiting for Parson Peterson to appear from his home. Gerrit was still in the house apparently getting ready for work, and I figured that Joy was still asleep. Gerrit, together with the Sloans, owned the local sawmill in LaPier. Gerrit did all the bookwork and got the orders, and Mr. Sloan took care of anything to do with labor, etc. After the day I had experienced yesterday, I genuinely needed to make sense of my life. My mind was so filled with fragments and pieces that didn't connect, that I couldn't understand it all. There was no way I could ask the man, who everyone called my husband, anything. I was terrified of him, and there just wasn't any trust demonstrated by him for my well-being. Sadly enough, there were only three people who I thoroughly trusted, and they were my daughter; the man I believed I loved, Thomas, and Parson Peterson.

The door suddenly flew open, and Gerrit stood on the porch with an umbrella in his hand.

"You're up early today," he said, acting unfazed by what had transpired between us just hours ago.

I didn't answer, but walked over to the far side of the porch where I could be the furthest away from him. I sat on the swing.

He continued down the steps of the porch and through the yard. He never looked at me nor said anything more as he approached the gravel road and left. It was Gerrit's routine to walk to town on the rare days when he would go to work. He'd walk no matter what the season as long as it wasn't snowing too hard. It was, however, misting rain today as I observed him opening his large, black umbrella. He walked briskly down the road until he disappeared from view. I sat on the swing for some time. The misty rain had now begun to come down in sheets, and each time my swing would sway past the porch roof, I would get wet. I calmed my swinging to a bouncing back and forth with my feet and sat listening to the gentle sound of rain showers. It was mesmerizing and my thoughts continued to churn inside.

After a while, I heard the sound of the barn door being opened next door. I looked and spotted Parson Peterson. He was running from the barn to the house with his shirt pulled up over his head, trying to keep dry. I needed to talk to this man. I noticed that he had hooked his horse, Emily, up to his buggy. He apparently had some calling to do today. I wrapped my shawl around my head and without delay ran next door, slipping secretly into the barn. Pulling off my wrap, I gave it a good shake, trying to get all the water off before it penetrated deeply into the fibers. I draped it around my shoulders. Emily neighed, acknowledging my presence. I looked over to where a ladder went to the upstairs loft and knew exactly where the letters were kept that Joy had talked about. How I wanted to climb up there and look inside that hidden door. I went over to the ladder as Justin approached the barn. I heard a loud stomping. He vigorously clomped his feet, attempting to free the mud from his boots. He spotted me, startled.

"Natalia, what are you doing here so early in the morning?" he asked, looking down and giving another stomp.

"I told you, I needed to further speak with you," I said, coming closer to him. Emily began backing up slowly with the buggy. "Whoa," Justin yelled.

He turned to me. "I'm off to go and visit the Morrisons and their new babies. You probably didn't hear, but, Mrs. Morrison gave birth to twin boys last night. She's been really ailing with her pregnancy, and the Doc never thought it would turn out this good. We've all been praying for that family!"

"I'm glad all turned out okay," I said, as I watched the rain falling outside the barn. "I'm sorry to change the subject, but I need to ask you something. I need to ask you about Thomas."

"What about Thomas?" Justin gave me a peculiar glance.

"Forgive my memory, Sir, but I know I love Tom Abendroth, not Gerrit Kappan. I have his picture in my mind, and I feel the love he gave me, and continues to give me. I am so lonely without him. I also need to know about my necklace. I cannot go on without knowing about Tom, yet to my horror it slips my mind as to where he is. And, Justin, why do I call out for Arie, when it is Thomas who I love?"

"Natalia, I have always been your friend, and I've always been honest with you. That is why you must trust me now more than ever. If you can't remember the past, please let it be known that God is protecting you from reliving things you don't want to relive. You seem so much better the last couple of days. If you feel love from the past, then feel very fortunate that you had found love. Many people search their whole lives and never find true love. You have a beautiful daughter and husband who love you. Perhaps now you could begin giving them part of your life and part of your love."

"That's not good enough," I cried out. "I know about the letters, Justin. I've read them."

He acted as though he didn't hear what I had said and seemed troubled.

"It's not important that I know where the letters are." I continued, "What's important is why I crave those letters, Justin, when they're not from Tom; the man I love? Why are they signed with the name Arie, and yet, I know they are to me? And, why does this necklace..." I pulled it out from under my blouse..."mean more to me that just about anything on this earth? I desperately need some answers."

"What if I told you that something tragic happened," Justin said. "So tragic that if you remembered, it would only sadden you more. Would you still want to know if it created in you such a hatred, even perhaps for your daughter, and put you in a mental state that made you unresponsive and aloof? You have been this way before, Natalia."

"If it has to do with me knowing where Tom is, then yes, I need to know regardless."

"Natalia, life is so very complicated. I truly don't know what ranks higher in life, love or forgiveness. For me, I think forgiveness is the greater of the two. In the last couple of years, I have had to make a great sacrifice also. I lost someone who I loved, almost more than life itself, to the mercy of someone who I despised and wanted to eliminate. And I wasn't even sure who that person was, if you could possibly understand that. Then, by the grace of God, I was given the opportunity to forgive that person, but I had to do it unconditionally, just as Christ did for us. It made me question my very being. But, do you know what would have happened if I hadn't forgiven?"

I shook my head.

"If I hadn't forgiven this person, I would have died, both physically and spiritually. It was my only option. I would have been eaten up by hatred and disgust for the rest of my life. I know I'm a better person for what I did, even though not one second of my life goes by without thinking of the person I lost."

I looked at Justin as he dried the tears gushing from his eyes. This pain he spoke of was so real to me also, as I remembered losing someone dearer than life. His name was Anthony, and I could vaguely remember experiencing an ongoing, agonizing pain regarding his loss. It felt as though a dagger from two worlds had just pierced my heart.

"As you can see," Justin continued, "this means more to me than just about anything, Natalia. And it all has to do with me not being able to tell you about your Tom. Please, know that he loved you, and if life would have been different, he would be with you to this day. He loved you with all that he was, and there is no denying it."

"You said he loved me as in the past tense...where is he, then, and does he still love me, Justin?"

"Love is eternal, Natalia. Yes, he still loves you."

"I had a vision last night as I was at the Sloans' farm. It was so real, so violent, and I know, without a doubt, that it happened sometime in my life. Please, Justin, I'm begging you ... pleading with you to help me sort out the questions about my life."

"Natalia, just as with all the things you ask me, this is another thing that is best left in the past."

"But, Justin, last night, when I was down on the path by the Sloans' pond, a figure approached me. It was too dark to see who he was, so I began returning to the house. On the way back, I had a vision, although I thought it was real at the time. I was defiled. I know I was. I could feel it last night as though it was truly happening all over again. I felt the presence of the evil within me and around me, and I heard the screams."

"You say you saw a figure?" he questioned.

"Yes, I know I did."

"Perhaps seeing the figure was your imagination?"

I noticed how he tried to make the statement into a question.

"I am quite sure what I saw," I responded.

He paused for a moment. "Well, we've been hearing the screams for a long time now, Natalia. I like to believe that possibly they are screams asking for forgiveness and not of an evil, torturous manner as everyone thinks. Please, do something for me, will you?" Justin Peterson came closer and put his arm around me.

"Live for the present, Natalia, and forget the past. Your daughter needs you and your husband needs you. If I were given the gift of forgetting some of the things from my past, I would accept that gift without question. And, I know it's hard to believe anyone except for yourself in that regard, but you must trust me. I have known you for a long time. Your state of mind, since I found you at Bitterwood School a few days ago, has been better than I've seen you relate to others for many a year. And I believe it is because God has taken your memory from you to relieve you of your pain."

"So, that's all I'm going to get from you?" I pleaded. "You're really not going to tell me anything?"

Justin shook his head. "I will pray for you, Natalia, just as I always do. If God wants you to remember, then He will allow you to remember, but let it be in His timing." He got into the buggy and grabbed onto the reins. I noticed again the unusual way he used his right hand. He always kept his last three fingers tightly tucked within, using his thumb and first finger to do everything. The hard rain had turned into a slight pitter-patter as I followed the buggy out of the barn. I pulled my shawl a bit tighter around my neck and over my head, trying to stay dry.

"There's no way I could ever love Gerrit Kappan," I said in disgust. "Who knows, I may even kill him someday," I said softly, remembering what I had experienced the previous night.

The Parson looked at me with a look of distain. "Don't ever say things like that, Natalia," he said sternly.

I didn't know that he had heard me.

"Do you understand? Saying things like that could get you into trouble! Love comes in many forms, just remember that." He looked at Emily and then back to me. "I will tell the Morrison family that you send your best. And, remember, live life as though it's a precious gift! You have so much to give, Natalia." With that, he gave a little, "Getty up." And he was off down the road leaving me with no more answers than I had started with.

I was greeted on my way back home by Joy, who had obviously just awakened. Her long, black, wavy hair was tousled, and she had sleep in her eyes.

"Mama, I was worried about you," she said with a yawn. "I thought you had gone to the gazebo again without telling us. Where is Papa; has he gone?"

"Yes, he walked down the road," I answered. "Joy, do I go to the gazebo a lot?"

"Ah ha; I wish you wouldn't go there anymore," she said, looking at me. "Before Parson Peterson found you at Bitterwood School, you would go there each and every night."

"Come," I said, taking her hand and heading back to our home. "Let's walk back over to the porch before you get all wet. We can sit on the swing and talk a while." Jogging back, I led my daughter to the porch where we were free from the spitting rain.

"Joy," I said, taking off the wrap that I had around myself and placing it over both of our laps. "You must tell me, because I've forgotten, but did I ever tell you why I go to the gazebo so much?"

"Mama, you always tell me it's your meeting place, but Papa and I have spied on you and no one has ever met you there. You sit and sit and say your little chant, and scare everyone that comes near to you. And, Mama, you sometimes even take the flowers home with you, and it makes Papa so angry."

"The flowers? Please, tell me about the flowers, Joy."

"You know about the flowers, Mama, everyone knows about the flowers. They usually appear at the gazebo in the morning if they're going to. Not every morning, but some mornings. Papa says someone leaves them late at night, but no one has ever seen who leaves them. Lillian says it is the spirit of Bitterwood Commons. It's the same spirit that screams so often through the countryside. I know most of the people of LaPier believe that. I don't let Papa know, but those screams scare me so much. I think it's because they remind me of how you scream, too."

"And, Joy, where do I fit in with all of this? Why do I sense that most of the people here are so uneasy around me?"

"Mama, you usually don't talk to anyone, and you scare people by the things you do. You changed so badly after that night when Papa found you ...The night of the killing." She turned her head away. "I wish we could talk about something else." Joy looked down and stopped pushing the swing with her feet. "Papa made me swear on the Bible to never tell anyone this."

"I'm not just anyone, Joy, and I really do need to talk about this if you think you could bear it for a few more minutes. You can tell me, anything, Joy. I'm your Mom."

"I know, Mama, but you must already know; you were there!"

"Just refresh my memory a bit, my dear." I tried with all my heart to persuade her.

"You must never tell Papa that I talked with you about this. He must not be aware that I know all of it. And you have to promise me not to scream like you do so often when I talk to you."

"Honey," I said, caressing her little arm. "I would never knowingly do anything that would harm you. You must believe me. I'm just having such a hard time remembering everything that I need you to help me sometimes. Now, you must tell me of that night. I will not scream, I promise."

Joy sighed. "Okay," then she sighed again, and began... "You had left us that night, Mama. There was such a terrible storm, but you sneaked out anyway. Papa thought you had gone to the gazebo, and he went out to fetch you as usual. I didn't want him to leave because the thunder was booming in the sky. This night was different than most of the nights when you ran off. Papa was out very late looking for you. I was here alone, and I was so scared because of the storm. I was also scared because for two nights in a row, I had seen a shadow of a man in the field behind our house."

"And who was the man?" I asked quickly.

"Papa said he wasn't real, just as he always tells me, but I know what I saw. I saw him before, too, many times. It was when I was a little girl and I would go with Papa into town. There have been so many times I could feel someone watching me. But this night, I was so scared that I crawled under my bed and held my dollies. I just knew that something had happened. I thought you were dead, Mama. I cried so hard, but I was so scared to come out from underneath my bed. Then, very, very late, Papa came home with you. I could hear him talking, so I finally came downstairs. He pulled all the curtains shut and seemed to be in such a hurry. I think you were hurt, Mama, because I saw blood on you, and Papa kept working the pump in the kitchen sink really fast. "Wash," he kept telling you…. "Wash it off!" he yelled.

"Then, quickly, I heard Papa bring in the bathing tub from the back porch. I wondered why Papa was doing that, because we always take our baths on Saturday night, and this was Wednesday. I asked Papa if I was to take a bath also, because we always took them together. He told me to get back to my room, and to not show my face until morning. Papa was very stern, even more so than usual.

"Later that night he came to my room. That is when he made me promise not to tell anyone what I had witnessed that night. He said, not even Lillian! Papa stayed up all night cleaning and doing wash. I kept peeking from my door. I cried that whole night, because I could hear you screaming and whimpering in your room. Papa never closes your door all the way, but he did that night and locked you in. I wanted to come to you, and even tried a couple of times, but Papa got even madder at me. He told me you were ill and would die if I didn't stay in my room and do what I was told. I still have bad dreams of that night, Mama."

"As you should, my dear," I said, holding her close, trying to keep her warm in my shawl. I was desperately troubled by what I had just heard and wanted her to continue, yet I felt the need to keep silent and just hold this little person for a while. What trauma she had been through! Finally, after some time, I needed to know. I turned to my little girl. "Joy, you must tell me, was someone killed that night?"

"Yes. Papa said it had been a couple of drifters who had gotten into a fight. Mr. Barnet came to our house early the next morning and asked Papa and I all about the night before."

"Mr. Barnet, the police chief?" I questioned.

"Yes, Mama, Gracie's Papa. She helps me with my numbers sometimes."

"Yes, of course," I acknowledged. "And what did you tell him about what you had seen?"

"I told him nothing. Papa told me you would die if I didn't do what he told me to do. Mr. Barnet looked around our house and even tried to talk to you. Don't you remember? You wouldn't say a word...all's you did was cry."

"And did Mr. Barnet talk to your Papa as well?" I questioned.

"For such a long time, Mama, he talked to him. Papa lied Mama, I heard him. He lied to Mr. Barnet. He told him that you stayed in the house all day and night and never left, but you did, Mama. Papa told him that you were sick, just as he told me."

I suddenly began shaking so hard in fear for what I might have done. "Joy, listen to me carefully; you mentioned something before about what the children said about me. Please tell me again, what do the children say that your mother has done?"

"Mama, I told you that some call you a murderer."

I continued shaking profusely.

"But, Mama," Joy said, hitting my arm repetitively and trying to get my attention. "Parson Peterson told me that when I hear the children saying those words to close my ears and know it's not true. He told me that you never hurt anyone, and I believe him. He told me that a man killed the other person, and it's been proven, Mama. He says he knows it in his heart. He just won't tell me how he knows. I've asked him and he told me that perhaps when I'm older I can hear the whole story. So, when the kids say those things about you, I just pretend I don't hear it. But, Mama, you won't hate me if I ask you something will you?"

"Of course not," I said, kissing her forehead. "Joy, I could never hate you...NEVER!"

"Then, Mama, just tell me one thing for sure." She looked up at me with misty eyes.

"You didn't kill that man, did you?"

In a split second, memories of the night before illuminated my mind. Memories of how I grabbed the letter opener from my nightstand and wasn't afraid to jab it onto the neck of Gerrit. If he hadn't stopped pursuing me, what could I have done? Was I capable of killing? I wasn't sure! I looked at Joy. My lips were quivering. "Honey, I won't lie to you. I would never lie to you, but, honestly, right now, I don't remember that night!" I began weeping and my little daughter, who acted as though she was 25 years old, consoled me. I was the one who was supposed to be consoling her, and yet Joy knew no other way of life. My heart felt as though it were going to burst. I honestly wondered if I was the one who killed this drifter. Why else was Gerrit being so protective of me? I needed to find answers, and I needed to do it now!

Chapter 10

The Outcast

J oy, I have an idea, if you're up to it," I said as we went inside the house.

"What is it, Mama?" She smiled.

I pumped some water into the sink and washed the sleep from Joy's eyes with a cloth. "It looks as though the clouds are breaking up," I said. "If the rain stops, would you like to see if Lillian would like to walk with us over to the Sloans today?"

"Mama, that would be fun! But are you sure you're supposed to leave the house without Papa?

"Of course I can," I answered. "I do it all the time."

"I know you do, Mama, but usually you sneak out when Papa doesn't know. Or you'll be swinging on the porch when all of a sudden we discover that you have left for the gazebo. I would love to have Lillian come with us, but I don't know if Lillian's Mama will let her come with you if Papa isn't going."

"And why is that, Joy? Obviously, she doesn't trust me, right?"

"I don't know," Joy answered reluctantly as I dried her face. "But let's go and visit anyway. Could we please? They just won't believe that we're taking a walk together!"

It had bothered me all the previous night that we were unable to take Lillian home from the Sloans. Although I was certain that Mr. Sloan had gotten her home safely, I was sure that Lillian's mother would think less of me for not getting her home in person. Having a daughter myself, I could totally understand how she might feel. It was as though I had let everyone down again. The sad part was, from what I had interpreted, that nothing was ever expected of me. So, even when something uncanny did happen, it seemed to be the norm when I was concerned. I wanted to change my reputation so badly, but wondered if it were possible anymore. After all, I wasn't even sure what brutality I was capable of causing. The murder would not leave my mind, and I knew I must find out the details from whatever source I could.

"We'll watch and see if the rain clears off," I continued. "If it does we'll go on our walk. How does that sound?"

"That's fine, Mama," Joy said, beginning to become very excited, just as she had acted the night before.

We made three loaves of corn meal bread that morning, as a good-will offering. I thought I'd bring one to the Sloans, one to the Posts, and keep one here at home. I couldn't believe the fuss Joy made because we were baking together! She said we had never done such a thing before. It was funny because it seemed so natural, and I enjoyed it so much! The sun finally made its way through the clouds in early afternoon, creating much heat and humidity. All morning long, Joy talked of going on our walk together.

No matter how hard I concentrated, I still could not put all the pieces of my life together. From what I could understand, I had been in a very wretched mental state for several years, and apparently within the last couple of days had begun to come out of it.

Perhaps it was the reason for all the unexplained people, places and emotions that kept flashing inside of me. There were just so many names bouncing around in my head like Anthony, Daniel and Arie. They were people who were so real to me in some way, and yet I had no idea who they were, and where they fit into my life. I was scared that during my previous mental state I had conjured up fictional characters. That is why I needed to go and visit Mrs. Sloan today. After all, I had lived there a number of years, and I was hoping that she could make sense of many things for me. I knew it wouldn't be easy; it was apparent that she didn't think too highly of me. Still, I had decided I needed to talk with her.

"Are you ready, Joy," I called. Her little face, beaming, peeked out from upstairs and Joy descended promptly. The walk to the Posts was about the same distance as was to the Sloans' farm. That meant that some backtracking would have to be done. It also meant that we were in for quite a stroll today. I was really looking forward to the walk. It just seemed like I was meant to walk or run, or something. I just hoped the rain held off.

The Posts' house was right around the corner from the Bitterwood School and Cemetery. As we walked by the area, a large hill on the other side of the school caught my attention.

"Joy," I said loudly, making her skipping stop. She waited until I caught up to her.

"Yes, Mama?"

"Did something used to be there?" I pointed to the spot in question.

"What do you mean?" she asked.

"I mean like a building...a gazebo perhaps?"

"Mama, the gazebo is just past our house on State Street. You know where it is. We were just there last night." I hesitated a moment, continuing to have the same premonition. Why did I feel like a gazebo once stood in this spot? "Yes, of course, Dear." I answered, shaking my head, and for the millionth time I questioned my sanity.

The Posts' house was a very pretty yellow home with brick pillars that encompassed the front porch. Geraniums bloomed in the flower boxes, and it appeared to be a cheerful place to live. There was a wicker baby buggy out in the front yard with a doll inside. Joy quickly told me the entire story about the doll and how it belonged to Lillian. The doll had originally been meant for Lillian's youngest sister, Verda, according to Joy. Verda had tragically died of the Spanish flu a couple of years prior, when it ravished the country. Lillian's aunt had sent it from England, but her sister had perished before it arrived. It was agreed that it would become Lillian's doll. Her name was Margaret, and in Joy's words, Lillian's favorite doll in the whole world. We climbed the steps and knocked on the door.

Priscilla Post, Lillian's mother, answered the door. "Natalia, what a surprise, and Joy! Where is Gerrit?"

"He's at work," Joy blurted out.

Mrs. Post acted uncertain. Before long, all three of Lillian's brothers were at the door along with a very excited Lillian and her older sister, Sarah. Lillian quickly took Joy by the hand and pulled her inside the doorway with her sister. "Did you hear of the Morrisons babies?" I could hear Lillian asking as they went farther into the house.

Suddenly I felt peculiar as I stood alone outside, being stared at by Priscilla Post and her sons. It was evident I didn't belong here.

"Here's a loaf of corn bread for you. It's fresh baked." I handed the loaf to Mrs. Post. She unwrapped the bread from the linen towel, took a whiff of the freshly baked loaf, and folded the towel back up, handing it to me.

"Matthew, please bring this bread into the kitchen," she said, handing it to one of her sons.

"It smells wonderful, Natalia! That was very kind of you to think of us," Mrs. Post smiled. "It's quite a surprise. Did you make the bread yourself?"

"I did," I replied. "Joy and I, that is." I paused a moment to get my composure. "I wanted to tell you that I was sorry we didn't get Lillian home in person last night. I wasn't feeling well, so Mr. Sloan said he would drop her off. I hope it all worked out okay."

"Yes, Lillian arrived home fine."

"I'm glad to hear that," I replied. "I was hoping you weren't upset. I had the best of intentions."

"Everyone's intentions are usually for the best," she

mused.

"Joy and I are off for a walk today, and we were wondering if you would allow Lillian to accompany us."

"Just you and Joy off walking, Natalia?" She sounded disturbed.

"Yes, we are off to the Sloans' house. I made her a bread also, and I wanted to thank her for having us over last night and apologize to her for what happened." Mrs. Post looked at the loaf of bread I was holding and then back at me.

"Yes, Lillian told us about your mishap last night."

"I guess my imagination got the better of me," I responded sheepishly, trying to excuse what had happened.

"Yes, Natalia, that seems to happen to you quite often."

I was sensing a very awkward conversation, as Joy and Lillian appeared back at the door.

"So, Mother, can I go?" Lillian asked as the two girls jumped up and down. Joy had apparently filled in Lillian regarding our plans.

"I don't think so," Mrs. Post replied. The girls stopped jumping and looked glum.

"I would assure you that I will take the best of care of Lillian, Mrs. Post," I said. "I don't know how you're used to seeing me act, but everyone tells me that I am feeling better these days."

"But what about last night, Natalia, and the nights before that?" She raised her voice. "How do I know I can trust..." She stopped talking and looked at Lillian and Joy, who had now sat down in the corner of the porch. Joy was crying and had obviously gotten Mrs. Post's attention. Hurriedly, she called out to Lillian's older sister. It wasn't long and Sarah appeared.

"Sarah, would you accompany Mrs. Kappan, Joy and Lillian on a walk to the Sloans' farm?" She asked. Sarah looked at her mother and crinkled her eyebrows in disbelief. "It's okay, Sarah. Lillian and Joy would like to have you come along," her mother insisted.

"Are you sure it's okay, Mother?" Sarah asked, sounding extremely puzzled, yet trying to be polite.

Her mother nodded her head. "It will be a fine, Sarah."

"Well, yes, of course, Mother," Sarah replied. "I can go with them." And, before you knew it, the two girls were up on their feet, jumping for joy again. They tried to get Sarah to join in with their antics, but it seemed she wasn't interested.

Now that I thought of it, I remembered Joy telling me about Sarah and how she had never forgiven herself for her sister, Verda's death. Apparently Sarah had been sick with influenza before Verda had come down with it. Sarah recovered, but Verda didn't. Joy told me how it really made an impact on the older sister. Sarah had confided in Joy at one time that she would do anything to get her sister back. She blamed herself for bringing the virus home and for causing Verda's death. Perhaps, that was the reason Sarah acted so subdued. I couldn't imagine such a burden on such a young girl.

"I will have them home before suppertime," I promised.

"Sarah, I'd like to speak with you a moment in the house," Mrs. Post said. She looked at me. "Excuse us, please, Natalia." She shut the door, and I could hear muffled talk going on inside. Finally they came out.

"I will see you, then, before supper, Natalia," Mrs. Post agreed.

"Yes, we will see you then," I guaranteed. The family stood in the doorway and watched us as we walked down the steps.

"Be good, girls," Mrs. Post called out. "And, Lillian, you do what your sister tells you. Do you hear me?"

"I will listen to her, Mother," Lillian promised. She walked over to the wicker buggy. "Shall we take Margaret with us?" Lillian said, picking up the doll and looking at the other two girls.

"Lillian, leave your doll here, please," her mother called from the doorway. Lillian laid the doll back down in the buggy and we proceeded to the road. The girls started skipping and I started jogging, and it seemed so natural and sweet.

We were hot and parched as we once again approached our

home, on the backtrack to the Sloan farm.

"Girls, let's go inside and get some water, and I'll cut our corn bread. We have some preserves we can spread on it. A little snack sounds good before we proceed," I suggested. Sarah leaned over and whispered something to Lillian.

"Lillian and I will wait outside, Mrs. Kappan," Sarah directed.

"But don't you need a drink? Wouldn't you like some bread?" I asked, looking at the girls.

"If you could have Joy bring it out to us that would be fine," she replied. I entered the house alone, feeling distressed that the girls would not come inside. I started pumping the water, waiting for it to turn cold. Joy soon joined me.

"They're not allowed to come in without Papa present," Joy whispered.

"Because they think I will harm them? Is that why, Joy?" I asked.

"Mama, remember what I told you that Parson Peterson always tells me...That when people say mean things, or do mean things, to just ignore them?"

"Yes, Dear, I remember," I said, bending down to kiss Joy's forehead. "I just don't want people thinking things of us, Joy, and yet, perhaps they have a right to."

"I understand how they feel, Mama. Sometimes I get scared of you, too."

There were absolutely no words that came to mind to console her. I just stood there with my head down pumping water. Joy could certainly sense my sadness, and after a while she said, "Don't worry, Mama...things are going to be okay."

I looked at Joy. "Honey, I'm so sorry for what I've put you through. How could you ever forgive me? You are just the most special little girl a mother could have."

She looked at me with bright eyes and hugged me with all her might. "Thank you for telling me that," she said, smiling. "You've never told me that before."

Why hadn't I ever told her that? I was definitely a miserable mother. How did this little girl get to this age without ever hearing this from me? I would have to make so many things up to her; that was very apparent.

We prepared the bread, spreading it with strawberry preserves, and Joy brought out two extra glasses of water for the girls. We sat on the porch enjoying the refreshments. Joy kept replenishing the glasses. Sarah was extremely quiet. I could tell that she was uneasy, but Joy and Lillian took right over for her with their non-stop chattering and happiness.

"Girls, just leave the glasses here on the ledge. I will tend to them when I get home." I laid my cup down next to the empty plate and the others followed.

"Okay, then, are we ready to go to the Sloans?" I said as I hurried down the steps. Everyone followed.

"Last one to the corner of Engle Road is Mr. Willard's filthy old sow," Joy blurted out as everyone laughed, including Sarah for a change.

"Joy Laural Kappan, I said, chuckling yet pretending to be disgusted at her language. We all took off running. It wasn't long before a horse and buggy came into view. We slowed down and were greeted by Justin Peterson, who looked concerned.

"Good day, Natalia, Joy, Lillian, Sarah," he said, looking at each one of us as he spoke. "Where are you off to on this fine, hot, summer afternoon?"

"Mama's taking us for a walk," Joy answered, trying to catch her breath.

"And does Gerrit know and approve of this adventure, Natalia?"

"I don't need approval for a simple walk."

"And, Sarah, does your mother know where you girls are?" he continued with his questions.

"Yes, sir, she does," Sarah said shyly.

I was suddenly very upset. "Why does everyone treat me like such a child?" I shrieked! "It disgusts me that you have to question these little girls as though I'm some criminal or something! If I am a criminal, then please, Justin, tell me!"

Joy knew I was troubled and came swiftly to comfort me. She held on to my waist and hugged me. Justin got down from his buggy. "Natalia, you are not a criminal. Look at me, please."

I looked at him and noticed that all the girls were watching intensely.

"You are NOT a criminal, and no one suggested that you were. Do you understand?"

I just stood there, looking down at the ground. He grabbed my arm.

"Natalia, you have had some problems in the past. We all have problems. No one is perfect! I'm just surprised to see you walking with the girls without Gerrit; that's all. He generally doesn't like it when you leave the house. You must believe me when I say that my only intention is to watch out for you and Joy's best interests. Please forgive me if you thought anything differently."

"I'm sorry," I said. "Please forgive me for my belligerence. I think there have been too many changes in my life in the past few days for me to comprehend. I was unfair to you, and I do appreciate you looking out for our well-being. I can't even remember the simple things in my life, although things are slowly coming back to me, let alone blame you for anything. I guess if the people who know my past are unwilling to share it with me, then they will have to deal with me the way I am." I looked at Justin and hoped that he interpreted my sarcasm. "We are on our way to the Sloans' farm," I continued. "As you know, something happened there last night that I wish to address with Mrs. Sloan."

"I already heard what happened to you, personally from Mrs. Sloan, Natalia. She was just leaving the Morrisons' house this morning when I arrived." He looked at the girls. "Please, girls, go on ahead.... She'll meet you in a minute."

It took a moment for Joy to leave me, but I assured her I was fine, so she went ahead to join Lillian and Sarah. "You're going to end up being the dirty old sow, Mama, if you don't hurry," Joy shouted, trying to cheer me up, as she caught up to her friends.

Parson Peterson gave her an unusual look, and I giggled, which seemed to surprise Justin and please Joy. The girls continued running on ahead.

"You're forgetting what I told you this morning, aren't you?" Justin said when he knew the girls were out of hearing range.

"I'm not forgetting but, I told you, I need to have answers," I replied firmly.

"Hop in the buggy, Natalia." Justin held the reins and helped me in, and then got back in himself. He turned the buggy around in the road and stopped a minute before proceeding toward the girls. As we were stopped, a Model T went by at quite a good pace. I could see the girls ahead waving at it, enthusiastically as it approached them.

"That's the wave of the future, Natalia," Justin said with a smile as he watched the car go by. "Now where were we? Ah, yes, I don't mean to be repetitious, but it's better that you have forgotten several things," he said again. "I also don't know if it's such a good idea for you to visit the Sloans today."

"And, why is that, Justin? Is it because Mrs. Sloan may tell me the truth?"

He relaxed the reins, encouraging Emily to go, with a tiny slap on her rear end and a brisk, Getty up. We said nothing more to each other until he pulled up alongside the girls.

"One of you can sit in here with us, and the other two will have to ride on the bumper. As for you, Natalia," Justin said, turning toward me, "I see you're not going to listen to me."

I looked at him and shook my head no, then turned to the girls. "Sarah, why don't you join us in the buggy so that Joy and Lillian can sit together in the back?" Parson Peterson steadied the buggy as the girls climbed on.

"I assume you're taking us to the Sloans then?" I questioned.

"Natalia, it's your call. I can either take you home, or take you to the Sloans. You know what I think is best."

"We are going to the Sloans," I said unwaveringly. "We can ride, or, we can walk. Either way will suit us fine."

"You're already in the buggy, so you will ride," he answered. I could hear Joy and Lillian clapping in the back.

"You girls hanging on good?" Justin said, turning his head to make sure.

"Ah ha," they said, laughing.

"I will take you to the Sloans then, Natalia. Getty up, ole' Emily." We started forward and quickly turned down Engle Road, passing the gazebo on the left.

Chapter 11

"Live for the Hope"

The girls, sitting on the back bumper of the buggy, giggled all the way down Engle Road. They claimed old Emily was deliberately looking for bumps to make for an adventuresome ride! I was glad that Joy was having a good time. Again today I was taking in the scenery as my memory of this place continued to return. Flashes of my childhood with the Sloans encompassed me, but soon were replaced with passionate flashes of Thomas. As we approached the farm, I could see Mrs. Sloan bent over, working in her garden.

"Good day," Justin said loudly, tipping his hat as we turned into the driveway. "It's a pleasure seeing you twice on such a fine day."

She stood up slowly, holding her back. She gave us all a wave. Justin halted the buggy and got out. The girls in the back quickly jumped off. Mrs. Sloan came over to us, brushing the dirt from her hands as Justin helped us down.

"Hello, Justin...Natalia, and everyone," she said, looking at all of us but paying special attention to me.

"Good day," I replied, handing her the bread that Joy and I had made.

"Well, thank you very much," she said, accepting it. "Are you feeling better today?"

"Much better, thanks," I answered.

"And to what do I owe this visit from all of you?"

"I would very much like to talk to you for a while if it would be convenient," I said.

"Natalia, you're always welcome here, you know that. This is your home." She looked at Justin to see if he was listening.

Whenever there were people around, Mrs. Sloan would go to great effort to act as though there was a great bond between her and me. In reality, however, that wasn't the truth at all. And I never for a moment thought of this as being my home.

"I'll leave you ladies here then," Justin said as he returned to the buggy. Mrs. Sloan looked at him as though surprised.

"You're leaving?" she asked.

"Natalia and the girls were coming for a visit without me," Justin said. "I intercepted them on the road. Ol' Emily wanted to go a little farther on this nice, hot day, so I thought I'd bring them over in the buggy."

"We are very grateful to you for the ride," I said, turning to Justin and wiping the sweat from my forehead.

"It is a warm one...I'll grant you that," Mrs. Sloan replied. "...Don't know why I picked such a day to be out here in the garden. Girls, if you'd like to go in the house, you can get yourselves some cool water, and Catherine brought over some of her delicious sugar cookies this morning. She is such a good baker! She thought up the recipe all by herself. I'm sure she will enter the cookies in the County Fair, and she will certainly win! That girl of mine is so talented in everything she does! The cookies are lying on the table... Help yourselves to one." The girls quickly ran inside giggling with pleasure as they went.

Catherine was Mrs. Sloan's oldest daughter, and not a favorite person of mine. I had certainly never thought of her as a sister, or even a friend for that matter, and, I'm sure she never thought of me in those terms, either. She lived just down the road with her husband and children; building a house on the

Sloans' property. As we were growing up, all the work was tossed my way, and Catherine had all the fun. Catherine was not an attractive or popular girl and was forever mean and degrading to me for one reason or another. I wondered if it was because she would see her father hugging me from time to time when I lived with the Sloans, something I never saw him do to her. I knew he didn't care for me; it wasn't that. It was obviously just a gesture on his part, but, I always wondered if it had made Catherine jealous.

It was very apparent that all the Sloans' love was directed towards their natural children. And, I didn't even know if I could call it love, it was more of a bragging to others about their children, and their possessions, and what they had accomplished. They seemed to live for attention in order to build up themselves and their reputations. I was always an outsider, and yet I knew I should be thankful that they took me in as they had.

"Natalia, are you sure you wouldn't like me to pick you up in a while?" Justin questioned. "It wouldn't be a problem."

"No, we can walk home accordingly. The girls would like that. Thank you, though."

"Stay as long as you wish, Natalia," Mrs. Sloan said. "I just hope Gerrit won't worry. He knows you're here, right? You have been known to be a constant worry to that man!" Mrs. Sloan grinned at Justin, making sure he was hearing her comment.

"Actually, he does not," I interjected. "It is not his business to know what I do every passing moment of the day."

Mrs. Sloan gave another surprised look at Justin as he got into the buggy. He raised his eyebrows and put his hands out a bit, signifying to Mrs. Sloan that he had no idea of my intentions. "Have a nice visit," he said, putting on his hat. Soon, he was off.

"Come, Natalia, we can sit in the backyard in the shade." Mrs. Sloan directed me in that direction, brushing some dirt from the garden off of her. "Would you like something to drink, or perhaps a cookie?"

"No, I don't need anything, but thank you for asking," I replied.

"Okay then, I'm just going to put your bread on the porch and see what the girls are up to. I'll join you in a minute. Did Joy or Gerrit begin baking?" She was almost sarcastic to me now that Parson Peterson had left, giving me no appreciation for the gift.

"Joy and I baked together," I replied firmly.

"Well, that doesn't sound like you, Natalia ... Never known you to be a baker...At least on your own, anyway. Catherine always had that knack!"

Mrs. Sloan entered the back porch, and I made my way to some wicker chairs in the lawn near the back garden. Some late-blooming delphiniums, lilies, and black-eyed Susans were in full bloom, as well as phlox. Mrs. Sloan's gardens were as lovely as usual. I remembered painstakingly pulling weeds here for hours as a child.

I strolled farther to the back of the garden and bent down to look at the intricate details of the tall delphiniums. Taking one of the stalks in my hand, I bent it carefully to my face to take in a breath of its fragrance. I stood up as something startled me. The sun's rays were so bright as to make everything appear to be in some sort embellished haze. I had never seen any type of fog or low-hanging cloud of humidity like this before. I turned, as I heard a noise. Then, to my utter surprise, there he was, standing there looking at me. His presence seemed to encompass more affection and longing than I had ever experienced. Everything was blurry, but I knew, without a doubt, that this was the face of Thomas. I began to tear up, and he embraced me. He had a strong, striking appearance, and I felt an eternal-shared longing like nothing before. Just from his presence, I now understood what love was!

"I've missed you so," I said in despair, while kissing his neck tenderly.

"I told you that you can't miss me." He looked at me with

such compassion. "I told you that no matter what happens in life, our love will always find a way to shine."

"But, Thomas, my life is not good. I am married to a man who I'm frightened of…who I despise, and everyone says I'm not mentally well. And, my dearest Thomas, you must tell me some important things. I am not certain of what I may have done, and am terrified of what I may be capable of doing! I fear that I have killed someone!"

He sighed and tried to speak when I interrupted him once again.

"And, this is the most upsetting thing to me," I said, looking into his eyes. "I can't remember! I try and I try, but I can't remember … Is Joy our child? A child's soul that is that sweet could not possibly belong to Gerrit."

"You did not murder anyone, Natalia," he said with complete certainty, uttering words with such a soothing voice that it sounded almost angelic. "You would never be capable of such a thing. You must believe me, for I know this without a doubt. And, as for Joy, just love that child, Natalia…She was brought into the world for a reason, and I love her because she is part of you. It does not matter if she is a part of me, or a part of someone else. Whoever's child she is, is unimportant. It's only her precious soul that matters."

"I so need to hear the truth!"

"Sometimes the truth is what lies within your heart," Thomas replied.

Just hearing him speak so matter-of-factly satisfied my questions for the moment. I looked deep within his eyes and kissed him passionately. He rubbed my back and a tepid feeling extended from my heart all the way through my entire body. This love I felt went beyond and exceeded all realms.

"Natalia, you must listen to me carefully. What I am about to tell you, you will not understand." He held my face in his hands and kissed my forehead. I kissed his lips and didn't want to quit. The haziness from the light was still present when I looked upon his face. It was almost as though he was brought to me from another dimension.

"I have to leave you once more, but, we will meet again...I promise."

"But, what do you mean? You can't leave me...I've finally found you...I finally found everything I've been searching for." I began to weep uncontrollably, embracing him with all my might.

"Natalia, you must be strong. You must give me the necklace. I need it so that I can make things right for us. Joy told me that one day in times past you took off the necklace and laid it on your dresser; she put it on and the prisms took her somewhere in another time. She could only remember that someone was desperately calling out for help! My mother told Justin, and Justin told me that the prisms worked differently when used by a child. The gypsies explained to my great-grandfather that things would be fulfilled, and good would be accomplished when a child would wear it, but only if it was God's will. And,... if the prisms would allow for time travel, they would take that child to the place where they were supposed to be without any, or at least much, memory left to substantiate it. Crazily enough, Joy found me in times past, and now again today. She was able to bring me here to you. Joy has since returned with the necklace, but now I am left without it! This is not my home right now, Natalia, not my place in sequence of time and space. I desperately need to do some traveling, and the time is right."

"I don't understand! What gypsies, and how can you not be in the correct time and space? As, for Joy, she is here with me; Lillian accompanies her along with Sarah. How could she have found you when she is here? You speak ludicrously!"

"I told you that you would not be able to understand, Natalia! Who could understand! Age and time...years and months...they are limitless and only a moment can separate each experience if you are allowed to use the prisms! Joy was even permitted to take someone with her, and I am that someone today!"

"I cannot give up the necklace," I said. "It is part of you, and it is part of me. It has become a part of my being. And, you're here! Why would you leave?"

He stroked my face and gently kissed my lips yet again.

"I am here, yes, but because I traveled with Joy from another time. The things of the past have not changed for me! Be strong, my darling, and believe that love can find its way through all existence if we have faith. Do you remember what I told you when I gave you the necklace?" He waited a moment and I didn't respond. "I told you to wear it always and when you had it on, I would find you through all time, through all space, through all eternity."

"I try to remember everything, but it's so hard," I confessed. "I will try to believe, Tom, but I can't have you leave me again...I just can't. I don't know how much longer I can go on without you."

"But, I have to leave, my love, and I know you won't understand, but to leave is going to make it possible to be with you again. I will only be gone for a whisper in time until I can make things right. Time and love have no distance. Natalia, you must remember that. Now, let me have the necklace...I need to take it with me to continue fulfilling its ultimate purpose. I need to go now while the sun is out. Please, you must listen to me."

"But, how will I find you again," I said sadly unclasping the necklace and reluctantly handing it to him.

"Natalia, I will find you, that is my promise. I will not let life, or death, or time come between us. You have to believe me, and you have to live for that hope. Do you understand?"

"Tom, I don't want to live without you anymore. What's the point?"

"Everything will be fulfilled in its time, Natalia. That's just the way life works. I believe this with all my heart, and I will not be stopped until that day. I have come to the belief that our lives are very special. I believe that we were put on earth to make things right, perhaps for someone, or even a multitude of people in other lifetimes. I know it's hard for you to understand. Just watch for the necklace to be returned to you, Natalia. It has been used by many people! It has powers beyond belief.

"I'm not sure how I will get it back to you or, how you will get back to me, but we will...I promise, even if I have to use powers from within the very depths of the supernatural. And, when you get it back, listen to your heart and follow the prisms. They will guide you. That's all I can tell you now, or it could change things more than we wish." Tom kept looking up at the sky. "I must go now, the clouds are beginning to make their way on to the horizon, and it's almost too late. You must be brave for me. Now promise me." He pulled me closer yet, and kissed me, and then tried to draw himself away. I wouldn't let him go and continued embracing him with everything I had.

In the distance, I could hear a door opening, and it brought back the reality of this place, of this time, of this existence.

"I love you, Natalia," Tom said with tears welling up in his eyes. "I love you with all my heart and soul." He pulled himself away from me, and I grasped on to his hand with mine. I could see through the openings in the shrubs and trees that Mrs. Sloan was approaching on the hill above.

"Be strong, my fairest flower, and know that someday I will return for you."

He pried his hand from mine and made a run for the path in the woods. I began to follow, screaming for him to stay. He outran me and soon disappeared into the forest with the haze still enveloping him.

I was roused again to reality by the calls from Mrs. Sloan. I had chased Tom down the path far into the tree line, much farther than I had thought. I had apparently fallen to my knees and had been weeping frantically for who knows how long.

"Please come up here, Natalia ... Come up here right now! I can't get down there to you with my bad back," Mrs. Sloan demanded. She had followed me into the woods as far as she could go. I could see her above through the trees on the hill. I wasn't exactly sure how long I had been kneeling that afternoon in the woods, but, I could tell that Mrs. Sloan thought I was the same extreme Natalia by the time I arrived back up the hill.

"What were you doing down there, Natalia? You looked as though you'd perished down there. Your child was wondering where you were!"

I didn't want to leave the edge of the woods. I just kept peering down the path, wondering if what I had just experienced had really happened. I felt around my neck. My necklace was gone! I had indeed been with Tom, but he was no longer here! I felt as though my heart had been tortured and ripped out.

Mrs. Sloan took my hand, trying to free me from my dazed emotion, and led me away from the woods and over to her wicker chairs. I welcomed her hand leading me. I would have welcomed anyone showing me kindness at this moment. I felt as low as someone could feel. At that moment, I pretended Mrs. Sloan was my mother...Someone who really did care for me instead of her false self. She pulled out a handkerchief from her apron pocket and handed it to me. Then, she sat me down hard in one of the chairs. I was numb, I was cold, and I was desperate. I wiped the tears from my face and blew my nose. Mrs. Sloan said not a word and sat down next to me.

"I sent the girls over to see Catherine when I knew you had run into the woods. They got a new puppy." Her words were non-existent yet echoed through my brain.

"Natalia, do you hear me?"

"Yes...yes, I hear you," I replied softly.

"Are you all right? Shall I send for Gerrit?"

"No," I yelled.

"Well then, get yourself together, and tell me what you wanted to talk to me about. I've been waiting for you to come out of that woods for over an hour."

I sighed and took a deep breath. My breath was shallow

from all the crying.

"Mrs. Sloan, I came here to ask you to help me find some-one...to find love. Ironically, I found what I was looking for without your help. I also now have reason to believe in the goodness of myself. I am innocent of the murder that occurred here, no matter what anyone thinks, and I was far too young to understand what I was doing when I married your brother. I've never loved him, nor will I ever love him. Now, it is my promise that I will continue to wait for the love that I always knew existed, even if it is the last thing that is allowed of me on this earth."

"You're looking for love? How dare you say that!" Mrs. Sloan sarcastically retorted. "You better remember what my brother did for you. He has been good to you, and you have never acted like a wife. He has needs, you know...Every man does. Besides, no one else would have had you. You've always used your dirty, promiscuous ways to lure men! He took you in pregnant and penniless."

I looked at her. "Tom would have me," I answered. "And he will someday."

"And who is Tom?" she mockingly replied. "Is that the young renegade that used to sneak by the house when you were but a girl? We all know about your escapades. Catherine, and even my husband, watched you many times you know... kissing and carrying on when you thought no one was around. My husband told me how you throw yourself on men! I guess the young man fled when he found out you were pregnant, huh?

"Where was this Tom then, Natalia? I wouldn't call that love if I were you. You're nothing but a TRAMP! And, I'm also glad you've convinced yourself of your innocence of murder. You certainly haven't convinced me, or, most of our town. Everyone knows what you did, Natalia. You need to look at my Catherine's life and make it an example to you. She takes care of her husband and they are very happy. She always had more integrity than you did. I always knew it. Have you ever thought where you would be today if my brother would not have taken you in? You would be scum on the street. You were pregnant and alone at 14 years of age because of your foolish actions. That young man had no respect for you!" She cackled. "If it weren't for Gerrit, you and your illegitimate child would be out on the streets. Natalia, you sicken me...you always have. You have no appreciation for what you have been given. How do you dare to say that you're looking for love?"

I stood up from my chair; my tears now dried in anger. "Thank you, Mrs. Sloan, for talking with me today. I now understand everything that I came here for, quite perfectly. If you'll excuse me, I need to go and find my child." I ran to the front yard, ignoring her replies, and proceeded down the road toward Catherine's house. I licked my lips as I ran down the street, crying. I could still taste the sweetness of Tom upon my mouth, intermingled with the salty, dripping tears. So many things were happening to me. Could it have been that Thomas was only a delusion from the craziness that everyone thought I possessed?

Live for that hope, were the words that wouldn't leave me, and I had to believe in my heart that Tom was real and that my life did have purpose. As I approached Catherine's house, I noticed Mr. Sloan's horse and buckboard parked in front. The girls were running in the yard with the puppy, and Catherine, Gerrit and Mr. Sloan were exiting the house.

"Joy, Lillian, Sarah, I want you to come with me now," I said loudly, ignoring the others.

They immediately stopped playing, and Joy came over to me at once, but the other girls stood there, looking at Catherine and Mr. Sloan.

"Did you hear me?" I yelled, but the girls didn't budge.

Gerrit made his way to where I was standing. "What were you thinking, Natalia?" He sneered. "You know you are not to roam from home without me. You took on way too much authority taking the Post girls with you, not to mention Joy. What if you had been besieged with one of your seizures?

What if you forgot where you were again?"

"I just have one question," I replied. "How did you even know that I had ventured from home?"

"Justin was concerned and came to the mill and told me," Gerrit replied. "He was concerned that you were out on such a hot day with those girls."

"That's what he told you, huh? What nonsense," I yelled. "I am very capable of caring for the girls! He, like everyone else in this town, is only concerned for one thing, and that is to make sure that everyone knows that I am mad! Look at me, Gerrit," I screamed, making sure Catherine and Mr. Sloan were included. "I am your crazy, sinful wife who gave birth to an illegitimate child and who murdered a passing stranger. I'm no good for anything. That's what you think, and what everyone else thinks as well." I looked at Catherine and her father standing in the distance and screamed, "Hades awaits all of you!"

"Mama, Mama, please," Joy said, tugging at my side. "I don't believe that."

"Get on the wagon," Gerrit commanded sternly. "You and the girls get on there too, Joy." I stood in utter disbelief, yet knew that I had no other option than to follow his commands.

"Get on there!" he yelled, pushing me toward it. Joy took my hand and led me on.

"She's going, Father; leave her alone," Joy insisted.

Catherine and her father stood in the distance. She had a snide grin on her face and was whispering something to the Post girls. Soon, Mr. Sloan and the girls approached and got on, too. Mr. Sloan waved at Catherine. Gerrit finally got on the wagon, sitting next to Mr. Sloan, and soon we were on our way. My life was a maze of mystery, although the mysteries were slowly becoming unraveled. No matter what anyone would do to me, or think of me on this earth, I would try to live for the hope that Tom made me so aware of. Without that hope, death was eminent!

Chapter 12

Reality

I'm not sure what happened to me, but the next days were a blur. It was as though my experience with Tom overwhelmed me and made me not want to live anymore without him. I was not living for the hope as he had told me to do. How could I, when I wasn't even sure that hope existed? Perhaps Thomas was just a mental specter that blew through the chasm of my mind to create in myself the justice for what I had been through. After all, Joy had told me that it was Arie's name that I had been calling out for and not Tom's. Nothing made sense.

Even through these darkest of days, Joy kept coming in and out of my bedroom, trying to keep me clean and nourished. She'd come in daily with a cloth to wash my face and hands. I had gotten to the point where I didn't even care about hygiene anymore. She also continued bringing me food and drink, which I had stopped partaking of. A few times a day, she insisted on taking me outside to the outhouse, although now I was too weak to leave my bed. A bedpan was now kept in my room for me to use. I couldn't actually remember the last time I ate more than a bite, or drank anything significant.

I had given up on everything, and Joy told me that everyone said I was wasting away. All I wanted to do was lie here and remember what I had experienced with Tom. Gerrit sent for the doctor, and Mrs. Sloan kept coming in and out of the house, ironically, whenever she knew someone would be around. She'd act as though she were very concerned for my well-being and the major caretaker of the house. I certainly knew better. It was definitely a show on her part, just as it had always been.

There was nothing wrong with me; is what the doctor told Gerrit. Nothing that is, except for my refusal to want to live anymore, and I heard him say that perhaps that could be the worst diagnosis of all.

"Be patient," I heard the doctor say to Gerrit in the hallway. "Sometimes people with these mental illnesses go through times like these. We'll put her on a heavier dose of Laudanum. Give it a few days, and if she isn't better, we'll see what we can do."

I guess things drastically changed that windy afternoon when I was visited by Justin Peterson. He came into my room and truly looked alarmed when he saw me. Gerrit was with him and Justin asked him if he'd please leave us alone for a while. Gerrit agreed, which surprised me immensely, since he didn't like me left alone with anyone, except perhaps Joy. I don't think Gerrit knew what to do with me anymore, and knew he needed intervention for me. I could hear Gerrit make his way downstairs and out the door. Justin poured a glass of water from the pitcher on my dresser and sat down next to me on the bed. He brought the glass to my lips. "Drink, Natalia, you must drink."

I refused and struggled to raise my head to look at Justin. I was so very weak. "I don't want to live anymore without Tom or without knowing about Tom," I said softly.

"Natalia, what you're doing to yourself is pure selfishness! Your daughter, Joy, she needs you immensely! Are you just going to give up like this and not think of anyone but your-self? Natalia, look at me," he shouted. Then he bent down and whispered in my ear, "Tom would have never dreamed that you would do this to yourself."

"How do you dare pretend to know what Tom would think?" I struggled to respond.

"Because, Natalia," he continued whispering, "Tom was my brother!" He lowered his head and bit his lip and seemed to be quivering.

I looked at him in disbelief. What was this man finally admitting to me? I looked down and began sobbing, then I looked back at Justin, fighting to raise my hand to caress his cheek. "What are you telling me?" I pleaded. I took the cup from his hand, almost too weak to hold it, and took a gulp. Then, slowly, I took another drink, almost dropping the glass. He took it from me, and my arm fell to the bed limply.

"Justin, do you realize what I've been going through? I wasn't even sure that Tom existed. I didn't know if I had made him up! You couldn't possibly understand how it is for me to know if what I've experienced in life is real or an illusion. You just don't know how it is to have everyone think you're unable to reason. After a while, you begin questioning what you think reality is, and think it's just a dream or a made-up lie. Now, I know that the love I have for Tom is more than I can fathom. Please, Justin, you must tell me more things. I need to put this puzzle... this book of my life together. The night of the murder, Justin, you and I were there, weren't we?" I looked at him through hazy eyes.

"Yes, we were there, Natalia," he answered softly. "And I'm sure you remember more than you think. Like I said, I think that God has temporarily taken the burden of knowing the truth from you, to save you from its tragedy. After seeing your frailness today, however, I know I must tell you what happened in order to save your life."

"Please, please ...what took place? I don't care if it's something that is too gruesome to imagine. I'm prepared to hear the entire story. You must tell me now more than ever," I pleaded.

"Natalia, I have not slept soundly since I heard of your refusal to eat or drink. People kept telling me of your fate, and

I can't bear it anymore. I stayed away hoping that you'd cure yourself, but it's been too long. I couldn't live with myself if something happened to you. You see, I promised Tom I would look out for you and Joy. You have to believe me when I tell you that I thought keeping the truth from you would benefit you. But, now I see your state of health, and that is why I'm here."

"Then, if you wish for me to recover, you must be honest with me. That's all I ask of you. Justin. If you loved someone and didn't know what happened to them, would you want to continue to live? Now that I know that Tom truly existed, I can have faith that Tom is still alive! I must!

"But Natalia," Justin interrupted.

"Let me speak, Justin. I'm not sure where his spirit roams, or how he will come back to me, but he promised he would. At least, I now know that he existed and wasn't a figment of my imagination. This may sound totally ludicrous to you, but Tom appeared to me. It was in Mrs. Sloan's garden, and he told me that we would one day be reunited again." I looked at the man sitting next to me and could feel his genuine compassion for me, yet I could also feel his unbelief in what I had just said.

"Natalia, things may not be what you think. I'm still not sure that revealing everything to you will help you, but I will say the most important words I know to utter to you," Justin continued softly. "If I were you, I would want to continue to live. No matter what you go through on this earth, there is a greater power guiding our lives. Perhaps we don't understand why things happen, but maybe it will all make sense in the next generation or even the next. I can't try to analyze the things that take place here on earth. I can only live my life in the best way I know how, and hope and pray that in doing so it will generate love to others. Now saying that, I've come to know that there are some things that I cannot keep from you anymore." Justin got up and went over to the open window. The drapes were swaying from the wind. He stood there for a few minutes as if pondering many things, then returned to my bedside.

"Gerrit's still outside with Joy," he said softly. He put his face into his hands and rubbed hard, then sighed. "The things I'm about to tell you are going to upset you, Natalia. These words are not to leave this room."

"I am prepared to hear it all," I said, grasping his arm. I noticed his right hand once again clenched into a fist. "I need to know that what I have been dreaming is not a lie. And I need to put all these names and places that I don't recognize back into some sequence in my life. Don't worry, Justin, none of the words that you will speak here will leave my earthly being."

He looked at me kindly, then began. "I first noticed this complete change in you, Natalia, the day I found you asleep at Bitterwood School not too long ago. I don't know what came over you, but from that day on, your mind seems to have changed. You began to make almost complete sense at times, something you hadn't done since the murder that occurred two years ago." Justin paused.

"Murder; so there was a murder!" I gasped, closed my eyes and shook my head.

"We will get to the murder later," Justin continued. "We first need to talk about when I found you in Bitterwood School. It was there that I noticed that you had forgotten most of your past. Since your mental stability seemed to have improved so much, I believed that it was a gift from God that you had forgotten. That is why, when you asked, I refused to tell you anything. I now realize that what you couldn't remember was the very thing that you longed to know to be able to continue living.

"I'm going to start as far back as I think will help you." Justin took a deep breath and then began again. "When I was 10 years old, my family traveled to New York City to establish a tannery. I was the oldest child, and it had been previously determined that I was to stay behind with my uncle in Colorado Springs where he ran a successful mining company. My uncle never married and had no children and wished for me to take over the business someday. I was to stay behind and become an apprentice to him. Some months passed and a telegram arrived. The cholera hit my family en route to New York. It was terrible, and no one survived. At least, that's what I was told. It was devastating news to me, Natalia … you can only imagine.

"Years went by, and my beloved uncle passed away, and the business was left to me. I was now left with no family and no one to call my own. Though, I had tons of assets, what is money worth when you have no one to share it with? In desperation, I did some investigating about my family's deaths and found a rather peculiar twist. There had been only four people buried from my family in the cemetery in New York. I boarded a train and went to New York promptly and found out that my youngest brother, Thomas, was unaccounted for. I learned, through much searching, that he had also become very sick but had recovered and was placed with a family somewhere in New York. I was ecstatic! I lived only to find my brother!

"I searched and searched and came up with nothing. It was like my heart was torn in two, because I believed that part of my family still survived, and yet I knew not where he was. I hired a lawyer and private investigator to help me find Tom. The lawyer said he'd get the word out on the streets and he'd list the information of the inheritance in all local publications. The lawyer was worried, however, because there were so many orphans, and people of disregard on the streets of New York at the time, that he was fearful many fraudulent individuals would turn up to try to cash in on the birthright. I assured him that if Thomas did appear, he'd be very easy to identify. If anyone showed up claiming to be him, I could definitely identify him positively. Very peculiarly, all of the Peterson children had been born with the pinky finger on their right hand deformed."

A tingling sensation went up my spine. Now I knew why Justin Peterson always held his last three fingers of his right hand closed. I smiled and took Justin's hand in mine. I gently pried open his fingers and outlined his pinky with my touch, as I had done so many times with Tom.

"Just like Tom's," I affirmed. "He wondered so often what had happened to his hand."

"It was a trait that our father had, as well as our uncle," Justin continued as he looked at me.

I continued gazing at his hand, and the familiarity of his finger made me get lost in the thought that I was holding Thomas' hand in mine. Justin became uneasy. He quickly pulled his hand away and continued talking. "Anyway, the lawyer agreed that this trait would definitely weed out any fraudulent characters who may try to claim the inheritance.

"Before I left New York he placed an ad to run indefinitely in all the publications throughout the city. They were boldly printed ads, created to catch anyone's attention, stating that an inheritance was being offered to be collected by a Thomas Peterson, and for him to contact the lawyer that I had hired. I would have done anything to find him, Natalia.

"After spending some time in New York, I needed to head back to Colorado. I couldn't leave the mine any longer. I hated the mine and all the danger it posed to the workers, and it seemed less and less that I wanted to keep it. Nothing was important to me except for finding my brother. Months passed, and I corresponded with the lawyer and private investigator in New York weekly with no luck in finding Tom. They said there was absolutely no trace of a Thomas Peterson anywhere in the entire confines of New York City with the stipulations I sought. There were a multitude of inquiries, as you can imagine, but at that time, there were no legitimate claims, or anyone who truly knew Tom.

"I was heartbroken and almost gave up, when a friend of mine invited me to a tent revival that was coming to Colorado Springs. I went that night, not knowing what I would experience, but I know now that it saved my life. The power of the words that I heard from the preacher who spoke that night overwhelmed me and made me know that I wasn't alone in this world anymore. I gave my life to God that night, Natalia. He saved my life.

"Not long after that I sold all the rights to the mine, and with the inheritance I had already received from my uncle, I would definitely be very well set for life. How I wanted to share it with Tom.

"I decided at that point in my life that I was going to attend a nearby seminary so that I could spread the Good News in which I had been gifted; which I did. After I graduated, I too began doing tent revivals here and there, from city to city, spreading the Gospel that had saved my life. I also used my travels to look for Tom. Then one day, my journey took me right here to LaPier. I set up my tent and proceeded to put up signs for the revival. You may have remembered the day I arrived."

I nodded my head, acknowledging that perhaps I did remember. "I remembered hearing that the whole town was talking about it." I answered.

Justin smiled, "Whenever I knew that I would be at a certain city for a while, I would leave word with the lawyer in New York that I'd be here or there for a time, just in case he needed to get ahold of me. I'll never forget this little city; for it was here that word came to me in the form of a telegram. I was told that information was collected from an orphanage on the outskirts of New York City. My brother Thomas was taken from that orphanage to live with a family; the Abendroths, Adolph and Ebba. There was a slight hope that Tom's name had been changed to Thomas Abendroth. Now I had hope as never before. I waited to hear more, continuing to conduct my revivals here in LaPier. Sadly, after a few days, word came to me stating that the Abendroths had returned to Germany and no one had accompanied them on the ship. It was confirmed on the ship's manifest that only two had boarded. My lawyer was unable to reach the Abendroths, and now we were back to where we started from again. My heart once again broke, and yet I didn't give up.

"I began praying fervently each day for Tom, more than ever, and decided that I couldn't continue roaming around the country anymore. I needed to plant my feet somewhere. Ironically, and almost eerily, I felt that God was speaking to me as never before, telling me that this community really needed a pastor. So, as you can see, after many months of traveling about, I decided to stay in LaPier. And, I'm still here today."

I was crying as Justin looked at me on the bed.

"Tom took care of me in New York, didn't he?" I sobbed.

"He did," Justin answered as he watched me wipe the tears from my eyes. "He loved you so much, Natalia. He told me all about your times in New York...How you cared for each other, when you had nothing."

"I can picture everything in my mind from hearing you speak. I remember it all now," I said in amazement. "I remember the tall buildings, the alleys, and the smell of the mornings on the streets. I remember the fights, and the people that would try to take me. I remember how scared we were at times. We would steal apples from the market and not be proud of it, but we had to eat. But, most of all...I remember Tom. He cared for me like no one else. The orphanages became too full and could not support themselves. There were no adults to care for the immigrant children, so we were forced to the streets. Tom would sell matches and newspapers and do anything he could do to make money. He'd always think of others before himself; especially me. He'd bring me food when he would do without. Those were terribly hard times." I continued crying and looked down, burying my head in the pillow. I sobbed and tried to gain my composure. "Justin, things are all coming back to me. Although, these memories aren't pleasant, I thank you for giving me my life back. I just had to know." I sighed and then continued. "My life in New York was anything but pleasant. I know that. But now I am remembering an even more terrible day." I rubbed my face.

"The children on the streets began noticing that the kids

we knew and grew up with were disappearing. There were rumors abounding of trains hauling them to strange destinations. Anyway, each day Tom would go out on the streets to find odd jobs and I would wait for him in the alley behind Mc Phearson's Market, with some of the other children. This particular day, constables appeared and took me and several other children off to a large, multi-story brick building. We were not happy, and they had their hands full as we kicked and screamed all the way.

"At the home, we were given baths and food, scrubbed for lice, and a doctor came in and checked our hearts and lungs. We were all given new clothes, but we were not allowed to leave this place for several days. The ladies in the home told us that we were very lucky children and that we were about to begin a new life. I missed Tom so. I didn't want to begin a new life without Tom. I knew he must be worried about me, and I didn't know how to tell him I was okay. I kept watching from the windows for him, but he never appeared.

"After some days, one of the ladies in the home came to me, and I was told that I was to go and live with a new family. I was to leave bright and early the next day. I was terrified. I was given a change of clothing and written directions, including my name and a brief summary of where I had come from, for this family that I knew nothing about. The next morning, I was given a lunch and put on a train. I now knew that I would never see Tom again! Oh, Justin, I was only 8 years old. The only true form of love I had known was from my mother, and from the love and caring that Tom had given to me. He was my caretaker; he was like my brother, my father, my best friend, my everything! Can you imagine how I felt when I was taken from him?"

"Actually, I can imagine, to some degree, Natalia," Justin admitted, with tears streaming down his face. "My family was taken from me, too; you know."

I tried to sit up on the bed, but I was so weak. Justin helped me by propping a pillow up underneath me. He stood up and went once again to the window.

"They're still outside," he said as he returned to me. "So, Natalia, if not for Divine Providence, how do you explain that the train took you to LaPier to live with the Sloans when you could have ended up anywhere else in the entire country? You were taken to this very city that I was directed to live in. You must believe that God directed you here, just as what happened next."

"And just what happened next? Please, Justin, you must continue. I think I know what happened, but you must make it true to me. Please continue," I pleaded.

"Well, as you know, you were taken to live with the Sloans, and in the meantime, my lawyers were continuing to monitor the inquiries from the ads that were put in the papers in New York City. It was late one night; I remember I was preparing my sermon, when I got a knock on the door. Two young drifters stood there in front of me. "Are you Justin Peterson?" one asked.

"I told them I was."

"I believe that you are looking for me," the other replied.

"The young man then took out a watch that was in his pocket and, holding it in his right hand, proceeded to show it to me. I didn't need to see the watch; I had seen his finger. I looked at him and at once knew that I was looking at the countenance of my brother. I was so excited that I couldn't breathe, but I knew that I had to keep him unaware of our relationship...at least for a time."

Presently Justin stood up and pulled on a tarnished, silver fob that hung from his shirt pocket. A watch was attached. He handed it to me, opened it, and showed me the engraving inside.

Without even looking, I spoke. "William Ingram Peterson. I know the watch well, Justin," I said, holding it in my left hand and caressing it tenderly. "Tom treasured it so. He never knew who it belonged to because he only knew his name as Tom Abendroth. If only, all those years, he could have known that it belonged to his father. If only he could have known his heritage. He pondered it so often."

"As you already know, then, Natalia," Justin continued, "the watch did, indeed belong to our father, although Tom would have never known that. He was too young to make that correlation without someone directing it to his attention. Somehow, some caring soul had put the watch in Tom's pocket after the rest of our family died. He had kept it all those years, as some type of heirloom, although he had no idea who it was from, or who it had belonged to." Justin paused and took a long breath. "That night, I got to know my brother again, although I continued to keep our kinship a secret from Tom. We chatted until it was morning light.

"The other young man, named Seth, who had come with Tom, had been sleeping through most of our conversation that night. Tom checked to make sure he was still asleep and then took me outside. It was then that I learned things I wished I hadn't, but, I also came to realize what integrity my brother possessed. Tom proceeded to tell me how Seth had found the writing in the newspaper in New York City regarding the inheritance from my family. Seth had gone to the lawyer's office and told the secretary that he may have a lead, but needed to correspond personally. Seth somehow conned my address out of the lawyer's secretary. That's how they found me here in LaPier.

"The unbelievable part of the whole thing was that Tom never believed that he was the true inheritor, for he only knew his name as Thomas Abendroth. Seth had thought the entire con game up, telling Tom to pretend to be Thomas Peterson, because of the engraving on the watch that he possessed. Tom stood in front of me, Natalia, admitting the entire story, not pretending to be anyone but the lowly orphan from New York that he believed he was. I took him in my arms, and told him what a miracle it was that he came here. I didn't care if it had been dishonesty that had driven them here. I told him it was no accident! Then, I put out my hand and showed him the abnormality of my finger.

"It's a family deformity," I told him. "Your father had it, your uncle had it, and our other brother and sister had it. He looked down at his finger and he wept, Natalia. Tom just wept, for he also now realized what a miracle it was that we had found each other.

"The next bit of information I learned from him was very troubling. Tom explained to me how he was in trouble with the law. There had been a robbery in New York City at a market there. Tom knew that Seth wasn't always to be trusted and feared that he was one of the kids responsible from the start.

"All the way to LaPier, Seth kept telling Tom bits and pieces of what had happened the night in question. There was never to have been any violence. Seth had made sure that no one was to be present in the market at the hour of the robbery. It was Tom's understanding that there was quite a squabble. This wasn't the first time that the market had been robbed, and the owner apparently had been waiting inside with a gun. When the kids broke in, the owner of the market began shooting. One of the kids overtook the owner and got the gun away from him. The owner then grabbed an axe and began to come after the kids, swinging. Seth apparently was the boy who had gotten the gun out of the hands of the owner and, out of fear for his friends' lives, he shot. The owner was killed instantly. Seth and the other boys ran from the building.

"It was just then that Tom had come looking for them. As they ran, Tom saw them and ran with them. Police arrived almost instantaneously and saw the boys running. No one was caught, everyone got away into the alleys and tunnels of the city. Warrants for open murder were posted for everyone in the street gang, and that included the warrant for Tom's arrest. The evidence was so incriminating, and Tom feared he'd never clear his name, so he decided to go along with Seth to LaPier to try and claim what they thought to be a fraudulent inheritance. And so you see, Natalia that is how I became reunited with my brother. It was all in God's will!"

"Could you please pour me a bit more water?" I asked, as I sat there taking it all in.

Justin poured the water into my cup and brought it to my mouth. I drank quit a lot. I sat there for a moment and said not a word.

"Natalia, are you okay?" Justin questioned.

"I am fine," I replied. "The story you tell...I now know it well. I have regained my memory of it. It was just as Tom told me. So, you must have been the one who allowed the boys to stay with you then; is that right?"

"Yes, Natalia, I hid them in Bitterwood School and Church for some time, and got to know and love my brother with all my heart. I didn't know what to do. I knew my brother was innocent. Seth was guilty of attempted robbery; there was no dispute in that. He was a somewhat seedy character but still a child and, although the murder had been committed by him, it had been done to save his friends' lives. It was out of desperation! It was never intended to have happened! But the story isn't finished. There is another miracle in all of this, too. Not a day would go by that Tom didn't talk of a girl that he had to find. She was a girl that he had cared for in New York City some years ago, and she had disappeared without a trace. I learned that her name was Natalia, and of course you know the rest of the story."

"Oh Justin!" I sobbed with all I had, and sat there for a moment as it all made perfect sense. "I first learned of Tom's arrival in LaPier when I was outside working in the garden at the Sloans' one day. I kept feeling a presence...someone watching me. It was a very eerie feeling. I used to love to walk down to the Sloans' pond and listen to the frogs croak in mid summer. It was always my get-away place. It was there that Tom first approached me. I couldn't believe my eyes. I knew him at once. I was so overwhelmed and thrilled to see him.

"He told me some things, as he did you. How he and Seth had journeyed from New York, and that it was a miracle that he had found me! He was, however, very secretive of so many things. He did make it very clear to me, however, that he was running from the law until he could get his name cleared. He told me he wasn't guilty of anything. I believed him, without a doubt. I never said one more word about his lawlessness, because I knew Tom's character, and I knew he was innocent!

"Anyway, it was as though we had never parted except for that we had now grown up somewhat. Our child-like love had now changed to something very intense, and I'd meet Tom every chance that I could down by the pond, or I'd sneak out in the night to meet him in the woods. That summer, Justin, was as though I was in heaven. Although, I was young, we fell so deeply in love! I never dreamed that love could be as it was. The passion that we shared was incredible, and we couldn't get enough of each other.

"But, through the ecstasy, a dark past always seemed to loom in our plans. I also had known Seth from my times in New York. He also cared for me, but not like Thomas did. I never liked him much, nor did I trust him. He always gave me a creepy feeling, but Tom told me to ignore him ... that down deep he was a good person. It seemed that Tom never saw the bad in anything, or anyone. He was, and is, truly remarkable." I smiled remembering him. "I still don't understand how Tom kept it a secret from me that he was your brother. He would never tell me where he stayed or where he ate, or how he survived. He told me he couldn't because he had to protect me, and I had to believe him. Now, I know he was protecting you, too, Justin."

"I know he was," Justin replied. "Natalia, do you remember anything more

"I remember so much pain, Justin," I replied. "...So much pain."

"Do you remember what happened to you one night at the Sloans?" he questioned. "I know this is hard for you, but you said you felt an evil there, and you've mentioned it to me before. Do you remember any of it yet?"

I closed my eyes and rubbed my face briskly, then opened

my eyes. "What I recalled at the Sloans' the other night was real, wasn't it, Justin? Even though it was only a mental re-enactment, I now remember what happened to me well." I began to shake. "I was only 14 years old when I was awakened by the sound of something hitting my window as I slept at the Sloans' one night. I went to the window and quietly lifted the sash. Seth was outside my window and told me he came bearing news from Tom. He asked me to meet him outside."

My shaking increased and Justin Peterson tried consoling me by putting his arm around me. I began to cry very hard.

"It's okay, Natalia, we don't have to go there now. You just need to get better."

"No, Justin, you don't understand; I must go there in order to get better! I was taken advantage of that night! I was violently defiled!" I yelled. "I snuck outside to meet Seth and was attacked from behind and thrown to the ground. I was gagged and bound. Seth didn't come bringing me news from Tom... He came to defile me!"

I was so very weak, and yet I was enraged!

"Natalia, please quiet down." Justin rubbed my back, then, got up and went over to the window. He could see Gerrit and Joy gazing up at the house. "She's okay," Justin hollered out. It was apparent that they could hear my frantic voice from the open window.

"What's going on up there?" I could hear Gerrit's voice, questioning.

"It's okay, Gerrit. Please give me a few more minutes with Natalia," Justin replied, and he closed the window. The room became silent without the rustling of the wind coming in, and Justin came back over and sat on the bed with me.

"Natalia, did you actually see the person who attacked you?" Justin questioned.

"It was Seth," I said loudly, "I know it was. Why else did he come to my window?"

"But did you see him, Natalia, during the violence?"

"Something was thrown over my face so, no, I never saw

the face of the rapist, but I know who it was." I didn't know if I wanted to continue with the conversation. It was becoming harder than I ever anticipated. I once again buried my head in the pillow. Justin sat beside me and knowing that he was there made it bearable.

After some time I continued, with the sheet still pulled up over my head. "That night, after I was attacked, Mrs. Sloan apparently was awakened by my screams. Mr. Sloan arrived first from what I understand. He had been in the barn working late, and said he had seen a boy running from the area. They blamed me for it all, Justin. Mrs. Sloan called me a tramp. She said if I hadn't sneaked out of the house this wouldn't have happened. She said I had asked for everything I had received. Mrs. Sloan wanted to know who the boy was, but of course my lips were sealed. They ended up calling the police. Mr. Sloan gave a complete description of a person to the officer, and demanded that they catch him. Of course they questioned me, but I couldn't tell them anything. I knew that not only would Seth be arrested, but it would be easy for them to find out the whereabouts of Tom as well. I was so young and so naïve."

"I know, Natalia. I know the story well," Justin acknowledged. "I remember how news spread fast around town of the rape. When Tom heard of it, he was enraged. I never saw him so disturbed. Tom and I felt right away that Seth was somehow involved. Curiously enough, Seth had never returned to my home that morning. The police were going door to door looking for the intruder. A complete search of the town was imminent. I told Tom that he must flee until I could assure evidence of his innocence from the crime in New York. I told him that everything would be all right, and that I would hire a multitude of lawyers if need be to gain his freedom.

"I gave him quite a sum of money to live on and told him to take anything else he needed. He asked me if it would be okay if he took one thing that I had previously shown him that had belonged to our mother. I told him to take anything he wanted. He told me he wanted to give it to you.

"Several weeks earlier, we talked of our mother's beloved necklace. It had been given to her grandfather by a band of gypsies while he was still living in Europe. Apparently her grandfather had saved one of the gypsy children from a drowning, and in return they insisted on giving him their most prized possession. They told him that it was a bridge between life, death and time...that the prisms emitted from this jewel could take you on a journey to your heart's desire if permitted by God. There were more instructions also given by the gypsies pertaining to the necklace, including the gift that a child could have in wearing it, but I don't need to get into that with you right now. Our mother always told us that it was magical, and that it possessed special powers that no one was capable of understanding. She was always a bit frightened of it, and for that reason, I don't think she ever wore it.

"Justin," I said, "Thomas told me of the story of the gypsies when he appeared to me in the garden. I didn't understand then, but now you've explained it!"

"Natalia, just listen to me, please." He paused, sighed and began again. "I knew exactly what Thomas wanted besides the money to live on. I quickly got Mother's necklace from the wardrobe and laid it in Thomas' hand. In return, he gave me our father's watch. I hardly had a chance to say goodbye. I had finally found my brother and now we were being torn apart again!"

"Oh Justin, this is so hard to relive!" I said, quivering.

"We can stop talking now if you wish, Natalia."

"No, I must ... I must continue." I shook my head and sighed. "It was the very next day, after the attack, and though I was terrified, I went outside in hopes that Tom would come for me. I just wanted him to take me away from the Sloans and from my pain! Mrs. Sloan was giving me peculiar attention, not letting me out of her sight. I remember Mr. Sloan joining her that day, and she told me to run along. They seemed so troubled, and I couldn't imagine it was due to my pain! She permitted me to walk around the perimeter of the yard alone.

That's when I spotted Tom in the bushes. I could barely function even walking, after what I had been through. Oh, Justin, I was so young!" I whimpered sadly.

"We just don't know the reasons for things, Natalia," Justin said, patting my back.

"No, indeed we don't," I acknowledged. "Anyway, Tom whispered for me to meet him down by the pond as soon as I was able. He was very distraught. Then, he took off running. I had to be so careful because Mrs. Sloan kept watching me now more than ever. I couldn't figure it out because I truly knew that she didn't care about me, and yet she seemed so concerned. I returned to Mrs. Sloan and told her that I was going in to lie down. I went in the front door, then exited out the porch door. I had to make sure no one was watching. I was terrified as I ran down the path to the pond. I knew it had been Seth who had hurt me, and at this point no one knew his whereabouts. As I ran, I kept feeling the presence of someone behind me, although I convinced myself that it was only my imagination.

"Finally I made it to the pond and was safe in Tom's arms. I told him everything that had happened, not knowing he already knew. He cried and cradled me to his chest. I could feel the ever-present love that we shared, but today I could also feel a horrible anger within him toward the person who had defiled me. He just kept telling me that he loved me...that he loved me, and that the person who had done this to me would pay.

"That was, without question, the saddest day of my life, for that was the day that Tom told me he had to leave. He took something out of his pocket and placed it around my neck. He told me it was his mother's and that it was very, very special. He said it had special powers. He told me that when I would wear the necklace he would find me through all time, through all space, through all eternity! He said that when he returned we would meet at the gazebo, and then he would take me away forever. He said he'd write to me, but from this day on I should know him only as Arie. I was told that his name must be kept secret until he was found innocent by the law. He asked me to believe that he would return for me, and that he loved me. I told him, of course, I believed him.

"Then he made me promise not to question what he had to do next. He told me I mustn't look for him or question anyone about him. He spoke so quickly, and that is when he told me again that he had to leave. Those words were like having my very heart torn from my chest. He hugged me as though he had pulled part of me within himself, and then, as though the earth shook him off, he was gone...just like that...he was gone."

"Oh, Natalia, I am so sorry for what you have had to go through!" Justin exclaimed. "I just don't know what to say."

"Justin, just having you be here with me, and now knowing that you are Thomas' brother, is more than I can ask for. Thank you ... thank you so much," I said. "I'm just glad that you're willing to confirm that what I thought were misty dreams of days passed, then turned nightmares in my mind, are all really true."

"It's all true," Justin confirmed. "Although I so wish some of it weren't, for your sake."

I looked at Justin. "And so now I know the rest, as you must, too," I continued. "I became with child. No intruders were ever caught by the police, and Mrs. Sloan became obsessed with getting me out of their house before I started showing the baby growing inside of me. Gerrit was Mrs. Sloan's brother and one day, out of the blue; I was informed that I was to marry him. It was as simple as that. I wasn't asked; I was told. I didn't even know this man, other than when he would come over, every once in a while, for Sunday dinner. He was a quiet man and I never gave much notice of him, but for some reason he gave me the creeps. So, in all my agony, over losing Tom, I was both married to someone I didn't know, and thought I despised, and gave birth to a little girl during my fifteenth year on earth. I didn't know how to be a mother. I was a child myself. I only lived to be with Thomas, and that is when I began to doubt my sanity."

Suddenly I heard the downstairs door open.

"We will talk another time about the rest, Natalia," Justin said softly. "But promise me that you will start taking nourishment again. You must promise me to eat."

"I know I must live for the hope, Justin. If I don't, there is nothing else to live for." I wiped my tears and gave a tiny smile to Justin as Gerrit walked in. I looked at Gerrit somberly, and wondered how this all could have possibly taken place.

"Please come and visit me tomorrow, will you, Justin? Please promise me that you will come. I could feel Gerrit's piercing eyes on me. "Gerrit, you will allow him to come, won't you?" I asked persistently.

Gerrit said not a word. I looked at him with pleading eyes. There was a silence.

"Is it okay if I check on her tomorrow, Gerrit?" Justin asked.

"Let's see what tomorrow brings," Gerrit mumbled. "She's been a lot of trouble these last few days." They started walking to the door.

"I will stop by tomorrow then," Justin said in a clear voice, turning back to look at me. "Let her rest now, Gerrit," Justin continued as he pulled Gerrit out the door.

My door was shut, and I knew it was Justin who had shut it. Miraculously, it stayed shut. How Gerrit allowed it baffled me. I could hear muffled voices going down the stairs, and then after some time, everything was silent. There I lay in the quiet room, with the memories of the man who Justin and I both loved so dearly. I longed for tomorrow to come, so that I could hear Justin read some more pages from the book of my life to me.

Chapter 13

Thomas Arthur Peterson

I awakened the next morning feeling renewed. I was so, so weak, but for the first time in days I felt a bit hungry. As usual, Joy came into my room as soon as she heard that I was up.

"Mama, you look better today," Joy said, with the biggest smile.

"I am better," I responded. "And, I'm actually hungry."

Promptly, Gerrit entered the room. He must have been lingering and listening in the hallway. "What are you hungry for, Natalia?" he asked.

"Some oatmeal with those summer raspberries that Joy picked yesterday would be lovely." Before I was even done talking, Joy had already made her way down the stairs to fulfill my wishes.

"What has made this turn around in you, Natalia?" Gerrit questioned as he lifted the window sash to let in some fresh air. "Was it something that went on between you and Justin Peterson yesterday? I don't like secrets, and I won't tolerate them in my house."

"There are no secrets here, Gerrit, except perhaps the secrets that you have kept from me yourself. I'm sure you're aware of pretty much everything you need to know that goes on in my life. Besides, it's not like we're a real husband and wife is it? It's not like we share things with each other...our passions, our fears, our needs. I don't even know you, Gerrit, or wish to know you fully. And I'm sorry if I never told you this before, but things could never work out with us. You certainly must know that. You keep me here like a caged being, and when I try to leave, you have the whole town watching out for me."

Gerrit looked at me and came closer to the bed. "You thrive on hurting me, don't you, Natalia?" He sat down. "Do you have any idea what you've put Joy and me through all these years? That little girl of yours... I've cared for her, and told her to love you, Natalia. I've given you and your daughter food and shelter and never have asked much of you in return. Most of all, I've protected you from your own self as best I could. I have to watch you, Natalia, because I never know what you'll do, or what you're capable of doing. Do you think I wish to treat you this way?"

"Gerrit, just tell me one thing. Why did you marry me? I was but a girl. I didn't know better! You didn't even know me! Why did you take on the burden of me with child?"

"I married you at the start because my sister pleaded with me to. I had no one before you in my life except my sister. She told me that you would be good to me and that I could finally have a family. She assured me that I could make you love me. She told me that your child would be the child I never had. Then, Natalia, after some time, I did fall in love with you. As crazy as it may sound, I fell in love with you. Even through your crazed tantrums and your calling out for other men, and your running away to that god-forsaken gazebo, yes, Natalia, I love you, and only God knows why."

I got out of bed on the other side from where Gerrit was sitting, and went to the window. I felt light-headed and had to watch my step. It was the first time I had been to my feet in days. It was another clear summer morning. The earth was shining, but my heart felt so shattered by what Gerrit had just said. Maybe I didn't know, or remember all the things I had done to this man. Maybe he truly tried to love me, and I wanted no part of it. Whatever the case, I would never love Gerrit; I could never love him, although this morning I had a strange, unexpected type of sorrow in my heart for him.

I turned to look at him. He had his head down. "Gerrit," I said, approaching the chair he was sitting on. "I'm sorry ... I'm truly sorry."

"Why can't you just love me, Natalia?" he asked in a whisper. "Am I not worth loving?"

"You can't force love, or create it from something that doesn't exist, Gerrit. I'm sorry it's just not possible."

I could hear Joy scrambling up the stairs. Soon she entered my room with a bowl full of raspberries, and she was carefully holding a cup half-filled with something else.

"Your oatmeal is cooking, Mama ...Sit... sit, I brought you raspberries and cream."

Gerrit stood up. "Try to eat, Natalia, it will do you good," he said softly, and then went out the door.

Joy poured the thick liquid cream over the raspberries, and I sat on the bed next to her. She handed me a spoon and watched in anticipation as I scooped the berries into my mouth.

"Good?" she asked.

"Very good, my little darling," I replied.

I managed to eat a good breakfast and even bathed by the wash basin. My hair was a ratted mess from lying for so many days, but Joy helped me to comb out the snarls, and I braided it and pinned it atop my head. I changed into some clean bedclothes. I knew I wouldn't be leaving the house for several days as weak as I was. I spent most of the morning just talking with Joy, and then found that I was too tired to do anything else.

"My dearest Joy, I need to lie down for a time," I told my little girl, and I did just that.

I must have slept far into the late afternoon. Gerrit, patting my arm, awakened me. It frightened me to see him standing there, but soon I noticed that Justin was standing next to him. I rubbed my eyes and quickly scooched up into a sitting position, trying to feel if my hair was in place.

"You have company, Natalia," Gerrit announced.

"I can see that. I'm glad you came, Justin. I was hoping you would."

"Are you up for some conversing now, Natalia?" Justin questioned. "I didn't mean to disturb your slumber."

"No, please stay. I need to speak with you in confidence. Gerrit, would you excuse us, please?" I said tactfully.

Gerrit looked at Justin and then at me. "Why is it so necessary that I leave? Is what you have to say to each other so private that I cannot hear?"

"Please understand, you just need to leave, Gerrit," I again tactfully spoke. "I need to get better, and to do that, I need to speak with the Parson alone."

He said not another word and, much again to my surprise, he left.

"I feel as though you've come to read me some more of the writings of my life," I said, watching Justin pull the chair up next to the bed.

"Did you do okay last night after learning so much, Natalia?"

"I'm doing pretty well, Justin, but I will do better after you affirm everything to me. It's a funny thing, because I don't remember things, but once you start telling me of my life, it's as though I knew it all along."

"Well, Joy tells me that you had a good breakfast and have been keeping yourself hydrated. I'm happy to hear that. I can already see that you're getting stronger. I was worried that perhaps I had done more harm than good by refreshing your memories yesterday."

"No, Justin, no matter what you tell me, even if it's dire, it will only do me good. It's hell on this earth to not remember or understand what has happened to me in the past. I remember completely where we left off yesterday ... how I became with child and how I ended up marrying Gerrit. Now, take me on the rest of my journey; will you please, Justin?"

"If you're certain you want to hear, Natalia. This will be difficult today."

"I'm very certain; please go on," I directed.

"Well, after Tom left, Natalia, you began to have a multitude of mental problems. Gerrit confided in me many times, saying that you'd spend most of your days out in the garden talking to a non-existent man. He'd watch you for hours talking to no one. I, of course, knew what you had gone through, and tried to understand your instability, but I was unable to tell Gerrit any of it. Doc was called to your house numerous times. He prescribed many medicines to calm you down, but in my opinion nothing has helped. Then you started roaming the streets of LaPier late in the evenings, and you'd sit at the gazebo in town for hours at a time. The children said you started chanting a peculiar chant, and no one including me truly knew what to do with you."

"But Justin, don't you see … I was searching for Tom. Perhaps in my own demented way, I was truly talking to him all those days. Perhaps he was really there just as he was the other day."

"Natalia, he wasn't there the other day, at least not in person. I know he wasn't! It just isn't possible."

"In your mind he wasn't, perhaps in my mind he was. Oh, how could you or anyone understand?" I questioned. "Just please go on, Justin."

He looked at me as though confused, and then began with the story again.

"After the baby was born, you were in a bad way. It was a hard childbirth for someone as young as you, and I truly believe you had a breakdown of sorts. You ignored your infant daughter, and Gerrit couldn't keep you in the house. The doc forbid you to go out because of the hemorrhaging that you were experiencing. You only wanted to journey to that gazebo despite your weakness. Gerrit was beside himself trying to care for you and the newborn child. Because of Thomas' instructions for me to watch over you, I decided I needed to be closer. It wasn't long after that, I decided to have a house built next door, so that I could look out for the both of you. I tried to help Gerrit by looking after Joy as best I could, while he tried his best to care for you. And, in the meantime, I continued to try and clear Tom's name of any wrong-doing by working with the authorities in New York. They said it looked very grim; the evidence was so incriminating."

"And what about Tom, Justin? Did you ever hear from him?"

"You never knew this, but, Tom secretly returned to LaPier when Joy was just about two years of age, and then one more final time. He never lost his love for you, Natalia, and watched you in your garden from my windows when he returned. He wept tears of sorrow seeing you. He wept violent tears! Knowing you were now married to Gerrit crushed him. Oh, how it tormented him! He wanted to come to you, but he knew that seeing each other would only wound you more, because he would have to leave again. After he left this time, he began corresponding with me by letter. He never left a return address, so I never knew where he was, but at least I knew he was safe and alive. You know of the letters don't you, Natalia?"

"The letters in your barn? Yes, I know of them," I affirmed. "I told you I did! They were written to me, weren't they, Justin?"

"Yes,...every time I'd receive a letter, there was another envelope tucked inside which was addressed to you. It actually didn't say your name, but they were to you. I knew you knew of the letters because I spied on you in the barn reading them several times when Gerrit was away from home. I even watched Joy, although she didn't know it, take the box to your house. How did you know they were there, Natalia? Was Joy the one who told you of them?"

"Yes, she did … It's not her fault, Justin, those letters kept me going. She found a couple of them one time on the ground. They must have fallen from the ones you were holding. She brought them to me. I knew at once they were from my Thomas. I made Joy return them to you, and told her not to let you know that I had seen them. I kept watching you that day, and in the evening I saw you go into the barn. I followed you in the dark and watched you hide the letters. My precious letters ... my precious letters!

Oh, Justin, where is my Thomas? You must tell me."

"Please brace yourself, Natalia. What I must tell you will hurt very much! My brother, and the man you loved, Thomas Arthur Peterson, was murdered one night. Murdered in cold blood."

"NO!" I got up and went as fast as I could out of the room. I was numb and it felt as though I was unable to hear. My heart thumped as though going through my head. I stood in the hallway shaking. I dreamed of what Justin had told me so often, but refused to believe it happened. Justin followed me. He laid his hand on my shoulder. "I'm sorry, Natalia, I knew this would be so very hard. I didn't know if I should tell you."

"But, he will find me," I demanded. I searched desperately around my neck for my necklace. Desperately, I fidgeted through my hair, trying to find it. "My necklace ... How will he find me without my necklace?" I panicked.

"Natalia, you must be quiet. Gerrit will come up here if you're not. Come; let's go back into your room."

Justin helped me, and I sat on the chair that he was previously sitting on. He stood beside me holding my hand.

"Just where did your necklace go, Natalia?" he questioned.

"I gave it to Thomas the other day, when he appeared to me at the Sloans. He told me he needed it to make everything right."

"Natalia, do you understand that Thomas is dead? How could you have given your necklace to him? Have you lost it? Please think where it could be!"

"I don't know!" I let go of Justin's hand and buried my forehead in my palms and began to cry. "I want to believe what you're telling me, but I saw him. I'm telling you... I saw Tom! Please, please," I said, tugging at Justin's shirt. "Tell me of the murder. You must tell me the details so I can understand."

I got up and walked over to the window. I turned and looked back at him. "Justin," I said softly, "I'm just as what everyone thinks of me, aren't I? I can't reason properly; I can't remember my life, and I have so many names floating around in my head, but I can't place the faces with the names. I'm insane, Justin, INSANE, aren't I?" I looked away.

"Oh, Natalia, our dear Natalia." Justin came to me and stroked my back. "You've been through so much. I'm not one to judge you in that way, but please, now, you must try to remember. I will tell you what I know of the murder, but I believe that you, and perhaps others who are still living, know the truth. You were there, Natalia. I believe that you saw the entire thing."

"Then tell me, Justin," I said, turning to him. "Tell me what you know, and I will try and remember. I will concentrate and try to remember everything, but tell me what you know."

"You have to consider that my information has been gathered from talking to anyone who knew anything of that night. I've pieced it all together as best I could. I was there after it all happened, Natalia. Doc sent for me, but I wasn't there when it happened. But, I believe you were!"

"I just can't remember," I said, straining to recall anything.

"I'll tell you then what I know of that night," Justin said, sitting down and trying to get comfortable. "It was a very stormy evening right around two years ago. I remember it well. We just don't see storms in these parts like that one too often. There were trees and limbs down all over the county. It was late when word came to me ... at least 2 a.m. Doc came by my home and told me to come with him. On the way, he proceeded to tell me what had taken place. There had been a gruesome stabbing at the gazebo and a man lay dead. His face and hands had been so disfigured that there was no way to identify him. Doc knew that I, as the parson in LaPier, came across just about anyone and everyone in town, and he was hoping that I might have been able to distinguish something about the victim as to his identity. Before I even got to the scene, Natalia, I had the eeriest feeling in my heart that Thomas was the man who had been killed. Do you remember what I told you about Thomas returning to LaPier twice?

"Yes," I answered.

"Well, he had returned for the second time the night before the murder. Why didn't Tom stay away?" Justin paused and looked as though he were looking up to God in prayer. Then, he began again.

"When I got to the gazebo with Doc, the police chief was there with his deputy and they were searching for any evidence they could find. Doc took his lantern from the buggy and we walked over to the gazebo. There, in a puddle of blood lay the victim covered with a sheet. Doc asked me again if I'd look at him. I knew I had to. It was why I had come, so I reluctantly agreed. He carefully uncovered the body. Before I looked at his face, or his body or anything, I looked down at the corpse's right hand. There were deep gashes on each finger, and flesh missing, but through all the gashes and blood, I could see without a doubt that his pinky finger identified him as my brother. I stood there, Natalia, and could hardly keep my composure. I began to cry uncontrollably, and asked who had done this. I demanded to know who had done this! That's when Chief Barnet stepped over and began talking with me. He told me that someone had spotted you, Natalia, in the gazebo earlier in the evening."

"ME...and, what did he mean by that, Justin?" I asked frantically.

"He meant nothing by it, and I don't want you to think otherwise. It was, however, the only lead that they had. That is why I asked you to try to remember anything about that night."

"Oh Justin, I just don't remember. I can't remember that

night as hard as I try."

"Try to imagine it again, Natalia. Try to put yourself back there. If you were there at the gazebo that night, it must have started to storm. Think Natalia, what happened next?"

I put my hand on my forehead and rubbed hard. I wiped the tears from my eyes. "Justin, I have completely blocked it out. Please don't think that I'm not telling you something. I certainly didn't kill the only man who I've ever loved! Justin, I couldn't have, could I? ... I mean for what reason?"

"Natalia, you mustn't think anything like that. Do you hear me?" Justin looked at me with concern. "Doc assured me that whoever killed this man had to have been someone with a very strong physique. He said that it would be very unlikely that any woman as small as you could have done the severe damage to a human body as was done to Thomas."

"But Joy told me some disturbing things about that night, Justin. Gerrit brought me home and bathed me. Joy said there was blood on me and my clothing. Then he locked me in my room. He made Joy promise to never tell anyone that I had been out that night. Oh Justin!" I draped my arms around him and sobbed.

Justin stood up, gently pulled my head back, and looked into my eyes. "Do you remember when I told you that I had to forgive someone in order for me to get on with my life?"

"I do remember, Justin," I replied.

"That someone, Natalia, was the murderer of my brother. I hate to incriminate anyone, especially after Thomas had been so wrongly accused, but I suspect it may have been Seth Maddison. I believe with all my heart that he had something to do with Thomas' death. I also believe that he still roams the streets of LaPier from time to time."

Shivers invaded my very being as I thought of the man who had raped me. Could this same man; this monster, now also be the one who had killed my beloved Thomas? Shadows passed my brain of that night, and I tried so desperately to remember. I HAD to remember now!

"But Justin, why would Seth have done these things to me, and then to Thomas? What could possess a man to do the unimaginable?" I questioned.

"I think that Seth loved you, Natalia. Thomas believed it also. I think that Seth was jealous of Thomas because he had the inheritance and he also had you. I think it was Seth who was there with you the night of the murder."

"Wait," I paused a moment and trembled. "I remember, I remember something! I am remembering quite a few things!" I sighed loudly and quickly began to give my account. "It was a stormy night; I remember the wind... the rain. I remember being badgered by it! But there is something very strange that Joy said to me that I now recall vividly. She said that she saw the figure of a man, in the field, watching the house for two days. I now remember, too! I thought that perhaps it was Thomas, and that this was the night I was to meet him in the gazebo. I was so very excited! I snuck out of the house while the lightening continued striking, and ran to the gazebo. The wind was blowing hard and tree limbs were falling. Some small ones hit me on the head and made a couple of gashes right here." I pointed to the small scar on my forehead. "I was dripping blood, but I was determined to go regardless of anything."

"So there's the explanation for the blood that you said you had on you that night."

"Perhaps," I acknowledged. I shut my eyes, again sighing, and then looked at Justin. "I now also remember sitting there on the bench of the gazebo while the wind and rain slammed against me. It was a hellish night." I took a breath. "When finally the wind and rain subsided a bit, I could hear talking in the distance. I rose and went into the woods, searching for the voices. It seemed I walked quite a ways. The rain started up again, hurling down harder and harder, and I couldn't tell where the sounds were coming from anymore. As I continued walking down a hill, I stumbled into a small stream. The darkness disoriented me and I didn't know where I was."

"Why, you must have wandered all the way to Pine Creek," Justin commented. "It's the only creek anywhere near that area! That's a good half mile from the gazebo."

"It could have been, I have no idea. I do remember that it was then, Justin, that I heard the horrific sounds in the distance. I heard hollering, and screams of terror and foul language and, worst of all, I heard my beloved's screams in the midst of it all. I followed the sounds back up the hill. It seemed to take me forever to reach, but soon I saw the clearing. I peered out of the woods and saw a man running from the gazebo. He never saw me come out of the woods, and I never saw his face. Oh Justin ... OH, JUSTIN, that must have been the killer! I went over to the gazebo and found a man in a pool of blood. He was unrecognizable! I bent down to try and revive him. Next to him lay a bent letter opener. I picked it up and studied it, then looked back to the gruesome scene. His face was gone, that's all I can remember is that his face was mangled and gone! It couldn't have been Thomas, Justin, I would have known, wouldn't I?" I sobbed.

"How could you have known, Natalia? I witnessed what you did. There was really no way to identify him unless you saw what I had ... his finger."

"I know, but you would have thought I would have known if it were my Thomas!" I took a deep breath. "I guess it was then that Gerrit found me. He ran over to me and tightly held me by my shoulders and shook me and asked me what I had done. By that time I was screaming, for it was finally dawning on me what had happened. Gerrit took the bloody letter opener from my hand and laid it next to the body. A stray lightning bolt lit up the grayish color in Gerrit's eyes as he bellowed at me... "Never, NEVER tell anyone that we were here this night." Then he grabbed me and put me over his shoulder and carried me all the way home."

"So the man that you saw running, where did he go?" Justin questioned intently.

"He ran in the direction of Engle Road. That's all I can tell you.

"Justin," I continued, "Joy has told me the rest of the story. The part when Gerrit and I returned home, and now I feel like I'm about to collapse. Our Thomas is gone, isn't he, Justin? He's gone from this earth?"

"His body is buried in Bitterwood Cemetery, Natalia. I placed a silver cross on the place where he lays. He is without peace; I can feel it each time I visit the grave. I never told anyone that he was my brother, Natalia; only you. I guess at the time, I was still in denial that it was truly Thomas, and I didn't want to tell the law anything in case he still lived. But it was he who died, Natalia. Thomas has perished."

"But you say that you're a man of God. Is that correct, Justin?"

"I try my hardest to be," he replied.

"Then you believe in the supernatural. Is that also correct?" I continued.

"Yes, I do believe in the supernatural. I believe that our Lord is omnipresent!"

"Then explain to me how I know in my heart that Thomas will come back to me."

"Natalia, Thomas cannot come back to you here on earth. If you believe in God, as I do and as I know my brother did, then someday you will be reunited in heaven, but you have to come to the realization that Thomas is gone from this world. I have no doubt, though, that his soul is in eternity," Justin said reverently.

"He will come back to me, to us, to Joy and I someday ... he promised and I believe him."

"You can't come back to earth from the dead, Natalia. I buried him. He is no longer here, and it's ludicrous for you to think he's going to return. You do, however, have to continue to live for what's alive, and I'm talking about your daughter. She needs her mother, and that's what I know for sure."

Justin Peterson seemed to become unnerved and restless. I had not ever seen him act like this before.

"I must go now," Justin said as he headed toward the door. "This is harder for me to relive than I dreamed. Natalia, we will keep in touch, that I can promise you."

I could feel him looking at me, and I sensed that Justin continued talking, yet his words became blurred. I sat there staring at the wall. After some time, I saw the shadow of the brother of the man I loved leave. I was alone again. I was alone with the thoughts of my beloved, Thomas Arthur Peterson.

Chapter 14

Garments From Another Era

The summer days proceeded, and I continued to gain my strength. My mind was a chasm of mystery within myself. Though I now knew and understood many things about my life, I still felt such emptiness without my Thomas. Along with everything else, something strange was going on that baffled me and was making me feel terribly uneasy. I seemed to possess emptiness in almost equal proportions for that of missing Thomas, for something, or someone, that I couldn't explain. Could it be another loss I had experienced? Could it be another secret that I wasn't told? I wasn't sure.

Perhaps there were other things that were being kept from me. How would I know? It was just another thing that I needed to get answered. Something from within my subconscious kept telling me that Thomas was indeed alive. Who, or what, was I to believe? I only knew that if I were to give up hoping and believing, I would no longer want to live; just as had been the case over a week ago.

Today, I had decided, would be the day that I would try to figure out some of the things that I was being accused of doing in the past. For example, the obsession I apparently had with going to the gazebo. I would visit there this morning before anyone had risen. Maybe I would feel Thomas' spirit there.

Maybe I would see him again! I had to find out why I traveled to the gazebo so often.

I was very, very quiet as I rose from bed. It was not yet full-morning light and the birds had just begun their first song of the new day. I had not been out of my bedclothes in a long time. I had been too weak. Now, after days of replenishing my health, I felt that I owed it to myself to begin anew once more. I was determined to begin my search for Thomas.

I quietly opened the drawer of my bureau and began to rummage around for some clothing that would keep me warm in the early-morning temperatures. Most of my summer selections were in the front of the bureau, and my warmer items were folded in the back. I reached back and pulled out a clump of garments. The light was just becoming visible in my room as I noticed some clothes that were unfolded and wedged within the pile. The vivid colors caught my attention, and I pulled the colorful fabrics from the stack. For some odd reason, I felt anticipation upon finding them, almost like they were a link to something. I quickly took them over to the window to inspect them better. Something immediately came over me!

As I continued to look at the clothes, thousands of haunting emotions invaded my thoughts. I felt more confused than I had ever believed was possible. Where had these clothes come from? I began shaking intensely. They were not from this generation, and yet, I knew them...they were familiar to me. I raised them to my face and smelled them. Who was this perfumer who had created this scent? It made me feel love again, but this love seemed to have been experienced with someone other than Thomas. Immediately, my mind raced back to what seemed like another dimension. I tried not to let my thoughts go there. I blamed it on my mental problems, but there was something wrong, something peculiar.

I held my head in my hands and cringed, for it seemed that I was in pain in that life also. Why did the name Anthony keep coming to my mind? I kept thinking and trying to remember.

I loved him! I loved this Anthony, but it was a love unlike the one I experienced with Thomas. It was more like the love I had for Joy. More names came to mind: Daniel, Colin, Libby... who were these people? I kept trying to think.

As the room became more illuminated, I continued to inspect the clothes. Were they mine? There was one way to find out. I quickly unfastened the buttons on my nightclothes and let them fall to the floor. Looking in the mirror, I put on the other garments. They had unusual fasteners and they fascinated me, and yet I knew exactly how to use them! The clothes seemed a size too big, but that would not be unusual because of all the weight I had lost. They also seemed to fit more formed around my body than the things I was used to, but they fit!

I turned around, trying to see what the back of the clothes looked like in my mirror, when my toe caught the post of my bed. I tumbled to the floor, trying to catch myself. It made quite a boom. I feared that I had awakened Gerrit and Joy. I lay there for a moment, listening, trying to hear if anyone had gotten up. All stayed silent. Usually the moment that Joy heard that I was awake she would be in my room. I got up, noticing that I had banged my thigh on the bed pretty hard. I'd have a nice bruise in a day or two. Once again, I focused my attention back to the mirror when my door opened slowly. There stood a droopy-eyed Joy looking at me.

"What are you doing, Mama?" she asked rubbing her eyes and staring intently at me.

"Nothing," I quickly replied. I grabbed the quilt from my bed and draped it around myself.

"Why are you doing that, Mama? What are you hiding? What clothes are you wearing? Are you ashamed of something?" Joy continued badgering me with questions.

"I'm not hiding anything, Joy," I insisted. "I just don't understand so many things! I'm going to show you something." I unloosed the quilt and laid it on the bed. "I want you to tell me if you know where these clothes came from. Are they mine?"

Joy came beside me and peered at my outfit, inspecting the clothes from top to bottom. Then, she gasped loudly. "Mama, where did you get them?"

"Shhhhh," I said. "I found them bunched up in the back of the bureau. Please tell me, have you seen them before? Have I worn them before? Where did they come from?"

"Mama, do you remember the day that Parson Peterson found you asleep in Bitterwood School?" Joy asked, looking at me.

"Of course, dear," I answered.

"Well, the day before that, Lillian and I were at the summer party at the school. It was the party our teacher, Miss Larson, gave for the children before she left LaPier. We left the party and were looking for something very important in the woods that I thought I had lost."

"Okay; go on, Dear," I said.

"When Lillian and I were looking, we saw a lady bent down on the path. She stared at us and we at her. She was no one we knew. She was unlike any lady we'd seen here in LaPier, and she had funny clothing on. The clothing was nothing like we had seen before, so we noticed it. Mama, she had that clothing on! She was wearing those clothes!"

"This clothing?" I inquired, surprised.

"Yes, Mama, where did you get it? It scares me that you have it! Please take it off." Joy began to cry. Suddenly, I could hear more commotion in the hallway. I ran to the door and shoved it shut. Almost at once, it reopened and Gerrit stood in the doorway. I quickly grabbed the quilt from my bed and wrapped it around myself.

"Joy...Natalia, what is going on?" Gerrit asked. "Why are you crying, Joy?"

Joy looked at me and tried to catch her breath. She was crying very hard.

I looked at Gerrit. "Nothing is going on, Gerrit. I just awakened early. I could not sleep. Joy heard me and came into keep me company. I'm sorry if I woke you up. I hit my toe on the bedpost and fell. I think Joy thought I was hurt. That's the explanation for her tears. Is that right, Joy?" I turned to her, nodding my head yes, hoping that she'd catch on to confirm what I was saying.

Joy inhaled and exhaled very loudly twice and then tried to speak. "I guess ... I guess. I thought Mama was hurt. Yes, that's why I'm crying."

"Please go back to bed, Gerrit, it's still so early. I will take care of Joy." Gerrit responded so softly that I couldn't hear what he said, and then he returned back to his room.

There I stood with my frightened daughter with absolutely no explanation for how I had gotten the clothing. I walked over to Joy and she stepped away. Once again, I tried to get close to her, and she headed for the door. What did she think of me? What did she think I had done? What had I done? It hurt so badly to think that she thought evil of me.

I thought Joy was leaving when she turned around in the doorway. "Mama, what happened to the lady who was wearing those clothes?" she asked between gasps of breath.

"I told you that I'd never lie to you, Joy. My answer is that I don't know. I just don't know what happened to the woman, nor do I know how I got the clothes!" I answered.

Joy ran from my room to hers, and I could hear her door shut tightly. Quickly I unwrapped the quilt, took off the clothes, and put on some of my usual ones. I snatched the garments in question from the floor and, grabbing one of the hatboxes that were underneath the bed; I stuffed the clothes inside. Spontaneously, I tucked the box under my arm and ran down the stairs and out the door. I got to the road and looked back up to my room, and I could see Joy in the window, looking at me and crying as hard as ever. She must have returned to my bedroom where the window looked out to the road to watch where I was going. I couldn't face her. I turned away. I didn't know why, but I needed to get rid of these clothes. They seemed to be nothing but trouble, and yet I longed to know of them.

I ran as fast as I could down the road to Justin's barn and grabbed a shovel. I walked a little way out into the field, where no one could see me, and began to dig a hole. I was sweating and began to cry. Why was I doing this? When the hole was big enough to fit the box, I dropped it in and covered it back up with dirt and grass. Quickly, I made my way back to the barn and set the shovel beside the building. Then I headed back to the road. I was sweaty and dirty and crying. I needed to go to the gazebo. Maybe there, I'd find some answers. I stood there, trying to gain my composure and attempting to block out everything that had just transpired. Suddenly, I heard the sound of footsteps on the gravel road. I turned around, and there I met Gerrit face to face.

"Natalia, get home!" he commanded.

Without any thought as to what he had said, I began to run. I just wanted to run. I passed our house and kept on going fast, then faster and faster. I didn't turn around to see if Gerrit was chasing me, I just kept running. It seemed that it was the only thing I was able to do. Right before I came to Engle Road, I saw a clearing that looked like a path into the woods. I turned down that path, never slowing down. The foliage was lush and I was sure that I couldn't hear anyone behind me. I was panting hard when finally I fell to the ground. I looked up. No one was there. What had I done? I truly must be insane. Why did I bury those clothes? What did happen to the woman who wore them? Had I done something to her? Suddenly, this life seemed unimportant, and the names I had remembered, Anthony, Daniel, Libby and Colin, seemed to take precedence over the events of this life. I knelt there beside the path and called out to God. "Oh, please, if you can hear me, help me," I pleaded. "I can't do this anymore."

I sat there on that path for a few minutes and then got up. It was a hazy day. Through the openings of the trees, rays of light shot down upon me with an almost uncanny beam. Perhaps it was an answer from God that He was watching over me. I certainly needed someone to watch out for me. Slowly, I continued down the path until I reached the road. I looked out from around the trees to see if Gerrit was anywhere in sight. When I knew it was clear I started walking, turning the opposite direction trying to elude Gerrit if indeed he was following me. I had a creepy feeling that he hadn't gone home at all, and that he'd reappear at any time. I walked briskly down Engle Road and kept on going up the hill. As I reached the top of the hill, the gazebo and State Street came into sight. It was still very early in the morning and there was nothing stirring anywhere except for the milkman making his run into town.

The lawn was wet with dew in the park, and the grass that apparently had been cut last night clung to my shoes. I slapped my feet on the steps, and then proceeded to climb the stairs of the gazebo. I was suddenly taken aback by what I saw! Laying on the bench within the lattice work of the porch were the flowers that I had heard so much about. I went to them at once and took them into my arms. I smelled their lovely, unusual fragrance, and had the uncanny feeling that they must have been left for me.

They were the most beautiful flowers that I had ever envisioned! Even though Joy had told me that I had seen them before, I hadn't remembered them. And, yet, they seemed familiar from another place, another time. I knew that seemed crazy, but then, I guess it went along with my mental condition just fine.

There definitely was a kinship I felt in being at the gazebo and holding these lovely flowers. Joy had mentioned that I sometimes took the flowers home with me. Could it possibly be that these flowers were a sign from Thomas to me? Was he leaving these flowers to make me know that he hadn't left me after all? From now on, I was going to believe that. Believing that the flowers were from Thomas would keep me alive. I brought the bouquet up to my face and kissed the delicate-looking buds. We will be together again, Thomas, I said to myself, looking up to the sky.

The wind began to pick up speed as I climbed down the gazebo steps. I embraced the flowers and instinct seemed to take over as I began to encircle the perimeter of the structure. I first walked slowly and then faster. Out of my mouth came words that were unclear to me. What on earth was I doing? Was I possessed? I began chanting softly: "The stones upon foundation stand for sun to prism onto land. And if you're in the perfect place, you'll be transported to another place." Over and over, I continued saying these words as I encircled the gazebo, grasping the flowers tightly in my arm. "Arie!" I shrieked as I made another circle around the gazebo chanting over and over again. I could feel the sweat streaming down my face and my heart was beating faster and faster, when someone abruptly stepped in front of me. I screamed. Gerrit took hold of me. He glared at me, furious.

"Natalia Kappan, what are you trying to prove?" He held me so tight that it hurt my arms, and I struggled to get free. Then he let go of one of my arms and pulled the flowers from my grip. He threw them to the ground and stomped them into the dirt.

"I told you to never, never touch those flowers or bring them home again. Do you understand me?" he yelled.

I backed away as far as I could, although I knew I was still in his clutches.

"Natalia, look at me!" he continued yelling.

I refused.

Gerrit grabbed ahold of me with both hands and started to shake me.

"Please," I pleaded. "Let go!"

It was at that moment that a loud, shrill, screaming sound began. It was as though a banshee was bewailing through the hills, challenging everyone to stop and hear its pleas. The sound seemed to make Gerrit stop shaking me, and he let loosened his grip. I raised my hands to cover my ears. When the screams stopped, I looked at Gerrit.

"Just leave me alone; that's all I ask of you. I'm not harming anyone," I said softly.

"You harm many, Natalia! You don't even realize what you do. I can't leave you alone, don't you realize that? I can't." Then Gerrit tightly took hold of my hand and began leading me home. I had no choice but to go with him. I had no one else in this life to turn to. What a lonely existence I had! Gerrit continued his harsh hold upon me and led me all the way home without either of us saying another word.

Chapter 15

Hopes Wrapped in Twine

Once again, my spirit had been torn down by what I thought was Gerrit's preoccupation and manipulation of me. I had no freedom whatsoever, and anything that I did that seemed out of the ordinary was blamed, without thought, on me having mental difficulties. Here I was, back in my lonely little room with only my window to view the world. I was truly a prisoner being guarded by my so-called husband, and this man also had the entire town keeping me at bay. And now, to make things worse, not even Joy ventured to my room.

What I didn't understand before was becoming perfectly clear as I gazed out the window's blurry panes of glass. How could freedom lay right outside this transom and yet be so hard to obtain? If I didn't do something to grasp what was going on, I'd simply dry up and die in this wretched place. As I had planned earlier, today would be the day I would begin my journey in finding out all my answers. I would do whatever had to be done to get out of here and find some sort of refuge.

I suddenly heard talking going on in the parlor and soon found out that Justin had come to pay a visit. I quietly went into the hallway and stooped down on the edge of the stairs, straining to hear what was being said.

"She ran from me this morning," I could hear Gerrit saying.

"I found her several minutes later at the gazebo right after day-break. She was doing that mystical chant that she does. She found more of those flowers. She was grasping onto them like she was holding a baby. I'm afraid Natalia's returning to the past."

"You mustn't think that, Gerrit," Justin replied. "We all have to hold on to our hopes and prayers."

I heard a little giggle come from Joy's mouth as Justin must have tickled her, or done something to amuse her. I'm sure he was aware that Joy didn't like the conversation, and he was trying to get her mind off of things. He was good at that.

"I don't find much conversation coming from you today, my little Joy," I could hear him commenting.

"...Don't feel like talking." Joy responded.

"Why are you in such a bad mood?"

"I'm worried for Mama," she said, as she took off running up the stairs.

Not aware that I was sitting there, Joy met me at the top, and I put out my arms to hold her. She had been ignoring me so much due to the incident with the clothes that I thought she'd run right by. But she flung herself into my arms as though that's what she was looking for, and I hugged her tightly. Children's minds are so resilient, I thought to myself!

Lowering my head, I whispered in her ear, "Please, Joy, you have to believe in me no matter what you hear. Without you believing in me, what would I have to live for?"

The commotion above soon brought Gerrit and Justin to the foot of the stairs. They stood looking up at us.

"Morning, Natalia," Justin said, giving me a muted smile.

"Good morning," I replied.

"Gerrit, I need to talk with Natalia today. That is the reason for my visit," Parson Peterson said, looking at Gerrit and then back at me. "I need to take her with me...it's a personal matter."

"She's not leaving this house," he retorted swiftly.

"May I speak with you in private?" Justin questioned.

I could see Justin put his hand on Gerrit's shoulder and pull him away. After that, the talking became too muffled to hear. I took Joy's head into my hands, rubbing her cheeks and gently turning her face to look up at mine. "I love you," I softly spoke. She looked troubled.

"Mama, where did you put those clothes? After you left, I looked for them and they are not here."

"Oh, Joy," I whimpered, "I hid them, Honey." I don't' know why, but I hid them."

"But why would you hide them if you were innocent of doing anything to that lady who wore them? I'm scared, Mama. That's the kind of stuff that you do that frightens me terribly."

"I know you are scared, and I am as well," I said matter-of-factly. "Joy, I don't have any explanation for the clothes, or for so many things, but I will assure you that I am going to find out everything, and I mean everything. Someday, I will make you proud of your mother. I promise."

"I hope so, Mama," she said, blinking back tears. "Please find everything out soon though, will you? My friends are always saying things, and those things make me wonder so much."

I could hear the door open downstairs and soon Justin was standing at the opening below.

"Natalia, I'd like to have you come with me today if you're up to it."

I hastily walked down the stairs and Joy quickly followed. "Will Gerrit permit me to leave with you?" I questioned.

Quickly, Joy interrupted, "Please, can I come too, Sir?"

"Joy, you'll have to stay with your father today," Justin said. "I will take you away another day, okay?"

She nodded her head sadly.

Slowly, Justin turned back to me. "In answer to your question; yes, he's allowed me to take you with me today. Please get your things." He sounded sterner than the last time I had been with him.

I bent down, looking at Joy. "Remember what I told you? I love you," I whispered.

I ran back up the stairs. I looked in the mirror that hung from decorative pegs off my dresser and saw Natalia Kappan, but oddly it felt like I was gazing at a completely different person. These were definitely the thoughts that made me question my sanity. I quickly ran a brush through my hair and washed my hands in the basin. They were still soiled with grass stains from earlier that morning when I had fallen on the ground. I grabbed my bag. What was going on that made Justin have to take me away? I truly didn't care; I just needed to escape this house.

Joy was sitting by the kitchen table, showing Justin a picture that she had drawn,

when I approached. "I'm ready." I kissed Joy on the forehead.

"I think you're on your way to becoming a famous artist," Justin said as he patted her head.

We walked to the porch. Gerrit was standing there next to one of the pillars, seemingly looking down the road.

"Thanks for understanding," Justin said to Gerrit as we left the porch. "I'll have her back promptly."

As we made our way next door, Justin kept very quiet. I turned around and could see Gerrit through the field, watching our every move. Justin had already made ready the buggy. Old Emily was waiting for us.

"Hop in, Natalia," Justin instructed.

I did, and we took off promptly.

As we passed the house, Joy and Gerrit were sitting on the porch steps. Gerrit was on the highest one, and Joy was on the lowest one. Joy raised her hand to wave a solemn wave. I returned the gesture.

"I'll be back soon, Joy," I said, as I gazed at Gerrit. He sat there with no expression at all; never giving as much as a hand signal to signify our leaving.

It was quiet in the buggy for some time. Something was

obviously bothering Justin.

"I'm very interested about this visit," I said as we began down State Street.

"Natalia, I should explain all of this. There has been a package left for me in town at the Hotel Saint Denis'. I have no idea who it is from or why it was left there."

"And what does that have to do with me?" I eagerly questioned.

"Well, the package wasn't exactly left just for me. It was left in two names, both yours and mine. I guess George Middleton was given precise instructions by a woman who left it at his hotel yesterday, that we both must be present to pick it up. She also instructed that no one else could be with us. I was talking to George Middleton last night at the prayer meeting. I guess the woman refused to leave her name and had left it yesterday around 2:00 p.m. He said her hair was tightly bound in a kerchief and he couldn't see what she looked like too clearly; although he tried. I told him that I'd come and get the package sometime today. I told him I'd wait to open it until you were with me, but he was adamant in having you present with me to pick it up as well."

"Justin, what could it be? Why would someone leave something for us at the hotel? Why wasn't it sent in the mail?" I was bewildered and knew I must have sounded overwrought in my questioning.

"I have no idea," Justin said, "but I guess we'll soon find out."

As we neared Engle Road, I could see the little path that I had gone down trying to flee from Gerrit just hours ago. I was amazed after what had happened this morning that Gerrit had allowed me leave the house with Justin.

"Did you hear about our confrontation this morning?" I said, turning toward Justin. "...Gerrit's and mine, that is?"

"Yes, I did." Justin answered. "I didn't think Gerrit was going to let you leave with me. I had to persuade him a bit. I told him that I needed to speak with you regarding religious matters, which is somewhat untrue. I do, however, always try to speak on that subject with everyone that I am with. We will have to cover that matter, too, sometime on this trip.

"What else did you speak about?" I asked curiously.

Justin looked over at me. "You heard us talking, didn't you?" He eased up on the reins a bit.

"I wasn't sure how much I had heard." I replied.

"We didn't speak long, Natalia."

"I had quite a few weird things happen to me this morning." I admitted. "I felt the need to go to the gazebo today. I thought that perhaps I could feel Thomas there, and I was right. His spirit was there, Justin. He left me flowers. I know they were from him."

Instantly, Justin slowed the buggy. He pulled it over to the side of the road and stopped. "I want you to look at me, Natalia," he said firmly.

I was a little shaken by his attitude, but I did what he wished.

"Thomas was not the one who left those flowers," Justin said sternly. "Thomas is gone. Do you understand that I buried his body? I'm not quite sure that you do. A dead man cannot come back to this earth. It upsets me so badly when you make these accusations. He was someone that I loved as well, you know. He was the only family I had left. I just wish you'd quit saying that he is coming back. You are living on false hopes and deceptive dreams."

I could feel tremendous resentment in his voice. What could I do? I had to believe that Thomas was going to come back for me, although I worried every minute how he'd find me again without my precious necklace in my possession. I knew it seemed preposterous, but I had to believe it; I had no choice. I wanted to say something so badly to comfort and help Justin, but no words came to my lips. The rest of our ride to the hotel consisted of almost no conversation except for some brief updates on how Justin had known the Middletons; the owners of the hotel, and other unimportant musings.

It was afternoon when we arrived. The Hotel Saint Denis' was a large building for LaPier. It had been built approximately 15 years ago and was quite a pretty brick structure. George Middleton, a timid, very religious man who Justin knew well, owned it. He was a member of Justin's church and a much-respected man throughout town. The hotel got quite a bit of business from travelers proceeding to Chicago, and he kept it in fine order.

"I don't think we have to worry about George telling too many people about the package. He'll respect our solitude," Justin said, helping me out of the buggy. "We'll take it with us and open it after we've gone from here. It's no one's business what's inside. I keep thinking that it has something to do with you and my brother's time in New York. Perhaps it's something from the lawyers. What else could it be?"

"I have no idea what it could be, Justin. I have no family other than Joy."

"You're forgetting your husband, Natalia," Justin said.

"I don't think of Gerrit as my husband," I said. "I never could! I can't think of anyone who would send me anything! My world is so limited." I paused a minute to catch my breath. "I was thinking...I know you said that George Middleton wouldn't tell anyone about the package, but I'm sure he'll tell his wife. You don't suppose we have to worry about her saying anything, do you? I'm thinking of the busy socialite that Mildred is. She's liable to tell Mrs. Sloan, and then it will get back to Gerrit and the entire town."

"Natalia, I don't know what we can do. What other people say and do is not in our control. You and I did nothing wrong. Let's get the package and take it from there."

Justin hitched Emily to the post, just right of the hotel, and proceeded to enter. George Middleton was standing behind the desk and noticed us at once. I could see him immediately bend down. I assumed that he was already fetching the package.

"Good day, George," Justin said, putting out his hand and

looking over the counter to see what George was doing.

George finally stood up, laid a small package on the desk, and accepted Justin's handshake. "I brought Natalia Kappan with me this time, so all should be in order," Justin remarked.

He gazed at me and I smiled and tipped my head. I had only seen George Middleton a few times. Mostly when he and his wife would come over when I lived at the Sloans. I hadn't seen him in years. George Middleton turned back to Justin, but then quickly looked at me again. I sensed that he was studying my face, and it made me feel uneasy.

"I'm so sorry if I inconvenienced you by not allowing you to take the package without Mrs. Kappan being present," he said apologetically, looking back at Justin. "It was just that the woman who left the package gave such strict instructions. She seemed so desperate! She asked me if she could trust me, and I gave her my word. She even offered to pay me a large fee for my services, but of course I told her no." He turned back to me. "I'm a bit embarrassed to ask you this, but I must, Mrs. Kappan. Are you sure it wasn't an older sister or relative who dropped off the package? The woman had so many of your traits...the nose, the eyes. She was hard to see from her coverings, she was older, but she looked so much like you."

"I would assure you, Sir, it couldn't be," I replied, surprised at his inquisition.

"Of course, I know I must have been mistaken," George Middleton said, acting truly sorry for what he had said. "There would be no purpose for a relative of yours to bring a package to the hotel instead of delivering it to your home. Unless, of course, she didn't know where you lived. I will say, however, that the similarities in appearance that you have with the woman yesterday are truly amazing."

"I assure you, Sir, I take no offense in your questions," I answered politely.

He smiled at me. "Anyway, I tried to take care of the woman's wishes at her request. Running a good business is what I strive to do." He looked at both of us and continued smiling. "You never know when someone will return to become your customer. Besides, God watches what we do at all times."

"George, you don't have to explain or apologize," Justin responded. "I applaud your integrity in keeping the woman's wishes. We would like to ask something of you, though, if at all possible."

"Most certainly," he responded. "What can I do for you?"

"I don't want you to think that there is something immoral going on here, because there isn't. Neither Mrs. Kappan nor I know what is in this package, or where it came from, but no one else besides us three needs to know about this. It may make trouble for Natalia or myself."

George Middleton handed the package to me and strung his finger across his lips signifying that his lips were sealed. "You two have a good day," he said as we approached the door. The door had almost shut when I heard Mr. Middleton shout. "Oh, wait."

Justin caught the door, reopened it, and we went back inside.

"There was something else I was supposed to tell you," Mr. Middleton said as he quickly approached us.

I stood there eagerly, listening.

"It didn't make much sense to me, for she spoke in broken English, but perhaps it will to you. That woman said to tell you something to this effect...To be sure to follow your heart, and follow the stone's prisms, for you never know what dreams will come true."

"I guess that's an unusual statement, don't you think, George?" Justin affirmed as he patted him on the back.

George held the door open for us and we proceeded to the buggy. "Yes, I took it as a strange statement indeed. But I was hoping that it would make some significant sense to you or Mrs. Kappan. I hope there's a real nice treasure inside that package for both of you."

I pondered everything I knew in my heart. Justin untied

Emily, and we got into the buggy.

"Thank you," I said to Mr. Middleton. It was nice seeing you again." I waved goodbye. I had a tight grip on the package. We both were feeling much anticipation!

"Let me get out of town a ways, and you can go ahead and open the package," Justin suggested.

The hazy day had just burst into a deluge of rain showers. Luckily, the wind stayed at bay, and we were kept pretty dry under the canopy of the Jenny Lind carriage. We passed Engle Road, and right beyond where the gazebo stood, Justin turned, taking Engle Road Path. Engle Road Path was a long, narrow dirt track that went all the way into the Bitterwood Commons area where the school and graveyard were located. On a rainy day such as this, it didn't seem like the best place to be taking Emily and the buggy.

"We better stop here, Natalia. I don't want to get stuck. I'm not going to go any farther with this rain coming down. At least we'll have some privacy here."

"Do you want to open it, or should I?" I questioned, looking at the box.

"Go ahead," Justin instructed.

It was a small, corrugated cardboard box tightly wound with twine. No writing or anything else about it was unusual. It took me a few minutes to unwind the cord. I fumbled as I tried too quickly to open the box. The container seemed empty, except on the bottom lay a folded piece of paper. I pulled it out with Justin patiently watching. I unwrapped the paper and two small items fell to my lap. I looked down, and to my utter surprise, there lay my necklace...My beautiful sapphire necklace! And, right next to that was a tiny gold heart pendant with no chain! I opened the pendant carefully, finding a child's picture tucked within the tiny gold frame. I studied it for some time, showing it to Justin for his interpretation. He looked at me and I began to shake.

"Natalia, I think that is a picture of you as a child," Justin said. "Look at the hair and the eyes."

I studied it as closely as I could. "Indeed," I agreed.

Then I grabbed the paper that the jewelry had been wrapped in. There were written words that read: Returned to you as promised. It won't be long. That's all it said.

It was quite some time that we sat there. I don't think either of us knew what to say or think. After some time, I once again shared with Justin of my experience with Thomas at the Sloans some days ago. It was the day that I had given him my necklace. I told him how Thomas promised me that he'd get it back to me somehow. I could tell that Justin was no more interested in hearing my story than he had been the last time that I had told it to him. Still, I knew in my heart that he had to have been imagining who had returned his mother's precious gem...which was now my precious gem.

"Natalia, I must ask you something," Justin said quietly. "George Middleton said that the woman who had left this package looked much like you. Would there have been any reason for you to have done this? I mean, did you wrap it up, also putting in the package a pendant of yourself, and then disguise yourself and deliver it to the hotel? Were you trying to prove that Tom was alive to me, hence making me believe that he had someone deliver it?"

I immediately felt crushed that Justin would even make such an accusation. I turned to him. "I have never owned a picture of myself at this young age, if indeed this is me. It boggles my mind to know where it came from! And, I feel I must say something to you." I cleared my throat and coughed nervously.

"Yes, go ahead," Justin said. "Please be frank with me."

"Do not ever say that Thomas is dead again, Justin." My voice was quivering. "I won't believe it. Love cannot die, it just keeps returning in one form or another."

I took the little gold heart pendant and strung it on the chain so that it hung directly underneath the beautiful stone on my sapphire necklace. I pulled the chain under my hair and around my neck and clasped it in the back. I closed my eyes and looked to the sky. I could feel Justin watching me. I could understand his confusion regarding who had returned the necklace, and this little pendant with a beloved child's photo inside, and how they had gotten these treasures in the first place. I knew he didn't believe me when I told him that Thomas had taken the necklace from me at the Sloans. But at least I wished he would have thought I had lost it, and a good Samaritan had returned it, or several other perfectly good explanations. But to accuse me of making up this entire story and even dressing up as another person and delivering it to the hotel to convince Justin that Thomas lived was heartbreaking!

I certainly knew that Justin didn't believe that I had been in his brother's presence just days ago. Justin Peterson believed that his brother was dead, but now I believed with all my heart that Thomas would somehow return for me. This was the sign I needed; the sign I waited for. Justin was silent. I knew he didn't know what to say. The rain had stopped and a tinge of blue sky broke through the clouds.

"I'd better get you home," Justin said. "Gerrit will be getting worried."

"Oh, please, Justin, I don't want to go back there. That house is so disheartening, and I keep finding things there that I don't understand. Sometimes I just want to take Joy and run away." I shook my head and closed my eyes and looked to the floor. "I want to tell you something." I cleared my throat nervously once again. "I know that everyone thinks there is something wrong with me mentally. I would lie to you if I told you I didn't wonder myself. But sometimes I believe there is nothing wrong with me at all. And, I know this will sound mad, but I feel as though I've been caught between two alternative worlds. Perhaps I'm lost between both of them. Are you absolutely sure that there isn't more I need to know, Justin? That I haven't experienced more loses, or deaths?"

"I've told you all that I know about you," Justin answered. "Of course I don't know fully what happened when you were in New York...."

"No, no," I interrupted. "This stuff that I'm remembering doesn't go back that far. These memories seem as though they were yesterday! There are these faces and names that I can't place together. There's this terrible, agonizing pain of loss, and yet another feeling of love, and they don't correlate with the people I have here. Do the names Anthony, or Daniel or Libby...or Colin make any sense to you?" I pleaded.

Justin shook his head. "No, Natalia, I don't know how to substantiate these memories or feelings you're having. I guess when you say these things like; feeling like I belong to two different worlds, it makes people right away not listen or believe you. These are not Christian beliefs, Natalia. And frankly, it's quite impossible. It's just plain bizarre!"

"But what if God had a purpose? A purpose for my life, but it could only happen when everything was in place...until everything transpired?"

"Natalia, God does have purpose for everything, including your life, and He will put everything in place."

"But I feel as though sometimes I'm being used. That my life is being used to narrow a partition to make things how they are supposed to be. Does that make any sense to you?"

"I'm sorry, Natalia, you're speaking very profoundly. You know, we need to be getting back."

Justin was scared that the buggy would get stuck on the path, so he got out and led Emily by hand, turning her around in the grassy area. Soon, we were back on State Street.

"If I showed you something," I began, "something remarkable...something that didn't look like it belonged here; and when I say here, I mean in this time period. Would you then be more open to my ideas about the two alternative universes?" I looked intently at Justin as we neared our homes.

"That's just plain silly talk, Natalia. What are you talking about?"

"Meet me tonight after everyone's asleep...probably around 2:00 a.m., in your barn. I will show you something,

Justin, that I want you to see. It's something I need for you to see. I need an explanation."

He turned into his drive. "And you can't just tell me about it? I have to see it?"

As soon as the buggy stopped, I could see Joy leave our home. She began running hard through the field, on her way to greet us. We both got out of the buggy.

"Just meet me here tonight at the time I mentioned, okay?"

Joy bolted into me. "Oh, my goodness!" I exclaimed as she almost pushed me over.

"Where did you go, Mama?" Joy asked, being somewhat out of breath.

"Parson Peterson just needed to talk to your mom, that's all," I said, brushing her dark hair away from her face with my hand.

I looked at Justin. "As I said, see you then?"

"Yes, that's fine, Natalia." He agreed.

Chapter 16

Recollections

My heart beat frantically as the clock approached one-thirty in the morning. Everything seemed to be working out. Joy and Gerrit had gone to bed not long after dark, and I sat here in anticipation, awaiting the time to proceed to Justin's barn at two a.m. My patience grew thin as I quietly got out of bed. The sky still hadn't cleared off. I could see no glow from the moon from my window. I was already dressed and ready to go. Now all I had to do was to get out of the house without anyone hearing me.

My biggest obstacle would be getting down the creaky steps. I stepped on the first one, putting a tiny bit of weight on it. All was okay and I proceeded. The next step gave way to some noise. I paused, trying to hear if anyone had awakened, then proceeded to the next one, and then the next, until I was in the parlor. I stood silent and still for several minutes. All seemed clear as I opened the door. A cool breeze of freedom met me and I breathed, welcoming it into my lungs. I wished the moon were out. It was very, very dark as I walked through the field to Justin Peterson's house.

"Natalia?" Justin whispered as I approached.

"Yes, it's me," I heard him coming closer, then I saw his silhouette.

"You better have adequate reason for this."

"Please, trust me...Do you have your lantern?" I questioned.

"It's in the barn."

"We need to go and get it," I said. "There is something I need to dig up in the field out there."

"Natalia, what are you talking about? I've not buried anything in that field."

"But I have."

I could tell that Justin was on edge and very uncomfortable.

"Well, what exactly is it?" He spoke out louder. "There's not something out there that you're going to get into trouble for, is there? If you get into trouble, then I will, too!"

"I don't exactly know what to make of it," I muttered. "But please come with me." I led the way to the barn and Justin finally followed.

"Stay here," he said. "I know my way around in there without light." He soon exited with the lighted lantern in hand. I grabbed the shovel that I had set aside that morning.

"Give me the shovel, Natalia," he said as he traded with me for the lantern.

The meadow grass was damp as we made our way out into the field. We kept the light at its lowest point, and I held the lantern close to the ground, searching for evidence as to where I had previously dug.

"I sure hope Gerrit doesn't see that glare from your house," Justin commented.

"We're behind the barn. It would be almost impossible to see this light from our house. If he sees it, then he would have had to have followed me over here."

"Well, let's hope that isn't the case," Justin said, bending to look at the ground.

"Natalia, something's over here. It looks like overturned dirt." Justin motioned for me to come his way.

I approached the spot, but I hadn't remembered leaving it so disrupted.

"This has to be it. Can you dig in there for me?" I asked.

"Before I will dig, you have to tell me what I'm digging for," Justin bargained.

"I buried a hat box there yesterday morning. There is some clothing inside that I wanted you to see."

"I'm digging for clothing?" He sounded perturbed, but he started digging anyway. "And what significance does this clothing have? And why did you bury it?"

"These clothes are unlike anything that you can obtain in this era, Justin. The fabric is very unusual; very bold. There is a very modern-looking fastener that closes the skirt. I've never seen anything like this clothing! But then, perhaps I have!"

"And how, exactly, did you acquire this clothing, Natalia?"

"It's a long, unbelievable story, Justin. I've been thinking and thinking long and hard. I want you to see the items before I tell you how I think I got them."

Justin dug for a while longer and then quit and looked up at me. "Well, I don't think there is anything in this hole," he concluded. "I can see where the dirt was overturned and re-placed, but I'm now down to new, hard dirt that hasn't been dug in before."

I dropped the lantern down closer to the hole and then looked up at my proximity to the barn. "This has got to be where I buried it."

"It is where you buried it, Natalia," Gerrit cried out, as he stepped out of the shadows. "But I unburied your package and now I have it."

Justin jumped back, and I wanted to run.

"And my fine Parson Peterson, can I ask what you're doing out here with my wife?" Gerrit demanded.

I was so glad it was dark so I couldn't see the hellish fire that seemed to glow in Gerrit's eyes when he was angry.

"I'm sorry, Gerrit. I should not be here," Justin replied awk-wardly. "I never intended for this to turn out as it has."

"So you were just intending to do this all behind my back?

Is that what you're saying?"

"I'm just saying, forgive me, please, that's all." Justin took a step back.

"And my dear Natalia. What were your plans with the hatbox and the clothing?" Gerrit asked sarcastically as he neared me.

I felt like a knife had pierced my heart. Just knowing that Gerrit had been watching me and had seen the clothing made me ill inside.

"I observed you yesterday morning. When Joy was crying, I felt something was wrong. I followed you over here and watched you bury the stuff...Why, Natalia? Where did that stuff come from? Why did you want to hide it?" Gerrit demanded.

I didn't answer him and he came to me and tightly gripped my arm.

"Why aren't you answering me?" he continued as his tone rose.

"You're hurting me, Gerrit. Please let me alone." His grasp got harder and I struggled to get loose.

"Gerrit, that does no good," Justin stated angrily. "Natalia meant no harm. She apparently didn't know where to turn. She was just seeking help from me."

"And why would I ever again listen to a man, especially a man who claims to be a man of God, who sneaks out with another man's wife?"

"I will not allow you say that about me, Gerrit," Justin adamantly interrupted. "We did nothing wrong, and you don't have the right to make a judgment like this. I would never take advantage of you, nor your wife."

"I know enough about you now," Gerrit replied, looking at Justin and holding my arm tighter and tighter. "I have nothing more to say to you. Do you understand? You are no more welcome in my home. You are not to come near my family."

"Gerrit, you're not being fair," I cried. "It isn't Justin's fault."

"Natalia, it will be okay," Justin said as he watched Gerrit get an even firmer grip on me. I kept staring at Justin, wishing he could rescue me from this so-called husband of mine. I wished he could see the silent plea on my face, but I knew he couldn't with the blackness of night. Reluctantly, I succumbed to Gerrit's hold. It did me no good to resist. In no time at all he directed me, with his tight grip, all the way back to our home. When we arrived, he opened the door and pushed me inside. I fell to the floor. Gerrit walked to the back porch and returned, holding the soiled hatbox. He threw it to the floor next to me. The top broke open and the clothes spilled out.

"Now explain this to me!" he shouted.

"Sir, I can't explain," I answered, choked up.

"Something is wrong, Natalia. You don't go and bury something like this unless you're hiding something. Now explain!" he hollered.

I was crying uncontrollably when I spotted Joy at the foot of the stairs. She gazed at the broken hatbox and the clothes. "Oh Mama," she frantically yelled, looking at me, and then she ran back up the stairs. Surprisingly, Gerrit went after her. From her reaction, I figured that Gerrit thought Joy knew something about the clothes. I knew I needed to do something right then and there. I hysterically picked up the clothes and ran out the door. I had nowhere to go but to hide in the darkness of the night.

It's funny, but when you own no freedom, you welcome any slight bit you can gather, even when you're running for your life. I ran down the road in those hours of darkness, heading for the gazebo. It was my place of solitude, the place that I hoped I would eventually be reunited with my Thomas, or, I should say my Arie. I tired fast, and soon slowed to a walk. It was amazing all the sounds I heard that mimicked someone running after me in this coal-black surrounding. An animal by the side of the road, the howl of the wind, or even an insect buzzing by, seemed to take on the sound of footsteps. My heart beat so fast that I didn't even know if I'd make it to the gazebo without collapsing. And, even if I did make it there, where did I go then? I guess it was the only place I could go. After some time, I knew I was coming close.

I needed no light; the familiarity of this place was uncanny. I put one hand on the wood of the gazebo, holding the mysterious clothing in the other, and started following the structure, going around and round. As I circled, I was careful not to get splinters. Soon I closed my eyes. There was no need to keep them open since I was following this endless sphere. Here, I could imagine anything; and imagine I did. Ever since the clothes had appeared from my dresser, I sensed another dimension, another world that I was a part of. Was this only possible with someone who was mentally deranged, or was there truly some weird phenomena that made it possible for me to experience another world...another time? Who was the woman the girls had seen on the path? Could it possibly be that she was me? After all, my memory of this life, of Natalia Kappan, was nonexistent right after the woman was seen on the path, and soon after, Justin discovered me in Bitterwood School. I sighed. Where did I even come up with such conclusions? It all sounded ludicrous, but how else could I explain the other people that I thought I knew and loved... this Anthony, this Daniel? They obviously weren't here. They weren't a part of this time period. And, then there was the issue of Thomas. I would give my life to be with him, but where was he? I knew better, just like Justin had said. I knew that after you died you could not come back to life, but if there was another life...If there was time travel...It was my only hope.

I started going faster around the circumference. Suddenly, the words that were so familiar to me came to my lips and I said them aloud as I continued to twirl. This time I pondered these words in my head as never before. "The stones upon foundation stand for sun to prism onto land. And if you're in the perfect place, you'll be transported to another place."

Where did these words come from? What exactly did they mean? Was I the one who had made them up? Suddenly, the vision of an old woman came to me reciting these very words. Who was she? I stopped circling, took my hand off of the gazebo, and felt to make sure my necklace was in place. As I touched it, I stood there alone and cried out to God to give me sanity.

Suddenly, there appeared a supreme existence of light. I looked up and saw a gleaming star make its way out of the clouds. Always believing that there were more stars in the heavens than sands on the earth's seashore, it was unique to peer up at this one, and only one, shining light. The clouds were dispersing, and the transparency of them dancing around the star mesmerized me. Perhaps it was symbolic of my life. Perhaps I was a light trying to escape this darkness. I climbed the stairs and sat atop the gazebo as a soft wind tickled my face. There was a mist in the air from the humidity, and I could feel the dampness settle upon me. I lay down on the floor, placing the clothes beside me, and looked up to the sky. Thankfully, slumber soon rescued me from this labyrinth of darkness.

I had no idea what time it was, or even what day it was when I awoke shivering on the cold, wood floor of the gazebo. I blinked my eyes trying to free them from sleep. Everything looked clouded. I sat up and looked next to me. Beside me were the clothes that had caused so much uproar, and on the other side was something beautiful and peaceful. A bouquet of flowers had been placed on the wood floor. The flowers looked fresh, as though they had just been picked. On the bouquet was a note. I quickly picked it up and unfolded it. The writing was untidy and illiterate and looked laborious. I studied the words and tediously put the sounds together. Finally I could make it out. I'm sorry for everything, it said.

Just what I needed, another piece to this unsolvable puzzle! Someone had been here while I slept. I shivered harder.

Someone had been in my very presence watching me. Someone was trying to give me a message but, most importantly, someone had left me these beautiful yet mysterious flowers. Quickly, I put the note in my pocket. I began to tremble. I looked up the hill and saw a buggy fast approaching. I prayed it wasn't Gerrit, but who else would it be? I ducked low as it halted. Footsteps soon climbed the gazebo.

"Natalia, you there?" I could hear Justin's voice. I quickly stood up.

"Yes," I quivered.

"Come with me quickly. I'll take you to Bitterwood Schoolhouse. We can talk there in private."

"But Gerrit will be coming, Justin. He'll find me with you again."

"Gerrit was in the mercantile already early this morning and said you had vanished once again. I must have just missed him. Anyway, he told Claire Malone that he was done searching for you. She asked me if I had seen you and said she was worried. I figured you'd be here. Are you okay?"

I began to cry as I made my way to him. In one hand I clasped the flowers and in the other I held the clothes. As I got to Justin, I looked up to heaven, dropping all the things in my hands to the ground. I could not take anymore; I needed aid. "Justin, please, help me," I cried.

Justin picked up the flowers and the clothes and we walked to the buggy and got in. Justin wrapped a blanket around me and Emily trotted the short distance down State Street. As we approached Engle Road, Justin halted the buggy.

"I know it's not the best of conditions after the rain we had, but I'm taking Engle Road Path so that we don't have to pass your house," Justin stated.

"But what if we get stuck?"

"I don't think we will if I keep out of the furrows and stay toward the grassy areas. There's no way I want to pass by your home with all that's gone on."

Engle Road Path was just that, a path that was hardly

big enough to accommodate a buggy. It circled through the fields and meadows and bypassed the houses on State Street. It was a bit treacherous traveling but we made it. We entered the Bitterwood Area, near the schoolhouse, and as we proceeded slowly down the path, my recollection of the clothes intensified. I looked down at them and the vision of the girls suddenly encompassed my thoughts. I remembered this path. I remembered being here and seeing Joy and Lillian and thinking what peculiar old-fashioned clothing they had on. The clothing that sat next to me now wouldn't have seemed unusual to me at that time at all. It was the girls' clothing that took me aback. A revelation overtook me. These clothes that now sat in the buggy had been my clothes, just as I had pondered! They didn't belong to another woman! But, how could it be? How could I prove it?

"Natalia, are you still with me?" Justin said, touching my wrist.

"Yes, yes, I was just thinking," I answered.

"We're almost there. If we can make it through this last bit of mud, we'll be fine." He continued carefully guiding Emily up to the drive that continued up the hill to Bitterwood Schoolhouse, which was also Bitterwood Church.

"It's cool this morning. I'll throw some wood in the burner and get you warmed up. Why don't you go inside while I get it, and I'll be there in a moment's time."

Justin tied the buggy to the post and walked over to the woodpile. Timidly, I approached the large wood doors of the building, continuing to hold the clothes in my hand. I had been here before. I had been here before as the other woman! I opened the door and entered...The desks, the blackboards ... the flag! I ran over to the calendar on the wall, making sure not to look at it. July 7, 1920, will be circled, I said to myself. It was the day that I came! I looked, and sure enough it was circled as I had remembered. I ran to the corner of the room where there were some quilts and blankets stacked on a shelf. I quickly pulled one down and brought it to my face, smelling it.

Suddenly the door opened and Justin entered with a stack of wood in his arms.

"This smells musty," I said, facing Justin, "just as I remember. It smells like 1920, not like the smells I'm used to where I came from." I let the quilt drop to the floor.

Justin quickly put down the wood and approached me.

"What are you talking about, Natalia?" he questioned, looking puzzled.

"I remember, now...I REMEMBER! I was here, Justin. I was here before."

"Of course you were here before. You were here many times," Justin retorted "You occasionally came here for worship service with Gerrit and Joy. And I found you here... remember, the night you ran away from Gerrit."

"That's what I was remembering, Justin...when I was here and you found me, I was wearing these clothes." I lifted them up to him and he took them in his hand. "Look at the closure on the skirt, look at the top. Pull the fabric, it stretches in all directions. We have no clothing like this here! Justin, try to remember...when you first found me, was I wearing this?"

He shook his head. "I just remember finding you and wondering why you didn't know your name. You kept asking me why I called you Natalia. I can't be certain as to what you were wearing because you kept a quilt wrapped tightly around you. I remember it distinctly because it was such a warm day and I thought you must be ill."

"And why do you think I did that, Justin?" I asked excitedly. I looked on the shelf and stroked the very quilt that I had wrapped around myself that day. "It was because I was wearing the clothes that you're holding in your hand. I knew they were not appropriate to this time period!"

Justin continued analyzing the clothes and looked at me. "So what are you saying?"

"Oh Justin, I don't know! You've got to help me! I know you think I'm not making sense, but to me it is finally proving to be real!" I pulled my necklace from within my layers of clothing. "It all has to do with this, Justin."

"So tell me what you're saying," he asked again.

"This necklace has powers. I know it does." I brought it to my mouth and kissed it.

"Natalia, I told you the story that my mother used to tell us of the necklace," Justin replied. "You probably think that it has powers because of what I told you."

"No," I insisted. "It is a barrier between times! Justin, you have to believe me!"

"Natalia, calm down and let's try and make sense of all of this."

"Okay, I'm going to try and explain to you what I think is going on, but you have to have an open mind and listen. Is that a promise?" I eagerly asked.

"I will listen," Justin agreed. "But as a minister of the Lord it is hard for me to believe these mystical things that you keep insisting upon."

"Just listen, Justin, that's all I ask of you. Do you remember when you found me lying here that morning?"

"Yes, of course," Justin agreed.

"I didn't know you. I had never seen you before! I didn't know anything about my life here. I had these clothes on when you found me. I remember now. I had to hide them in the dresser. I didn't know who Joy or Gerrit were either, Justin. Everything was a blank."

"So you experienced some type of amnesia. That's not unusual," Justin suggested.

"No, it wasn't that. I remember seeing myself in the mirror that day and gasping. The face I saw wasn't mine."

Justin shook his head. I grabbed ahold of his shirt. "You have to listen to me!" I pleaded. "How do you explain Joy and Lillian seeing that strange woman on the path who disappears, never to be seen again, and then I appear in the schoolhouse?"

"So, if you were another woman transformed into Natalia Kappan, where then, did the real Natalia Kappan go, and furthermore where did the other woman go?"

"I don't know!" I screamed. "Don't you understand, now I am Natalia Kappan!"

"You need to stop this," Justin said, laying the clothes on the shelf. "This is nonsense."

"Just tell me one thing, Justin. You said that I had changed since you found me. Is that right? You said that I now made sense. Joy said it, too. How exactly did I act before you found me? Please tell me that."

"I've told you before. No one could reason with you, Natalia. Gerrit had almost given up on you, sadly, just as he has now. People would find you roaming the streets and you were obsessed with that gazebo. You were obsessed with the flowers, and you were always found chanting, encircling that gazebo."

"So, don't you see?" I exclaimed. "Natalia, the real Natalia, was searching for something as well, and we both know what it was. She was searching for her love, just as I have been. I feel her spirit within me, Justin. It's almost as if she is using my other person to fulfill something that had to be done in another lifetime, and perhaps here as well. I know it's crazy and scary, but I feel it!"

"It's nonsense, and I won't believe any more of this talk," Justin concluded.

"So what if you could have your brother back? What if you could have your family back? Wouldn't you want to look into every aspect of it? Justin!" I said loudly, once again pulling on his shirtsleeve to make him look at me, "Look at this necklace! This necklace has powers! Thomas told me. Your mother told you. How do you explain the package with the necklace and the pendant that was returned to us? How do you explain the woman who appeared to George Middleton looking just as I do? Perhaps she was me in another time, traveling back to return the necklace, or someone else who had found out how to use its powers!"

He walked away from me and seemed to be ignoring me. I

followed him.

"I've been thinking; whenever the necklace has been off of me something has occurred. When I first got here...When I was on the path and saw the children, I was not wearing my necklace. I found it, Justin, lying in the weeds. I remember Joy telling me that she had lost something that day. I think that Joy must have been wearing that necklace and had lost it. When the necklace was off of Natalia, perhaps it opened a prism into another dimension. Perhaps it let someone else in, to fulfill what she so deeply wished for. Or... I just thought of this, perhaps it was also helping someone else to fulfill his or her wishes. The possibilities are endless."

I grabbed a piece of parchment paper that lay on the teacher's desk. I made two holes through it with my finger, in two different places on the paper. "Imagine if these two holes represented two different time periods; two different dimensions. I'm here, and she's there." I pointed to the different perforations. Then I took the paper and folded it in half making the two holes become one on the paper. "What if somehow this happened, Justin? What if these times combined and I was allowed to enter another life?"

"So are you now trying to tell me that you are not Natalia Kappan?" Justin asked.

"No, I think I have turned into her, Justin. I truly love your brother, and I love my daughter, but I still feel as though I have another life somewhere else. I have experienced in my soul everything that she has gone through, but I can't explain it. I've also gone through another life somewhere, I can feel it."

"If I were to believe you, Natalia, then I would have to believe in reincarnation, or something that isn't of God. I cannot believe that nonsense. Do you understand?"

"Oh Justin, suppose it is of God. Suppose it is a path that He is directing me on. Please, you need to think about this!"

"I think I need to get you home," he said, shaking his head again.

I grabbed the clothes that Justin had laid on the shelf. "But

Justin," I said, crying. "I have no home without Thomas. I have no home here."

"I just don't know what to do with you anymore, Natalia," Justin said, guiding me toward the door. "I will continue to pray for you, that's all I can do. We better not stay here. I need to take you home now." He lifted my head to look at him. "Do you understand, I need to take you home to your family?"

"Do what you need to do, Justin. If I'm right, events will start changing, and you'll see. You'll see that I'm not a lunatic after all. I promise you."

Chapter 17

Fleeing Death

*E*verything was beginning to make sense to me. At least to some extent, although questioning my sanity was a constant ongoing battle. How could I ever be certain that I wasn't living in complete mental derange? At least now, with the appearance of these clothes, I had some physical evidence that what I was thinking, and telling Justin, was real and not just a fragment of mental deception from my subconscious.

Justin had dropped me off, and much to my surprise there was no one to "greet me" as I entered the house. Gerrit was at home. I could see him in the study. I knew he heard me return, but not a word was said as I smuggled the clothes and the flowers up to my room. I didn't know the whereabouts of Joy. I didn't hear or see her anywhere. My guess would be that she was at Lillian's house.

Although it was evident that I had inherited much of Natalia's life, I most desperately wanted to know of my other existence. I lay down on my bed and tried to collect my thoughts. The old woman, once again, came to mind. It had been the old woman that I had first heard the chant from. I closed my eyes and tried to ponder more. What was her name? Where did she come from? What part did she ever play in my life? Everything was blank except for her face. I got up and poured water from the basin into a vase that sat next to my dresser. I tried to arrange the flowers, attempting to make them all fit. I reached into my pocket and uncrumpled the note that I had found with them, and read it again. I'm sorry for everything. Who was trying to convey this message to me? Someone here, in this life was apparently sorry for something that they had done to me. Could it be that someone knew details of the rape, or something else that I wasn't even aware of? I definitely was bound and determined to find out who this note-writer had been. And, if I found that out, I was hoping it would solve the mystery of the flowers as well.

I tidied up, washing in the basin, and put on fresh clothing. Shockingly, for the first time, it dawned on me that I had never taken on the role of being a wife, or even a mother. I looked at the stack of clean clothing lying on my bed and knew that either Joy or Gerrit had laundered, folded and placed them neatly in my room. I apparently never did the wash, or the cleaning, or much of anything here. Everyone else always took care of me. Why was I the way I was? Why hadn't I noticed?

I brushed my long black hair and gazed in the mirror at the smooth olive skin that was now a part of my being. I looked into the pretty, deep-brown eyes I had. Why did I think they should be green? I shook my head, trying to free myself of this craziness. Quickly, I picked up the skirt and stretchy top that I had smuggled into the house and hid them between the mattresses. I desperately needed to find my daughter. I longed to make her love me one more time, and I also longed to let her know that I loved her. Would she believe me about the clothing? I wasn't sure, but I wanted to try and explain the whole thing to her anyway.

Once again, I quietly made my way down the steps. Gerrit had not been to work in some time. Apparently, he had been doing his bookwork at home and giving the finished paperwork and bids to Mr. Sloan in the evenings on his return from the mill. That was the reason for his frequent visits each night. Sometimes, I wondered why Mr. Sloan put up with so much slack from Gerrit. It had to have put undue pressure on him by being his business partner. Mr. Sloan must have allowed it so that Gerrit could keep his eye on me. I just wondered why Mr. Sloan tolerated such things.

With Gerrit at home, I knew he'd never allow me to leave. I just had to make a break for it. I didn't say a word as I snuck out the door. As I started down the road, I looked back to find Gerrit gazing at me through the parlor window. I turned and kept walking. He never screamed for me to stop, and as I made my way around the curve, I turned around to see that he had not left the house. Perhaps it was just as he had told the woman at the mercantile...That he was done with chasing after me. As fast as I could, I ran past Justin's house and continued onward. I wondered if Justin had seen me go by.

I always felt that I was in a terrible rush to get wherever I had to go, and this time was no different, in fact it seemed worse. I knew that all the eyes of the town were upon me. Somehow, however, I was beginning to be at a freaky sort of peace, for I now believed, with all of my heart, that this life wasn't the only life that I lived for. I took a breath and slowed down. If Gerrit were going to come, he'd find me whether I ran or walked. It was a humid summer's day, and I was tired. I was physically, emotionally and in every way possible, exhausted. I kept walking down State Street and soon approached the area where the Bitterwood vines climbed up the trees. In a couple of months they would turn the prettiest crimson color imaginable. I remembered them from years past. I remembered them from Natalia's mind.

As I got to the place in the road where I could either stay on State Street or turn up the path that led to the schoolhouse, I once again noticed the large hill. I had such an uncanny feeling that this was a place of significance; a place I knew well in a time before. It made me quiver, and I climbed the hill, raising my head to the sky. The wind subtly brought in the sound of the Post children playing not far off, and I was in hopes that I would find Joy there as well. I reflected from the hill one more time, and then carefully climbed down. I crossed the street and made my way to the Post house.

The flowers in boxes that lined the front porch of the Posts' property had grown since the last time I'd been here. Toys and dolls were lying haphazardly on the wood decking, awaiting their children to come back and play with them. I stood there in silence, listening to the laughing and happy shouting in the back of the house, and so wished that I were the mother of this household. It gave me comfort that my precious little Joy could spend so much time here. Why couldn't I just make my house this way? I guess it was a futile thought, for this was not the life I had been given. I bent down to pick up one of the dolls when the front door opened wide.

"Natalia, you scared me to death," Mrs. Post said, grasping her chest.

I stood up. "I'm sorry. I was just listening to the children."

"Do you wish to come in? Do you need something?" she asked, seeming surprised, continuing to hold her chest with both arms crisscrossed.

"As a matter of fact, I need my daughter," I continued. "Is she here?"

"Indeed," Mrs. Post replied. "She's at play with Lillian in the back woods.

"I need to see her, Priscilla. I know that I am not the kind of mother that you are, and I treasure the fact that you share with Joy how a normal family should live. I just want you to understand that I am a very mixed-up person. I could tell you things about myself that you would never believe or understand, so it's better left unsaid. But I do love my daughter. And I need to tell her that right now if it would be at all possible."

Priscilla Post unclasped her chest and gave a sigh. "Your husband dropped Joy off here early this morning. He said Joy was pleading with him to come and play with Lillian." She shook her head. "Natalia, don't you understand what you're doing to that child of yours? I don't mean to be rude, and I don't know if it's because you can't help it, or what it is, but that child of yours is scared to death. Between you and I, she told Lillian that she thinks you killed the woman that the children saw on the path some time ago, and that you have her clothes hidden somewhere. Where that child gets these things I just don't know, and, is there any truth in this? I think she finds safety here. I think it's best if you just leave her alone for a while."

I looked straight into Priscilla Post's eyes. "I killed no one," I stated. "That woman on the path was me that the girls saw."

"Don't be silly, Natalia," Mrs. Post said, giving a subdued smile and a tiny chuckle. "Lillian came home that day and told us of the stranger on the path and her description was nothing as you look."

"But don't you see, I told you that you wouldn't understand." My voice became louder.

"Natalia, I think you need to go home," Mrs. Post suggested. "And I will admit to you that I have not stopped thinking of the claim that Joy told Lillian. Where did that woman on the path go?"

I felt so helpless. What could I say? "I will not return home without talking with my daughter," I demanded.

Presently, two of Lillian's brothers appeared on the porch. "Is everything, all right, Mother?" one of the boys questioned.

"I do believe so, Matthew, but please stay here on the porch as I escort Mrs. Kappan on her way home, will you?"

"Priscilla, I told you that I'm not leaving without talking with my daughter," I persisted. I pushed her aside as the Post boys aided their mother, and I entered their home. Just inside the door stood Joy and Lillian, who apparently had been listening to our conversation. I ran to Joy and attempted to hug her, but she darted away. She and Lillian stood down the hall, looking at me from a distance

"Joy, what is the matter?" I asked.

"Mrs. Kappan, Joy is frightened right now," Lillian suggested, taking hold of Joy's hand.

I bent down, keeping my distance from her. "You don't

need to be frightened of me, darling," I pleaded with Joy. "I'm your mother, remember?"

"Oh Mama, I don't understand. I'm so tired of not understanding. I just want to stay with Lillian. Please Mama... Please, let me stay here. Just go home to papa. I will be all right here; I promise."

I wasn't aware of a more hopeless moment in my life than what I was experiencing at that moment. The only one who I felt truly a part of me, besides my Thomas, was now rejecting every bit of my being. I was worthless, and I cried. I hadn't noticed, but Priscilla Post and her sons were now standing directly behind me.

"Sarah, please take the girls up to your room and close the door, will you?" Priscilla insisted.

"Yes, Mother," she replied.

Quickly, Lillian's sister took Joy and Lillian by the hand and led them up the stairs. A tearful Joy turned on the steps and glanced at me before disappearing on the upper level. Suddenly, I felt very light-headed and fell to the floor.

"I have nothing, Priscilla," I said, looking up..."Nothing!" I screamed.

"Natalia, you must get hold of yourself," she softly said, bending down and caressing my back. "You can make things better for your family. You just need to change. God knows you need to change!"

Priscilla Post's sons stood surrounding me as if guarding their mother from a raging lunatic, and perhaps they were doing just that. Priscilla offered me her handkerchief and I accepted it and rubbed my eyes roughly.

"I will leave now," I stated, trying to get my balance to stand up.

Priscilla Post gently touched my arm and escorted me out to the porch. "Natalia, you must sit for a while and regain your strength. I don't feel right letting you leave like this."

"I will be fine," I insisted.

"You know, Joy's welcome to stay her indefinitely," Priscilla softly commented. "We love her." She took a step back as if pondering something. "And Natalia, I'm sorry for what I said about the woman on the path. I had no right. There is no evidence."

I closed my eyes and bit my lip. "Thank you," I whispered. "I know I make people think the worst."

I turned to descend the porch steps. I hung my head and didn't know where or who to turn to as I crossed the street and took the path that led to the schoolhouse. I had just made a scene at a house where the people were good and wanted the best for my daughter. Why would anyone take me seriously? Why would anyone take me for a sane person? I continued walking on the path, passing the school and nearing the cemetery.

Perhaps the only one who had ever truly loved me in this life now lay lifeless here in this place. Perhaps Justin was right, that the visions I had of Thomas and the hopes I tried to hang on to, were worthless. I searched the grounds for the evidence that I didn't want to see...The single silver cross that Justin said he positioned on the grave the day he buried his brother. The clouds were once again rolling in, and I could hear thunder in the distance. I continued searching the graves, now almost frantic to see if what Justin had told me was true, or just something else that my mind had made up.

Finally, in the far corner of the cemetery I spotted a glare. Even though the sun was not present, something caught my eye. Tucked away on the edge was a plot surrounded by trees draped with Bitterwood vines. And there, on that plot, stood a single silver cross marking the grave. It appeared that the cross had been cared for. I assumed that it was Justin who kept it polished. So, this was where my Thomas lay. I could somehow feel his presence and it wasn't in a good way. I shivered and wanted no part of this place. Quickly I walked away. I could feel death and despair here. I screamed and began to run. It was like death was hovering all around me and now it followed in my very steps.

Rain began to fall in torrents and thunder boomed. Mud on the pathway seemed to suck at my shoes, and with every step I had to hold them tight against my feet for fear of losing them. It was hard to keep my balance, but I had to keep going. All I could feel was desolation behind me. I made my way past Bitterwood School and decided to take a shortcut through the woods that led to the back of Justin's property. It was supposedly right before you got to Engle Road Path. Joy had told me about it many times. She liked the fact that not many of the town's children knew the path was there, and they marveled at how fast she was able to get home.

With the storm as it was, I needed to find shelter. In going this way, I wouldn't have to pass the Post house again. I had put the Posts, and Joy, through enough agony for one day. I looked for the opening in the bushes as the rain continued to drench me. My hair was so saturated with water that the weight seemed to pull my head down each time I'd bend to free my feet from the oozing mud. Lightning beamed and thunder clapped hard. I raised my hands over my ears. I looked up and finally saw the opening in the woods that would eventually lead to Justin's property. I quickly turned down the path. It looked like Justin hadn't been down here with his sickle in some time. It was very overgrown, but at least the weeds on the ground helped with the leeching mud.

It seemed I had walked a long way when I finally saw a clearing ahead. Out of the bushes I stepped onto the rear of Justin's field. I could see the back of both Justin's house and Gerrit's house in the distance. The storm seemed to be blowing over as I made my way to Justin's barn. Drenched, exhausted, and mentally distraught, I entered the barn. I looked in the buggy and pulled out the blanket that I had used that very morning. I slipped off my wet clothing and wrapped the blanket tightly around me. I hung my clothes over some boards. Old Emily was keeping a sharp eye on me; however, she didn't give out her infamous whinny. There was something I needed to do in here today. I knew I needed to do it the minute I laid eyes on Thomas' grave. I knew the letters were here. They were hidden in this very barn. Those letters, I now believed, were the fence that may have connected my lives; these time periods that I was unwillingly thrown into.

I quickly climbed the ladder that led to a primitive loft. There, I found a small door in the floor. I knew this place. I opened it to find a box...a box of letters. My adrenaline sky-rocketed. I pulled out the box, laid it on the floor, and pulled out the top letter. I read the words to myself. Immediately, it was as though I could hear Thomas' voice saying the words aloud to me. I could no longer keep my composure and fell face-first onto the floor. I wept uncontrollably. After some time, old Emily began to whimper, and I knew I must be quieter. For hours upon hours, I must have sat up in that loft, reading all the letters from the man I so desperately loved. Dusk had once again descended. I needed to get home, or I knew a posse would be sent to find me like a rabid dog. Care-fully, I placed all the letters back in the box and carried them under my arm down the ladder with me. These words from Thomas would never leave me again. I didn't care what I had to do; they would stay in my presence forever.

There was just enough light in the barn for me to find my clothes. They were still quite wet. I had no choice but to put them back on. I swished the blanket back over another board to allow it to dry, and put on the wet garments, shiver-ing as I went. I grabbed my letters and proceeded to the door. A cold front must have come through, for the subtle change in weather met me at the door and made me tremble even harder. I could see a faint light inside Justin's house as I exited his property and made my way home. How I wished I could just stay with Justin. He truly was a friend, and sadly to say he seemed to be the only friend I had.

I knew I had no choice but to make a beeline up to my room as soon as I entered the house. If I did it fast enough, I wouldn't allow any time for Gerrit to see that I had the box of letters under my arm. I opened the door and made a mad dash through the parlor and up the stairs.

"Mama, you're okay!" I could hear a little voice rejoicing as I reached my room. Hurriedly, I slid the box under my bed and prepared myself for what would happen next. The door soon opened and Joy entered.

"Mama, we thought you were dead. I thought something happened to you in the storm. Right after you left Lillian's house, when the wind picked up, Mrs. Post hitched up her buggy and we went out looking for you. We were so worried. Where were you, Mama?"

Without time for me to answer, Gerrit made his way into the room. "A fine day again you have made for all of us, Natalia. It seems most of the town heard of your disappearing in the storm. You have disrupted many folks. I hope that makes you feel good."

"I never asked for anyone's assistance, Sir," I responded. "I am capable of caring for myself."

"Indeed," Gerrit quipped. He looked at me, shaking his head. "And I warned you before about those hellish flowers that you had up here in your room. They are not to enter this house. They have been destroyed. Do you understand me quite well?" He slammed his fist into the door as he existed the room.

Joy stood near the door, shaking profusely. She was clutching her porcelain-faced doll.

"I took the shortcut home," I said quietly, looking at Joy. "That's why you couldn't find me."

"I see. I'm glad you're home, Mama," she said, giving me a subdued smile.

"Joy, I want you down here now!" Gerrit yelled from downstairs.

"I must go now, Mama. I'm glad you're home."

As Joy left the room, I called out her name. She stuck her head back inside the doorway.

"I needed to tell you all day that I love you," I said quietly. "No matter what happens, you need to know that."

"I know, Mama, Lillian's Mama explained that to me." She carefully closed the door to the span that Gerrit would allow and left me alone.

Chapter 19

A Figure in the Storm

I sat on my bed and was comforted by reading my beloved letters. They were precious words that took me right into the arms of my beloved, and they eased so much of my pain. I kept the letters underneath the bed, retrieving one letter at a time. I could easily slip the paper under my pillow if someone entered. The humid weather continued even though the temperature had gone down drastically. The distant rumble of thunder continued to promenade throughout the countryside. Much to my surprise, neither Gerrit nor Joy came to see me for the rest of the night, and I was left alone surrounded with Arie's love through these writings.

A flash of lightning suddenly swept across the sky, and I couldn't help but be mesmerized by its magnificence. I put the letter I was reading aside and walked over to the open window. I had been opening and shutting it all evening, depending on the force of the wind and rain. Now the wind was starting up again, and I watched trees and bushes being blown around like toys. I closed my window sash and stood there thinking. Although I had called out to God many times, I was still not a believer in the things that Justin so adamantly spoke of, and yet I wondered who could make these storms at their command. If there was a God, I marveled at the miraculous powers that He held within his hands. I pondered what Justin kept sharing with me about this faith. It was this faith that he so desperately wanted me to find. I wondered if it could be real.

I blinked and peered out of the window again. Something was out there! And, as I continued to focus on it, I could see that it wasn't something, it was someone! I kept trying to recognize if it was Gerrit venturing out to use the outhouse, or if he was gathering something that had blown away due to the winds. I got as close to the window as possible and opened it again. Debris began to fly in as I tried to guard it from blowing into the house with my hands. I kept squinting and trying to focus. I desperately needed to know who was out in the yard.

The figure stood erect, and even though the wind and rain darted down, the person seemed to be unaffected. I shivered. This unknown being seemed to be looking directly up at me. My thoughts drove me to that unsettling feeling of death that had seemed to chase me from the cemetery some hours before. Could it be that it now stood below, waiting to claim its prize? I gasped and looked harder. Another bolt of lightning emblazoned the sky and enabled me to see clearer. The figure was definitely a man; not the grim reaper or spirits of demise come to take me away. It was a man and he appeared to be looking up at my window! My heart seemed to skip a beat. I immediately turned down my lamp to the lowest level. Whoever, or whatever brought this individual here, I knew he was able to see my face in the window. I shivered, extinguished the flame in the oil lamp entirely, and gazed out the opening once more.

Each time lightning glared; I could make out something new about him. He was tall and had dark clothing on. His face was shadowed, allowing me to only see darkness upon it. I so wanted to holler out, but I knew it would awaken Gerrit and Joy. Could this be the person who had been in my presence at the gazebo as I slept? Could it be the person who had left the flowers and the note? I kept staring. Could it be Arie?

Perhaps they were all one and the same! I felt for my precious necklace which also included the little gold pendant now. It was around my neck and I pondered all the many times that Thomas...or Arie...had told me that when I wore the necklace, he would find me through all time, through all space, through all eternity. Perhaps he was here to do just that!

Thunder clapped hard and made me jump back. I fell against the bed. I hoped I hadn't awakened anyone again. Quickly, I got up and returned to the window. The figure was gone! I frantically gazed around the yard, searching every part. I couldn't just let him go and never find out who he was! I raced down the steps, through the parlor and out the door, ignoring the noise. The rain drenched me and I ran to the spot where he had stood.

"Please Sir, don't leave," I pleaded in a loud voice trying to be heard through the clamor of the storm. A lightning strike seemed to turn the entire countryside red. My mind was in another frame. I didn't see any danger here; I just wanted, needed, to be with the person who had appeared to me. After some time, the wind began to die down, and the fragments of leaves and rubble ceased. It was then that I heard his voice.

"Natalia, please don't come near me," he said. "Just listen carefully." He was hidden in a clump of trees on the side of the house farthest from Justin's property. I couldn't see his face. I went closer, and he spoke again.

"Please stay afar."

I stood there, obeying his words. "But please, Sir, who are you? What do you want from me?" His voice...it sounded somehow familiar, but it wasn't as though I had remembered my Thomas' voice.

"I know everything, Natalia," he stated through the whistling wind and rain. "And, I love you! I must be with you, Natalia."

Quickly I ran toward him, and he dashed away. "Arie," I hollered... "Arie, don't leave me!" Lightning streamed again and thunder clapped, and suddenly, I was face-to-face with none other than Gerrit. He grabbed ahold of my nightclothes and shook me. I screamed, and just as I did the piercing screams from another's lips ripped through the fields. They got Gerrit's attention and allowed me to free myself from him. He still had a grasp on my nightclothes and they ripped as he held on. I ran off. I ran hard to the trees and ducked down within them. The screams, which didn't appear to be too far off, continued and terrified me. But they didn't terrify me as much as Gerrit's pursuit.

"Natalia Kappan, show yourself!" Gerrit commanded. The wind once again was beginning to pick up. It was hard for me to hear just where Gerrit was. I continued ducking in the bushes. Debris began flying again, and another wave of the storm seemed imminent. The screaming was close, and I wanted to follow it so badly.

"Die out here then, if you wish," Gerrit yelled. "I don't care if the Apparition of Bitterwood takes you away. I have had it with you, Natalia." I watched him circle the yard one more time, coming close to me at one point, and then he approached the house. Finally, he went in, slamming the door behind him.

The screams seemed to be coming from Justin's field, and I quickly made my way over to them. They were haunting and made me tremble.

"I am here," I called out, and the screams instantly stopped. I could hear rustling nearby in the weeds.

"You mustn't look upon my face," The man said, standing a ways away in the darkness as the storm again ripped around us.

"If that is what you wish, then I will do as you say," I replied. "Please, you must tell me, who you are?"

"I am one who has come to free you," he said softly.

"Pardon, me please, Sir," I said, with anguish upon my heart. "But do I know you? Do I love you also? Are you my Arie? Oh, please, let me come near to you." I took a few steps forward in anticipation.

"No," the voice lashed out. "Stay as you are."

"But why don't you want me to see your face. Has it been so disfigured that you don't wish for me to view it?" I asked excitedly, now believing that it was Arie who stood in front of me. Could it have been that Justin didn't tell me the whole, true story? Could it have been that Thomas lived, and Justin was protecting me from him because of my marriage to Gerrit? Or perhaps it was Thomas who made Justin tell me that he had died, in order to protect me from his horrendous appearance from the outcome of the stabbing. Could it be that the love of my life stood in front of me and was mortified to let me see the ravages of his countenance? Didn't he know that I didn't care? His voice probably sounded differently due to the violent cuts that had torn through his mouth and face. I just wanted to be with Thomas no matter what he looked, or sounded like.

"Natalia, I wish to give you my love. Will you meet me at the hour of one a.m., in two nights' time from tonight, at the gazebo? If you say yes, it will quench my screams forever and permit the flowers to finally have a heart to love. You don't deserve what this life has afforded you. You deserve my love forever, just as I have always wanted to give. If you decide to do this, we will go away from here and live in peace forevermore. I promise you, I will give you all that I have."

"But, my daughter," I cried. "What will become of her if I leave? Oh, Arie, we must take Joy with us, too."

"You don't have to give me your answer now. I will be waiting for you at the gazebo in two nights. It will give you a chance to think. If you show up, I'll know you will be forever mine. If you don't, I will understand and go away from here forever. I must go now."

I began to run with open arms toward Arie.

"Please," he shouted, making me stop. "For now, you must stay away." I could hear him run away from me.

"I pray that I will see you in two nights," he said, and then he disappeared into the darkness of the storm. I once again stood alone, drenched, freezing, and dazed at what had just taken place.

It must have been around three a.m. as I walked through the field. I gazed at Justin's house and saw the light still ablaze in his parlor. I wondered if it would be too impudent of me to knock on his door and see if I would be able to stay with him the rest of the night. I was so scared to go back to my home. I just never knew what Gerrit was going to do, but I didn't want Justin to get into any more trouble, either. My heart pained for Thomas as never before, and I knew without a doubt what my decision would be. I reached Justin's porch and quietly climbed the steps. I was trembling and soaking wet. I wondered if Gerrit was somehow watching me as I knocked quietly on the door. Justin didn't answer, and I waited. Finally, I knocked again. I could see him coming as I watched through the window. He saw me and came hurriedly.

"Natalia," he said as he opened the door. "Did you hear the screams? What are you wearing? No more than a nightgown? Have you been out there all night? You're soaking wet and shivering! Come in...come in."

"I had nowhere else to go, Justin," I said, falling into a chair.

"You need to get those wet things off, Natalia," he insisted, looking at me. He quickly went in the other room and returned, holding a crocheted afghan. He handed it to me. "Please cover yourself up...your nightgown is ripped. I think you should go home."

"I'm frightened of Gerrit, Justin," I said sadly. "I think he would do harm to me tonight if I went home."

"But, Natalia, what have you been doing out this late? Didn't you hear the screams a few minutes ago? They sounded as if they were coming from my field."

"They were coming from your field, Justin," I replied.

"And how do you know that?" he asked, looking at me intently.

"Because I was with the person who screamed those screams of agony," I answered.

"You saw him?" Justin said with anguish.

"No, he would not show his face. Justin, the man who screams.... You must tell me...Is that man Thomas?"

Justin looked dumbfounded at me. "Natalia, I've told you numerous times that Thomas is dead. What you say is impossible." He shook his head, seemed agitated and went to his lamp, turning down the flame. He went back into his bedroom, this time coming out with some clothes.

"Listen...go and change into these, and get a good night's sleep. You can have my bed for the night; I'll sleep in the parlor. You'll feel better in the morning. We'll have to figure out what to do with you then."

"Justin I know that Thomas is alive," I stated, looking intently at him.

"Natalia, go and change, I don't want to hear any more of this tonight."

Justin acted even more frustrated. He opened the door and went out on the porch. No more screams interrupted the night's fury. Only the distant, ever-present thunder seemed to serenade me to sleep as I lay in Justin's bed, safe but alone.

Chapter 19

The Time Capsule

*J*ustin confronted me as soon as I awakened to tell me that he had journeyed over to Gerrit's in the night. I guess when I saw him go out to the porch, he was heading over to let Gerrit know that I was safe and asleep at his house. I should have known that such an honorable man as Justin would have gone there, even at that late hour, not even thinking what Gerrit's response would be. Apparently Gerrit was furious, raising his fist at Justin and accusing him of unreasonable things.

I felt so sorry for Justin, for our relationship was so completely opposite from what Gerrit perceived. In all reality, Justin was a precious friend who would never take advantage of anyone, especially me. He was the most upright person I could imagine. If anyone should represent God in this town, if there truly was a God, I was glad it was Justin. I certainly could see the traits in Justin that had made me fall so desperately in love with his brother. I kept wondering how I was going to show my face back home, and how Gerrit and Joy would respond to me after staying out all night.

It felt like a brand new day today. I had tons of planning to do, and many people to see. In just two nights, I would be leaving this place with the love of my life...my soul mate...my Thomas. I would be leaving this misery behind, and I could not wait. I wasn't sure of all the details, but I knew in my heart that my days here were numbered. I kept thinking about the letters, and how Arie had said to follow my heart and follow the prisms, and to wear my necklace so that he could find me. Now I knew he had found me, and it was just a matter of days until I would be with him. Perhaps everything that I was unable to put into sequence before would all fall into place now. The names of people and faces that I couldn't place; maybe they would all make sense in this new life I would have.

I guess there was only one thing that troubled me, and that was Arie's response to my question about Joy. He certainly had to have known that I would never leave my daughter for good. I had decided that I had better make provisions for Joy with the Posts, at least for a time, until I was settled. When all was right, I could send for her. I also was going to mention all of this to Justin, before I left this morning, to see what his response would be. Why was he so adamant in making me think that Thomas was dead? My only explanation was that he was too good, too moral, and that he simply could not justify a married woman leaving her husband to be with his brother, or, for any other man. Couldn't Justin understand that Gerrit had never really been a husband to me, and that I never loved the man?

I examined the ripped nightgown that I had hung over Justin's bed-frame last night. The wetness had left a mark on the wood finish of the bed. I hoped it would go away after it dried. The nightgown was still quite damp. I took off the man's shirt and pants that Justin had given me to wear and exchanged them for my soggy nightclothes. I sure had been wearing wet clothes a lot as of late. I'd only need to wear them until I got home. I folded the others up; tidied the bed, and proceeded to the kitchen, wrapping the afghan around me.

"Thank you, Justin," I said, handing him the clothes. "I hope I didn't ruin your bed. I hung my nightclothes over the post to dry last night, and the moisture from them seemed to have marked up the wood."

"Don't worry about that, Natalia. Aren't the clothes you have on still wet?" he asked, perceiving that I had put them back on underneath the afghan.

"Yes, damp, but I will be fine until I get home. I didn't want to have to explain to Gerrit or Joy why I was wearing your clothes."

"No, I agree with you and completely understand. So, you're going home now? Do you want something to eat?"

"I suppose I am. I have no choice," I replied. "I have many things to do before tomorrow. And, no thank you on the food. I'm just not hungry."

"Is tomorrow a special day? Are you planning something?" Justin asked.

"What would you say if I told you that I was leaving LaPier tomorrow?...Leaving with your brother." I looked at him fix-edly.

Justin turned away, and then looked back at me as if to respond, but then he turned away again and shook his head. "Honestly, Natalia, where do you come up with these mon-strous lies?"

"Justin, I was with Arie, I mean Thomas, last night. We are going to go away together."

"Ah ha, and where are you going, may I ask?" he asked sar-castically.

"I'm not sure of that yet. I don't know if we're going to another town; and I know this will sound bizarre, or if we're going to another dimension in time. I honestly don't know." I sighed.

Justin just stared.

"Please don't look at me like that," I pleaded. "You looked at me just now as all the others do; as though I'm a lunatic. I can't have that from you, Justin."

Justin made his way to me and put his hand under my chin, forcing me to look at him. "Natalia, I'm worried for you. I'm worried that you've lost sight of reality again. Listen to the words that I speak, okay? Thomas is dead, Natalia. You cannot go away with Thomas because he no longer exists on this earth."

"Then perhaps it's his spirit that comes to snatch me away. That would be the explanation as to why he wouldn't permit me to look upon his face last night. Unless, of course, you're not telling me the entire story. I don't believe you, Justin, when you tell me that Thomas is dead. I can't. Who knows… Perhaps, Thomas and I will leave this entire millennium…this year of 1920, and enter another place in time." Justin stepped away.

"It's futile for me to try to talk sense into you, Natalia. You believe what you will." Justin seemed very perplexed.

I approached him again and laid my hand on his back, holding the afghan around me with the other. "It's okay, Justin. I understand your concern for me to be with your brother. I know I'm married to Gerrit, but I will not let anyone know that I have left with Thomas. I will not allow this to spoil such a solid reputation that you have maintained in this town. It is between you, me and Thomas, but I need to make sure that Joy will be cared for until I can send for her."

"And what do you want me to agree to?" Justin said, turning around. "Do you want me to agree to take care of Joy while you run away with a dead man? Natalia, this is crazy talk!"

"Stop!" I yelled. I put one hand to my ear, covering it, wishing the other hand was free to do the same with my other ear, and I walked away. I rubbed my face hard and then turned, facing Justin. "I will no longer bother you with this, but please, just tell me one thing. If you find me gone in the next couple of days will you promise that Joy is taken care of?"

"And you claim to be going with Thomas? Is that right? You're not going with anyone else?" Justin questioned. "And if Thomas isn't going with you, you aren't going either?"

"Of course not." I replied earnestly, stepping away.

"I'll tell you what then, Natalia. Since what you're saying is impossible, I will agree. If I find you gone with Thomas in the next couple of days, yes, I will see to it that Joy is taken care of." He shook his head.

"Thank you, Justin," I said, looking at him with teary eyes. "That's all I needed to make sure of. I will return the afghan to you when I can." I said no more to my friend, and quickly exited the house.

Finding the door locked as I returned to my so-called residence, I knocked loudly. I could hear someone inside and waited. I waited some more and knocked again. Finally, Gerrit opened the door.

"What are you doing here?" he said sternly. "How do you have the audacity to return here?"

"I'm sorry for last night, Sir. I needed to stay at the Parson's house."

"Our Parson and yourself are quite familiar, aren't you?"

"Gerrit, it's not like that," I said as he grabbed ahold of the afghan which was wrapped around me. He pulled it off my shoulder and saw the ripped nightgown underneath. "Your clothes are wet and torn."

"I was out in the rain last night, as you well know. And my ripped nightgown is due to your actions, Sir. I am going up to change. Please permit me to do so," I pleaded. He continued to bunch my clothes in his hand drawing me closer to him.

"Where is Joy?" I asked hastily.

"Joy is not here. She's at the Posts again. She wanted to go there already at daybreak when she found out that you didn't come home last night. I don't know what will become of that girl of yours if you don't straighten up." He looked straight into my eyes. "It is just you and I here, Natalia."

The afghan was so tightly gathered up within his hand that he drew me upward, lifting me with the fabric. His lips met mine and I vigorously pulled my head away, wiping my mouth forcefully with my hand. I let go of the afghan and it fell to the floor.

"What's the matter, did you get enough of that with our Parson?"

Furious, I reached up and slapped his face with all the power I had.

"Well, I'm your husband, and I deserve a bit more from you." He took my hair in his other hand and held my head firmly as he kissed me again. He was panting wildly.

"Please," I yelled out between advances. "I will not stand for this." I pulled back as hard as I could, feeling some hair being plucked out from my head. His other hand held on to my nightgown, and as I bounded back, more of the fabric ripped off in his hand. I was able to free myself. I ran to the fireplace and grabbed a fire iron to guard me.

"You are good for nothing, Natalia Kappan!" he screamed.

"I will not be here long, Sir," I said, trembling and pointing the poker in his direction. "You will not have to put up with me too much longer. Or, should I say, I will not have to put up with you, Sir."

Suddenly a knock came at the door. I stood there, relieved and anxious.

"We will resume this at a later time. I will promise you that," Gerrit said, looking at me. I put down the fire iron and ran up the stairs. I stood there, listening to see who had come over. I was sure it would be Justin.

"I hope we're not interrupting something," I heard a woman's voice say as she entered the house. "Is everything okay, Gerrit? We could hear commotion coming from in here."

"Yes...yes, don't mind that, everything is fine," Gerrit replied.

"I'm sorry, Gerrit, Joy wanted to come home and see if Natalia had returned yet."

I could now hear that it was Priscilla Post talking below in the entry. She must have brought Joy back home already.

"Has she come back yet?" Priscilla asked. "Joy was so worried."

"She is here somewhere," he answered as Joy gave a quick smile to Mrs. Post. Joy stopped where the afghan lay on the floor and picked it up in her hands, and then quickly ran up the steps. She met me at the top, and I put my finger to my lips signifying for her to be quiet. I could see her gazing at my ripped nightgown. She took hold of it, feeling the damp fabric. She handed me the afghan. I put it around myself, then sat listening with my daughter on my lap.

"You've sure been having ample problems with Natalia as of late, haven't you?" Priscilla Post asked.

"Natalia is very difficult to care for," Gerrit said softly.

"You knew that she came for a visit to my house yesterday, didn't you? She was acting quite peculiarly."

"And what's new?" Gerrit quipped.

"Well, please let me know if I can be of any more assistance to you. You know that Joy is always welcome to stay with us. Lillian thinks of her as her sister."

Lillian...Lillian, I thought to myself! The old woman who I had first heard the chant from in another place and in another time...her name was Lillian! It was as though I kept forgetting and it had just dawned on me again. Her face went through my mind and I remembered the small birthmark on her right cheek.

"Joy," I whispered. "Lillian has a mark on her cheek, doesn't she?"

"Yes, Mama, you know she does," Joy replied softly. "Why do you ask?"

"Shhhh." Once again, I motioned for her to be quiet.

All became silent downstairs, and I could hear footsteps making their way over to the steps. I quickly got up and entered my room dropping the afghan on the floor. Joy followed.

"Joy,...JOY... is your mother okay?" Gerrit called from below.

"Yes, Papa," Joy answered, peeking her head out from my door.

I sat on my bed with my head buried in my hands and pondered my thoughts. I now realized that I had been with the same Lillian Post, but ironically it had been almost a century later! She had the same birthmark; the same name...they were one and the same! Somehow, I had become a part of two lives that spanned a century! Now, I was certain of it.

I heard the door shut downstairs and figured that Priscilla Post had now left.

"Mama," Joy said, putting her hand on my shoulder.

"Yes, Dear." I looked up at her.

"What happened to you and your nightgown? It looks like you had a fight." She seemed to peer through me with expressive eyes.

"I just had a little accident; that's all. I'm not hurt....see." I gave her a small smile.

"You fetched the letters again, didn't you?" Joy asked.

"Why do you ask me that, Joy?"

"Because I heard you run down the stairs late last night. I didn't know what was going on, and I came into your room. On your bed sat one of the letters. I read it, Mama. Who is this Arie? No one will tell me...Not you, not Parson Peterson." Joy squinted and looked troubled. "Anyway, I was scared that Papa would find the letter, so I reached underneath the bed to hide it and found the entire box of them. Mama, what would Papa do if he found them? He would be so angry, and I don't want you to get hurt by him! I can't stand it when you fight!"

"Oh, my dearest Joy, how could I ever explain everything to you? All I can say is that you must trust me."

"Trust is probably the hardest thing for me to believe in, Mama. Sometimes I don't know who I can trust. That's why I feel safe at Lillian's house. No one yells there. Her mama doesn't run away, and her papa is kind." Joy looked down to the floor. I felt I was having a conversation with someone who was equal to my age.

"Joy, you must listen to me," I continued. "Your mama might be going away for a time."

"Away where, Mama? Is Papa going with you as well?"

"No, I will be going alone," I answered.

"But, Mama, where are you going and why will you be leaving us?"

"I will send for you, Joy, but you must keep it a secret. Do you understand what I'm telling you?" Joy seemed distraught and didn't answer.

"Joy, are you all right?"

"Mama, I'm not sure that I want to go with you." She kept looking down and I knew she felt uneasy.

"But, I want you with me, Dear. You're my daughter; we belong together."

Joy finally looked up at me. "But would I have to leave Parson Peterson and Lillian and Papa?" She looked even more upset.

"Well, yes, you would, but we would be together," I answered.

"Mama, just stay here where we can look after you." Joy kept fidgeting and started getting very emotional. "I don't want to leave LaPier, Mama." She ran out of my room.

My head was spinning, yet I knew that the decision I had made to leave with Thomas was the only logical solution to my life. Even though I was married, this marriage to Gerrit meant nothing to me. I was but a child when he forcibly made me his wife. There was no love here, no caring...not anything! It didn't even seem as if Joy would miss me from the way she had acted. I listened for voices coming from downstairs but heard nothing. I was chilled and took the damp and ripped nightclothes off and changed into something dry.

I scrunched down on my bed and hugged the feather pillow tight. I had to think...I just had to think. How could I have come into this world; this time period, and not known anything or anyone? Yet, mysteriously, I had taken on the identity and very soul of a stranger? Why was my old life so blank? The only evidence I had of it was the strange clothes and perhaps some misty memories, and now my recollection of Lillian Post. Was I directed here for the single purpose of finding my soul mate? I still had so many questions, and the more I pondered them, the more mixed up I became. I looked at my necklace. I still believed that it had powers capable of doing miraculous things. I still believed that this magical stone was the bridge from here to there, wherever there might be. My heart beat fast as my thoughts turned to Thomas. I will be with you soon, my love, I said quietly to myself. But first I must make everything right.

I got up and looked at myself in the mirror. I was young and beautiful, but those seemed to be the only attributes I possessed. I was a horrible mother. Not one person took me seriously, and no one respected me, except perhaps for Justin. At least I hoped he did. To be with Thomas again would be like becoming reborn. I shivered, thinking of being in his arms. I went over to the armoire and pulled out the soiled and broken hatbox that I had buried the clothes in some time ago. I would make a time capsule for Joy in this box so that if I never returned, she would never forget me.

I stuck my hand into the mattress and pulled out the hidden clothes from another era. I folded them and put them in the box. Next I placed a photograph of myself in a pearly frame. On the top, I would place a note. I went to the desk and began to scribble down some words. A tear hit the paper, for I suddenly realized that these might be the last words that Joy would have to remember me by for a while. "I can't write this!" I said, closing my eyes and crumpling up the paper. I tossed it under the desk. I started anew.

The words were so hard to write. I just had to focus and know that I was doing the best thing for everyone. It almost broke my heart, but I finished and folded the paper in half. I couldn't just put it on the top of the box. I pulled out the frame and stuck the note inside the frame alongside my picture. Surely, after some time, Joy would become curious and open it, finding the hidden writing. I put the crumpled top back on the box and fastened it with four ribbons. It would be adequate to keep the box closed until, and if, Joy should need to find answers someday. Now I needed to make a journey, and it definitely would not be an easy one.

My hopes were that Gerrit was still so disgusted with my

actions that I would be able to walk right out of the house again. I hated that man, and he scared the very bones within my body. I walked nonchalantly down the stairs, carrying the hatbox in my arms. Joy was sitting at the kitchen table drawing, but Gerrit was nowhere to be found.

"Joy, where's your Papa?" I asked.

Joy was very aloof and would not look up at me. "Joy," I said again, "Where is your Papa?

"I don't know, Mama. I think he may have gone to Parson Peterson's."

That's all I needed! I would have to pass Justin's house on my way to where I was going. Hopefully, they would be in the barn and not notice me. And furthermore, why would Gerrit have gone to see Justin in the first place? The thought made me very uncomfortable.

"Joy, I need to go away for a little while. I will be home promptly," I said, nearing the door.

"Where are you going with that hatbox?"

"I need to take care of some business," I said, using the hatbox to help push open the door. "I will be home soon. Don't worry about me. I will return home, I promise."

I quickly started down the road as Joy yelled from the porch, "Mama, be careful."

"Of course," I said, as I hurried farther down the road.

Chapter 20

The Altercation

I laid the hat box down and knocked on the door of the Post house. This visit was an important task I needed to address before I could even think of leaving with Arie. I now noticed myself saying and thinking of Arie and Thomas randomly; knowing now that he was one-and-the-same person.

Although Priscilla had just left my house not long ago, I was hoping she'd be home by now. After all, she had taken her buggy, and I had walked the entire way. Unless she had stopped at the mercantile or gone visiting somewhere, I was in hopes that I would catch her here. I knocked again on the door in anticipation. I could hear noises inside. Just as I lifted my hand to knock a third time, the door opened and Priscilla Post stood there looking at me.

"Why, Natalia, I just left your home about an hour ago. Is everything all right...Joy all right?" she questioned.

"Yes, Joy is fine and nothing's wrong...at least nothing I need to tell you about. I needed to come over here today because I need to speak with you about something very important. This is a private matter, and I'd appreciate it if we could go somewhere alone." I glanced inside, wondering if her children were listening.

"Of course, Natalia," Priscilla agreed. "I don't think anyone can hear us, but we can shut the door and walk in the front yard together if that would be more private for you."

"That would be fine," I replied, picking up the box.

Priscilla shut the door. "It looks like you have your hands full, Natalia. Would you like me to take that hatbox for you?"

"If it's okay, I'll just put it back down here on your porch as we walk," I suggested.

"Of course," Priscilla answered.

I carefully laid the box next to the cement rail by the flower boxes. We walked down the stairs and onto the lawn. There was a view across State Street from this area. It was the area where I felt the unusual sensation that a gazebo used to stand. I stood there staring for quite some time.

"Is everything okay, Natalia?" Priscilla questioned.

"Please tell me if there was ever a structure built over there?" I asked, pointing to the area in question.

"No, it has always been unoccupied land. It's all unoccupied land until you get to the Bitterwood Cemetery. Why do you ask, Natalia?"

"No reason, I guess. Can we sit?" I asked. I neared some Adirondack chairs. They appeared to be newly painted white and were in the far corner of the front yard. "These are dry, aren't they?" I asked.

"Oh, yes...my husband painted them last week....please sit; be my guest," Priscilla Post said pleasantly as she sat down. "Is everything all right at your home? I heard shouting coming from within when I was dropping off Joy. It sounded like you and Gerrit were having a spat."

"No, it's never all right, Priscilla. I don't belong there. I never did. I definitely don't belong with Gerrit. I know that everyone in town thinks that I have problems, and perhaps I do. I don't even know myself anymore. If I have problems or not, it's irrelevant. I don't want to be with that man. I should have never been with him. You see I believe that I've been caught between two different dimensions in life. And I know what you must be thinking of me right now but please, listen if you will."

"Go on, Natalia, I'm listening," she said softly.

"I believe that sometime in the future there will some sort of structure built over there...A gazebo perhaps." I pointed once again across the street.

"I guess we don't know that, do we, Natalia?"

"But you see, I do know that, because I was already there. I already saw the future of that land from a time in the future," I said impatiently

Priscilla Post took out a fancy embroidered handkerchief and gave a slight cough into it. She acted uneasy.

"And just what did you want to talk to me about, Natalia?" she said. "I certainly hope it's not more of this silliness."

"You can call it silliness if you wish. I know what is true. I won't bother you with anymore of that. What I need to talk to you about is Joy. I will be leaving here soon, Priscilla, and I need to know that Joy will be taken care of."

"Leaving here? What on earth are you talking about?"

"I can't give you any details, because I'm not sure how it will all take place. Who knows, I may enter another time and just disappear from this life. I may have to go to another town and live. It's all unclear to me right now."

"I'm very, very confused," Priscilla admitted, looking puzzled and almost fearfully at me. "And so where do Gerrit and Joy fit into all of this?"

"Gerrit will not be a part of this, Priscilla, and I don't know yet what will happen with Joy. That's why I'm here."

"Go on," she instructed.

"I just want to make things clear. If I should turn up missing, or seem to disappear from this world, would you watch out for Joy for me? Joy loves it with your family, and I know she feels safe here. She can't feel safe with Gerrit, Priscilla. No one could."

Priscilla Post put her hand on my arm softly. "Natalia, people don't just disappear, dear. I'm having a hard time knowing what to say to you."

I closed my eyes and sighed heavily.

"I could go into depths with you about what I think is going on, but you, or no one, would believe a word that I'd say. You'd only think it was nonsense. I believe I'm a part of a huge plan. Perhaps a plan that spans many generations. It's too awesome to even comprehend." I put my hand in my blouse and held tightly to my necklace. "I love my daughter, Priscilla, and although you may not be able to figure out why I'd leave her, I feel that it will benefit her in the long run. That's the only way I would ever leave her."

"And, have you talked with Gerrit about all of this?" she continued to question.

"No, I will not. I will talk to you and have already talked to our Parson about Joy. You are the ones she loves, and I feel you love her as well."

"Of course we love Joy, but like I said, I really don't know what to say to you," Priscilla said, unclasping her hands. "I mean, of course, I will look out for Joy for you, if Gerrit would agree. But, Natalia, nothing's going to happen to you, dear. People don't just disappear!"

"The box that I brought today. Will you take it for me and give it to Joy just in case what I say happens... Please? That is why I made this journey today."

"I'm not going to take that from you, Natalia," Mrs. Post said, standing up and turning to look at the package on the porch.

"I'm pleading with you to take it for me," I said, standing up and taking Priscilla's hand.

"What's in the package? Can't you leave it for Gerrit to give to Joy?"

"I would never be certain that she would get it if I gave it to Gerrit. I trust you, Priscilla."

"I feel very uneasy about this." Priscilla said. "Natalia, no sane mother would plan to leave her children. Plus, this disappearing stuff is downright insane. I feel that I must get you help, Dear."

"Tell me something," I said sincerely. "Has anyone ever truly sought help for me before? I know better...few people truly care for me."

I began to make my way to the road. "I will leave the box with you, then. Please don't tell me no. Just care for it for me, and do what I ask. Thank you very much for helping me."

Priscilla Post was speechless as she watched me walk away.

Joy was sitting silently on the front porch as I got home. She appeared to be very upset.

"What's wrong, Joy?" I questioned as I made my way up the steps. Before she could answer, Gerrit burst out of the house. He was holding something in his hands and looked furious!

"Explain these!" he hollered as he threw some letters to the porch floor.

I shivered and looked at Joy, for I realized that he had found the letters from Arie. I wanted to run.

"These are from Justin, aren't they?" he demanded. He walked up so close to me that I could feel his breath as he spoke. "Aren't they?" he demanded.

"No, Sir, I assure you that they are not from Justin. You must believe me."

"I demand to know who this Arie is," he continued shouting.

I took a step backward as he clutched my arm once again.

"You're hurting me," I whispered, hoping that Joy couldn't hear.

"Joy, go next door at once," Gerrit commanded.

"But, Papa, you told me I mustn't go over there anymore," she said, her voice quivering.

"I'm telling you NOW to go!" he hollered.

"But I don't want to leave Mama," she said in tears.

He held more tightly to my arm. "Tell her to go, Natalia. Tell her that I need to talk to you, NOW!"

I was trembling from fear and didn't want Joy to see this.

Gerrit could end up killing me, or even worse, Joy, as angry as he was. I couldn't let her stay in this situation. Besides, if I told Joy to go to Justin's, I knew she would tell him what was happening and perhaps he would come to my aid.

"Joy, you must listen to me, Darling." I sobbed as Gerrit tightened his grip. "Go to Parson Peterson's as your Papa says. I...I will be fine...I promise."

"Papa, let go of her," Joy said sternly.

"You mind your own business, and get next door," he continued to demand.

Her crying intensified. She looked at me and then Gerrit, and took off running. Gerrit pulled me into the house and threw me against the parlor table. My back hit it hard.

"I knew you were entertaining gentlemen, Natalia. It's the reason you never want me, isn't it?" His voice now seemed to calm. "How many have you had without me knowing?"

"It's not what you think. I never wanted you, Sir, because I never loved you. I cannot help that."

"But you love this man, this Arie character, don't you?" he screamed with all calmness gone.

"I do love him," I cried. "Oh please...please let me alone."

Gerrit approached me again. I leaned back against the table as far as I could go, and my body became stiff. Very tenderly he began to caress my arm. I shivered and looked at him, trembling. His hand now reached for my face and he stroked my neck and cheek. All was silent.

"Please," I whispered. His stroking motions became lower as he touched just above my breasts. I was shaking so hard; I felt that I would faint. I wanted to hit him...I wanted to kill him. I wanted to run, but it was as though I was numb. He pushed himself against me hard and kissed my forehead.

"I would have written you letters like those, if you would have permitted me, Natalia," he whispered in my ear.

"Allow me to go upstairs, please," I continued pleading.

"We could go up together." He continued whispering; now holding onto my arm.

I could no longer stand this. I felt as though I was going to get sick. Suddenly, all the emotions came over me that I had experienced when I was raped. This wasn't going to happen again. I raised my head up and placed my lips on Gerrit's. As I did, he began returning the kiss and released me from his grip, just as I had hoped. I jolted sideways, freeing myself from being pinched against the table. He came at me again.

"I knew I could make you love me," he bellowed.

I ran out the door and he followed. Justin and Joy met me on the porch. I was panting.

"What's going on here?" Justin questioned.

I noticed that Joy quickly picked up the letters from the floor.

Then, suddenly, Gerrit walked over to Justin and swung at him, hitting him in the head.

"Gerrit, what's wrong with you!" Justin yelled, wiping his face with his hand and looking to see if there was blood.

Gerrit swung at him again, but this time Justin fought back. Joy was screaming and it all seemed like a horrible nightmare. I grabbed ahold of her and pulled her inside. She laid the letters on the table and continued screaming. I couldn't let her see this.

"Mama, why is he doing that?" she squealed. "Why is Papa hurting Parson Peterson?" I kept watching from the doorway, as Gerrit would not give up. Justin tried not to fight, but it looked as though he had no choice. He took a second swing, and Gerrit stood motionless, then fell to the floor.

"Natalia, get some cold water!" Justin yelled, trying to help Gerrit while wiping the blood from his own face. Joy ran out to the porch. I cranked the kitchen pump back and forth until a steady stream came out. Finally, the water turned cold. I grabbed a cloth, soaked it in the cold water, and ran to the porch. Justin was holding up Gerrit's head, trying to revive him, and Joy sat on the swing, crying hysterically.

"Put the cloth on his forehead," Justin instructed.

I looked at the battered face of this man and honestly

hoped that he was dead. It was as though all was in slow motion.

"Natalia, put the cloth on his head NOW!" Justin demanded.

I laid the cloth on Gerrit and sat back, legs crossed on the porch floor.

"Is Papa dead?" Joy said through her cries.

"No, Joy," Justin confirmed. "Why don't you go to your room?" She didn't move.

I continued to get cold rags, exchanging them for the warm ones. Justin continued to hold up Gerrit's head. I hadn't noticed until now, but Justin was bleeding profusely from his nose. I ran inside and grabbed another towel and wiped Justin's face gently.

"Are you okay?" I asked.

"I am fine...Don't worry about me. I certainly didn't mean for this to happen, Natalia. I was worried for you after what Joy told me. I never really comprehended that Gerrit would respond to me so violently. He's acted like he was going to strike me in the past, but never acted on it. I thought we had begun to made amends after his visit today."

Gerrit started slowly moving, then he opened his eyes. Justin was still holding his head, and I sat next to him with the cloths.

Gerrit focused on Justin. "Get away from me." Gerrit sat up slowly and felt his face.

"Allow me to help you into the house, Gerrit," Justin offered.

"I will not allow you to do anything! Now leave my property, before I kill you."

"Papa, please don't say those things," Joy said, now stooping next to Gerrit, continuing to cry.

I followed Justin down the walk. "I'm so, so sorry," I said, shivering. "I took the letters from your barn yesterday and he found them. He thinks they are from you."

Justin shook his head. "How could you, Natalia? No wonder he's furious!" Justin looked at me in disgust. "Take care of him. You'll have to." And he made his way through the field back to his house.

Chapter 21

Sour, First Fruits

Gerrit lay down for the rest of the day on the floor of the room where he did his bookwork. I passed by now and again just to make sure he was breathing. Joy offered him some bread and meat and drinks throughout the day, but he didn't want anything. Joy seemed very withdrawn toward both Gerrit and me. How could I blame her with all she had seen and gone through?

Even with everything that had taken place in recent days, I could think of nothing but being with Arie. I would only have to get through this night, and the following evening I'd be in his arms. I began planning and went to the armoire in my room. I pulled out the white dress that had gotten my attention when I had first arrived here. It was lovely; all white, yet simple with elegant design. I would wear this garment to meet Arie. Without having to worry too much about what Gerrit would see today, I took the dress outside. My plan was to hang it on the line until dark to air out. I wanted it to smell fresh and lovely for our reuniting. Soon, my attention was diverted to the road as a buggy neared. It was Priscilla and Lillian Post.

"You're still here, I see," Priscilla commented. I knew she was referring to the comments I had made to her about me leaving when I was at her house. I noticed that she and Lillian were looking at the dress hanging on the line.

"I'm here, yes," I answered. "But not for long."

"What a pretty dress," Priscilla commented.

I didn't answer.

"We were coming by to see if Joy would like to come and spend the night tonight with Lillian," Priscilla continued. "Mr. Post has erected a tent for the children. They want to have a campout with some of their friends. With all the storms we've been having as of late, I thought they should take advantage of the day's nice weather."

Joy must have heard the buggy and had quickly made her way outside.

"We're sleeping out of doors tonight," Lillian said excitedly, looking at Joy. "We want you to come. Father has put up a tent in the yard."

Lillian's bliss was taken aback by Joy's sadness. "Papa is ill," Joy responded. "I should stay with him."

"Is Gerrit okay, Natalia?" Priscilla asked.

"He will be fine in time. He needs his rest."

"Well, do you need help? Should I send for his sister?"

"No, please, don't do that. He'll be fine in time. I will care for him." I looked over at Joy. "Joy, you're welcome to go with Lillian. It would be better for your Papa if you left. That way the house will be quiet."

"Are you sure, Mama?" she asked, with eyes open wide in anticipation.

"Yes, go and get your stuff."

"You better bring some warm things, Joy," Mrs. Post interjected. "It may get cold out in the tent at night. We'll wait for you while you go and get your things together."

Quickly, Lillian got out of the buggy. "I will help you, Joy," she said, as they ran into the house together.

"So, please tell me, Natalia. What exactly does Gerrit have? ...A cold, flu, what?"

"Oh, Priscilla, I'm embarrassed to tell you. Gerrit had a fight with someone."

"A fight? What kind of fight?" she questioned curiously.

"I really don't want to talk of it," I declared.

"Well, was the fight with you...Joy...who?" She continued to pry.

"Gerrit and Parson Peterson had a disagreement. I don't want this to be told around town, Priscilla."

"Justin Peterson!" Priscilla exclaimed. "Of all people! There's not an argumentative bone in that man's body! Justin's not hurt is he?"

"No, just a bit bruised I'd assume. I haven't actually seen him since it happened. It was Gerrit's fault. Justin just got in the middle of something between Gerrit and I. I just would appreciate it if you would keep this to yourself. There's no need spreading gossip about a good man."

"I do not gossip, Natalia," Priscilla Post said sternly.

"Then I'm glad this will go no further," I replied.

We stood there waiting for the girls for some time, as neither of us said another word.

"We're all ready," Lillian shouted, coming out of the house holding Joy's hand. She was carrying a bunch of things.

"It looks like you are," I said, as I helped the girls into the buggy with Priscilla Post and their load of things.

"She will be home tomorrow some time, won't she, Priscilla?" I asked.

"Oh yes. I will have her home by afternoon, if that's all right?"

"Yes, but she must be home by afternoon," I said, looking at Joy. "I need to spend some time with her tomorrow."

Priscilla nodded her head, agreeing to my request. "Oh, and Natalia, I know it may be awkward in this situation, but if you need help with Gerrit, please go next door and get Justin, won't you?" Priscilla directed.

"I will, but I'll be fine caring for him myself." I kissed Joy on the cheek. "Have fun, my darling." Joy didn't answer me, and I could tell that she was relieved to get away from this house and the agony that loomed here. The buggy took off as the three of them looked at me and waved goodbye.

As I went into the house, I looked down on the table. Joy had picked up the letters and laid them there during the fight, but I just realized they were no longer there. I ran upstairs and looked under my bed. The box was gone. I was very upset that Gerrit had managed to get up and dispose of them somehow. I really didn't think he was up to doing that. Quietly, I searched the library where he slept on the floor, to no avail...no letters. Then I went upstairs and entered Gerrit's room and began to search for the letters in there. I knew there was no way he was able to get up the stairs in his condition, but I had to check anyway. The letters had disappeared.

For the rest of the evening while Gerrit slept, I searched the house for the letters, going over the same places two and three times. It wasn't as though they'd be easy to hide. The box that held them was sizable, at least sizable enough to be found. I searched in every cabinet, every cupboard. They were nowhere! It was getting dark. I went outside to the clothes-line where my dress hung, dancing in the breeze. I pulled it off the line, inhaling the fresh scent in fabric. I couldn't wait until it adorned my body and Thomas could see it on me. Would he think I was beautiful? I certainly hoped that would be the case.

"Natalia." Faintly, I could hear Gerrit saying my name as I entered the house. I laid the dress down and went to the door-way of the room where Gerrit was still on the floor.

"Is there something I can do for you, Sir?" I asked quietly.

"Come near me" he said, motioning to do so.

Reluctantly, I went in.

"Would you sit here, please," he said.

I sat on the floor next to him.

"Do you wish for me to get you a drink or something to eat or another cold towel?

"I wish for you to sit with me. That is all. Where is your daughter?"

I tried not to let him see that I was once again trembling. "She went to Lillian's house for the night."

"So then we're alone?" he asked.

"Yes," I replied. It frightened me, although I knew he was in no shape to move just yet.

He turned his head slowly, keeping it on the floor, and looked at me. "I never intended to hurt you. You will never understand that, but I never have. I'm sorry that I was never able to give you the love like you found from the man in those letters."

I turned away. "Just get better, Gerrit. That is what I pray now." I answered.

"Natalia," he continued, "If those letters are from Justin Peterson, then I will understand. He is a better man than I. I had no right to do what I did to him."

It was as though Gerrit had experienced a spiritual revelation.

"But, Gerrit, they are not from him," I said sincerely. "Justin cares for you. He would have never been untrue to you."

"I believe you, Natalia." He turned his head back to face the ceiling and, after some time, he dozed off to sleep.

I sat looking at Gerrit. Even though I was terrified of this man, that same compassion came over me for him that I had felt before. I sighed and went upstairs. I began thinking of all the things that Justin had told me about faith, love and hope. I knelt beside my bed and said a prayer. Even though I didn't doubt the decision I had made to leave with Thomas, I wanted to know that it was right in God's eyes as well. I had to let my heart lead the way, but I was hoping that this loving God that Justin spoke of would direct it as well.

I had a restless night's sleep but awakened to believe that this was the day I had been waiting for my entire life. I could hear someone downstairs and peeked down the steps. Gerrit was in the kitchen, which was a good sign. I was afraid that he had suffered a concussion or worse, and I had decided that if he was no better today that I would need to fetch the Doc. After our conversation last night, I had mixed feelings toward the man. Did he truly love me? I just didn't understand how he could love me and treat me the way he did. Was I perhaps overlooking how I treated him? Was I even capable of knowing how I treated others? I was just so scared to be around him, for I never knew what to expect. Especially now, since I was alone with him in the house.

I returned to my room. The humidity was high and I could tell it was going to be another hot day. Priscilla Post was right about catching the good weather while they could. Yesterday had been the only day in the entire week that it hadn't stormed or rained, and it felt as though something may be brewing again today in more ways than one. I looked at my dress that hung from the armoire door and a chill went up my spine. I thought of nothing but my time with Arie. My prayer last night had not changed my feelings. I felt that it must be God's will for me to proceed in my plans. Tonight I would be in Thomas' arms!

I took my pitcher downstairs to fill with water. The pump in the kitchen seemed tight this morning.

"I'm glad to see that you're feeling better," I said to Gerrit as we crossed paths in the kitchen.

"Yes," he answered. His face looked battered and blue, but at least he was upright and able to walk around today.

I let go of the pump handle, pulled the full pitcher from the sink and began to make my way back upstairs.

"Do you wish for help with that?"

"No, I'm fine," I answered, climbing the steps. "You cannot make it up here. You rest!"

I washed myself with lilac soap today. I couldn't remember the last time I had used it. I hadn't had a reason to smell pretty. I kept it wrapped in waxed paper, and the fragrance was still sweet. I patted my face dry, grabbed the towel and soap and proceeded to go downstairs. There would be ample rain in the barrel for me to wash my hair. I felt as though I was a young girl in New York City again, waiting for Thomas to return to me after his day on the streets. Even though I was so young, I even loved him then. Our love only grew stronger

when he found me once again here in LaPier. I could only imagine how our love together would be now, at this age, when I
truly understood the meaning of love for this man. It would be
euphoric! It would be paradise!

I was rinsing my hair in the rain barrel when Gerrit came
out.

"I am going to try and make things better here," he said,
standing beside me.

I carefully twisted out the water from my hair and
wrapped the towel around my head.

What could I say? I looked at the man and gave a subdued
smile. I didn't want things better with Gerrit. I didn't want to
be with him, period. I left him standing there and went into
the house.

I got some of my things together and hid them on the floor
by the far corner of the armoire, next to the wall. I also put
some things into a large purse; my powder and some undergarments, etc. I laid my soap on the window ledge to dry out.
I'd wrap it later and pack it to take along. I was excited, yet
strongly sad as well. I wanted to get away from Gerrit more
than I could explain, but now that the time was coming closer,
there was an eerie sadness in leaving him. How could that
possibly be? I had just come to depend upon him and Joy for
everything, and now all was going to change. I knew he was
abusive, but it was all I had known living here.

I unwrapped the towel from my head and the smell of lilac
encircled me. I breathed it in, feeling elegant. I laid the towel
over my rack and began to brush out my long black hair. I
looked at myself in the mirror and wondered what my mother
had looked like. I didn't remember. I was so young when she
had left me. Was she still alive and searching for me, or had she
passed on? Who could the woman have been who left me the
locket with the picture of myself inside? I wondered so many
things. I pulled the necklace from around my neck and kissed
it. "I have been waiting so long for this day," I whispered.

For most of the morning I sat on my bed and gazed out the

window, just waiting for time to pass. I had eaten no breakfast and Gerrit didn't offer any. Usually he did all the cooking, but in the last year, Joy had begun doing many of those chores as well. I was hoping that Joy would be returning soon. I needed to spend this day with her. I needed to share what was left of my life with her.

I went downstairs and grabbed an apple from the basket which lay on the cupboard. Gerrit must have picked the first apples of the year. These Yellow Transparents were always very sour, first fruits, and made my mouth pucker. I took the apple outside with me to the porch swing and continued feasting. My taste buds soon adapted to the flavor.

I could hear talking and looked to the rear in the field. I could see Gerrit and what looked to be Justin in our small orchard. Gerrit was pulling weeds from around the trees, and the other man stood beside him. They were apparently in heavy conversation. I walked in the back where I could see well. It was Justin. I was relieved to see that he was okay. He waved at me, and I returned the gesture. Gerrit seemed to be tolerating his visit, and I hoped, with all my heart, that he had apologized to Justin. After all, it was almost entirely my fault that the fight had happened in the first place. If I hadn't taken the letters home, none of it would have happened. Now I longed to know where the letters were. I guess that after tonight I could ask Thomas himself to recite the letters for me. Tonight he could tell me in his own words how he felt.

Throwing my apple core in the field, I returned to the porch to find that Priscilla and Lillian Post were in front of the house with Joy. I hadn't even heard the buggy pull up. Joy hesitantly got out, and Lillian handed her things to her. I approached the buggy and gave Joy a hug.

"Did you have fun?"

"Yes, Mama, we had a big fire, and we played hide and seek. No one could find me two different times."

"She was a good hider, I will say that," Mrs. Post said with a smile.

"Tell your Mama about Matthew," Lillian quickly broke in.

"Matthew burned his finger, but, he's okay."

I looked at Priscilla.

"It was just a small burn...Playing in the fire, you know....nothing serious," Priscilla confirmed.

"Oh, that's too bad, but I'm glad he's okay. I'm glad the weather cooperated for your party. It sounds like the kids had a lot of fun...except Matthew, maybe." I looked up. "Those clouds are furiously rolling in again."

"Yes, and the wind is picking up again as well," Priscilla said. "We thought we'd better get Joy on home before any more storms came along. How's Gerrit today, Natalia?...and Justin?"

"He is much better. I appreciate you asking. As a matter of fact, he's out in the orchard with Justin right now. I'm hoping they've reconciled."

"That is great news," Mrs. Post replied.

"Joy, would you run in and grab a few apples for Mrs. Post and Lillian to take home? They're on the cupboard." Joy handed me her things without hesitation and ran into the house.

"Make sure you have one for each in the family," I hollered.

"Did Gerrit pick apples already?" Priscilla asked, seeming surprised.

"They're the early ones...Don't have a lot of taste, but it seems nice having them anyway," I replied.

Joy returned with a basket of apples. "There's just enough for everyone in your family, and one extra so you can have two," she said, handing the basket to Lillian.

"Thank you, Joy," Mrs. Post replied. "Tell Joy and Mrs. Kappan thank you for the treats, Lillian."

"Thanks," the exuberant Lillian called out.

"Well, we better get on home. That sky isn't looking too good. Hopefully, your father has that tent taken down," Priscilla said, looking at her daughter.

"Thank you for having Joy," I replied.

"Don't thank me, we love having her. I will return your basket promptly," Mrs. Post said as they pulled away.

"I had so much fun," Joy said, as we walked into the house. "We stayed up late and Lillian's brothers told ghost stories about the Phantom of Bitterwood. I didn't even get too scared, Mama, but Lillian did. Lillian's brothers and their two friends said I was much braver than Lillian and even Sarah. The girls had to awaken their mother because they were so frightened. Mrs. Post got mad at Lillian's brothers for scaring us. She made them go inside.

"This morning Mrs. Post made a chocolate cake, and it was so good. She let Lillian and I frost it, and we licked out the bowls. Then Lillian gave me a new package of paper dolls. She bought them just for me. We cut out all their clothes and pretended they lived in the big city...Perhaps New York, perhaps Chicago. It was so much fun. Would you like to see them?"

"I would love to see them," I answered. I laid her stuff on the parlor table and she pulled out a booklet with the paper dolls and their attire inside.

"This is Margo...She's French," Joy apparently had decided. She pulled out another doll. "This is Amanda; Margo's friend. I love this dress she has on."

I gave Joy a hug and listened to her nonstop chatter regarding the fun time she had with Lillian. Her talking became a blur, and I looked at this little girl and thought about leaving tonight. A tear came to my eye, and Joy noticed it at once.

"Please don't cry, Mama," she said softly. "What made you sad?"

"Don't mind me, darling. These tears are tears of joy because that is what you bring to me. That is why you are named the name you are. I want you to know something. I see how happy you are at Lillian's house. How their family loves each other and takes care of each other." I took Joy by the arm. "Joy, look at me. Whatever I do, I just want you to know that I'm doing it for you. Do you understand? Remember how I told you that I had to leave for a while?"

"Mama, must we talk of this stuff again?" Joy seemed irritated.

"Joy, I will send for you. No matter where I am; I will send for you, but you'll have to be patient."

"I asked Lillian's mama about this stuff you say about leaving. She told me not to pay any attention."

"And, do you believe her before you believe me?" I asked.

"I do," Joy answered. "Mama, sometimes you say and do things that scare me so much. I just wish we had a family like Lillian's. I can count on what Mrs. Post says."

I wiped my tears and looked at Joy. "I guess I'm kind of like those Transparent Apples in the orchard. Compared to the other apples they don't have much flavor, but they are the first to ripen, and so we enjoy them for what they are. I know I've never been a very good mother, Joy. I try to be, but it seems that something always gets in the way. I am, however, the only mother you have, so, I'm hoping that you take me for what I am and love me because of it."

"I do love you, Mama," she said. "I will always love you." Joy yawned and stretched. "Could you rock me in the big chair?" Mrs. Post did that with Lillian last night when she was scared. Lillian told me that whenever she is scared her mama rocks her and it takes her fears away. I'm scared right now, Mama, because I don't like you talking about leaving and stuff."

"Then I won't talk of it anymore." I took ahold of Joy's hand and led her to the claw-foot rocking chair. I sat down, put a pillow under my arm and pulled Joy onto my lap. She continued telling me of her time at Lillian's and the hopes she had for the future. I wanted to tell her so much; explain so much, but I had promised her I would be silent. Before long her head began to bob, and soon it lay nestled against my arm, moving back and forth with each motion of the rocker. I stopped rocking. I looked at her angelic face. She slept in peace, and I knew I would remember that priceless expression on her face for all eternity.

Chapter 22

Anticipation

I sat with Joy in the rocker for almost an hour while she slept. Today, more than any day, I treasured being in her presence. She must have had so much fun with her friend Lillian that she was all worn out. Gerrit had come in while I was sitting with Joy and brought me some bread and pork. I should have been hungry after eating only a sour apple for breakfast, but I was too wound up to eat. It was approaching late afternoon, and I could barely keep my composure. I had many things yet to be done before I would meet my beloved tonight. Gerrit was in the study doing bookwork, and I rose quietly, carefully lifting my sleeping daughter. Tenderly I lay her on the floor, placing the pillow I had under my arm beneath her head. Gerrit heard the activity and came into the parlor.

"I can't believe that she stayed sleeping," I whispered looking down at Joy.

Gerrit signaled for me to come into the study. I adjusted the pillow under Joy's head to make sure she was comfortable and followed him to the other room.

"I talked with the Parson. I know you saw us in the orchard," Gerrit said as I went into the study, or library as I called it.

"Yes," I answered.

"I asked for his forgiveness. I told him I had no right." Gerrit spoke very directly.

"That was for the best, Gerrit. And I'm sure he accepted your apology. Am I right?" I questioned.

"He did." Gerrit came closer to me and I shuddered. "You smell of flowers," he said, stroking my hair.

I stepped back.

He put up his arms as if in defense. "I will stay away from you. Don't worry," he stated, looking at me. Slowly, he put down his arms. "I owe you an apology also," he said, coming near and putting his hand on my shoulder.

"You owe me nothing," I said, turning away and thinking of how upset he had gotten finding the letters.

"I told you, I wish to make things better for us. I don't want you to contemplate running away from me any longer. I don't want you to be scared of me. I just want you to think of me as your husband. Natalia, I love you." I wondered if Justin had said something to Gerrit in regards to my plans of leaving. His remarks seemed odd considering the circumstances.

"Please, Sir, I need to go upstairs and finish some things." I so wanted to get out of this conversation; after all, it would be only hours until I would be gone.

"Do as you wish, Natalia. I just wanted to let you know about the Parson, and make you aware of my feelings to you."

"Thank you, Sir," I replied. I scurried upstairs, trying to make sense of what Gerrit had just said to me. I snatched the lilac soap from my windowsill and made sure it had dried out properly. I wrapped it in the wax paper and placed it in my white brocade bag. I noticed that the dark clouds that were so evident when Priscilla Post had dropped Joy off had somewhat dissipated. I was so hoping it wasn't going to rain. I wanted to appear beautiful to Arie when I saw him tonight, and I couldn't look as I wanted if I were soaking wet.

The time seemed to be standing still and I just wanted night to be upon me. I could only think of being with Thomas. The sensations that enveloped my body were incredible, like feelings I'd never had before. Euphoric was the only word to describe them. I felt that I could conquer the world. I sat by my desk and scribbled my name next to Thomas's and then scribbled them both out again. It wouldn't be long.

Joy ended up sleeping a good four hours, and soon it was close to dusk. We had dinner late. Gerrit prepared a simple meal of eggs and ham. Everyone was very quiet as we sat together at the table. I hardly ate a thing. I just wasn't hungry. I was full of anticipation.

"Joy and I will clean up," I said to Gerrit when we were finished.

He looked at me rather peculiarly and then without a word got up from the table and entered his study.

"Mama, you usually run upstairs directly after dinner if you even eat with us at all," Joy said, looking at me. "Most of the time you wish to eat upstairs all alone. I'm glad that we can clean up together. Lillian says she and Sarah always help their Mama. Usually Papa does it by himself. What made you decide to do it tonight?"

"I want to spend as much time with you today as I can," I answered. "I wished all these years I had been different, Joy. I would hope, with all my heart, that you would remember me in a good way if I were gone. Would that be at all possible?"

Joy brought some dishes from the table and set them down in the sink. "Why do you ask me these things, Mama? I don't want to answer them because I think you're going to leave me. I keep thinking of what you said to me. Mrs. Post said to just ignore you when you talk this way. She said that you weren't going anywhere."

I caressed her cheek. "Please, if you can get yourself to do so, please, think of me in a good way. That is all I pray," I said softly.

Not much conversation occurred after that as we finished the dishes. Joy seemed preoccupied and went outside to the porch as soon as she was done drying, and I put the last pieces of china away. After a few moments, she burst back into the house, scaring me and causing me to stumble.

"There is a man out there!" she exclaimed. "I saw him!"

Quickly, upon hearing Joy's comment, Gerrit grabbed his shotgun, and made his way as fast as he could to the kitchen and then out the door.

"Was it Justin?" I asked.

"No," Joy said, looking alarmed and panting for breath. "He's a stranger; I've seen him here before. I've also seen him in town. Why is he at our house, Mama? Do you know this man? Is he the man you cry out for at night?"

Strong shivers shot up my spine, and I hurried to the porch to see for myself. I prayed that the mysterious man would not be caught, for I knew in my heart who he must be.

Gerrit met me at the door as he was coming in. "There is no one out there," he said, shaking his head.

"There was someone there, Papa!" Joy said. "As I got out on the porch, I felt someone watching me. I looked over to the tree ridge and there was a man."

"I think it's nonsense, as usual," Gerrit said loudly. "You seem to see this man quite often. Don't you think it's funny that no one else sees him?" With that, Gerrit returned slowly, still in obvious pain, to the study.

Joy stood there quivering even more after Gerrit's comments.

"I believe you, Joy," I whispered. "I know you're not making up what you see."

"Then, Mama, explain it to me. Why is he at our house? What does this man want from us? I see him, but Papa says there is no evidence of him."

"Then perhaps he is an angel. Perhaps he's been guarding us all along," I answered.

"What do you mean, Mama?" Joy asked.

"There are forces in this world, Joy, that we aren't even aware of. Forces that make one thing happen to offset another. Forces of good...forces of evil. I want you to talk to Parson Peterson about this someday soon. He is a good man. Do you promise me that you will do that?"

"I promise, Mama."

"And I want you to be a very brave little girl from now on. Everything happens for a reason, Joy."

"I always try to be brave, Mama. Parson Peterson also always tells me that." She came over and gave me a hug. "I'm going to go up and play with my dolls now. I'm going to pretend that we are in Chicago or New York or some big city somewhere and are having a grand ball."

"That sounds spectacular," I answered, giving particular notice to my daughter's beautiful face. I had been capturing these mental pictures for several days now. I wanted to remember everything about her until we were reunited.

I knew that what Joy had seen was not a real angel as in cosmic terms. But I did believe that he was my angel, my Thomas, that she had envisioned. Most certainly, he had secretly come by the house to see if I was making plans to meet him tonight. I knew exactly how he felt. I couldn't wait, either! I truly did wonder, however, if he had been guarding us all these years. I also wondered why he had waited so long to come for me. Soon, these questions would all be answered. Night had fallen, and I sat on the porch swing looking at stars shooting in and out from behind the clouds in the heavens. Gerrit had gone to bed, and I hadn't heard from Joy since she had gone upstairs to play. I wondered if Thomas was watching me right now from somewhere beyond my sight, off in the darkness. I turned my lamp down and placed it on the floor in the corner of the porch. I would take it with me on my way to the gazebo tonight.

I walked down the porch steps and picked some blossoms of newly opened hydrangeas. They were white, tinged with pink. I would place them in my hair for Thomas. I hoped they would look lovely with my white dress. As I walked back up the steps, I thought I heard something rustling in the field. I wanted to call out but instead I'd adhere to his instructions and meet him at the stroke of one a.m. at the gazebo. I smiled, looked off into the darkness and entered the house.

All was quiet. I went upstairs. Gerrit's door was shut. I entered Joy's room, and I found her asleep on the rug. She was clasping her porcelain-faced doll tightly in her arms and her paper dolls surrounded her on the floor. She must not have slept at all at Lillian's party to be as tired as she had been today. I was a bit concerned that she would have wanted to stay up late into the night after her long nap, and perhaps hinder me from leaving. I guess that wasn't going to be the case. I put down the delicate flowers that I held in my hand and carefully pulled the doll from her clutches. I placed Joy in her bed. I set the doll next to her. I pulled the sheet over her and gazed at her countenance. She was the true angel that God had given to me. How could I have ever denied that there was a God, with the precious gift He had given me lying right here! I would be sending for her soon. "I promise," I said. I kissed my fingertips and touched them to her forehead. "I love you," I whispered as I picked up my flowers. I quickly departed her room and began to cry.

My room was dark and I lit the lamp inside. I looked around. I would not be seeing this place again after tonight. I wiped the tears from my eyes and laid the flowers on my dresser as I looked at myself through the sullen light. Taking the white dress from the hanger, I laid it on my bed. I took off my other garments and carefully exchanged them for the dress. It fit perfectly! I never remembered having it on before. I took the hair brush from my dresser and began brushing my lengthy locks of black hair. I grabbed the hairpin that Joy loved so much and pulled some of my hair back, fastening it with the pin. In the pulled-back space, I attached the flowers with some smaller pins gracing the flowers all the way to the back of my head.

I turned, looking at myself in the mirror. Something was missing. Quickly, I pulled on the chain of my sapphire necklace, which hung against my bare skin, and let it hang on the outside of my dress. The clasp seemed to be stuck in my hair, and it pinched the back of my neck. I gave it a gentle nudge, freeing it. I looked in the mirror again. The stone glistened even in this delicate light. Perfect, I thought to myself. Now everything is perfect! I didn't know this woman. She looked like a duchess from a wealthy country all ready for a royal ball.

For the first time in ages, I looked happy, and I felt happy! I pinched my cheeks several times, trying to achieve some color, and then glanced again to see how I looked. I was almost ready to meet my soulmate, my true love, my Arie. I untied my everyday shoes and put on some lace-up boots that were off-white in color. They were the fanciest ones I owned, yet I would be comfortable walking in them. I opened my white-drawstring bag in which I had already placed some of my things and pulled out the lilac soap. I unwrapped it and rubbed it against my skin quite a few times until I could smell the scent reflecting on me. I also rubbed it subtly against my neck. I could remember how Thomas would kiss me there and it made me tremble. I wanted to smell good for him tonight. Wrapping it back up, I placed the soap in the bag and pulled the drawstring tight. I had a larger bag in my armoire. I took it out and placed all the other things that I had gotten together in that bag. These supplies would hold me over until I was able to shop at a mercantile for more.

I was ready. I couldn't believe it. I was ready! I knew it was a bit early, but that was fine. My goal was to go early on and sit at the gazebo until Thomas came for me. I couldn't let anything interfere with these plans!

I was especially apprehensive tonight trying to get down the steps without awakening anyone. I noticed that the heels on these boots made a clapping tone as I stepped, so I unlaced them and took them off. My hands were full now as I carried two handbags and my boots down the stairs. I got to the parlor and instead of standing there to see if anyone had awakened, as I usually did, I ran out the door. I couldn't let anyone get in my way tonight. I laid my shoes and other things on the floor of the porch and grabbed the lantern, which I had placed off to the side earlier. I sat on the steps and put my lace-up boots back on. I sighed deeply and grabbed my things. I threw my bags over my shoulder and walked out to the road. The moon was in the crescent stage tonight, but still gave out a nice light. The stars sparkled amongst the clouds. Apparently, and thankfully, it wasn't going to rain.

I stood in the road and gazed up at the house that I had lived in, but never truly called home, and thought of my daughter sleeping upstairs. Would she be okay when she found me gone? I couldn't let myself think of that again. I would be sending for her promptly, and hopefully then I'd be able to give her a normal and fulfilling life. That's all that mattered. I started down the road, keeping the lantern turned off. My new life was now beginning.

With the load I was carrying, I knew it would take me longer than usual to get to the gazebo tonight. I was relying on the chimes from the Baptist church's clock to let me know when one a.m. arrived. Even though the town of LaPier was farther down State Street from the gazebo, I knew from experience that you could hear the clock's chimes when at the gazebo. I looked around. I was finally here! I laid my belongings down and opened my purse, taking out a matchbox that I had placed inside. I lit one of the stick matches and ignited the lantern. It gave out a flash, lighting up the sky and my surroundings. I turned it down to the lowest level, sat on the steps in expectation, and looked to the sky. God, please help me to be doing the right thing, and give me strength, I said to myself.

It seemed I sat there for some time when the chime striking one startled me. My heart raced, I felt faint and I looked around but saw nothing. I climbed the steps, walked around the gazebo, and finally sat on the bench inside. I continued sitting there until finally I heard a voice.

"Natalia," I heard someone say. He must have been standing outside the gazebo, off in the brush.

"I'm here," I replied. "I'm here, Thomas."

"I hoped, with all that's in me, that you would come. I have waited for this day for almost my entire life."

"As have I," I answered. I walked over to the side of the gazebo where I heard his voice. "Please, don't be afraid to let me see you. I love you no matter what you've done, or how you look. I just want to hold you. Please come up here to me."

"We must talk first, Natalia. Then we can be together. We have things to straighten out," he continued.

"Then, please do your talking, so that we can be as one. Please!" I said.

"I have loved you since our times in New York. I've never stopped thinking of you, never! You don't know this Natalia, but I know all of your secrets. It has been so hard for me to know of all these things and know the pain that it has brought to you. I know you inside and out. I know about the rape. I even know the person who did it to you, for I was there. I know who the father of Joy is."

"You were there? What are you talking about?" I said in dismay. "It was Seth Maddison who abused me. I know it was him."

"You are wrong. You are very, very wrong!" he hollered.

"Why have you waited so long to come for me? Why did you keep this from me for all these years?" I couldn't stop asking questions. I couldn't stop wondering what was going on!

"Do you remember when you lived at the Sloans' house and Seth threw the stone at your window and asked you to come outside? He told you he had news about Thomas."

"Yes, of course, I remember," I said. "The news Seth was supposed to be telling me was about you!

"Seth came to tell you something entirely different, Natalia," he continued. "He came to tell you how he felt in his heart about you."

"He came to defile me, that's what he came to do," I screamed. "He wanted nothing more from me!"

"No! Natalia, I was watching the whole thing. I was there!

None of it is how you perceive! You must believe me! As you came outside and passed the barn, I was waiting for you, but apparently Jonah Sloan was also waiting in the shadows."

"Mr. Sloan?" I yelled, alarmed.

"Yes, it was him. He grabbed ahold of you and placed some type of material over your head to cover your eyes."

"No, No!" I yelled.

"Listen...I must tell you this. It's for your own good," he demanded. "He threw you to the ground and gagged you. I thought you had died, for your body became lifeless. It was him. He was the one who raped you, Natalia. It wasn't Seth! Seth would have never done such a thing to you!"

I turned from the edge of the gazebo as panic enraged me. I screamed. Then I screamed louder. "What gives you the right to tell me this? If you watched the entire thing, why didn't you help me?"

"What gives me the right to tell you, is because I know the truth and I can't live having you think it was Seth that did this to you. Why I didn't help you is because I thought Jonah Sloan had killed you, but also because I am a coward. I have been a coward my whole life, but that will change tonight. No longer will I live in this discontent. No longer will I scream the screams of despair. What I say is the truth, and I know that Agatha Sloan knows the truth as well.

"I saw her come out of the house that night. She walked over to the barn, apparently looking for her husband. I assume that Jonah Sloan heard her coming while he was committing the crime. She looked on the ground and spotted him with you. Mr. Sloan was in terror upon having his wife see him, and he quickly fled from you. She knew what had happened, Natalia, but Agatha Sloan did nothing. She put her hands to her face and ran back to the house. As she was running, she saw me. I ran to you and unfastened the fabric from around your head and saw that you were still breathing.

"It was then that Mr. Sloan approached me and started hollering, blaming me for raping you. The children awoke and came outside, and Mrs. Sloan followed them, acting as though it was her first time seeing what had happened. I, of course, had no choice but to run into the woods. I have been running and screaming ever since, Natalia. The authorities were called, from what I understand, but from that time on, Mrs. Sloan denied her husband had done anything. They blamed the rape upon this stranger they had seen. And you must have believed it as well."

I was crying frantically now. "Then, what you're saying, is he, Mr. Sloan, the man who pretended to be my father, is actually the father of my child?" I was in complete denial, and yet thoughts of how Mr. Sloan always wanted to be physically near me invaded my mind. I had thought it was peculiar, and yet I put his behavior aside and pretended he was trying to give me fatherly love. I screamed again, and stomped my feet frantically.

"Natalia, I am not telling you this to upset you. I'm telling you this because I care so deeply. You must, and deserve, to know the truth!"

"Thomas, I just want to see you. Come out to me. Don't hide in the shadows any longer. I need you to hold me! I can't bear this alone!"

"Don't you see, Natalia? That is why Agatha Sloan arranged for you to marry her brother, Gerrit. That is why she always harbored such hatred for you. It tidied the whole mess up. Seth Maddison, although they never knew his name, was blamed for the entire thing."

"I just can't deal with this!"

"I'm not finished...there's more...much more," he continued.

"How much more could there be! How much more can I take?" I exclaimed.

"The night of the murder. Do you remember it?"

"Why must you ask me these things now?" I bellowed.

"Because I must clear a good name and make you aware of the evil that dwells amongst us. I was also there the night of the murder, Natalia."

"I know you were." I answered. "But there was no murder, right? Why didn't you tell me that you survived? I would have never cared how you looked. I just wanted to love you, Thomas."

"Thomas didn't survive, Natalia. Thomas was murdered in cold blood. He was killed by the hands of the very man who raped you."

I screamed again. What was the use of going on if this were true?

"It was Jonah Sloan who killed Thomas," the man confessed. "He ripped him from piece to piece because of his desire for you. Jonah Sloan used to watch you when you'd leave the house in the dark to be with Thomas. I know, for I secretly watched you as well."

I picked up my lantern. I tried to shine it into the bushes and brush to see who I was conversing with. Finally I realized that I may not be in the presence of my beloved. It felt as though a stake had been driven through my heart, and I didn't know where to turn. I set the lantern on the edge of the latticework and turned it up full-force. I stared intently. "Please come out and show your face!" I commanded. At once, I heard something fall. I looked down to find that the lantern had tipped off the edge and kerosene had spilled all over the base of the gazebo. The flame had ignited it.

Immediately the figure I had been conversing with jumped out of the brush and I saw his face. It wasn't my Thomas, my Arie. I kept staring at the man, and then finally realized that it was Seth Maddison! I was helpless; completely helpless! Why was this man here? If Seth was here, then where was Thomas? I finally came to the realization that I hadn't wanted to face. Could what Justin said about Thomas be true? Was Thomas truly dead? I couldn't stop screaming. The flames had now reached around the whole base of the gazebo, and I stood there in shock.

"But why..." I hollered. "Why did you lead me to believe

you were Arie?"

"I never pretended I was someone else," he screeched. "I only let you believe what you wanted, so that I could have the opportunity to talk to you...To make things right."

Seth valiantly tried to douse the flames. He tried to get up the steps, but the inferno was getting higher. "Natalia, you need to jump down," he demanded, but I ignored his pleas. He hurried to the other side. I was glad he couldn't reach me. I just wanted him to stay away! How could I know that what he was telling me was true? He ran around to the other side and frantically began to climb the edge. I watched as the smoke choked him down once again, and he fell into some flaming shrubs. He smothered the flames singeing his clothing as he tried again to climb the gazebo. All seemed to be in slow motion. It was uncanny, for I felt no fear for myself.

Suddenly the Post family appeared along with many other townspeople. I stood on the wooden seats in the gazebo; the highest point. I could see everything as plain as day from up here. The flames roared and people tried to get to me. I could hear them crying JUMP...JUMP! A multitude of them cried these words.

Suddenly, within the smoke and the flames, beautiful prisms appeared. They seemed to be dancing fancifully around me, as though it were a kaleidoscope! I felt for my necklace and remembered the powers it had. Were these the prisms that Thomas had spoken of in the letters? Had they finally appeared to show me the way out of this? I searched frantically for my necklace. It didn't seem to be there! I was helpless without it!

Revelations suddenly overtook me, and I remembered how it had seen the prisms from the sun against the stone of my necklace that had allowed me to travel in time. I was here on an amazing journey to connect with the love of my life. And now, Arie would never find me without my necklace! "Arie," I screamed. "Arie, I'm here!"

Frantically, I began looking on the floor next to me. I

remembered how the clasp had stuck in my hair when I was dressing to come here tonight. Perhaps my necklace had fallen off, but where? I got on my hands and knees and searched through the smoke. I searched and screamed and yelled for Arie until it seemed there was no more breath within me. I couldn't see anymore. Tears streamed from my eyes, and I was suffocating, but I kept searching by patting my hand on the hot floor over and over and over. Please, God, help me to find it, I prayed to myself. Finally my hand came across something! I grabbed it and stood up, coughing non-stop. Quickly I rose to stand on the highest bench again. I tried to take a breath but continued to cough exhaustingly.

I looked in my hand, trying to get just one look through the smoke. My eyes burned. A strong breeze blew in and filtered the air a bit, but the wind also intensified the flames. I brought my hand to my face. Through the opening in the smoke, I could see that I was now holding my necklace again.

Suddenly, it was as though the volume of the world had been turned up. I could hear screaming of people and cries of children that before had seemed to be muted. I looked down below and could see that Joy and Gerrit were there, panicked. I wondered why they were so troubled. I didn't feel that I was in danger, at least not from the fire. Mrs. Post was holding Joy back, and my daughter screamed at the top of her lungs. Gerrit ran through the flames up the collapsing gazebo steps. He looked as though he was a mad man. He almost reached me, but fell back down as the wood broke and buckled in the flames. He screamed tremendously, and I thought he had burned to death, but he rolled out of the rubble and people threw blankets and coats over him to douse the flames. He stood up and tried once more to get up to me, but fell over in what looked like excruciating pain. It seemed that I was numb to it all.

"Papa," Joy screamed and she tried to run over to him. Mrs. Post continued holding her back.

It was then and there that something miraculous happened. The flames, the screams, my gasping for air, it all seemed to cease in my mind as a figure appeared as though fused amongst the kaleidoscope-like prisms in the smoke. He appeared to be an angelic being, a child with eyes of the purest green. I noticed them at once. He reached out to take my hand, and I accepted it. I stood tall and unafraid and was now able to breathe. Then, it was as though all the forces of earth and heaven intermingled and I seemed to be sailing through an ocean of wind, yet all was serene. I could see the people's frantic faces, looking at me. I could see Joy and Mrs. Post. I could see Gerrit rolling on the ground.

Then I looked and noticed a face more pronounced than anyone else's. It was the pure face of evil. It was as though the face of a devil was looking up at me. It was the face I now remembered pouncing on top of me when I was fourteen years of age. It was the face of Mr. Sloan! At that moment, everything was clear, as if God was revealing to me where my true pain had come from. I knew I must forgive Seth Maddison. I knew in my heart that what he told me was true. I frantically searched the ground below the gazebo for Seth and finally spotted him off to the side and alone. He was bent down in tears and looked as though he had been praying. He looked up and screamed at me when he saw that he had my attention, yet I could not hear his pleas. Our eyes and hearts met, right at that moment, and I smiled at him through the smoke and flames. At that point in time, I was certain that he knew without a doubt that I had forgiven him, for he smiled back through his tears. He now seemed contented.

The smoke now bellowed up higher and higher and flames ripped alongside of us. Pieces of the gazebo were falling to the ground. I kept holding tight to the precious child's hand even though I could no longer see his angelic body. All of the things that Justin Peterson had constantly reminded me of in this life came so vividly to mind. I am your child, Lord, I said to myself! I suddenly knew, without a doubt, that the hand that I was holding belonged to a true angel that had finally come to rescue me.

I stopped searching the ground for people's faces as the smoke and flames made it almost impossible to do so anymore. I felt more content and safe than I had ever felt in my life. I screamed no more. It was as though a wet cloud encompassed me and drew all the heartaches from my life. I no longer felt that I was Natalia Kappan, I was now a new being... A new person, a new soul with no more pain. Suddenly, it was hard to breathe again. I gasped. Now, the screams and pleas from the people, the commotion, and everything stopped, as did my heart. The gazebo collapsed, and my life, my history, and my very being were buried in the rubble of this place.

Chapter 23

Rebirth

I awakened in the dead of night, around 2:45. I was screaming, and the nurses and night workers ran in to check on me. Everyone was scurrying to do this or that when they found me to be suddenly responsive. They said that my skin appeared reddened, and I was sweating profusely! Cool towels were brought in and placed on my face. They said I kept screaming a man's name over and over again. It was the only word I was saying that they could make out, for my speech was slurred and disoriented. I knew exactly what name I must have been screaming. I was screaming, Arie, through the flames until I awoke in this place!

I think we've probably all experienced it. Every few years you hear on the news, or read on the Internet, or in a publication, of a remarkable, unbelievable story of a person's recovery after being in a comatose state for many, many years. They finally awaken to a world unfamiliar to them and try to make their way out of this mind-boggling condition.

It is everyone's hope that after so many months, or even years, they become miraculously normal again, both in mind and body. They regain their recognition of loved ones, familiar places, and precious memories and have all physical abilities restored. This, believe it or not, is a story that I can relate to, for they tell me that I was in this comatose state of mind for many years, only to have been reborn into a world I'm trying to make sense of.

I could see from my appearance and I could feel in my heart that I had taken on another body, and perhaps another soul. I kept hearing the staff talking among themselves. They said it was a miracle; almost unheard of, and I assumed they were speaking of me. All was in a frenzy as they ran to call the doctor and my family. One of the workers in this assisted living home, where they told me I had been cared for all these years, stayed with me, holding my hand. How could I tell her that just moments ago my body and soul had had the identity of another woman? How could I explain to her that I lived in another era; another place so far from here? Neither she, nor anyone else would ever believe that the night Natalia Kappan's heart stopped in that brutal fire in the year 1920, was the night that I had apparently come back from a remarkable journey as well.

They told me my name was Emma Barker. I knew my name, and immediately upon the nurse saying it, sadness encompassed me as I remembered my son Anthony's death. Everything suddenly seemed intermingled. I remembered my life here to some extent, but I also longed for parts of the life I had encountered just hours ago. Yet, in reality, a century had passed. How did this all take place? If I was now Emma Barker, what had become of Natalia Kappan? Did she just cease to exist, or was she given the chance to live her life in a whole new beginning as well? Most of all, my heart ached for my little Joy. What had become of her?

I began to cry, and the woman who held my hand asked what was wrong. I told her with words that were long and drawn out, that I feared someone had died in a fire tonight, and I didn't know how to find the place where it happened. I didn't know how to help the people who loved the woman who had perished. It was very apparent that she could not understand my garbled words. I don't think she knew what to say to me. She changed the subject promptly and told me not to worry, for I had been through a lot.

I was asked by some of the workers if I remembered my family. I tried to tell them that I had three children, but that one had been taken from me when he was a child. My speech seemed clear enough, so I wondered why they couldn't understand what I was saying. They all seemed to dismiss my statements. They told me that my family visited me regularly, especially my son. Apparently he came the most to visit, especially when my husband was out of town. In fact, as the nurses informed me, he had been here reading to me earlier this night.

I had my vitals taken and much fuss was made over me for it seemed a good hour. My temperature was highly elevated which they successfully brought down. Finally, I heard talking in the hall and Daniel appeared in the doorway. I recognized him at once. He looked the same as he did right before I went to LaPier. He ran to me and hugged me and acted as though he had seen a ghost. Tears streamed down his cheeks, and he couldn't stop looking into my eyes.

"You've finally come back to me," he said, kissing my cheek. Then, he asked me many questions. I tried my best to answer, but just as it had been with the nurses, my words were slurred and I had to think so hard for the answers. I wondered if I was making any sense.

"Just rest," Daniel said. "The children will be here soon."

I wasn't able to rest. A woman, who I found was my doctor and another associate, gave me quite an extensive evaluation. They told me that what I had experienced was extraordinary, and that I was among only a handful of people who had encountered a "waking up" as I had. They seemed thrilled and just kept smiling at me.

"I'll bet you're eager to see your children," my doctor said. "They have grown to be fine young adults. Don't be surprised if it's hard for you to recognize them. No one expects you to adapt to everything right away. And your speech, too, Emma...take your time trying to talk. Your speech may be slurred for a while. Your brain needs time to catch up with your thoughts and actions."

Why did she talk of my children this way? I was very aware that they were fine young adults. I wondered what she was referring to. She spoke as though I hadn't seen them in some time, and I had just said goodbye to both Libby and Colin before they left on their trips for the summer. After a while, the doctors stopped fussing with me and gave their health analysis to both my husband and me.

"After giving you a short evaluation," one of the doctors began, "it is our hope that you're going to be fine, Emma," the doctors smiled, looking at both Daniel and me. "It will take a lot of work and time; speech therapy, physical therapy, getting your muscle tone back, but you're a fighter, Emma. And, please don't dismiss counseling if you need it. You have been gone from us for a long time. Things certainly change, and you may need some help in dealing with that. We'll leave you alone with your family now. If you have any questions or concerns, don't hesitate to press the call button." My doctor's associate pointed out where it was. Daniel thanked them, and they gave him a hug.

I wanted to walk and use my arms and hands so badly. I couldn't understand why my limbs seemed like rubber, unable to hold me up. It was as though I had forgotten how to use them. Everything was boggled up in my mind. I looked at the clock. It was still very early morning, almost dawn of a new day, but it didn't matter. Time was oblivious to me.

Daniel continued to stare at me, and it made me uncomfortable. Did I look so hideous after lying here for so long? I hadn't been able to look at my face in a mirror, although I had semi inspected my body. I'm sure when I did see my face, I would no longer be as young and lovely as I remembered.

Finally, some commotion in the hallway broke the silence. Daniel got up and opened the door a crack. "Emma, you have company," he said excitedly. "Are you ready to see the kids?"

I was tired and weak, but I smiled. "Yes."

Daniel motioned them in, and soon I saw Libby and Colin, and someone who appeared to be a friend of theirs, come into the room. They all appeared surprised, overwhelmed and a bit apprehensive. But I could also sense that the room was filled with love and sweet emotion. They quickly came over to me. Even the friend approached; in fact, he was the first to come near me. I looked at him, and I looked at him again. He was so very familiar, and yet unknown to me. His eyes... his beautiful green eyes! I shuddered and felt even weaker. It couldn't be! I looked at his eyes again and slowly tried to motion for him to back up. I wanted to inspect him further. I trembled, put my head down, and sobbed. I realized this wasn't just a friend of my children's!

"Mother, it's me, Anthony," he spoke, as he again moved close to me and cradled my head in his hands. "I know it's been a long time. You've been asleep, Mother, for so long, but I've been with you so much! We've all been with you so much. Do you remember anything? Did you hear me reading to you tonight?"

I looked up. "Anthony!" I whispered, although I wondered if what I said was understandable. I couldn't stop staring. "My Anthony." I shouted his name this time and tried to raise my hand to touch his hand, which was still holding my face. "I thought I had lost you forever! It was you, as a child, in the prismed fire at the gazebo, whose hand I held, wasn't it? All of the things that took place. They all happened so that you could live! Now I understand!" I wept. To me, I was saying these words so plainly, yet I wondered if they were coming out in clarity.

Anthony looked at his father as if wanting help in understanding what I had said. By the emotions on my face, I'm sure he could tell that I was speaking from my heart.

"It's okay, Mom. Don't try to talk right now; just rest," my beautiful daughter Libby interjected, handing me a tissue.

I just couldn't stop staring at Anthony, and I wouldn't let

go of his hand even when Libby and Colin bent down to comfort me.

We sat in that room, in the dead of night, trying to catch up on so many things. I was trying hard to understand, for it was as though the past life I had experienced here with Daniel and the kids, preceding Anthony's accident, had now never taken place as I remembered. That terrible, unbelievable moment in our lives when we had lost Anthony had been erased! But what had taken this tragedy's place was that I had fallen into a deep sleep for apparently many, many years! I had never divorced Daniel, either. The kids laughed when I asked that question. I guess there would have been no reason to, for I always believed it was Anthony's death that had drawn us apart. Everything indeed had changed!

"So, how long has it been?" I asked, trying to stretch and look at the kids. "How long have I been in a coma?" I had to repeat myself before they finally realized what I was asking. I tried to raise my hand to my hair; it felt kinky and curly. I no more had the smooth, black strands that I was used to brushing out.

Daniel cleared his throat. "It would have been going on 16 years," he answered. He sighed, putting his hand on my arm, trying not to disturb my fragile body. "It's a miracle, Em."

16 years! How could it be, I thought to myself? The kids and Daniel kept talking, but it all became a blur as I blocked out their words and sat there trying to contemplate the last 16 years of my life. I had not been in a coma. I knew better. I had been living in the early 1900s! I had been living in misery, but I had been living! Presently, I interrupted everyone.

"Please...I don't recall what happened to me," I said, trying to speak very, very slowly this time. I looked at Daniel and then at each of the children. "What made this happen to me 16 years ago?" They seemed to be getting better in recognizing my speech.

"You don't remember, Em?" Daniel said, seeming to understand. "You don't remember any of it?"

"No, it's completely blocked from my mind."

It was as though I had very sticky glue in my mouth, making me unable to unstick my tongue from the roof of my mouth. Apparently, even the muscles in my tongue were not working right from all the years I was mute. With each word I said, it was a challenge to both speak and use my mind to know what the correct word should be to get my point across!

"Your doctors told us that if you came to it wouldn't be uncommon for you to have forgotten a lot of things. Don't worry about it, Em. We'll refresh your memory whenever you need." Daniel sighed and smiled. "Oh, where do I begin?" He scratched his head. "Are you sure you're up to hearing all of this?"

I gave out a very drawn-out, "Yeaaaasss."

Daniel sat on the bed, next to Libby, and began. "We were on a perch fishing trip on the big lake," he started the recollections. "The kids were young, and you had refused to let me take the kids out on the charter boat without you. You had decided to come along. I guess you were there to supervise because, God knows, you never liked fishing." Daniel appeared to be joking a bit.

Anthony adamantly interrupted, "You came with us because of that letter that Grandmother saved. That's exactly why you wouldn't let dad take us out alone."

"Perhaps that was the reason," Daniel agreed. "We've talked about that mysterious letter so many times. I don't think your mother remembers that anyway, do you, Em?"

I shook my head as best I could. What letter, I thought to myself. I hadn't a clue what they were talking about.

"Anyway, we were already out on the lake when the wind picked up that day," Daniel continued. "You were being very protective of the kids with the waves as they were. We had quite a perch-catch going on, and everyone was having fun. All was fine, except for the weather."

"We were on Lake Michigan, weren't we?" I questioned two or three times before they could understand.

"Yes, Em, Lake Michigan," Daniel confirmed. "You always were in wonderment of its notorious undertow and all the shipwrecks that occurred there. It is a lake to be respected."

"So, what happened next?" I asked even more slowly.

"Mom, don't you remember what happened to me?" Anthony inquired. "You saved my life that day!"

What I remembered couldn't possibly be true, I thought to myself. I tried to shake my head, no.

Daniel continued, "Anthony, of course, was having the most fun that day. Colin and Libby really didn't do much fishing. They were still so young and had more fun playing in the boat with you, Em. But Anthony and I kept pulling in the perch that day. They were really biting. All was fine until that terrible moment occurred. I had left you guys for only a couple of minutes to go down into the boat to get more bait. I wasn't there to help Anthony with the net. I've prayed so many times that I would have been. The accident happened so suddenly, Em. Anthony was all excited. He had a big fish on this time. He got it up to the edge of the boat with no problem, or so it seemed. He leaned over the railing to see what was on his line. He lost balance and began to fall overboard. Everyone panicked, and you ran over to him at once. You hoisted yourself over the railing, grabbing onto one of his legs and tossed him back into the boat. As this was happening, his rod cracked in half and the special reel that your father had given to him started to fall into the water. You kept trying to reach for it.

"By that time, some of the crew and I got near to you, but it was too late. You tumbled into the water, Em, hitting your head badly on the side of the boat. Thank God, you were wearing a life vest because you were knocked unconscious. The waves were rough, and the water was cold and crashed around you. The waves and wind pulled you out into the lake. I dove in and tried to get to you, but I kept being pulled under despite my life vest, just as you were. As the waves crashed against my face, all I could see was your head bobbing in the water far ahead of me. Finally, the crew got to me and then, after some time, they got to your lifeless body as well. They got us both back into the boat. We all feared you were dead."

"It was horrible, Mom," Colin commented, reaching out to hold my hand. "I was so small, yet I still remember that day!"

I lay there listening to this new chapter in the book of my life that I had never heard before, and I trembled.

"Your body was lifeless, but you still had a pulse," Daniel continued, trying to hold back the tears. "Paramedics and an ambulance awaited us on the dock. You were rushed to the hospital. Their prognosis was that you had been without oxygen for some time, had inhaled a lot of water and had a concussion. They told me that they doubted you'd survive.

"The kids and I began praying along with so many who had heard of our plight. We never gave up hope. They told us that the next few days were crucial to see what the future would hold. You were never put on a respirator. You were able to breathe on your own, but you were in a coma, Em, and you had no signs of coming out of it."

I lay there in amazement, listening to the accounts of what had happened to me. How could I thank God enough for changing the events in my lifetime? He gave my son, Anthony, back to me, and kept me alive also.

I lay there the rest of that early morning reliving through the words of my husband, and children, the lives they had led for the last 16 years. I tried to have no regrets for what had happened. How could I? Anthony was now alive! And even though my body apparently lay there helpless on that bed for numerous years, I knew, without a doubt, that my soul had experienced another lifetime and changed the events of my family's lives and possibly history itself!

Chapter 24

Bittersweet

fter almost five months of vigorous physical therapy sessions, psychological evaluations and you name what else, I was finally trying to get on with my life. Daniel had raised the children wonderfully, and they seemed to be well-adjusted and beautiful. I was so proud of each of them. I tried not to show partiality to Anthony, but I constantly wanted to be with him and talk with him. It certainly wasn't because I loved him more than Colin or Libby. How could I explain it? I had already raised Colin and Libby once. Perhaps it was only in my subconscious, or in my coma-laced dreams, as everyone had told me, but I was sure I had raised them. Anthony, however, had been taken from me, and now I was given a second chance!

My relationship with Daniel was totally different as well. Libby confided in me that her dad had never been the same after the accident. He had blamed himself, all these years, for what happened, even though it wasn't his fault. When he wasn't out of town on business, he had been by my side every chance he could. He had never lost hope or strayed from me in our relationship. Now that I was back at home, I was falling in love with Daniel all over again. Even though I had had to travel to another century and back, be it a fantasy within my mind or be it true, I had finally found what I was searching for; my true love, my soul mate! He had been there all along.

Despite my accident and everything our family had been through, Daniel's estate business had thrived. He had put his heart and soul into it after the accident. It had become a cause for living for him, secondary only to the children, of course. Daniel decided, however, to take a leave of absence from it all so we could spend some long-awaited time together. Peter, our business associate and longtime friend, and his wife, Marcy, would be taking over for us. Of course, I made Daniel tell me the entire story of how Peter and Marcy met. Apparently they had married many years ago and had a beautiful family. I was so happy for Peter. He never deserved being alone in this world. Knowing Peter was happy and loved tamed any thoughts I may have had about him, and I realized our relationship had always been purely platonic, at least this time around.

For these last months I had done so much searching for answers. I knew in my heart what had happened to me. I felt it was true, but there was no way to confirm anything. I was told by more than one renowned psychologist that sometimes during a long comatose state, dreams can take place and take precedence in our subconscious. Perhaps I did dream everything up. I knew that I should believe that in order to concentrate on my life, here and now, but I still struggled.

I refused to take Daniel's word for it, but after doing my own research, I confirmed that there had never been an estate purchased by Daniel in LaPier, Indiana. If there had never been an estate, then there never was a necklace or letters... and, well...that was beside the point, for I knew better; at least I thought I did. Despite all the advice I was given, I was not ready to give up my search yet.

After my muscles had regained much strength and I was able to walk pretty much on my own, I told Daniel that I wanted to make a trip to the little town of LaPier, Indiana, as soon as possible. I also told him that I wanted to go alone. I didn't know it at the time, but it would be the first of two trips

I'd make back there within a year's time. Daniel wanted to go with me, especially after taking the leave of absence from the business, but I was adamant in making this journey by myself. Nonetheless, I was surprised that Daniel never questioned my judgment, or told me that I shouldn't go. I truly believe, after telling him so many stories about the early 1900s, that he also thought I had made a remarkable journey, although he believed that it all happened in my mind. I think he thought it would be a good healing process for me to get it all out of my system. So he encouraged me to go, and I hurriedly made my plans.

It was hard to leave each other; perhaps harder for Daniel it seemed, as I drove out of the driveway and begun my journey. It was as though it was yesterday as I turned off the highway onto County Road 312. I continued driving anticipating the park just ahead. Bitterwood Commons, I said softly, taking a breath. Once again, I observed everything about this place from the window of my car. Directly ahead, a decorative wrought-iron fence caught my vision. I turned the corner and entered the park passing two old stone towers on each side. There was a sign on one of the towers. I squinted to make it out. What did it say? I backed up to read it again. The sign read: Bittersweet Commons is a Community Park. I shivered contemplating the change in the park's name. I couldn't help but stare at the confusing plaque. After a few minutes I proceeded.

It felt as though this was the first sign to me that things were not as they were supposed to be in my so-called dreams. However, Bittersweet Commons was very similar to Bitterwood Commons! How could I have made this up when I supposedly had never been here before? I regained my composure and told myself to settle down. After all, it was only the name of a park! Still, where had the name Bitterwood Commons gone? And why was it changed? I tried to focus on the gazebo, which would be just ahead. When I parked there, I would have to stop and get out. That was very apparent to me. I would have to revisit that place! Of that I was certain!

I continued driving through the park. I passed the area where I was sure that the gazebo stood. I searched and looked, but it was nowhere to be found. I kept driving and before I knew it, I was on the other side of the park. The gazebo, where had it gone? I turned around and searched again; this time driving more slowly. "It's gotta be here," I declared out loud. But, it wasn't. My stomach felt so strange, and yet I couldn't believe how familiar this place was to me.

I continued driving out of the park onto State Street, now searching for the homes that would be recognizable to me. I needed to see the house where I lived with Joy and Gerrit, and also see Justin's house.

I drove down State Street and my heart pounded as I approached the area. I stopped the car and stared out the window. There was no longer a home where Justin lived; no evidence of one ever being there. The house that I had remembered so well, that I had lived in as Natalia Kappan, still stood straight and semi-well kept. I looked up to the window that had once been the eye to my room. It had been the very place where I looked out on the world for so many days, perhaps even years.

I parked the car, turned it off, and hesitantly yet excitedly, got out. I opened the back door and retrieved my cane. They told me I was doing amazingly well physically; however, at times my legs felt incapable of holding me up. I made a pledge to myself that someday I'd be able to walk without this crutch, but I was thankful for it now. I stood in the yard and closed my eyes. The memories were incredible! They were overwhelming, and they were real! This was not just a figment of my imagination. I had been here. I had lived here! I looked upstairs, once again, to the window where my room used to be, and I began to cry. I need to know about this house, and I need to know about it NOW, I whispered to myself as I quickly approached the door and knocked.

An elderly gentleman answered.

"Hello," I said through the screen door, wiping tears from my eyes.

"Is everything, okay, ma'am?" he asked as he noticed my dribbling, red eyes.

"Oh, yes," I answered, continuing to wipe my face. "My allergies are killing me!" I sniffed, trying to brush off his question with a smile. "I was wondering if you could help me. You see, I'm looking for a family who used to live in your house, or, I should say, I'm seeking any information about them."

"Oh...?" he said, looking amused.

"Yes, the mother's name was Natalia Kappan. She lived here in the early 1900s."

"The 1900s, huh? ...A long time ago. You must be mistaken though, ma'am. This house has been in the Kappan family; you're right about that, since it was built. But there was never a Natalia Kappan that I knew of."

I shivered, for how would I have ever dreamt up these places that existed, or these names? I just had to figure this out! "Was there a Gerrit Kappan?" I asked.

The old gentleman looked surprised. "Yes, he was my uncle down the line. The originator of this house, I do believe."

"And his wife...what happened to her?" I questioned, looking into his eyes.

He looked even more surprised. "Gerrit never married. He lived here alone...left the house and land to my father."

"But he had a child. Didn't he have a child? A child named Joy?" I must have sounded quite demanding.

The old man laughed. "If he did, it would have been news to everyone."

"What about his sister?" I continued probing. "He had a sister named Agatha...Agatha Sloan. Do you know of her and her family?"

"Oh, yes. Agatha married Jonah Sloan. They are, or I should say were, relatives of mine. Their family members still farm the land down on Engle Road there. They were, and are good people, quite involved in the community and the church. Agatha never turned away anyone in need from what I've heard. That family even took in one of those orphan children back in those early years from New York City. That was back when people were pretty lacking and hardly able to scratch up enough food for their own plates."

I began to shake. "The orphan...what was her name? What became of her?"

"Oh, the orphan wasn't a she. His name was Earl. He was a boy. I don't believe he ever took on the Sloan name. As I remember, he wanted to keep his own last name, but I can't recall what it was. But now that you mention it, they were expecting an orphan girl at one time. It was the talk of LaPier as to what happened. As the story goes, they went to meet her one day at the depot, but no child arrived. After some days, they got a telegram stating that a young pastor appeared unexpectedly at the orphanage house in New York City where the child was being housed. Apparently the pastor was seeking his younger brother, who was also a friend of this girl's. The girl, the pastor's brother and another boy, who was also their friend, were taken in by the minister.

"I don't know any more details of the girl, but it was only a few days after that that the boy arrived, and then a few days after that when the accident occurred. I remember hearing all of this from my father many times. I guess you don't forget stories of accidents like this."

"The accident?" I questioned. "Please tell me what occurred."

"Yeah, it was bad. Jonah Sloan, who was married to Agatha, had a farming accident down by Bog Hollow. They say the wagon's brakes failed. There was absolutely no explanation for it. If you knew Jonah, he kept all his equipment in tip-top shape. It had been parked on a hill and rolled on top of him while he was pulling out some stumps. They say it was almost like someone pushed the wagon right on down. He was killed pretty gruesomely. It was the boy who found him; the orphan child."

I stood there in utter dismay, trying to put all the pieces together. The sequence of these lives had changed so drastically. Could it be that through all of Natalia's time travels that she had made everything right? Could it be that Justin had found the three of them, Natalia, Thomas and Seth, before everything transpired? Could it be that I was somehow responsible for these changes? That the power of the necklace had permitted Natalia Kappan, Joy or perhaps even Thomas or Justin Peterson, through the course of time, to travel and change events in this world forever?

Suddenly I gasped, realizing something, If Jonah Sloan died, then I could never have been raped by him, either. I was elated, then surprisingly saddened. If I wasn't raped, then Joy had never been conceived or born, unless perhaps Joy was Thomas' child! Thomas and I, or I should say Thomas and Natalia, had only been intimately together one time. It was only for a brief second until I put a stop to our young passions that had obviously gotten out of control. It was almost impossible that I could have become with child from that one time... wasn't it?

In disbelief, I looked at the man by the door. What he told me couldn't be true. "Sir, this may sound strange, but I know that an orphan girl-child came to live with the Sloans." This man had to have been mistaken. I remembered it all so clearly. Why was he telling me the wrong story?

"You can think what you must, but I am certain that the child who was sent here was a boy named Earl. He ended up marrying one of the ladies right here from LaPier." He continued adamantly, "No,...the girl-child never arrived."

I, of all people, knew better. Joy had been born. Joy was Natalia's daughter. She had to have been born, hadn't she? I again became agonizingly confused. I missed that child so very much! I had prayed in my 'heart of hearts' that Joy had been given the opportunity to live her life, and now I blamed myself, to some degree, for perhaps not giving her that chance.

Had I taken on Natalia's body and changed the course of things so drastically that Joy was void from existence? I couldn't let myself think that; instead, I had to be glad that Jonah Sloan's life had been snuffed out, hopefully, before he was able to do harm to anyone like he had done to me. Perhaps, everything did change, and Agatha Sloan had turned out to be a loving woman without that evil man by her side, just as the man was telling me.

I turned back to the man behind the screen door. "And what, Sir...What happened to Gerrit?"

"Gerrit Kappan? From what I understand, he took over the mill after Jonah Sloan died. He sold it when he was old and lived like a miser right here in this very house up till the time of his death. He lived to be an old man. He's buried over in Bittersweet Cemetery."

He opened the door a little bit. "You certainly are asking me a lot of questions. ...Not sure of your intentions, but I suppose I should be attending to some things in the house now."

I didn't want to leave, but I could tell that the old man was becoming jittery with my constant badgering of details.

"Just one more thing, please," I said, smiling anxiously. "I also knew a family here named the Posts. They used to live on the other side of Bitterwood Commons, just down the road from here."

The man gave me a funny look.

"You mean Bittersweet Commons," he chuckled.

"Yes, I suppose I do...I'm sorry," I answered, shaking my head. "Anyway, this family, they lived on State Street right across from the park and the gazebo."

"That's downright impossible, Ma'am," he stated. "There is no gazebo in the park. The only gazebo we have is the one on the edge of town."

"But it burned," I insisted. "It burned didn't it? Didn't the town have to rebuild it? Perhaps it wasn't rebuilt in Bittersweet Park, but it must have been rebuilt somewhere, wasn't it?"

He chuckled again. "Not that I know of, and that's something I would definitely know. No, the old gazebo is right where it's always been. It's a really old structure. It's a historic structure. It has a sign on it stating when it was built and all. They keep it well preserved as a monument of our town's history. No...it's still there." He cleared his throat. "As far as this Post family that you're asking about: I know everyone around these parts. I'm not aware of any Posts living on State Street, especially not just down the road from here. They could've lived there in the past though, I suppose."

"It's a big yellow house with brick pillars that went across the entire front porch," I said. "There were flower boxes with geraniums that were well taken care of, freshly painted lawn chairs, and toys strewn in the yard. It was such a happy place to visit. You must know of it?"

"A doctor that runs the clinic in LaPier and his family moved into the house that's across from the park many years ago," the man continued. "They had the whole place gutted out and built on a large addition. It does have the brick pillars, but it's a blue/gray house, not yellow. How long ago are you talking, ma'am, that these Posts lived there when the house was yellow?"

"It would have been in that same time period; right around 1920."

He gave another laugh. "It sounds as though you visited that house yourself in that time period. How did you know it was such a happy place?"

I looked sheepishly at the man. "I knew a woman very well who became acquainted with and loved these people. Please forgive me for asking so many questions. I should have gone by the Post house myself instead of cutting through the park."

"Well, you can still ride past that house if you wish; it ain't goin' anywhere. Now, if you would excuse me, I have some eggs boiling on the stove. Probably, rock-hard-boiled by now." I could tell he was again becoming annoyed at my numerous questions.

"I'm sorry to have taken up so much of your time," I apologized. "Thank you so much for answering so many of my inquiries."

"It's a little strange to have someone knock on your door and ask all these things," he admitted. "A little frightening this day and age. You should be glad that you're a pretty woman and not a burly man, or I may not have been so forthcoming with answers." He gave another laugh.

"Please know I wasn't trying to pry or interfere with your business," I answered. "But before I leave, I must ask permission of you to return here if I have more questions?"

"Like I said, that was a long, long time ago. I'm not sure I can answer everything that you're wondering about, but I suppose I can try and help you if you need it," he answered hesitantly.

"Thank you again," I said, turning back to look at the house and all its surroundings. "Good day, Sir."

The man shut the door, shutting out my link to the past.

I put my cane in the back seat of my car and started it up. There was one more place I needed to visit this day. It was a place that seemed to be calling out for me. I drove west of town and began looking for the sign. I wasn't sure if the nursing home would still be there. I guess any change from the past could have affected the outcome of anything. As I approached the entrance, I was relieved to see the sign for Pinewood Manor. This was the place where I had spoken with Lillian Post in her elderly days. My faint hope was that she was still here. I parked the car and proceeded to the entrance. It was deja vu as I approached the front desk. I wanted to go directly down to room 124, but I stopped. Lillian Post was very likely not to be here. She was probably deceased by now, or who knows what the changes in the past had created in her life cycle.

"Can I help you?" a woman at the counter asked. She was a different woman than the one who had helped me here before.

"I'm here to speak with a Lillian Post. I'm in hopes that

she's a resident here. Could she perhaps be in room 124?" I asked.

"No, she's definitely not in room 124. We have an elderly gentleman who resides in that room. Who did you say you're looking for?" She picked up a stack of stapled papers and started going through them. "I'm sorry; I've only been here for a few weeks. I'm still not familiar with all the residents."

"Her name is Lillian Post," I said anxiously. "She'd have to be a very elderly woman. That's all I can tell you."

"I'm sorry, there's no one here by that name."

I felt terribly downhearted and paused, having the distinct feeling that she was indeed here and that I was about to miss her.

"Thank you," I said as I began to slowly walk away. I had almost reached the door when something came to me. I turned around and went back to the desk. "Is there any resident here with the first name of Lillian? Perhaps the last name is different. She would have a small birthmark on her face. She is a dear, dear friend of mine."

The receptionist's face suddenly lit up. "Oh, you mean Lillian DeCopla. She just turned 100 this year. She is actually in room 141."

I closed my eyes and sighed, smiling ear to ear. "Can I see her?" I asked expectantly.

"Certainly, Lillian will tell you if she's had too much entertaining." The woman laughed. "She's very outspoken."

"She always has been!" I replied. I wanted to run down the hallway, but I made my way slowly with my cane, trying to keep my composure. Could this actually be the Lillian Post I knew, or would I find a stranger? I entered room 141. There she sat in a wheelchair; her hair braided and wound on top of her head.

"Do you remember me?" I asked, as I entered the room.

She looked as though she recognized me immediately, but then kept staring and replied, "I'm sorry, my dear; at first, I thought you looked familiar, but I can't seem to place how I know you." She still had that burly, firm-toned voice that was unexpected.

"My name is Emma Barker." I put out my hand and gently took hers in mine. "I visited you not long ago. I brought some letters from the past for you to read. You remembered my necklace at the time. It was a very unusual sapphire one. The stone was orange."

She squinted at me. "I'm sorry, my dear, I don't seem to remember our visit. I know you will think differently because of my age, but I don't forget things too regularly, and I'm very proud of that!"

"No, no, please, pardon my ignorance," I said. "I just recovered from an illness several months ago and am trying to piece everything in my life back together. I actually was a friend of Jill Vandenberg. You know her, right?"

She pondered for what seemed to be a very long moment. "No, I can't say that I do know anyone by that name. I'm sorry. Am I supposed to know this Jill?"

"I was certainly hoping that you did, Mrs. Post," I answered.

"Oh, darling, are you sure you don't have me confused with someone else? My maiden name was indeed Post, but I have been a DeCopla for years and years. Perhaps there was another Lillian Post that you were looking for? Perhaps she knew this Jill Vandenberg?"

"You used to live in the big yellow house, didn't you?" I questioned. "The house with the pillars and the flower boxes?"

"Yes, how did you know that? My mother couldn't stay there anymore after a sad event happened in our family. We moved across town but yes, I did live in that house. I loved it there. I always thought of it as my home."

"Then I do believe that you are the Lillian that I've come in search of," I affirmed.

She looked at me with an expressionless face.

"I have one more thing to ask you, Lillian. Did you know

a woman named Natalia Kappan? Please, think really hard." I sat on the edge of the chair, awaiting her response.

She seemed to be pondering that name for several moments, not able to respond. Then, finally, she answered. "No, ...no, I don't believe so." She acted a bit confused as if she wanted to answer yes. "Of course I knew a Gerrit Kappan," she said. "He was a bachelor, never married. He owned the mill in LaPier way back when. As a matter of fact, my husband was sort of related to him; you might say, although they were not close in the least. The Sloan family adopted, well, I should say, took my husband in just before Jonah Sloan was killed in an accident. Gerrit Kappan was Agatha Sloan's brother and Agatha Sloan was my husband's adoptive mother. She was a good woman."

"So you married?" I asked in amazement.

"Oh, yes. Why do you sound so surprised? I was really quite lovely in my day." She gave a hearty laugh.

"Oh, I meant nothing by that comment. I know you were lovely. Please, I'm sorry I said that."

"Well, there's no way you could have known how lovely I was. That was far before your time." She gave another laugh, "Oh, never mind, I didn't take your comment in a bad way. I will assure you of that." Lillian continued laughing. "It was love at first sight for me as far as my husband goes. I remember the day when my mother told me that a boy was being sent here to live with the Sloans. It had been the second time that the Sloans had applied for a child from an orphanage in New York City. The first child they were supposed to receive never showed up, so my family went along for moral support, just in case the second child didn't arrive. We were all at the depot when the train stopped. I saw him immediately when he got off. His name was Earl, and crazy as it may sound at that age, it was love at first sight for me. We were inseparable from the start and married as soon as it was permissible for us age-wise. He ended up being a writer, but not the kind he dreamed of being. He wrote manuals for various mechanical products, but his real love was writing poetry. He wrote me some of the sweetest poetry imaginable! We were married over 60 wonderful years."

"You always wished you had been wooed by poetry," I answered, remembering how she had told me that she loved poetry after reading my letters. "I guess your wish came true."

She gave me a very peculiar look. "Now, how would you know that?"

"Oh, I'm sorry, I was just imagining. I'm a hopeless romantic. I remember your family well," I continued. "I mean, I heard about them from the Kappan family." The conversation was becoming very awkward.

"So, that is why you're here?" Lillian questioned. "You were friends with the Kappans?"

"Yes, with someone who knew Gerrit Kappan very well," I responded.

"I see," Lillian said.

"Could I ask you whatever happened to your sister, Sarah, and your brothers?" I continued probing.

"You are very well informed, aren't you?" Lillian said, clearing her throat. "No, I don't mind you asking. Unfortunately, I am the only one of my siblings remaining. They have all passed on to better things. You must mean my sister Verda, however, don't you? Sarah died of rheumatic fever when she was very young. It was before her teen years. That's the reason my family left the house on State St. There were too many memories of Sarah there. My mother couldn't take it. My brothers all had long lives, and I just lost my sister, Verda, two years ago. Hopefully, we have all left legacies through our children. All of us, that is, except for Sarah, who was never given that chance."

"Your sister Verda...Was she your younger sister? Did she have a doll that was sent to her from an aunt in Europe? The doll's name was Margaret, wasn't it?"

"How would you know that, my dear? If I didn't know better, I would have guessed you knew us from being right there when we were children." She now looked at me as if amazed and paused for a time. "In answer to your question, yes, Verda did have a doll named Margaret. I had forgotten about Margaret! It was given to her right after she recovered from a long illness. As a matter of fact, my mother and father didn't expect she'd live. And, you haven't yet answered me. How do you explain knowing this?"

At first, I didn't know how to respond. After all, I couldn't tell her that I knew Joy or Natalia Kappan. They didn't exist as far as this woman was concerned. At least they didn't exist in the world that she now knew. "I told you," I began. "I was a friend of someone who knew Gerrit Kappan."

"I'm just amazed how anyone would know the things you tell me besides someone in our immediate family. I guess people talk more than we know, but, it was such a very long time ago. Why is this your concern?"

I could tell that Lillian was becoming a little restless with me. I needed to be careful what I said. "I've come to believe that time is a matter of the mind, Lillian, and not entirely a matter of the body."

She again looked at me rather peculiarly. "I must say you fascinate me, dear child. You've brought me back to years ago. It's almost as though I know you, in a very strange way."

It was becoming harder for me to answer. "I suppose I've imposed on you long enough," I stated. "I should be going." I went over to the old woman and kissed her on the cheek.

"I just have such an uncanny feeling about you, my dear, Ms. Emma Barker. It's like we truly were together sometime in the past...friends, perhaps? But that's silly isn't it; taking into account our age differences?"

I smiled, wanting to say so many things. Should I continue with my stories, hoping something I would say would rekindle her memory? Was it even possible for her to remember if time and space had changed? I was beginning to think it wasn't. I took her hand in mine. "I guess you never know when a life passes someone else's. Perhaps we forget due to forces unbeknown to us." I looked at her. "Oh, never mind. I suppose it is silly." I smiled tenderly again at the old woman, let go of her hand and politely thanked her for the visit.

"Come again, my dear," she suggested. "I somehow feel akin to you."

"I hope I can," I answered.

I wanted to ask her so many more things, but I just continued smiling, contemplating everything in my mind, and exited the room.

Chapter 25

The Missing Chapter

$\mathcal{I}$ returned home and stayed there for several months, continuing to recuperate mentally, spiritually and physically. I now could walk pretty well without my cane and had gained some much-needed weight. I was feeling pretty good in my physical being, but my mental being was another situation. I had frequent nightmares, and daydreams of LaPier invaded my thoughts and visions almost without ceasing. But what was the most upsetting thing of all was not knowing what had happened to Joy! I now had my son, Anthony, back, but my sorrows seemed to switch from losing Anthony to losing Joy. I needed to know why this sadness prevailed and if there was reason for it. Was this constant sorrow over Joy truly valid?

I spent much time on the Internet, searching anything and everything about LaPier, Indiana. There was nothing about a murder, or the legend of Bitterwood Commons, or mysterious flowers being found in the town. I couldn't find any information about a fire; nothing at all! I would not give up hope. I was still convinced, from my first visit back to LaPier, that I had lived there! It would be so much easier if I could just abandon that belief. I kept trying to persuade myself that trying to solve this mystery was only taking precious time away from being with my family, who had been through so much with me already.

It was a rainy, late afternoon. Daniel and I were taking it easy, watching an old movie, when I remembered something very peculiar.

"The night that I came out of my coma," I said to Daniel. "Do you remember when you were telling me about my accident, and Anthony referred to a strange letter that my great-grandmother had received and saved from many years ago?"

"Yes," he answered. "Of course."

"I'm not aware of the letter. I was hoping you could tell me about it," I said, curious.

Daniel got up and went into the other room. I could hear some fumbling of things in the desk when he finally returned. He was holding an old tin box. He opened the ornate lid and pulled something out, holding the parchment in his hand. He stood in front of me gripping an old envelope and carefully handed it to me. I looked at it with interest. It was addressed to 88 State Street in Rolling Falls, Michigan, to my great-grandmother. It looked like it was written hastily and some time ago.

"This has been a mystery letter for some generations, Em," Daniel said. "You say you don't remember it, but I know that you do. That's why I thought it would be a good thing for you to visit the town of LaPier, Indiana. It's the town that this letter was sent from. That's why I let you go alone. I didn't want to say anything to you until you asked, because before the accident you were consumed with this letter. When Anthony mentioned it, the night you came out of the coma, I just didn't think an explanation was timely right then. Anyway, Anthony believes it's because of this letter that you saved his life!

"Ironically, it was not our son who had perished, but it could have been." Daniel continued. "You were the one who we almost lost! This letter was sent to your great-grandmother sometime in the early 1900s with a distinct warning. She never found out who sent it, but she believed, with all her heart, that it was important to pass down to all generations;

which it has been. Open, it, Em...Read it for yourself. I'm pretty sure you will remember." Daniel stood there, watching me.

I carefully untucked the little note from within its protective, crumbling, yellowing cover and read the words in front of me. I shivered, for there was no question in my mind who had written this notation. I skimmed over each word. I remembered holding the old ink instrument, quickly penning each swish and swerve on the letter, knowing exactly what was to come next. The person who wrote this letter was Natalia Kappan. The person who wrote this letter was me! I read the words:

Someday, perhaps years or generations from now, there will be an accident that will claim the life of your son and take him from your family. He will fall into a lake and drown. Always be prepared so this doesn't happen. This is my warning to you. Pass this down to your children and to theirs, and make sure that you heed my advice. If you don't, doom will follow your life forever!

There was no signature. I quickly turned the envelope over. Faintly, but still visible, stamped on the front was a postmark of July, 1920, sent from the town of LaPier, Indiana. I shivered again. "Justin mailed my letter," I whispered to myself. I looked over at Daniel.

"What did you say, dear?" he asked.

"Nothing,...I was just talking to myself," I replied. I felt faint.

"This letter you have in your hands," Daniel said, "your grandmother, your mother, and even you, always felt that someone was watching over us, even though it was written so long ago. Anthony is also convinced of it. That's why you came along with us on the boat all the times when we would go fishing. You thought you needed to protect the children. Can you remember now?"

I couldn't respond. My fingers tingled, and I just sat there and wept, holding my letter.

"We always thought it was ironic that this accident happened to you, Em. The kids and I asked so many times why the letter warned of a boy and not of you. I know it's silly that we even take relevance in that letter. It could have been sent to your great-grandmother by mistake. I would assume people mistook addresses a lot during war times and way back then, it probably wasn't that unusual." Daniel tried to comfort me.

I looked up at him. "It was no mistake Daniel." My voice held no doubt.

"Maybe not," he continued. "We know all things happen for a reason. Anthony is convinced that something grave would have happened to him that day if you hadn't been there. He is convinced the letter was addressing him specifically and that you saved his life because of it. That boy spent so much time with you while your mind was away from us. It changed him into such a spiritual being. He would read to you non-stop whenever he could. Anthony had just finished the last page of a novel that he had been reading to you the night you awakened. Do you remember any of the book, Em? It was called Bitterwood Commons."

I gasped. "What did you say?" I said abruptly, drying my tears.

"The book...the book that Anthony was reading to you was a novel called Bitterwood Commons. Do you remember any of it?" Daniel repeated.

I thought I was going to faint for sure and I suddenly felt very short of breath.

"Em, are you okay?" Daniel ran over to me and began rubbing my back. "Take a deep breath, Em, you're as white as a sheet. Do you want me to get you some water?"

"Is the book here, Daniel?" I cried. "I need to see the book immediately."

"Calm down, Em, and we'll talk about the book."

"Why are you being so elusive about this book?" I demanded. "Why didn't I hear of this book during all these months since I came out of the coma?"

Daniel shook his head. "I'm not being elusive, Em. There was never really a reason or opportunity to mention the book before today." He took a deep breath as if contemplating much. "The doctors had told us from the beginning of your accident that sometimes reading could stimulate the brain of comatose patients. Anthony never gave up hope that it was true and, like I said, he read to you whenever there was a chance. He read anything and everything that he could get his hands on, that he thought you could relate to. He was very excited when he discovered this fictional book he located at an Internet book store written about a town in northern Indiana. We thought this could have been the very town that the mysterious letter that was mailed to your great-grandmother came from." Daniel sighed again. "Are you certain you're okay?"

"Yes, I'm fine," I said, taking a few more deep breaths. "But I'm upset that no one has reminded me of these things! I feel that it could have helped me. Didn't you wonder that, Daniel? Didn't you wonder why I had to go there?"

"I'm getting to that, Em. When you awoke from your coma, the nurses believed that you thought that you were actually living the life of the woman who Anthony read to you about in the novel. The night you awakened, they said that you thought you were involved in a terrible fire that was depicted in that book. Your physical traits even appeared to be so, with your elevated temperature and reddened skin. Their fear was that you somehow equated this fictional book into your subconscious and turned it into the reality of your life. They said it was probably best not to mention any of this to you...that sooner or later you'd ask about it if you needed to. They were hoping that your subconscious would right itself. We really didn't see a reason to remind you of any of this unless you asked, Em."

"This is all so confusing," I said. "Daniel, is the book here?" He nodded his head yes and got up. I quickly stood up and went with him into the library.

Raising his arm to the third shelf from the ceiling, Daniel pulled down a book. He handed it to me, and I accepted it quickly, placing the letter addressed to my great-grandmother inside the cover. I went back to the den to sit down.

"It's quite a tale, Em. I read it from top to bottom two different times now. I wanted to know for myself what you thought you were experiencing when you came out of the coma. This book was the first literary effort by a relatively unknown author named Amanda Maddison Kelly. It was written some years ago now, and to our knowledge only a few copies were printed. Amanda Maddison Kelly's grandfather was a well-known preacher, Seth Maddison, who traveled throughout the country holding tent revivals and crusades near the turn of the century. It's kind of a dark tale!"

Goose bumps covered my skin. All of a sudden, something dawned on me. The first time I had ever traveled to LaPier, be it imaginary or real, was when I stayed at the Hotel Saint Denis'. The man at the desk told me of a woman who had come to LaPier to write a book. I had asked about her and he told me that he believed she was from California. It had to have been Seth Maddison's granddaughter; the author of this book!

Stunned and amazed, I began thumbing through this narrative for what turned out to be six consecutive hours. Some things had changed, but so many, many things that I had experienced during my time in LaPier were recorded on the pages right here in front of me. They were not words written from Natalia Kappan's memory, but everything seemed to be described through the eyes of Seth Maddison. I felt sick and confused. Was it possible that I had actually regressed into a fictional novel during my coma? Had I put myself in these very places while Anthony read this book to me? I rubbed my face harshly. I just couldn't accept it, and yet it made perfect sense.

I finally got up and logged on to the computer. I needed to find out about this author, Amanda Maddison Kelly. Was she indeed Seth Maddison's granddaughter? I typed her name in the search. Three pages down, I found her bio. My adrenaline was so high that I could barely click the mouse to her name. I began reading:

Amanda Maddison Kelly was raised in San Francisco, California. Bitterwood Commons was her only noted fictional piece of writing, published in 1985 just before she passed away of lung cancer in 1986. This book was adapted and created from true and fictional legends that her grandfather would tell her as a child.

I kept reading.

Her source of inspiration was her grandfather, a Baptist minister, Seth W. Maddison, who conducted many tent revivals and crusades along with mining-tycoon, turned-minister, Justin Peterson, during the early part of the 20th century.

I flung my head back and closed my eyes. Justin lived! Seth lived! I kept repeating to myself, looking back to the screen to make sure I wasn't being deceived. There was proof right here that the two men lived. If Justin and Seth lived, then Thomas and perhaps Natalia and even Joy did, too! Now there was no doubt in my mind that I needed to make another trip back to LaPier. And I needed to make that trip as soon as possible!

Upon my second and final trip to LaPier, Indiana, I stayed in a 10-bedroom farm home that had been converted into a bed and breakfast. Daniel once again wanted to come along with me, but I was hoping to find closure and needed to go alone. I had read on the Internet that the owners of this bed and breakfast were history buffs in regard to local affairs, and I was eager to talk with them about the history of their town. I told them of my letter, saved from my great-grandmother, and how it had been postmarked from LaPier in the year 1920. I told them that the letter, and the book that my son had read to me, had been the cause for my trips here, and though it was partially true, I knew in my heart there were far more reasons. They, as everyone else I had shared my story with, thought it was remarkable and believed it had been some sort of omen or spiritual journey set out for me, associating my life with this town and these occurrences.

My main reason for returning this time, however, was to visit the Hotel Saint Denis'. I remembered, from my visit there, that the owner said that he had kept the registration books back to the start of the century. I wanted to see for myself if indeed it was Amanda Maddison Kelly who had come here seeking information for her book. Did she stay here? I needed to find proof. Perhaps she, too, had been mesmerized by the strange tales told to her by her grandfather, Seth Maddison, of the occurrences of LaPier.

Perhaps she needed to account for something by writing this book to substantiate her grandfather's stories. Could it be that even Seth Maddison found a way to borrow the necklace and use the prisms to his benefit? If God had allowed someone, or even a multitude of people to change the course of history, and I believed most certainly He had, then most of the memories and a number of occurrences that truly took place must have been voided out upon each different time travel. Perhaps, little by little, everything came to fruition with only a few clues left behind to give us claim to our sanity.

Could it be that only certain things were voided out because of the number of people who had used the powers of the necklace? Even though I knew without a doubt that I had signed my name just below Peter's on the registry, it might not be here today. I just needed to know so many things, most importantly if Natalia Kappan had truly perished in that fire.

I entered the hotel and, much to my surprise, the same man who had helped me when Peter and I had stayed here, stood at the desk. In my mind it was only a short time ago, when in essence it could have been a lifetime in comparison to everything else. I approached him, but I knew he wouldn't recognize me.

"Good afternoon," he greeted.

"Good afternoon," I said with a smile. "I have a rather strange request. I was wondering if it would be at all possible to view your guest books? I'm trying to find out if some relatives of mine stayed here in the past."

"It's funny you should ask that…almost ironic, as a matter of fact," he began. "My son is somewhat of a history buff and also a computer genius. I have all of the hotel's guest books going back to when this business opened around the turn of the century. This hotel has been in my family since it began. Anyway, my son thought it would be neat to categorize all the information from within these books, so that we could see how many return clients we have had through the years, and also to see what cities our guests came from. He logged everything onto software. I have everyone's name who ever registered in this hotel right at my finger-tips."

"Oh, that was such a great idea! It must have taken your son weeks to accomplish such a thing," I remarked.

"Well, he's only 14 and has some time on his hands in the winter months around here. It's good to keep the boy busy."

"I can understand most perfectly," I replied, smiling. "So, would you be able to look up a few names for me to see if they stayed here? It sounds like it will be a lot easier the way you have the info stored. I thought we'd be looking through books for quite a while."

"Can I ask you how you even knew I had the books?" the man inquired.

At first I really didn't know how to answer. "…Just was hoping, I guess. Anyway, I had family who lived here years and years ago, and I also believe a friend of mine came to LaPier in the '80s and stayed here. She wrote a book called Bitterwood Commons. Her name was Amanda Maddison Kelly."

"Yes…she was here! I don't have to look up her name. You're right, it was in the '80s. We enjoyed having her stay with us. Do you know that she has since passed? It was so sad to hear."

"I do," I answered.

"I'll never forget her because she asked so many strange questions about our town and then we found the strange events she inquired about right in her book. She was a really nice woman, but she wrote a very dark novel. She sent me a copy of the book about a year after she had stayed with us, and I still have it in my library. It has a deplorable ending the way they printed it the second time. Have you read it?"

"Indeed I have," I answered. "I feel as though I lived it!"

"I can see how you felt that way. She wrote a very real depiction of all the events! Did you know that there was an omitted chapter to that book?" he asked. "Most of the copies in circulation have been printed with the omitted last chapter. The publishing company that agreed to publish her book in its entirety printed only a handful of copies and then went out of business. Amanda Maddison Kelly was given some of these first-run prints of the book, to give out to family and friends, and that's how I received the book before they omitted the chapter.

"The company was sold to another publisher. The new company printed one more run of the book, but omitted the very last chapter to give the story closure; they said. The version I have is very rare!"

I sighed and bit my lip. "So, then, since you have the first-run edition, you must know what the other chapter is about?"

"Oh yes, I do. She sent the book to us right here at the hotel."

I was so blown away that I could barely stand there. "So, please, the woman in the book who was killed in the fire... what did the omitted chapter say about her; about her child? Was there anything?"

"It was very strange, just as was the entire book, in my eyes. If you equated these events with our city here, it really gave LaPier a black eye! I really think it was a good idea that the publishers omitted that chapter. At least it has finality the way it was printed the second time. The last chapter that was omitted was very, very short, and concluded the accounts something like this...and I will paraphrase it, of course:

After the fire, the little girl obtained the necklace. Only God knew if, between then and the time she grew old, she stood in the prismed light. Only God knew if she was able to return to the past and use her childlike faith to let the prisms make good out of evil, and to spare her mother from the tortuous inferno. And only God knew if she was able to change the course of history forever.

"There was a little more to the chapter, but this is basically what it said. Like I implied, printed that way, there really is no end to the story. It is infinite! It pretty much leaves you to draw your own conclusions. If the little girl had the necklace, she also had all the power she needed to time travel, or even to share the necklace with others so that they could travel in time! Perhaps she even took them with her."

I was shivering and felt so cold. "Perhaps there was no end! Perhaps I would never find an end!" I began to cry.

"...You okay?" the man asked.

"Yes, of course," I answered, rubbing my eyes.

"So you can see why they omitted it," he continued.

I evaded his question. I had one thing on my mind. "Please, could you look up a name for me? I very badly need you to look up a name for me. Please see if the name Emma Barker is on your log of people who stayed in your hotel."

The man began fidgeting with the computer. "It will be just a minute." He popped in a disk, and brought up the information on his screen.

I could barely wait to hear the outcome.

"Okay, now, let me search alphabetically.....Nope, there was never an Emma Barker who stayed here," he said, continuing to hit the keys.

I knew my name wouldn't be listed. That spectrum of time when I had first visited LaPier had been voided out from history. My theory was proving to be correct, and yet I was hoping to see my name there!

"Is there another spelling it could be under?" he questioned. "Does this have something to do with the book?"

"I'm not sure...I mean, yes. I... I just don't know." I continued to make no sense.

"I don't know what I can do for you," he replied. "I can tell that this book has surely impacted you, though."

"You just have no idea of its significance. Thank you for everything you have done for me today," I acknowledged. "I can't even begin to thank you for what you've done." I began to make my way to the door.

"I really didn't do much," the man called out. "Have a good day."

"You, too," I said as I exited the hotel.

I returned to the quaint bed and breakfast, still bombarded with thoughts. As I was going up the stairs on what would be my last night in LaPier, I was admiring the many historic photographs taken of the town. They covered the walls on each side of the stairway and continued into the rooms. The entire downstairs was also adorned in numerous pictures, and it seemed the owners could tell an elaborate story about most of them. Instead of turning toward my room, this night I turned down the opposite hallway. I hadn't looked at the pictures in this part of the house yet. I followed the pictures with interest into the other unoccupied rooms. In a large, rose-colored room on the farthest side of the dwelling, I was drawn to a picture hung by a tapestry ribbon on the west wall. I looked at it intensely, squinting my eyes and studying it. I tried to take it off the wall but noticed that the ribbon was attached with a decorative nail. I immediately ran to get one of the owners of this place. Promptly, she returned up the stairs with me. I showed her the photo that I was so interested in.

"Please,... please, tell me of this picture," I begged, excitedly.

She looked at me and smiled. "Oh, I can't tell you as much about this picture as most of them in the house. I know some details, though. It was early after the turn of the century, probably between 1910 and 1920. You can tell by their clothing." She pointed to the handsome couple in the photo. "This, I was told, was a preacher and his wife. They visited our town from New York."

"And this?" I pointed to the faces of the other man, elderly woman, and woman with a little girl on her lap. I anxiously awaited her response.

"This was the pastor's brother, we were told, his wife, and I assume their child." She bent down closer, continuing to observe the details. "And this looks like it would be the wife's mother from their similar beauty, long-flowing hair and Asian descent," she explained as she continued examining the picture and pointing to each figure as she spoke. "These younger boys must have been the rest of their children. Lots of boys, huh? I don't know which couple they belonged to." She pointed to the other six youngsters in the photo.

"He; the pastor that is, never lived in LaPier. At least that's what I was told. That's probably why we don't know his name. He apparently made quite a sum of money in the mining business, but gave it all up to conduct his revivals from town to town. There was a very famous minister around that time period, however, named Seth Maddison, but we don't believe that's who this is. We do know for certain this group traveled from New York City, though, and I imagine they passed through our town as lots of revivalists did in those days. Why are you so interested anyway?"

I avoided her question as I quickly spoke up, dazed. "I can help you somewhat in your search for the facts of this picture. I know these people." I closed my eyes and sighed deeply. "I believe the name of your pastor is Justin Peterson, although I don't know his wife's name." I pointed at the picture and circled his face with my finger. "This was his brother, Thomas Arthur Peterson, his wife Natalia, and Natalia's mother! They were reunited after all. And this..." I continued, pointing to the little girl on the lap of her mother as my tear hit the frame. "Her name was Joy. She had to have been their child all along. She was the love of their lives, and she must have lived a beautiful, loved life with all these brothers and cousins."

The woman gave me a rather peculiar glance. I smiled and my face puckered up as I tried to contain my tears. "Would there be any way that we could take down this picture so that I could inspect it with a magnifying glass?" I asked urgently.

She told me to wait there a moment as she left the room. My heart beat in anticipation as my eyes froze on the yellowed photograph. Soon she returned with a hammer and handed me a black-rimmed magnifier. With a couple of pulls the picture was off the wall.

"We can lay it over here on the dresser. The light is much better," she said, carrying it in that direction.

There was only one thing I wanted to see, and if it showed up on the picture, I would be forever contented, no longer in search for answers. I put the magnifying glass down on the picture, directing it above the beautiful Asian woman with the smooth-as-silk, flowing black hair who held the little girl with so much love. I focused on Natalia and there it was, as plain as day. She wore the necklace! Natalia wore the Padparadscha sapphire proudly around her neck! Then I turned the magnifier to the older Asian woman; perhaps my mother in another life. I focused and could see that she was wearing the tiny gold pendant heart that was returned to me in the box along with my necklace: The pendant that was the home to the tiny picture of Natalia as a child!

Most of the pieces finally fell together in my mind. Joy did find the necklace after Natalia perished in the fire. There was now evidence of that written in the disregarded one-page chapter of the book. Joy, or someone, obviously did make it back through time to save her mother, sharing the necklace; the mystical gift from the gypsies, with many different people in order to make things right. They were able to use the power of the prisms, working together with the Padparadscha sapphire, to be allowed travel in time.

These powers had been allowed to alter things so that Natalia, Seth and Thomas had never left New York City. They were united with Justin and Natalia's mother, and Natalia was never taken away from her beloved Thomas after all. These journeys had freed so many people on this earth from a life of torment including my own. It would explain almost everything!

I picked up the photo and held it near to my chest. "They must have only visited LaPier for a time, traveling with their crusades. They look so happy and blessed," I said to the owner.

"Would you like for me to have s copy of this photo made for you?" she asked. "I can tell it means a great deal to you."

"Yes, I would like that very much," I answered.

"I will have a copy made and have it sent to you. I so appreciate you enlightening me about the people in the photo. Now I can share its contents with other historians in the area."

I now could take comfort in knowing that Joy, Justin, and even Thomas had journeyed back after I had taken on Natalia's bodily being, to rescue Natalia and Anthony, and even Agatha Sloan, and perhaps many others from a world of despair. I looked once again at the precious face of the little girl in the photo. You saved my Anthony, didn't you? I said to myself. I now knew without a doubt that Joy lived a happy, fulfilled life.

I didn't allow myself to question any more about the things that had happened to me from that time on. Everything did happen for the best, and for a reason, to those who had faith, and to those who put their total trust in God. This was an empowering truth that I now embraced. Perhaps Natalia and Thomas, Joy, and even myself had traveled much in time using the powers of the Padparadscha sapphire, combined with the prisms of this earth to make everything right. It would explain the package at the Hotel Saint Denis' that I now believe was delivered directly from the hands of my mother, to fulfill her promise to me that she would return, and so many other strange happenings from that time period. Perhaps lives and times somehow were intermingled to create just the exact prism to allow the bad to have a new beginning. Maybe our childhood imaginations and fantasies are far more than we ever fathomed they could be. I couldn't get the words that I believed Lillian Post had once said to me out of my mind.

When the sun was in the perfect spot and hit the crystal stones used on the foundation, we'd stand in the glow of the prisms and pretend we'd be taken somewhere in our imagination. Oh, the places we'd go! Oh to be a child again!

How everything took place was now no longer my business. I finally was at peace and rest. I now had my faith back, and I would never question God's abilities to direct my life again. Did these things all really happen to me? Did the precious sapphire necklace get buried with Natalia upon her death, or has it reappeared unknowingly through time to others as it had done to me? I would never know these answers, but if need be, I would always have an escape from these questions, blaming these events on my unresponsive mind while I was away in my deep, deep sleep.

The night I returned home from LaPier, I went out on our back porch. The twilight orchestra of insects was once again serenading the countryside with a constant echo. This evening, the moon hung high in the sky. I walked onto the grass and noticed something standing out within the greenery, highlighted from the moon's beams. I bent over and to my surprise found a lonely flower coming up out of our freshly cut, manicured lawn. There was one single bloom; no more, no less. I knew this flower well. I took it in my hand, caressed it, and pulled it free from the soil. I brought it to my face and gave it a gentle kiss. It would be the last time I would ever see this unusual bloom again. I knew that for a fact, for I knew in my heart that it was the final sign to me that all had finally been fulfilled.

The End

About the Author

Entrepreneur and artist Marike Mitchell grew up embracing the eerie romance of the Great Lakes. Going on holiday to Historic Mackinac Island for many a summer, she treasures the bygone nostalgic feelings that flood her soul from visiting there. While walking the hauntingly beautiful cemeteries on the island, a local once told Marike that one can almost hear conversations from long ago being said, both in French and English if one sits quietly and listens. Watching the freighters and hearing the warnings of their horns as they escaped through the fog enabled her to envision similar ships that have been voyaging these treacherous waters centuries before. Marike truly believes that history and another era are only a dream and perhaps a narrative away. Classics such as Jane Eyre, Wuthering Heights, and Pride and Prejudice are three of her favorite reads.

Many inspirations in Marike's faith-based life have come together in her new book, Bitterwood Commons. Marike lives in rural Michigan, directly through the forest from where she was raised. The meadow that she walked as a teen is now home to her and her husband's hobby farm. Marike's interests lie in creating various art forms, special perennial gardens, and self-sufficient farming; but, most of all, she enjoys putting pen to paper. Family is her greatest treasure, and she has a very special love for her precious Dachshund, Leah, who goes everywhere that Marike goes.

42257674R00194

Made in the USA
Middletown, DE
16 April 2019